About the author

Alice Berman is a New York-based author who grew up in Washington, DC. A graduate of Choate Rosemary Hall and the University of Pennsylvania, Alice lived in LA for five years, where she worked in fashion. She now resides in Tribeca.

I EAT MEN LIKE AIR

Alice Berman

I EAT MEN LIKE AIR

Vanguard Press

VANGUARD PAPERBACK

A CIP catalogue record for this title is
available from the British Library.

ISBN 978-1-80016-552 9

Vanguard Press is an imprint of
Pegasus Elliot Mackenzie Publishers Ltd.
www.pegasuspublishers.com

First Published in 2023

Vanguard Press
Sheraton House Castle Park
Cambridge England

Printed & Bound in Great Britain

Dedication

For my family — in greatest thanks for their endless love and support.

Prologue
Tyler
June 2017

Tyler found Alex Sable three hours after he was officially declared dead. Before they removed him from the grandiose bedroom with the portraits of someone else's ancestors — after two of the groomsmen had hauled him out of the tub and onto the once-pristine carpet.

"There's no protocol around suicides, any more. Could be a homicide. Could be an accidental death," Detective Sean Strickland told Tyler, as they cruised down the cool highways of New Hampshire.

"I don't think six cuts to the interior of the wrists is accidental, Sean," Tyler replied. Sean wanted everything to be a homicide, loathed the overdoses that Tyler had come to this part of New England to investigate, had a healthy suspicion for everyone and everything, including the organic yogurt Tyler had been eating at Sean's desk when the call came in.

Sean grunted and rolled his window down a few inches, inhaling the beginning of summer. "Last year some guy made his *suicide* look like a murder," he said, as if this, a thirty-year-old who'd bled out in the bathroom at his best friend's wedding, was exactly that.

Tyler laughed. "You only know that because I did an episode on it," he said. Sean had been prominently featured in Tyler's first season of *Crime and Question*, the podcast which amassed over a hundred fifty million downloads. It was a cold case from the 90s, which Sean had spent a good three years trying and failing to solve before Tyler came along. Together, they squeezed a confession out of an old lady who had done it for the money. They'd both been disappointed by the result — in that case, it really was the most obvious suspect — not just because they'd shared many teas at the lovely cottage her murder money had bought. She made a great spice cake, dispensed useful advice about marriage, and killed her uncle. Now she was dead, Tyler's voice was a minor celebrity, and people sent Detective Sean Strickland long emails asking how best to interrogate witnesses.

Sean nodded. He *did* only know that because Tyler had done an episode on it, and it wasn't even one of Tyler's favorites. Everything felt stale these days, too much murder, too much violence, too many forgotten crimes that people begged him to resurrect. He'd come to New Hampshire to research the opioid epidemic in New England, which his producer said no one would listen to, and spent most of his days hanging around the Hanover County Police Department, talking about crimes and questions. Tyler had been recording — Tyler was always recording — because he thought he might be able to assemble something decent.

This call, on a Saturday mid-morning of a golden June day, wasn't really of interest to Tyler, but Sean had said "could be an overdose" and mentioned that the house was a beautiful, historic one, privately owned, so Tyler's idle curiosity landed him in the car.

Tyler clicked on his tape recorder. Sean recognized the noise without acknowledging it; that was one of the reasons why Tyler didn't use his phone. The first season had been built on this tape recorder from Amazon, and it held a mythical significance for him still.

"So, Sean, tell us what we know so far. Where we're going, what information we have, why a detective like you is on this case." Tyler put the recorder in the cup holder.

"What we know, nothing until we get there. Never believe a report. Always wrong. *Always* wrong. What we think we know, rich kid up here from New York for a wedding found dead. Won't know the cause of death until we do an autopsy, which they'll probably skip, because it *looks* like a suicide. We should be asking a lot of questions, finding out if the victim fits the suicide profile. Probably they're just out there contaminating the crime scene. Let me tell you something; people think it's a suicide, they get lazy. They're not looking for more questions. They're happy to have the answer right there."

"Have you encountered any suicides that were actually homicides?"

Sean paused. "No. Not personally. I've heard stories, though. It could even be an accidental death," he repeated.

"I guess we'll see when we get there," Tyler replied. "How do we know that little tip about his family?"

"So the house we're going to," Sean explained, talking more to the tape recorder than to Tyler, "is a pretty big deal around here. Been in the family since the seventeen-hundreds. They've redone it — beautiful place, huge. The people who own it are a bunch of rich New Yorkers who come up here once a year. This kid, they told me, has a famous dad, or something. Fifteenth richest man in the world, the cops on the scene said earlier. We're getting to the scene late," he explained to the cup holder. "Because people *always* forget to call the detective for a suicide. They just want it nice and neat, all packaged up with a bow on top."

"I guess we'll see when we get there," Tyler replied, and stopped the recording.

"Feels nice to be doing this again," Strickland said, looking at Tyler, looking at the cupholder. "Maybe you should stay out here for the summer. Dig into another cold case. Someone was murdered in this house, you know. Like eighty years ago."

"Everyone associated with the case dead?" Tyler asked.

"Pretty much." Sean sighed.

The house was beautiful, like something out of a BBC show — the definition of an ancestral pile, which Tyler hadn't even known existed in America. He expected frenzy and sirens and uniformed policemen and defeated-looking wedding guests, but it was silent when they pulled up — one cop car, one Range Rover, both empty of people.

"Quiet," Tyler commented. Sean looked around without reply and led the way into the house, through the double doors that could easily have fit a horse. Or two.

It was decorated for the wedding, flowers everywhere, in any direction you turned. A breathless woman who introduced herself as *the wedding planner* explained that everyone was upstairs, keeping to themselves. "Such a shock," she said, clutching at her heart. "I've *never* had a wedding with a suicide. Of all times to kill yourself! It's very selfish," she admonished, turning to Tyler like *he* was the one who had committed suicide. "The *best man*. Do *you* know anyone who would do something like that?"

Sean cut in. "You know him? Alex Sable? Interact with him much?"

"Well of course I *know* everyone in the bridal party," she replied, leading them up a flight of stairs, where there were finally signs of life. "But I don't know any of them *well*, except for Will and Jessica. The bride and groom," she explained to the blank looks from Tyler and Sean. "I'm sure you know who Lulu Swanson is; she's famous, pretty, and from a good family. *She's* here. What a trial for her, poor thing."

"Actress?" Sean asked. They stopped at the top of the landing, where only closed doors greeted them.

"Instagram influencer," the wedding planner told them, and knocked sharply.

"An Instagram influencer," Sean murmured. "That's a first. Is that what we're calling *famous* these days?"

Tyler chuckled softly. The door opened a two-inch crack, and the face that looked up at them was instantly detectable as the girl in question, Lulu. She had waist-length blonde hair and looked well-groomed in the way that famous people do, skin that seemed to glow from within and eyes that took up at least a third of the real estate on her face.

"*You're* Tyler from *Crime and Question*," she said immediately.

The wedding planner turned with renewed interest to look at Tyler. "Most people don't know me by my face," he said. It was the voice that his listeners got to know, not him, and he had a generic voice, in his opinion — nothing you could identify immediately. "Tyler." He offered a hand. She inched into the hallway, shut the door behind her, then took it. "This is Detective Strickland."

"Lulu," Lulu replied, in that way that people who don't want to be associated with their last names do. She wore a flimsy, pale slip that almost brushed her ankles. "Carol, we need some sustenance up here; they're all dying." The wedding planner took in this task enthusiastically and departed. "Oh, dear. Is this really worthy of a *Crime and Question* investigation?" Lulu asked.

"Would that be a bad thing?" Sean countered.

"Well, it's already sort of a horrible situation. I wouldn't want to have to live through it all over again, via podcast. But, I suppose, if it shines a light on the danger of the stigma we hold around mental health in America, it's worth it." It was a surprisingly eloquent thing to hear from this small, vapid-looking person. "I suppose that's why you're doing it, right? To focus on suicide prevention?"

"Still developing the story," Tyler explained.

Lulu looked up at him again, her huge eyes unwavering in her heart-shaped face. "How funny," she said, suddenly. "Alex loved *Crime and Question*. And his father will absolutely hate this. Death is full of the oddest ironies, isn't it?" she asked. "How can I help?"

"We're here to see the crime scene," Strickland explained. "Then talk to all of you who were here in the house with him when it happened — go from there. Get a picture of it all."

"The crime scene is three doors down on the left," she said. "The police did mention that we couldn't leave until we'd spoken to someone. Everyone's fairly anxious to get out of here. I don't know why they need to talk to *all* of us. Surely just the ones who *knew* Alex."

"Did some of you not know Alex?" Tyler asked. "Aren't you all here for a wedding?"

"Well, I mean, one of the groomsmen, for example, really isn't… in the core group. He actually tried to sue Alex earlier this year, incidentally, but of course that went nowhere. And—"

"Do you mind if I record?" Tyler interrupted.

She looked at the recorder in his hand and looked at him. It was a protracted, measuring look that made the silence before her answer too long. "I don't know," she said, finally. "I wouldn't mind but — I have a feeling this would be the kind of thing my parents would kill me for. And I do have to worry about my followers. Plus, I can't see the Sable family being very… happy about your involvement. And I certainly don't want to get crosswise of them," she explained.

"Why?" Tyler asked.

"I'm dating Alex's cousin," she explained. "But they're also, just, you know. The kind of people I'll be encountering at dinners for the rest of my life. I would like it to be amicable." She started down the long hall. "And, of course, they're famously litigious."

"*Litigious*," Sean repeated. "Huh. So, how well did you know Alex?"

Lulu stopped a few feet before the open door. "I don't know. I knew him as well as you know anyone like that. We've known each other forever, I suppose, but we were never close; we both grew up in the same place—"

"Where's that?" Sean asked, glancing at Tyler taking notes.

"New York. Uptown. He's older than I am, obviously," she said, and studied their faces to see if they agreed that she couldn't look thirty, which she didn't. "But we knew each other mostly in LA. Oh, we both lived in LA until recently. Anyway, I've been dating his cousin since — well, since we were all up here for a weekend in February, kind of a pre-wedding party that Jessica, the bride, put together. Alex is sort of unknowable, though."

"What do you mean by that?" Tyler asked. He and Sean had been working together for so long that Sean relied on Tyler's notes and Tyler asked the questions he knew Sean was thinking.

"He's one of those people who's always… in search of the best time, I suppose. Making a party out of nothing. 'Constantly in pursuit of fun' would be a better way to phrase it. And when he's not… partying," she chose the word with care, "he gets very maudlin. He sort of mopes around until his next exciting venture. And by venture I don't mean *job*. I don't think he's had a real job — well, maybe ever." Lulu looked to the open door. "I should probably use the past tense now. Now that he's dead. He doesn't *feel* dead, though, does he?" she asked.

Neither Tyler nor Sean addressed this thinking-out-loud. He certainly felt dead to Tyler. "What kind of *partying* did he do?" Tyler asked. "Is this an opioid thing? Drugs? Or just drinking?"

"*Just drinking*." Lulu repeated, laughing. "As if drinking wasn't a killer on its own!" Sean shifted his weight towards Tyler, a silent commentary. "Look, I don't want to expound on anyone's drug use. That's how you end up with a libel case against you. If we need to get into things like that, I'll want a lawyer. Anyway, you don't need any of us to tell you that. You'll get a toxicology report, won't you? Tyler's done that on, like, six episodes I can think of, just off the top of my head."

Tyler *had* gotten six different toxicology reports, and hearing her spit the exact number at him unnerved him. Lulu unnerved him, she looked like she should say *like* every ten seconds and instead she dropped words like *expound* and *maudlin*. She looked like she would be breathless and pretty and thoughtless enough to just talk, but here she was, already asking for a lawyer. Afraid of a *libel* case, nervous to talk about Alex's drug use, which of course meant that he had been a drug user. "I'm doing a piece on the Fentanyl epidemic out here," Tyler explained.

She hesitated for a moment and then said, "Between us. Strictly to *never* be repeated and to be used off-the-record, I don't think he was a Fentanyl user, or that kind of thing, really, at all. So I don't know if this fits into… your story."

"Might be a better one right here," Sean told her. "Sounds like he doesn't fit the profile of suicidal tendencies."

Lulu stepped up to the door of the room, deliberately keeping her back to it. "He's… he *was*, sort of, well, dramatic. A person of extremes, I should say. Anyway, I don't want to see it again, so just come knock if you need anything else from me. We're all kind of desperate to go home at this point. I'm having anxiety being in the same house with a dead body for so long," she said.

Strickland pushed past her, into the room. "Why don't you want to see it again?" Tyler asked.

"Aside from the fact that it was… *gruesome* to behold… it's a terrible thing to see your friend dead. Hard to look at. Hard to process it. I don't want to make more memories around Alex *dead*. I wish I'd never walked in there in the first place. But one of the boys screamed and we all just sort of went running. If it were me who found him, I wouldn't have wanted anyone else to see it. But I guess you never know how you'll react in the moment. I did faint when I saw it. Which probably would have been a lot worse for someone else to find. If I'd been the first person to walk in. Anyway. Sorry for all the rambling. I hit my head when I fainted, and Yael said that I may be minorly concussed." Lulu gave him a strange half-smile and tilted her head to the side to look at him again. Tyler felt like he was in a scary movie, and this beautiful thing in a pale slip was really just a ghost, here to show him around the house where death came to call. "Good luck," she said. "I really am a fan."

She walked away and he wondered if Sean would want to question her again. He found her compelling, and he loved the way that she spoke, in a light, easy voice which would have translated well to a recording — but he had the impression that Lulu Swanson was the kind of person who wouldn't tell you anything, really, except for exactly what she wanted you to know.

Tyler walked into the bedroom. It was very large and filled with the bright light of the dawning afternoon and on the rug, as if he were part of the decorating scheme, lay a body bloated with water and patched with the rusty stains of drying blood. There was only one cop, a guy who Tyler recognized from his recent days around the station, who sat in a velvet chair by the window. Tyler took another step in. The double doors to the bathroom were wide open, and there was the *gruesome* scene to which Lulu had referred, blood littered with broken glass on white tile. It looked like the bathtub had bled out and died.

"He crawled out of the bath?" Tyler asked. "Decided he didn't want to die?"

"No," Sean said, immediately. "These idiots pulled him out. Told Sanchez here that it was the first thing they did in case he was alive. No one thought to check his *pulse*. No integrity left in the scene. There were ten, twelve people just in the bathroom, at one point, Sanchez says."

"Look at this cut on his hand," Tyler pointed. There was a four-inch-long gash down the middle of his palm.

"Happened last night. Playing a drinking game. One of the girls, Yael, is a doctor," Sanchez shared. "She said she tried to stitch him up; he wouldn't let her. This morning, she checked his pulse, but I think she came in after they'd pulled him out. The coroner stopped by on his way to golf. Said the time of death was around one a.m., give or take half an hour. His watch is broken, stopped at 4,11 — probably broke on the bath when he lost consciousness."

Tyler laughed. "That's straight out of an Agatha Christie," he commented. "Why slit your wrists, but leave your watch on?"

Tyler and Sean peered down at the body. The cuts were below his watch by almost an inch; Sean reached a gloved hand out to check his wrist. "Four eleven. Pat-tek-Philip. Never heard of it."

"Patek Philippe," a girl said from the doorway. Like Lulu, she wore a long slip and had bare feet. "It's probably a fifty-thousand-dollar watch. Leave it to Alex to break even that." She leaned against the doorjamb. "Sorry. I was dying in that room, with everyone." Her eyes flicked to the body, flicked to the tub. She registered nothing on her face. "Lulu said you were here, and I thought I'd peer in. Ask when we can leave. Isn't it odd that his parents didn't come up?" she asked.

"Tough thing for a parent to see," Tyler replied.

Sean made a noise of dissent. "Left it to a bunch of kids to clean up," he said.

"Oh, *we* won't clean it up," she told him. "Someone else will. Or do you all do that?"

She took a step into the room. Sean put out a hand to stop her. "Still haven't found the weapon," he said. "Still a crime scene."

"We were all in here, before. For like an hour. Lulu fainted. Utter chaos. My husband should have warned me not to come in, but he didn't and now here we are," she said. She stepped up to the body, to Alex, and looked down into his face. "I thought he would look so different, dead, but he's really just *him*, isn't he?"

"He doesn't look different to you?" Tyler asked.

"Looks like a corpse, to me. Bloat from the water. Pale from the bleeding," Sean put in.

"I don't know. Not as different as I'd thought. I didn't really look until now. The cuts are so deep." She bent over.

"Don't touch him!" Sean yelled. "They look like varying depths to me. We just need to find how he did them."

"Maybe it's one of those things, like he did it with an icicle and the icicle melted. One of those riddles," the girl said. She sat down next to the body. Strickland didn't stop her.

"Probably dropped in the bath. Someone's gotta fish around in there before we drain it, so it doesn't go down the drain." Sean looked to Sanchez. "You got long gloves with you?"

The girl on the floor shuddered at this. "Shouldn't they send a forensics team, or something? That's what they do on CSI. Why is it just you three? Is anyone else coming?"

"Even *she* knows," Sean said. "They don't send the whole team out, for a suicide. Department only has so many resources."

"And it's a Saturday," the girl said, shrewdly.

"What's your name?" Tyler asked her.

"Maxie Stein-Golden. I would stand, but I'm already sitting." Maxie smiled. "It's been a long day. And now we'll probably have to drive home with Lulu and everyone, because Alex was the one with the plane." She sighed and looked around the room. "What happens next? If no one else is coming. Where does the body go? Do you ask us questions?" She seemed more bored than anything else, not emotional or even tired. She sat next to Alex's body like it was a piece of furniture and waited for her answers like she was waiting for a waiter.

"How well did you know Alex?" Tyler asked.

"I mean, we all knew *of* him. His dad is Cornelius Sable and Alex was sort of a mini celebrity when we were in high school, because of the Chris Newman thing." She stood up. "But I just knew him from this wedding. We met at the party Will and Jessica had here in February."

"Who's Chris Newman?" Tyler asked. "Do you mind if I record?" Sean was in the bathroom, gloved hands on his knees, peering into the opaque water of the tub.

Maxie shrugged. "Don't use my name, please. But sure. Chris Newman is this guy who went to Dalton with Alex and was accused of raping a bunch of girls, like, blindfolded, so the girls never saw his face, apparently, but Alex finally… saw it, I guess. And Chris was one of those scholarship kids; I think he'd gotten into Princeton, then of course he went to jail for most of his adult life and died there. In jail, I mean," she clarified.

Tyler took his own careful turn around the room. It *was* a mess; it looked like it had probably been a mess before whatever happened, happened. He wasn't convinced it was a suicide and he wasn't convinced that it wasn't; the whole thing was so strangely out-of-place, like he'd stumbled into someone else's life. Yesterday he and Sean had revived a man with Naloxone in a Stop-N-Shop bathroom. Today they were in the grand bedroom of a family mansion with the dead son of a billionaire laid out on the floor like a turkey on a platter. Now a girl named Maxie Stein-Golden was telling them that Alex, the dead man, was a hero. Tyler saw no broken glass in his feet, although it littered almost half of the bathroom floor. There were undone lines of cocaine, still pristine, on a John Derian coffee table book next to the bed. A large vase of flowers had spilled onto the floor, an abandoned bow tie adorning the scattered lilies.

"There's another watch here," Tyler called, peering at the bedside table.

"One is a black-tie watch, and one is for every day," Maxie Stein-Golden told him. She got up and joined him on the far side of the bed, on her tiptoes, following closely behind him. "What else? I feel like we're in *True Detective*."

"Got the weapon," Sanchez held up what looked like a fancy carving knife, dripping in water.

Maxie giggled and covered her mouth immediately. "I'm so sorry," she said, "I know it isn't funny. But Jessica went *on and on* about how expensive these Japanese steak knives were. They had to buy one for every guest at the rehearsal dinner. And now here it is. She would die." She paused. "Maybe don't tell her. She doesn't have to know, does she? You won't put this in your podcast, will you? Don't say that it was one of her knives. She would never use them again. And she really cares about them."

Tyler didn't know if any of this would go into his podcast; it was the first active crime scene he'd ever been on. The dead body was starting to weigh on him and he wished that whoever was supposed to take it away would do it already, perform the autopsy, let them creep around the room *without* a corpse in it. It had already been tampered with beyond repair; the only thing they could hope for, Tyler thought, was a tox screen with results. He squinted at the label on the open-but-full champagne bottle next to the bed, it was Dom Perignon.

"What a waste of good champagne," Maxie said.

"You probably shouldn't be in here," Tyler told her.

"You probably shouldn't be, either," she replied.

"Valium over here," Sean said. Tyler, tailed by Maxie, went into the bathroom. She avoided the glass with care and scanned the room like she was searching for something.

"What are you looking for?" Tyler asked her.

"Clues," she told him. "Isn't that what we're supposed to be looking for?"

"We're doing a thorough report of the scene," Sean explained. "We have to talk to you guys about what happened, how the night went leading up to it, if he fit the profile of someone suicidal."

"Well, we're all going to die here," Maxie said, cheerfully. "Beautiful place to die, at least. Let me see what I can tell you. People have said that Alex was bipolar; that was the rumor, anyway. I can't speak to that, but he definitely had some dark turns. Last night, he was late to dinner, showed up with Rob, who is the third in their little trio. They seemed like they'd done mushrooms or something; they were definitely high. We had a long dinner with prime rib, and everyone had one of these steak knives. A bunch of the boys started playing some stupid drinking game with the knives and a tree; you can probably still see it on the front lawn. And then Victoria and I went to bed, and, in the morning, I heard someone scream, maybe Will, the groom. My husband and I came in from across the hall, and here Alex was. Rob and Will and my husband decided to pull him out of the tub. One of the bridesmaids is a doctor and she kept saying he was dead. I think she's the one who called 911. I'm not sure when Lulu fainted. Maybe it was because Yael kept saying *he's dead*, although it was pretty bloody, anyway. And then a bunch of people swarmed in and now we're just waiting to go home."

She took a breath. Tyler looked to Sean and Sean to Tyler. It was a fairly comprehensive answer, with a lot of *my husband's* making a star appearance, maybe borderline practiced, maybe made out of sheer desperation to leave. "It's getting to be more and more uncomfortable, in my opinion, the longer the Sables don't show up. They just want the body cremated and shipped home. Which is funny because Jews don't traditionally cremate. Anyway , what were the other questions? I have no idea what suicidal behavior looks like. Alex does more drugs than probably you should, and he has terrible comedowns from coke because he takes tons of Valium to sleep."

"Do you know who prescribed it to him?" Tyler asked. "I don't see a pill bottle."

Maxie swept the floor with her eyes. "No. I'm sure it's easy to get, though, like Adderall. I mean, without a prescription." She was moving across the bathroom, towards the glass.

"Be careful of your feet," Tyler warned.

"Don't go over there!" Sean told her.

"Detective, come on," Sanchez said, probably because he wasn't thrilled that he'd had to go shoulder-deep in bloody, cold bathwater.

"Let's talk to these people and get out of here. They want to leave; we've got three reports on a meth lab that they need back-up on. He's just another sad rich kid. Open and shut."

Maxie made a noise. Tyler had been looking at Sanchez; she was standing, inexplicably, by the toilet, in the worst of the glass, fiddling with something on her wrist. "*Just another sad rich kid.* Very *Cruel Intentions*. I don't know anyone who's committed suicide. I mean, personally." She said it with all the entitled arrogance of someone who considered herself a rich kid, perhaps a sad one.

"What are you doing over there?" Sean asked. "You're going to get glass in your foot." Tyler thought this was an unacknowledged agreement with Sanchez's opinion, but Sean wouldn't say it was a suicide until he had a full report on the body.

"I thought I saw the medicine bottle," she said. "But it was nothing." She hesitated, obviously wanting to say something but not wanting to say it. Tyler took a few cautious steps her way and looked around the toilet, on the white marble, where there was nothing but glass.

"Excuse me," a voice came from the door. "I'm Iskander Khan, the lawyer representing the Sables." Tyler stepped out of the bathroom. The man was trim and wearing a suit even though it was a Saturday. "We — my clients and myself — didn't want any trouble here. Mr Sable knows there is an undue amount of interest in his family… and that there can be difficulties around a suicide. Mrs Stein-Golden, I suggest you return to your room. Gentlemen, may I have a word?"

Tyler expected Maxie to say something like *why*, or simply refuse to leave, but she dusted off the bottom of her feet and walked out of the room, pausing only once. "Goodbye," she said, suddenly. "It was nice to meet you. I think Alex would have loved that you were here." She drank in Alex's body for a moment, and then she was gone.

Iskander Khan wanted two things, the entire *unfortunate incident* to be kept as quiet as possible, for the sake of the family, and the wedding party to be able to go home. As he said it, Tyler heard the crunch of cars on gravel, and floated to the window, the Range Rover had pulled up directly outside the front door. Lulu was climbing into the passenger seat, Maxie already in the car, door open, calling out to someone who was probably the oft-referenced *husband*. They'd put on sweaters over their slips; Lulu wore sneakers. Tyler watched as two boys got in and the Range slowly pulled off and out of sight. He didn't investigate rich people just for this reason, barriers like lawyers and the entitlement that allowed you to casually leave when law enforcement asked you to stay. Tyler didn't know what standard protocol was for a suicide. Probably most people didn't kill themselves in a house full of their friends, but Alex didn't sound like *most people*.

They talked to staff who didn't know Alex from the other guests, and to the parents of the couple, who seemed more shaken by the incident than surprised. *No one* seemed particularly surprised. Maybe it wasn't surprising. Maybe it was evidence. Tyler could understand how it might eat away at you, knowing you were the reason why someone was in jail, even if it was justified. He thought it must have been worse that Chris Newman had *died there, in jail, I mean*, as Maxie had put it. If your mind was unbalanced enough he could see how you might come to feel responsible for his death.

It was all just speculation, Tyler supposed. People listened to *Crime and Question* for the speculation, for the hour and a half Tyler would later spend in the guest room at Sean's house, dictating what he had seen, what people had said, why he could understand a suicide from this perspective, from feeling like you'd killed someone. Even if that someone was a rapist, eighteen when convicted, although there was a mistake in his Dalton records that said he was seventeen. That was the biggest drama in what was now a sealed case, to protect the victims. There was little about the case anywhere, except that Alex Sable was the son of a prominent billionaire and private equity genius. Alex had no LinkedIn and no track record of what he'd done after USC. His Instagram was private.

Chris Newman had been a scholarship kid at Dalton, who traveled into Manhattan to attend classes. He was the star of the baseball team — which Alex was on — and a straight-A student. When he was indicted, his scholarship and acceptance to Dartmouth were revoked.

It was almost deliberately difficult to find information on the case; Tyler wondered if Alex's father wanted to hush the whole thing up, instead of hailing his son as a hero. There were no interviews from Alex, nothing except an article in the Dalton school paper about the baseball team taking sides, some for Alex, some for Chris. Newman was accused of blindfolding and raping six girls, and attempting a seventh. There was no forensic evidence, because the previous rapes were long past, and he never actually got past the blindfold on the seventh victim. Alex Sable himself punched Newman, knocking him out, and untied the blindfold, holding the shaking, crying girl in his arms. Or so *The Daily Mail* reported, in their one piece on the trial.

Chris was sentenced to forty years, no parole. He was a legal adult when he committed four of the rapes. He died of internal bleeding in 2016. The internal bleeding, it was speculated, was caused by a fight. The prison he spent over ten years in was one of the most brutal in the country.

While they ate frozen pizza for dinner, Tyler and Sean studied the photos of the scene that had been taken before they got there. Tyler clicked through them on his laptop; Sean shuffled around print-outs, which he claimed were superior.

"What do you think?" Tyler asked.

Sean nodded his head from side to side, chewed a little, nodded a little. "Looks like a suicide. Coroner says it looks like a suicide, though we won't know for sure until we get the tox screen back."

"But," Tyler prompted.

"Kid like this," Sean put down his pizza, "has *absolutely everything.* Son of a billionaire. At his *best friend's* wedding. Would he do it? Either he's dark, dark and twisted, or there's something more here. Those creepy girls hanging around us. That lawyer appearing out of thin air. Something feels off to me." He took another bite, spoke around it as he chewed. "But I don't know anyone like this, anywhere. Maybe they're all just... bored. That girl today. Stein-Golden. She seemed more bored than anything."

Tyler wasn't sure. She seemed a little strange, he thought, zooming in on the bathroom, on the toilet. There *was* something in the corner, underneath the toilet paper roll He scrolled in until he could see it, then hit the button to unblur.

It was round and metallic, maybe a piece from the bathroom, maybe something else. Tyler emailed it to his team in New York and had another slice of DiGiorno before he got the response. A single photo, perfectly clear, of a diamond and platinum bracelet. *Golden*, it read, in sparkling stones, and then a date from the previous September. Tyler Googled *Maxie Stein Golden wedding date* and of course she'd had a *Vogue* write-up on her wedding, with the date, with the photos of the bride getting ready, with a close up on the bespoke diamond bracelet that her father gave her as a wedding day present. It said *Golden* in the same looping letters that the one on the bathroom floor did, the same date, the same everything. It was the same bracelet.

"Did anyone find this? Anyone bag it?" Tyler asked Sean, turning his computer to face the detective.

Sean scanned a list. "Nope. Nothing like it."

"Mrs Stein-Golden might have picked it up today," Tyler noted.

"Did you see her with it?" Sean, ever nitpicking, asked. Tyler closed his eyes, trying to draw up the memory.

"I don't know," he said, finally. "But it was definitely in the bathroom this morning, and we definitely didn't see it by the time we got in there." Tyler *had* looked over there, *right* there, and no bracelet had glinted at him.

"You think one of the guys took it?" Sean shook his head. "They're a pretty honest bunch."

"I think… a lot of different things. At a minimum, she was in there and didn't want anyone to know. Whether he was alive or dead when she was…" Tyler let his thoughts trail to nothing.

"List of people who were in the bathroom today." Sean passed over a list with eight names on it. "List of people who were in the bedroom today." This one had almost fifteen. "Never seen a worse crime scene. I hope he killed himself, because, if he didn't, this would be a hell of a homicide to solve."

Tyler nodded. It had the makings of something good, the stopped watch, the missing bracelet, but those were usually the kind of things that you devoted one or two dead-end episodes to, tangents you spent a month on that led to more questions which would never be answered.

By the next morning, the scene had been cleaned up. The chief of police himself had talked to Mr Khan, esq., and he thought it was best to let *this family* put their son to rest. He told Strickland in no uncertain terms to *leave it alone* and was frustrated at the delay getting the body back from the autopsy. Alex went to cremation and then home to New York. Tyler pawed through the evidence bags, held the watch in a gloved hand, stared at the broken face. By 4,11 a.m., the watch had to have hit the side of the tub hard enough to crack the crystal face. He wondered how difficult it would be to crack the face of a fifty-thousand-dollar watch. The family hadn't even thought to ask for any of these things back, things like his wallet and his cufflinks, which now sat in labeled plastic bags in a box. It was amazing how quickly you could box up someone's life.

Part I
Lulu
February 2017

Lanserhof Lans couldn't prepare you for a 'weekend away with your friends from college, who hadn't seen you since your boyfriend tried to kill you, and himself. To be fair, Lulu thought, to Lanserhof Lans, probably very little could prepare you for that. To be fair, Lulu thought, to Carlos, he said that he didn't think purposefully crashing the tiny plane would kill them, and it hadn't. To be fair, Lulu thought, to Carlos again, he had always had little regard for his personal safety, so Lulu should have *calibrated her expectations* of him. That was something they taught you at Lanserhof Lans, in one of your three-hour intensive therapy sessions.

'Rehab for non-addicts' was how Maxie described it when Lulu tried to explain. You went there for two weeks, and they healed everything. They healed you inside and out! She had one friend who'd stayed for six months. Lulu would have stayed longer, but Carlos was going there to recuperate as well, and Lulu was afraid of him in a way she had maybe never been afraid of anyone. He wasn't the kind of person to go to 'rehab for non-addicts' and she felt, as she had in the weeks since he'd crashed the plane and left the two of them in the desert, that he really was following her. That he was after her. Out for her blood.

I wasn't trying to kill anyone! Carlos explained in the hospital in Las Vegas. *It was about her love. She doesn't love me. She doesn't love anyone! See how she looks at me now. With the eyes of a corpse.* He'd said it to her father and her father calmly told Carlos that his life may be a soap opera, but Lulu's was not. Afterwards, her father said *please avoid lunatics like that in the future* and when the box arrived with the ring they both looked at it and fell into gales of unlikely laughter. To think that she would marry him! *To think!*

It was such an embarrassing story to tell; that was the worst part. There was no way to recount it that didn't sound conceited or silly or just mortifying. This was a person who she'd shared a home and a life and *years* with. It wasn't really fair because Lulu didn't have a lot of options, being referred to in *Daily Mail* articles as the *Swanson drugstore heiress* kind of narrowed the pool. You lived in the assumption that anyone who was interested in you and wasn't from your background had ulterior motives. Lulu had spent the better part of age fourteen onward being described as *rich, smart, and fun* by the friends and friends and friends who tried and failed to set her up successfully. She'd started dating Carlos when she was twenty-three and still carried fat heavily in her cheeks and her thighs and her arms. When her hair was the color of movie theater popcorn, and she hadn't made the life-changing discovery of *skincare*. Pre-veneers, before she caved and made her Instagram public. *Before*.

Now, packing to go home, back to New York where everyone knew the person she'd been, waiting for Carlos to be escorted through their formerly shared house for the things he claimed Lulu hadn't sent over, she felt that clenching anxiety like right before the waxer ripped a strip off your bikini, a fear so palpable she could actually smell the turquoise wax that Kim used at her place on Melrose.

Lulu wasn't sure what to do because Lulu never knew how to deal with confrontation. In her family, confrontation usually ended in sarcasm and a really good meal because she came from the kind of family who ate dinner together every night at seven thirty and said *I love you* to each other every day. Maxie always said *no wonder you're such a mess* because Lulu expected this kind of behavior from everyone, which, her best friend from Harvard explained to her, was *utterly unrealistic*. That was the kind of thing they would tell you at Lanserhof Lans. Maxie admonished Lulu for telling Jessica, the bride-to-be and mastermind of this dreaded weekend, that she had spent two weeks at rehab-for-non-addicts. *She'll tell Will, and then he'll tell all his friends, and then everyone will know that you're a disaster*.

Lulu heard Carlos buzz himself into the stairs to her house. She listened while the security guy talked to him in a low, calm voice and she thought that, all things considered, she wasn't really a *mess* or a *disaster*.

She was the sum of the things that had happened to her, and as their absurdity increased, so did Lulu's tolerance for it. His feet were dull on the stairs, *thunks* and *clunks* that sounded exaggerated. He put his key in the door for effect, because it was unlocked, and the security guy was there.

They'd told her not to be here, but she'd needed to be. You couldn't confront your fears if you didn't believe in them — that was what you learned at Lanserhof Lans. She believed in Carlos, in the existence of violence, in the psychopathy that bought both of them a matched set of hospital beds, but she had *blacked out the trauma*, or so her doctors said. Lulu in fact remembered every moment of it, but it was easy, easier, to erase it, evenly and slowly, from edge to edge. She'd always been good at erasing people and the things they did that took you from your bright sparkly self to something dark and wispy.

Carlos' steps were quiet on the carpet of the guest room; his voice was quiet in reply to the security guy. He was being deliberately quiet to gaslight her, to make her believe that *she* was the delusional one. He was back in the hallway.

Weren't you allowed to perform magic in your own mind, to make something like a purposeful plane crash disappear? Maybe Carlos was right, and she was a corpse, blank and hollow.

He moved through the office, feet too loud again, making her wonder what *shoes* he'd possibly worn. Maybe the sum of the things that happened to you made you that way or maybe you became nothing when you spent so much time curating your life on social media. All that happiness and light and joy had to pour itself onto Instagram from somewhere. Maybe it didn't matter because if you could actively forget, if you could lay in the sun by the spa at Lanserhof Lans and close your eyes and see only nothingness, it meant that there was nothing left to hurt you.

When he walked into the dining room, where she stood at what used to be *their* French doors, the first thing she checked were his shoes. He was wearing riding boots and it was so purposeful she wanted to slap him. They'd met when she was twenty, living in London and spending her weekends riding at one country house or another. He was a good rider, but she was better and when she ran into him again, years later, in

LA, he'd offered to take her to Malibu for the horse-fix she'd been craving. When she looked at him now, he was so small in comparison to the picture in her mind. It was funny how loving someone could change them so much for the worse, as she had changed him, and he had changed her.

He was still too handsome for her and still very dashing and still really looked like a Disney prince, and in the end she was so disappointed in herself for being taken in by all of that. By the family and the accent and their beautiful winter home in Punta del Este and the way he said *I will love you more than anyone ever could.* She'd always thought *you won't love me as much as my parents*, which was something that they told her she needed to *work on* at Lanserhof Lans. She hadn't worked on it. Her parents had known her through every iteration of bad to worse and they loved her still.

"Lulu," he said, in his dashing, Disney prince way, and she took four steps up to his symmetrical face and slapped it once, very hard. It hurt her hand more than she'd been expecting and the worst part was that it didn't even leave a mark. He smiled at her with his even white mouth. "Is that a yes?"

She'd returned the ring. Probably if he hadn't tried to kill them both she would have said yes, been like Maxie and Jessica, chosen Lenten roses and shades of white and flavors of buttercream. Instead there was the searing heat of the sand underneath the desert sun and the floating, errant thought, as they waited for the ambulance, of a book she'd read called *Empty Mansions* about an heiress from the early nineteen-hundreds whose father invented Las Vegas. She couldn't remember how he invented Las Vegas, just that his last name was Clarke and he used to sell eggs. That was what Lulu had thought about, laying on the sand that left burns along her exposed skin and that was what Lulu thought about now, searching for the red mark on his face, for the slightest sign that hitting him had *done* something.

He physically moved her like she was a doll and sat down at the dining room table like he still lived there. He took out his Juul and smoked it like a cowboy smoking a Marlboro. He traced the burns on the table from some accident he'd never explained away that happened while she was on a Revolve trip. The table had cost five thousand dollars on

1stdibs, and she thought often that she couldn't wait to be rid of all of it, to empty this house of the beautiful things she'd filled it with and start over. He opened a hand to reveal a palm of jewelry that he'd given her, and she quirked an eyebrow.

"Really?" she asked.

"I know you'll just give it away if I don't take it. Bad juju, right, Louisa?" He said her name like *Luisa*.

"I hadn't decided yet," she said, even though she'd already given four pieces to her cleaning lady.

"No, no. You don't *decide* superstition. Here you are, waging the war against *bad energy*. Fighting like Glinda the good witch. Burning the sage, lighting the candles, paying attention to the full moon. Did you ever think, *Louisa*, that maybe the bad energy is *you*?" He continued smoking his Juul. She wanted to smack it out of his hand, out of his mouth, but instead she removed it with the tips of her fingers. "In the end they'll find out who you are. That it's all just smoke and mirrors," he told her, in the cryptic way that once upon a time had been alluring.

"Take all the jewelry. Take anything that's yours. I never needed you, you know."

"That's the problem," he said, and stood. "That's the problem that you can't even *see*. You can't pay the doctors to make you whole, Lulu. You can't fix something that never worked. You think I did this to you, this… " he motioned to her, to nothing. "But you, you did this to yourself. You were always careless, always vacant. You can pretend you're better than we are, but that's just a good charade."

It would have been better or maybe easier if he'd yelled and screamed and tried to throw a candlestick at her head. She'd hoped in some shameful part of her mind that they would sit down and talk about the mistakes and misdeeds and the dark woods they'd traversed together. That she would ask him how he'd gotten foot-long scorch marks on the dining room table, and he would ask her if she'd ever really loved him. That she could say *yes, I really did, once* and then take responsibility for growing out of love with him and not doing enough about it, for complacency, for carelessness. It was easy to be careless when your life was full, and he was guilty of it too. When she looked at him now, she couldn't even see the parts of him that had been so transcendently exceptional to her. She couldn't remember what his face looked like when he'd crashed the plane and she wasn't sure that this was a person whom she'd spent years upon heaping years of her days with. He felt so alien to her, like the desert outside Las Vegas, like something she'd never encountered before. She wanted to say a grand and sweeping *I'm sorry,* but she wasn't sorry for anything she'd done, not when he was saying these things to her, things that were maybe true.

"Do you have everything you need? I have to get back to packing."

He took her small face in his soft hands, and she tried to pull away. He held it too tightly. She didn't call for security even though she felt like she should, and she knew immediately that he had won because of it. "I will always be the person who loved you more than anyone could," he told her. "And you will be the stupid girl who found in that something to be afraid of."

It was so crashingly dramatic, that all she could think about was her father's words, *Please avoid lunatics like that in the future.*

"I'm not afraid of anything," she lied to him. "Least of all, you." He dropped her chin in disappointment. "You could have killed me, you know," she said, almost conversationally.

"What a waste that would have been," he replied, boots smacking against the glossy wood floors, "of my life, I mean. Not yours."

When he left, he slammed the door with all the emphasis of an episode of *Grey's Anatomy*, except Shonda Rhimes would have written him to be better than that, to be redeemable. Lulu decided to accept what the universe had presented her with and call her team in Austria, her team of doctors, not the team of people who attended to her Instagram influencer needs. Before she could, she had to go sit by the pool and smother her face with a Missoni outdoor pillow so that the roaming security wouldn't hear her crying.

The scariest thing of all was the idea that he might be right about her.

Rob
February 2017

Rob shifted the blazers in his half-empty closet and thought that he really should use his paycheck more carefully. He'd been working for almost ten years now, and he didn't have a single bespoke blazer to show for it, or even a $1200 one that he wouldn't be embarrassed to wear in front of Alex. Alex mocked him relentlessly for his Topman, J.Crew, Rag & Bone wardrobe, for the Gucci sweatshirt he'd bought off The RealReal, for the Saint Laurent varsity jacket from the same resale website, which Alex had gotten the day it came out. By the time Rob bought it, Alex had stopped wearing his — probably lost at a party in Palm Springs with a bunch of famous people who would casually tag Alex in their photos. Tags that Alex would never check, a jacket Alex would never find, wool-blend sweaters that he would shamelessly mock Rob for. Rob used to share Alex's clothes, back when they were freshman-year roommates, lifetimes ago. Before Alex decided that everyone was taking advantage of him, and the cost of bottle service at Bootsy Bellows should be shared.

"What are you doing?" Ronnie asked. She was wearing Uggs and leggings and chewing gum in a way that Rob thought might kill him one day. It wasn't making noise, but it was revealing the inside of her mouth, and every time he saw her tongue moving he was disgusted by her. She was like the blazers in his closet, something he didn't want, but all he could afford to have. Once you spent enough time with Alex, he ruined everything for you. "Hel-lo. Rob."

"Packing," he said. Ronnie was not the kind of person to whom he could explain the need for him to have better clothes; she already thought he didn't spend enough money on *her*, which was part of her reasoning behind them moving in together. She wanted the big velvet Gucci bag with the Gs on it, and if they were sharing one rent, that was a much more realizable objective, she told him. He could never reconcile her Long

Island housewife way of speaking with the occasional finance term that emerged from the cavernous hole that her gum was currently rolling in.

She shuffled up to him and rubbed herself against him, which would have been a lot more interesting if she hadn't been wearing the ugliest shoes imaginable and tilting her gum-chewing face up to his. At least she was objectively hot, crazy skinny, skinnier than any of the girls Alex had dated, and she dressed well. She had a decent face. Jessica seemed to like her, which he thought was an endorsement. Jessica had even posted a video of the four of them from a college friend's wedding.

"Need help?" she purred in his ear. Ronnie had no sense of what he wanted or when he wanted it; sometimes he thought her entire point of reference of what a girlfriend should be came from old Bond movies. "Baby," she hissed. Rob hated the word *baby* when anyone used it, but it was particularly bad when it referred to *him*. "Can't I go with you? Jessica won't say no when I get there."

Rob turned back to his closet and resolved that he would use most of his next paycheck to go shopping. He wished he could ask Will to help him, or even Jessica, but that was too embarrassing. He wished that Ronnie understood what he wanted, the demure ease with which Jessica and Will dressed and traveled and acted and lived their lives, a way of being that was utterly opposite to Rob's Miami upbringing. If only his father hadn't been a *dentist*. Everything would have been easier if he had just been able to casually say *he works in finance*. If they'd lived in a house with a pool instead of an apartment. If Rob hadn't been Rob, but someone better, someone shinier. If Ronnie were as great as he pretended she was when they were in public.

"Baby?"

"Please don't call me that," Rob said. He shook his head. "I'm packing. You can't go. I've told you fifty times. You're not invited. You can't go. You can't just *show up*."

"I can't just show up? They don't even *like* you, Rob, they just keep you around to make fun of you. God, you're such a fucking idiot sometimes. It's like you can't even see how little they *think* of you, and your sad job as a trader. A *trader*. I mean, I could be a trader." She stuck out a hipbone and balanced her scary-thin arm on it. "They're only *nice* to you because you've been friends for so long, and Will, like, doesn't have any friends. But Alex literally treats you like trash."

"He doesn't treat me like trash," Rob countered. "And this isn't a good way to convince me to live with you."

"I shouldn't have to convince you! You should want to date me! I'm a commodity, Rob. I am a goddamn commodity."

It was going to kill him that she cursed so much. He'd noticed Jessica flinched at it the last time they'd hung out together. He didn't understand how Ronnie could want so much to be rich, to have nice things, but only in an obvious way, the anti-Jessica, the things that everyone knew they were supposed to want. All the worst of anything over a thousand dollars.

"He treats you. Like. Trash. And you suck up to him like everyone else because he's the son of a billionaire, and you want the trips on the private plane and the random gifts and the free Postmates." She made a clucking noise with her tongue. Rob thought that this was a little harsh. He didn't *mind* those things when Alex didn't mind sharing them.

"I'm sorry you feel that way, Ronnie," Rob said, folding a pair of socks in half, and she took this excellent moment to burst into what felt like very insincere tears.

"You have *ruined* me, Rob. All you do is tell me that I'm not fucking good enough. I can't come to your stupid weekend, and I can't hang out with your friends, and you don't want to move in together. All you want is for me to be Jessica. Well, I would *love* to be Jessica, but my dad isn't worth five hundred million dollars, so it's a little challenging, okay? Like, did you maybe ever consider that *you're* not good enough for these people, that you don't belong, that your standards are absurd? That you don't deserve the life you want when you treat the people who try to love you like *they're* trash?"

Rob tried to up the pace of his packing. Will had told him to bring a tux, but he decided a suit would be fine. "Ronnie, they're not *these people*; they're my best friends. I've been friends with Alex and Will for almost ten years. They just want the best for me. And I'm not telling you you're not enough, but, like, have we been together long enough for us to justify moving in? It's been, what, a year?"

"Sixteen months, you piece of shit," Ronnie spat, and her gum almost left her mouth. He was impressed she hadn't swallowed it during her rant. The worst part was that she was right; he *did* want a Jessica. Will was handsome and came from a slightly better family than Rob's, and, anyway, he was more *refined*, as Alex put it. Will got the better girl, the girl who got him his job, but that didn't mean that Rob wasn't allowed to *want* that, to see it and say *I should have that.* Instead he had Ronnie, hair like feathers from starving herself, face stretched into some weird semblance of anger, words cutting and relentless. She intended a fatal blow, but these were just surface wounds. Ronnie was upset that she wasn't invited. Rob had often been upset that he wasn't invited. You said the things you didn't mean when you hated yourself the most, that much he knew, that much he'd been doing since he'd switched to private school in ninth grade.

"Ronnie, I love you. I think I treat you as best as anyone could. I don't know why you have such a personal vendetta against my friends, because all you do is suck up to them and beg to hang out with them," he said.

"You think you're better than I am because you have the honor of being Alex Sable's little minion. Alex Sable is a fucking creep, Rob. He's a loser. He has no job. All he has is a rich dad, and you think that's the best thing in the world. I hope we don't move in together. I never want to be like you. I want what Jessica and Will have. Love and mutual respect and a good life with everything they want. You want to *be* Alex. Do you know how messed up that is?" Ronnie demanded. He was almost finished packing. She stamped her foot as he zipped up his bag. He should have bought an Away bag, because that was the cool suitcase that Alex and Will and Jessica all had ten of, but he kept forgetting to upgrade his old gym bag. He could already hear Alex talking to him about it, *What, out of garbage bags?* And wondered if he had time to run down to the Away store before the train.

"I love you, Ronnie," Rob repeated. "I'm sorry that you feel this way." Alex had taught him that, apology without acknowledgement. "Why don't you go to SoulCycle? That always calms you down."

She rolled her eyes. "You don't listen when we fight. Like, I'm literally saying things that should rip you apart, because they're so *true*, and you just don't even *hear* me. You don't hear me, and you don't care. Sometimes I feel like I'm just a placeholder until you can convince some rich girl that you're worth her time."

Rob thought that *all* the time. He thought that Ronnie was starting to know him too well. He thought that Ronnie wanted all the same things he wanted, she just wasn't friends with a billionaire, and she was jealous.

He kissed her goodbye and went twenty minutes out of his way to get the Away suitcase. When he met Alex at Penn Station, Alex pointed at the sticker on the top of the case and laughed. "Just get it?" he asked. "Finally run out of Hefty bags? Or did that scary gym bag of yours just disintegrate at the dry cleaners?" He slapped an arm around Rob's shoulder and produced a flask from which they drank something that tasted like lighter fluid. They met two girls on the train and played a drinking game that was less game, more drinking. Alex took one of the girls into the disgusting Amtrak bathroom and Rob reminded himself that Ronnie was skinnier than that girl, skinnier than anyone that Alex had dated. Ronnie was fine.

Alex
February 10th, 2017

Alex inhaled the dregs of last night's coke by sticking his nose into the tiny plastic bag and snorting.

"You sound like a pig," Rob commented.

Will turned away from the wheel in panicked confusion. He was a bad driver, and the car skidded a little on the winter roads as he did. Alex licked his finger and ran it over the inside of the bag, then onto his teeth. "You can't do that in my car. What if we get pulled over?"

Alex looked out onto the empty road in front of them, at the abandoned landscape around them. "Then you'll be glad I did the drugs. Can't arrest someone for an empty plastic bag." He put it in the glove compartment.

"Take that out," Will commanded. Alex didn't listen. His mouth was starting to numb but there hadn't been enough left to make what was a *dark* few days ahead a little more palatable. He should have thought it through and gotten more. He needed the serotonin boost.

"It's the middle of the day. What's the point of doing cocaine in the *middle* of the day?" Will asked. Rob bobbed in his seat. He sat in the middle of the backseat in a desperate bid to be included, leaning too far forward. If Alex were driving, he would have stopped suddenly so that Rob would hit his face and they could laugh at him for still, after all these years, trying *so hard* to be their friend, even though he already was.

Alex ignored Will. Rob wiggled in Alex's direction. "Tell Will what you said on the train."

There was snow on the ground and in the air. Alex wondered if they would get snowed in and if that would make it better or worse. He wondered if there would be enough snow for sledding. The funny thing about coke, good coke, was that it relaxed you while it upped your anxiety. You were happy and free and floating, floating but aware. The comedown from last night had been exacerbated by the claustrophobia of a shared train car with bobbing Rob, but Alex felt better now, like he might be able to make it through.

"I said a lot of things on the train," Alex replied. He unlocked his phone to a text from his father, *Sunday dinner is a mandatory performance. No excuses.* He rolled his window down a centimeter and back up.

"What are you *doing*?" Will yelled, like he had grabbed the wheel and tried to run them off the road.

"Rolling down my window. Jesus Christ. Do you need a Xanax?" Alex asked. Now that the thought had occurred to him it was all he wanted to do, take the wheel, turn it too far.

"He said that he was a truffle pig for yeast infections," Rob put in, butchering the line so artfully that Alex actually managed a little embarrassment.

"That's disgusting," Will replied.

"If you'd heard it in context, it wouldn't be," Alex told him. "Rob didn't even know what a truffle pig *was*."

"I know what a truffle pig is," Rob said, even though he didn't. Alex turned up the podcast.

"*Maybe people were right, and what I missed all along, in the bubble that I didn't know surrounded me, was the bare fact, there are some wounds from which you will never recover. From the producers of The America Game and Successive, this is, Tyler Carroll, for Crime and Question.*" Alex opened his eyes and flicked to the next chapter.

Rob leaned in between the front and passenger seat. "Come on," he said. "Can't we turn it off? I don't know how many more boy prostitute murders I can take."

Will hit a button. "That was *The Alienist* on Audible. This one wasn't even about a murder."

"It's all just… creepy." Rob said. Rob didn't have a creatively empathetic bone in his body, so *of course* parsing the psychology behind a crime wouldn't be interesting to him. Alex sighed.

"We can turn it back on, if you really want," Rob said, in his *way*, which was suddenly so annoying. In the months since Alex had been pulled back to New York, everything and everyone was annoying, the way his mother insisted they all brunch on Saturday, how he had to have check-ins with his dad's financial managers like he wasn't almost thirty, the friends who'd picked boring girlfriends and wives to fill their time and space and asked that they all pretend to like each other, the society parties that no one worthwhile showed up to, the lack of decent rice bowl options. After LA, Disneyworld for adults, it was all dark grey and exhausting. He woke up at noon most days to the same cold and drab New York of 1896, or whenever *The Alienist* had been set. It was smoky and dirty and just *boring*, an endless loop of life that he had already lived.

Will hit the same button on his pathetic BMW dashboard. Alex didn't know anyone in LA who had a BMW; it was the car of *Clueless*, not 2017. The temptation had built within him and now his mind was entirely occupied by the idea of messing with the car, with Will. "This podcast is brought to you by—"

Alex turned it off himself. He knew he was going to have to pull it together, because it was Will's goddamn bachelor party, and knowing this new Will, Will who wanted to be a Supreme Court judge, this would be his only wedding, which was the kind of annoying thing Will would do, get married at twenty-nine and stay married to his sniveling excuse for a bride for the rest of their lives. Just like Will would have a *shared Valentine's Day weekend* bachelor party *with his wife*, in the ridiculous mansion they were renting for their wedding, to *lay the base of memories*, which was a line they all knew Will repeated verbatim from the ninety-five-pound Jessica. If he did land them in a ditch it would probably just prolong everything. Maybe it would be better when they were with other people. Maybe it wouldn't.

"Is your four-wheel drive on?" Rob asked.

"Yeah," Will said. Alex moved his seat back, ostensibly so that he could stretch his legs out, in reality to take him away from the siren song of the steering wheel.

"Valentine's Day weekend," Rob said, leaning forward again. He smelled like Ivory soap, which was the soap he'd used in college, which was the first time Alex had ever encountered such weird, powder-scented body gel. "*Real* original."

"At least you have an excuse not to be with Ronnie," Will replied. He held the wheel at ten and two and even *that* pissed Alex off, because no one held the wheel at ten and two; it wasn't comfortable. Alex never actually learned how to drive, but he still knew that from the one time he'd had to drive back from Coachella, when they'd all been too hungover, and he was the only one with enough confidence to be able to eat three burgers and keep the car kind of steady. "And it'll be fine. Wait until you see the house."

"How'd you find this place?" Rob asked.

"Drop a pin in the middle of fucking nowhere and build a tent around it?" Alex suggested. They were three and a half hours from the nearest commercial airport, two from the train station, and a full eight-hour drive from New York.

"It's one of Jessica's friend's, friend's houses," Will said, eyes shifting to meet Rob's in the rearview mirror, to exchange a look about Alex that Alex could *see*. Because they rarely did anything more than drink, Will and Rob acted like drugs incapacitated you completely, like you couldn't *see* what was directly in front of you. He wasn't in a k-hole.

Alex seized the wheel as Will was looking at Rob, turning them off with a sudden sharpness into the whiteness that bordered the road. It wasn't particularly exciting, because the car was moving fairly slowly and there was nothing for them to hit, but it still caused Will to erupt into a barrage of angry squawking.

"What is wrong with you? Do you need to be in rehab, or something?" If Alex could have beaten the self-righteousness out of Will he would have done it until his hands were bloody and bruised. "Please don't try to *kill* us because you're having a quarter-life crisis." Will slammed into the accelerator, annoyed; the cars' wheels spun in the muddy snow. They were stuck.

"I hope I don't live to be a hundred and twenty," Alex replied.

Rob hit Alex on the shoulder appreciatively. Alex rolled his eyes. "Or even a hundred." Rob's humor wasn't humor. It was just modified repetition of something someone else had said.

"There was a chipmunk in the road. I thought you wouldn't want to hit it," Alex told Will. Will shook his head. "Why else would I have done that? It wasn't dangerous. God forbid we take you on a rollercoaster. You might wet your pants."

"There was no *chipmunk*," Will said. He pulled his phone out and started dialing.

"There was," Alex assured him. "You didn't see it because you were looking at Rob. I mean, seriously, *why else* would I have done that?"

Will looked at the road again, phone hesitating in his hand. Rob bobbed and nodded, nodded and bobbed. "I saw it," Rob told them. "I think it ran that way." He pointed to the left.

There was such satisfaction in watching Will struggle to decide if the chipmunk was real. It played across his unremarkable features, not believing Alex but feeling like Rob was a credible witness, hearing the question in his own head, hoping that his supposed best friend wasn't that far gone. Will lifted his phone back up and hit a number.

"Hey," he began. "We're a couple miles away and skidded off the road." He looked at Alex for a beat too long. Rob's memory was like Silly Putty; he would always believe what he hadn't seen. People would believe anything if you said it with enough conviction, and once you'd gained the conviction of one person you won the entire game. "I think… we're east?" Will said. "Hold on. Let me check the compass." Will turned to Alex. "Bring up your compass app."

"I don't have a compass app."

"Everyone has the compass app. It comes with your phone."

"Can't they just go the way you would go to pick someone up from the train station? If we're on the main road, surely they'll be able to find us? Or we could, I don't know, *drop a pin*?"

"Oh," Will said into the phone. "Alex points out that I can share my location with you. I'll share it with Jessica, then can you send someone for us?"

There was a dangling *please*. In the six years since Alex had left New York, Will met Jessica and went to law school and started going to trials and it wasn't just that, it was that he'd cut off all his floppy hair and stopped just doing things to do them. He lived in pursuit of an existence that was clean and controlled, right down to his college friends, Alex and Rob. Rob who played the part perfectly, Rob in the button-down shirt he wore today, like he was an off-duty trader. He *was* an off-duty trader, that was the thing. They were all the things they weren't supposed to be, the things they hadn't wanted to become.

There was a sense of possibility that you had when you were twenty, an idea that you could be more than a watered-down version of your father, that there was a wide world of creative pursuits waiting for you. There wasn't. That was where it stemmed from, the sinking despondency that you had all failed in being something *interesting*. That was it, this was all it ever would be, key bumps and bottles of scotch and Socialista after Cipriani and waking up at noon. That your friends weren't the eager-to-please sidekicks, up for anything, that even the best parties were just groups of circulating people, that there was no great mission awaiting you. What was compelling at age eighteen was still supposed to stimulate you at thirty. Life didn't open up like a flower and reveal to you something incredible. This was it.

"Too bad that guy Adam is coming," Rob commented inside the over-heated car as they waited. "He tries so hard. It's awkward."

"You try so hard, it's awkward," Alex replied, without missing a beat. Rob apparently decided that Alex was joking, so he laughed.

"He's a weird guy, Will. I don't know why you're friends with him," Rob continued.

"I don't know why I'm friends with you, most of the time." Alex looked from one to the other. "Either of you, but, Rob, you're the bigger offender."

"He's nice. He's normal. You just don't like normal people," Will accused Alex.

Alex held up his hands. "I'm not the one complaining about it! Take it up with the guy in the J.Crew blazer."

Will didn't take it up with Rob and Rob didn't say anything, probably because the blazer *was* from J.Crew. Alex wondered if life was always this mundane, a series of tasks and conversations, or if it was just that life in New York, with these people, was unlivable. He wished he could tell his nineteen-year-old self what it would be like, the endless rounds of weddings and mandatory events, the handshakes and the pitter-patter of small talk. You thought that adulthood meant everything you could want, but what if your only *everything* was something different and exciting, something that made you actually actively *feel?* Maybe the real problem was that Will and Rob had changed and Alex had not. Alex was in pursuit of all things *glorious* and heart-pounding; Will and Rob wanted the trappings of becoming a Respectable Person In The World.

It took twenty minutes for a middle-aged woman named Carol to get one of the groundskeepers down in a Range Rover for them. He told Will not to worry about his car and they piled into the heated seats, Alex taking the front.

"There've been two murders at the Heathcotes' house," Will said. "That was one of the biggest reasons why I didn't want to do it there."

"I don't think there's such a thing as scandal by proxy," Alex told him. "If there were, you'd have a problem with me."

"You were the hero. There's also no such thing as heroism by proxy."

Rob leaned forward again, in between Alex and the man driving them. "I'm surprised they didn't get you on the show, to talk about catching a victim."

"Catching a victim? He caught a *rapist*."

"You know what I mean."

"Since Chris is dead, I don't know how that would work on *Crime and Question*." Alex turned his face to the window. He didn't know enough about jail to say it definitively, but he felt like people weren't supposed die in jail, not in America, and especially not bright young things like Chris Newman, who used to juggle baseballs during practice.

"I mean, half the people they talk about on the show are dead," Will said. "Maybe they could interview the victims—"

"I don't think most rape victims are trying to be interviewed about what happened to them, especially a bunch of Upper East Side princesses who just want to grow up and get married and pretend it never happened," Alex shot back.

They all knew that Will wanted to ask who it was, the girl he'd found being raped by Chris when he was eighteen, the girl who was shaking on that freezing balcony above the city, looking up at Alex like he had saved her life. He hadn't saved her life, and he certainly hadn't saved Chris's, so the least he could do was protect her, let her get a chance at the sad, boring life she wanted. Get married, move into a penthouse like her parents, send her kids to the same schools she had gone to hope they didn't get raped.

"How do you know the Heathcotes?" the groundskeeper asked politely.

"My fiancée's best friend, Lulu Swanson, is a good friend of Phillip's," Will replied, voice equally measured, like they were at a tea party and the groundskeeper was a guest to be condescended to.

"We haven't seen Miss Swanson in years," he said, nodding. "It will be nice to have her back."

"She's changed a lot," Will replied, and there was a weight to his tone that Alex didn't miss.

"What do you mean?" Alex watched the whiteness blanketing the road in front of them.

"Oh, yeah, how do you know her, again?" Will asked.

"She's just one of those people you know."

"She's an Instagram celebrity," Rob put in. Alex felt his fingers twitching.

"She started a jewelry line, I think, and always goes to fashion week," Will commented.

"That's what they all do," Alex said, letting his forehead drop against the cold window. "Start a jewelry line, go to fashion week, write for *Harper's Bazaar*." All those girls standing behind that cheap wooden podium, swearing on a Bible like it meant something, talking about Chris. That moment Allie Makersman said it, *it was him, it smelled like him, like his soap; I always smell it in class* and Alex thought of *Atonement*, which came out a year later, *you saw him, or you know it was him?* How he hadn't even noticed people's soaps before, how strange he smelled that first week of college when he used Rob's Ivory, how foreign. Alex didn't have one soap specific to him, *his soap*, he usually ended up borrowing someone else's, until he couldn't stop hearing it, her stupid nasal voice, *I always smell it in class* and suddenly he needed a soap that would be odorless and colorless and flavorless and wouldn't remind him of that line, *you saw him, or you know it was him?*

Alex saw him.

Lulu
February 10th, 2017

Lulu missed winter in a way that was making her sick. She missed New York in a way that was making her sick; she was permanently sick, permanently nauseous, and no number of over-the-counter pregnancy tests or vials of drawn blood were giving her the answers that would have been easy. She put her cheek against the cold of her childhood window and closed her eyes. Being at her parents' house made her feel like something was *really* wrong, which was ironic, because all she'd done lately was try to convince herself that *nothing* was wrong. It felt like being home sick from school but not really being sick, just waking up overtired, eyelids heavy and throat raw from too much talking, wanting to stay in your room and watch TV and have Molly bring you up tea and biscuits and orange slices. It had been such a luxury, staying home from school on an icy day. When she went to boarding school there was no option of that, there were no sick days. *The world doesn't stop because you're sick,* her freshman dean told her, and that must have changed her, that puritanical hardness that she sometimes heard in her mother's clipped Connecticut consonants.

Now here she was, across the country from her real home that didn't feel like hers any more, frozen in indecision. There wasn't indecision at boarding school, either; there wasn't indecision in New England. Lulu pulled on socks and the matching top to her cashmere sweatsuit and Chanel combat boots and creaked the door to her room open. "Mom?" she called. "Mother?"

No one replied, even though Lulu heard the distinct noises of at least three staff members in the house. She left her room, tromped down the two flights of stairs, and rummaged through the coat closet until she found an old full-length fur that looked decent enough and a Gucci purse that someone had definitely given her mother as a gift because it was *way* too gaudy for Mrs Swanson. It had forty-three dollars inside. Lulu swung it on her shoulder and snapped an Instastory in the hall mirror, de Kooning in the reflection behind her, giant phone covering her unwashed face. *My mother has better taste than I do*, she typed.

The walk to Yura was longer than she'd remembered — a lot longer, and that wasn't just because she never walked in LA. It was long and *empty*, empty of people, maybe because it was ten a.m. on a Friday in February, but still. She'd done this walk every day for more than half of her life; it seemed unfathomable that New York, her New York, could ever be so empty.

Lulu stopped in the E.A.T. gift shop and bought a pair of heart sunglasses for eleven dollars. It was warm inside and smelled like the baking bread next door and she decided that she didn't care about going all the way to Yura when it was freezing outside and she still felt so exposed and raw everywhere, like she had in the desert. She went into E.A.T. to go and got herself a pain au chocolat and a coffee and a cucumber and chevre sandwich for later, and then she was basically out of money from her mother's purse.

She ordered herself an Uber Black and dropped onto the leather seats. "Only four blocks," the driver said, shaking his head.

"It's cold," she replied. Her phone rang; it was her agent, Cassidy. She put it on speaker.

"Hey. You're up early."

"It's eight a.m."

"Oh. Then I'm late."

"So I talked to Shane. He says he has to meet with you again."

"I'm away," Lulu said.

"You're not away forever," Cassidy replied. Lulu wanted to tell her very melodramatically, *maybe I am*, but she always tried to be manageable instead of exhausting to the people who got her paid.

"Why does he need to meet? It's a simple collab. They approached *me*."

"I know."

"Maybe we could remind them of that."

"I will."

They were both silent.

"He thinks you're cool. Just see him again, fluff his ego, whatever. You'll be the one laughing all the way to the bank." Cassidy always said this — *You'll be the one laughing all the way to the bank!* any time Lulu was asked to DJ something other than a fashion party, which was the only thing she actually enjoyed doing. "Let him feel cool because he gets to hang out with you."

Lulu snorted into her undrunk coffee. "I'm not cool," she said, and it sounded pathetic when she said it, because they both knew that the reason for her hundreds of thousands of followers was her intrinsic, unpurchaseable coolness. Her most recent write-up, in *W*, was entitled *The Last, Best Cool Girl.*

"I'll schedule it for when you're back. When are you back?"

"I don't know." Lulu sighed onto the window. Her breath made a heart. "Tuesday, I suppose."

"How are you doing?"

There was such weight to this question, now; such dense *meaning.*

"I'm okay. How are you?" Lulu knew Cassidy was thinking all of the things, things like *I wonder if he really did propose* and *how horrible it must have been for her to see him with June* and all the things everyone was thinking when they saw her now, things that were more tragic than this lowest-of-low version of herself.

They pulled up outside her house, behind a beaten-up Honda. Yael was grabbing a suitcase out of the back. "I should go," Lulu told her agent.

"I'll set the meeting for Wednesday."

"Can you make it a day meeting?" Lulu swung the car door open with her foot.

"Hey," Yael said. "I didn't recognize you with your hood on." Lulu reached up and felt the cashmere around her head. "Sorry, I'm early. I came straight from the train station." She wasn't early; she was on time. Lulu was late.

"Don't worry," Lulu said, looking at the suitcase, feeling dull and like she hadn't washed her face. "Thank you, sir," she told her driver. She still had Cassidy on the phone.

"Don't take Uber four blocks!" he yelled before he sped off. Lulu shut her eyes behind her stupid heart glasses.

"You took an Uber four blocks?"

She started up the walk to her house. "I've got to go, Cassidy," she said, hitting the red button even though her agent had been speaking about *day meetings*. "I borrowed a purse from my mom and ran out of money," she told Yael, and as she heard herself say it the monumental symbolism welled up inside of her and made her want to laugh. "Sorry. I'm jetlagged. I just woke up and rolled out of bed to get coffee." Lulu pushed the door to her house open. It smelled like fresh coffee and blueberry cake and the last thing in the world she wanted to do was get in a car and drive seven hours to New Hampshire to have some kind of weird Valentine's Day weekend with Jessica and her uptight husband, or husband to be, or whatever it was that they were meant to call Will these days.

"It smells like coffee here, too," Yael said.

"Someone must have just made it," Lulu replied. "Would you like anything? I need to go ask them to bring the car around."

"Oh," Yael looked at the marble floor, at the gilt-edged mirror, at the ugly Richter painting above the fireplace. "I'm good. But we can go get the car; seriously, Lulu, we don't need someone to bring it around—"

Lulu tried to wave her away in a hostessy way, but it just ended up looking wan and limp. "No, no. That's what they're here for!" she said faux-cheerfully, and then ran into the kitchen where she could drop her uneaten food and open the top of her coffee with one shaking hand and breathe in the blueberry cake and remember that it was up to her to make it all fine, wasn't it? Wasn't that what they told her at Lanserhof Lans? *You control your life*. If they said it at Lanserhof Lans then it had to be true and if it was true then she could control the spinning way she felt, like she'd come unstuck in time and she wasn't sure how to stay still any more.

Maxie
February 10th, 2017

Maxie could not believe that she had just flown halfway across the country to attend a Valentine's Day bachelorette with Jessica and *her* fiancée, and no one else's plus-one. Jessica told Maxie it was because this wasn't a *real* bach, it was just a weekend, and, anyway, they didn't want to upset Lulu or Victoria, *did they*? So then *Maxie* was the bitch who didn't care about her best friends' simultaneous break-ups and nervous break*downs*, because Maxie wanted to spend the weekend before Valentine's Day with her husband. Or, at least, Maxie wanted to spend the weekend before Valentine's Day without Jessica's husband.

She felt herself getting irrationally frustrated and decided to call Freddie, while she was thinking of him.

"What's up," Freddie answered.

"Hi, babe," Maxie said. She *hated* when he picked up like that. "I'm on my way to Lulu's. I thought I would call and see how you are."

"Good. You leave this morning?" Freddie shifted the phone mid-sentence.

"No. I took a red-eye. Didn't you notice I wasn't in our bed last night?" She tried to keep her tone light.

"Kind of a big week over here. Hey, are you bringing a cake for that brunch my mom is having? She said you should."

"No. I'm out of town. And it's so stupid for me to go to the *same* bakery that your mom is going to go to on the day of *brunch*" — she couldn't keep the derision out of her voice—"so that she feels like I'm fulfilling some sort of wifely duty. She can just buy the cake herself. I'll happily pay for it."

"It's not about *paying* for it. You know that. It's the effort. It's not that hard. Just have it delivered." Freddie sounded distracted *and* annoyed, a winning combo.

"They don't deliver, Freddie. Nowhere in the one-horse-town we live in *delivers*. It's *Chicago*. It's not New York."

"As you remind me. Every. Single. Day. Look, Max, I need to go. Can you just deal with the cake?"

"Freddie. I will be in New Hampshire. I can't deal with the cake. I literally have no means of getting a cake to your mother on Sunday morning unless *you* want to go get it."

"Thanks," her husband replied. "Super helpful. Bye."

Maxie dropped her iPhone into her lap and rested her head against the window. People told you not to get married so young because men were so immature. People used to get married even younger. Freddie was just young; Freddie would change. Freddie would be fine, and she would be fine and *together*, they would be fine.

Her phone dinged. Victoria, *Lulu's lost so much weight.* Maxie sighed. *I think I found all of it,* Victoria's message continued. Maxie didn't want to open the text yet because that meant she would have to reply. *She really does look like a DJ.* And then a picture of Lulu, her waist-length hair tucked into a hood, cutting a piece of Molly's blueberry cake. She looked exhausted. *I wonder if it's coke?* Maxie opened the text; Victoria was typing. *That got her so skinny?*

Lulu moved to LA after college; she was the only one in their ten-person friend group who didn't go to New York. While the rest of them got engaged and moved to Chicago and Boston and Philadelphia to be with their significant others, left their jobs for the new city, curated a life for themselves around engagement parties and family vacations and the Hamptons, Lulu wore weird outfits and stood behind tables at parties while they all pitied her, mocked her, whispered about her. Then she started dating a dashing Brazilian with a tequila brand, then she was kind of famous, then she was a person to brag about knowing instead of deride for pleasure. People had been excited that she was a bridesmaid at Maxie's wedding in July, so excited that it was almost annoying, except Lulu got Maxie her *vogue.com* article, so she couldn't really be annoyed, could she?

Maxie felt a pounding in her temples when she thought back on resenting that stupid photo of Lulu and Carlos dancing on the beach at her wedding. After you got married, there was so much less to do, so much more time for *thinking*, and while Maxie set up her new life in Chicago, her wife-life with Freddie's family and their puppy and grocery shopping and the trappings of living for two, she thought about Lulu and Victoria and what they would do, try to make their careers a focus, find a boy to marry, give up on everything and move to London… ? Maxie had always wanted to be famous — had always *known* she'd be famous — but where was that now? She wasn't pretty enough to act, had no discernible talent, eventually thought that maybe she could land herself on the cover of Forbes, until she left college and started working at Goldman and realized immediately that being Freddie's girlfriend was *a lot* more fulfilling than staring at Excel until ten p.m.

Some days she worried she was like Victoria and Lulu, with only *some* of the trappings of a full life. She didn't want to go back to work, and she didn't want to learn how to cook, and it seemed like all the options that piled on top of each other in their first year at Harvard, all the things you *could* do, had receded to one very short multiple-choice question, *What should Maxie do? a) Work really hard and fight for some minor recognition, or b) Be the belle of the ball, the fun wife, the cool mom, and the queen bee wherever she is?*

Lulu was standing outside her parent's brownstone when Maxie pulled up, looking like something out of *The Royal Tenenbaums*. She lolled against her parents' gate like she was smoking.

"Are you pretending to smoke again?" Maxie asked. Lulu *did* feel particularly thin in Maxie's arms — not as thin as Maxie herself, but still too bony and sharp around her shoulders. She *did* look like a DJ, with her two-toned cashmere sweatsuit and her heart sunglasses and a pair of weird dad-sneakers that she annoyingly pulled off. There was an air of tragedy around her that made Lulu somehow more compelling, shinier, like you could just tell by looking at her that a man loved her so much he tried to kill them both. Lulu would say, *he didn't try to kill us; he was just being an idiot* and do some weird breathing technique that made you feel dizzy just watching it, but Maxie knew the truth. Maxie almost wished she had a big fat truth like Lulu's, a story that made you somehow glamorous and beautiful even when you weren't.

"No," Lulu replied, too defensively. "I'm directing the packing of the car." Ravi, Lulu's parents' driver who used to take them back to

Cambridge, was stacking suitcases, already shoving Maxie's into the trunk around shopping bags and cardboard boxes.

"What's with the sunglasses?"

Lulu took them off and examined them, as if she didn't know what was on her face. "I don't know. I bought them today when I was walking." In the morning light, her dark circles looked more like bruises, a mauvey-pink that smacked of sickness. Lulu offered Maxie her coffee cup; she drank. It was black and bitter, and she decided unequivocally that Lulu was still deep in the self-loathing phase if she was drinking coffee without milk.

"You look like shit," Maxie said, lifting her own sunglasses. "What about that, like, emotional rehab thing you did?" She expected Lulu to put a hand to her brow, which was always a sign that she was trying not to cry, but instead she turned to her friend with her huge eyes and her now-sharp cheekbones and Maxie realized that in the six months since they'd seen each other, Lulu had become something akin to beautiful.

"I don't know. I think it made it worse, or something. The only thing that's actually going to help is time."

"And someone new."

"And not driving to New Hampshire for the weirdest weekend of anyone's life."

"I can drive," Maxie offered. Now that she lived in Chicago, she sort of knew how to drive. It felt like a true accomplishment.

"That's so weird," Lulu replied. They watched Ravi lay garment bags neatly on top of the suitcases. "How are you — feeling about everything?"

Lulu was the only one who knew about Maxie's paradoxical predicament, having a life that she didn't want in trade for ease of existence, which felt more like failing than inertia. "It will be different when we have kids," Maxie told her with completely false confidence.

You didn't *have it all* until you had it *all* — didn't she know that better than anyone? Being at the top of her class at Horace Mann wasn't enough until she got into Harvard and being at Harvard wasn't enough until she found a serious boyfriend and having a serious boyfriend wasn't enough until she got engaged, and so on and so forth, which was why Goldman had been soul-crushing. Maxie, as it turned out, didn't have enough force of will to claw her way onto a cover. She was never going to be famous, so she had to settle for being famous in her own world. Lulu pulled her hood up. It was starting to snow.

"God. I can't believe we have to participate in this sham of a weekend. It's like when Jessica used to put together sit-down lunches in the middle of exam week." What Maxie didn't say was that she would never be able to comprehend how Jessica managed all of it, ploughed through every aspect of her life getting exactly what she wanted in half the time it should have taken.

Lulu exhaled dramatically. "I mean, yeah. But she was never gonna get married any other way, it's always been like this, and we're the people who choose to accept it, to masquerade as her friends. At least she's *getting* married. I feel so behind."

"Do you ever regret it?" Maxie was the one who told her to leave Carlos, ditch the ring, and never speak to him again. Maxie was the only one; she was the only one who actually knew that the fabled institution of marriage wasn't worth the *whoever can get me to the aisle* mentality they had all seemed to fall into in the past two years.

"Sometimes I regret… I don't know. Sometimes I regret all of it. Sometimes I can spout my Lanserhof Lans bullshit and be at peace with it." Lulu exhaled like she was exhaling cigarette smoke, up into a stream frozen air.

"Isn't it weird that Alex Sable is Will's best man?" Maxie drank Lulu's undrinkable coffee, winced, and handed it back to her friend. The car was loaded and ready.

"Talking of regrets?"

"Chris Newman *died*. Did you hear that?"

Lulu nodded. She was still staring off into space. "I read it in the paper."

"I wonder what Alex is like."

"I used to date that friend of his." Lulu, pre-Carlos, had dated everyone; she was a three-month girl, and usually had the next boy lined up before the current one was over. "He was fine."

"Fine," Maxie repeated.

"I always felt sorry for him."

"Why?"

"What a horrible thing, to feel some small share of responsibility for the imprisonment of an eighteen-year-old and his eventual, untimely death. It's like *A Prayer for Owen Meany*. It must be kind of crushing to be an instrument of karma."

Maxie rolled her eyes. Lulu's failed career as a poet was the worst thing about her. "I don't think he minded being a hero who saved a girl from getting raped."

"I guess," Lulu said, turning into the gate. "It didn't feel as real, then. Rape."

"Knock on wood." Maxie touched the side of her head. "Kine-ahora."

"I meant then."

"We were so young."

"*They* were so young." Lulu paused on the steps to her house. "I think we all became the shadow versions of ourselves," she commented, which was such a heavily-therapized thing to say that Maxie didn't bother to reply. "But maybe everyone does when they get older. You find out that the best part of being an adult is eating cookies for dinner. All the rest of it is just… exhaustion." She swung open her front door. Victoria stood next to the fireplace, eating a piece of blueberry cake and dripping crumbs onto the marble floor.

"You guys were out there forever," she said, hugging Maxie with a full mouth. She *had* found the weight Lulu had lost — but her break-up had been more recent. "Lulu fake smoking again?"

"Yeah. And we were talking about Will's best man. He's the one who found Chris Newman raping a girl on the Walkers' balcony when we were sophomores." Maxie brushed crumble off Victoria's chin. "Well, *I* was talking about him. Lulu was waxing sentimental on how much we've changed." She didn't want to say that Lulu was right. They were the same people they'd been at twenty except lacking in the hopefulness of future excitement. You learned so quickly that life was a series of check marks next to dry tasks which purported to have meaning.

"Now I'm fat and single after fifteen years of dating the same person who I thought would take care of me for the rest of my life. That's how *I've* changed," Victoria declared. "Lulu, I told you I would start to cry. Why do you always make us talk about these horrible things?"

Maxie arched an eyebrow at Victoria, *really?* and then, inexplicably, Yael Tarrance emerged from the powder room, smelling like Sephora. "What things?" Yael asked. She was one of those perfectly nice people who had been adopted by Jessica after college but was never *really* in the group — and Lulu was too wishy-washy to say no to anything, which was why it was so obnoxious of Jessica to inflict this stranger on them for the entire seven-hour ride.

"Now we're just starting rumors," Lulu said, in her low voice, with that edge of *maybe-just-maybe I'm joking*, which was the voice she used around the rest of the world, instead of the flat, hoarse, toneless one that came out with Maxie and Victoria. It was as if, in the presence of an outsider, Lulu got that sparkle back in her eye, one dimple winking at you, the promise of *fun to be had*.

"I'm sure you know the story," Maxie said. "This guy was blindfolding girls and raping them — mostly Dalton kids, not Horace Mann — he went to Dalton — and Will's best man, Alex, caught him, and even though it was a hundred years ago we all still talk about it like it was yesterday."

"Because we still don't know *who* was raped," Victoria put in. "And why he did it, just that there were *a lot*."

"Rape is like a disease," Yael said, in her overbearing doctor way. "It's a need for control that exerts itself physically."

"Tell that to a rape victim," Maxie replied. "Shouldn't we go?"

"The sooner we leave, the sooner we get there," Lulu said, but when Yael looked at her she flashed that *maybe-just-maybe* smile, and it occurred to Maxie that the real reason why she would never be famous was because it wasn't worth all the goddamn effort of faking it even after you made it.

Rob
February 10th, 2017

The house rose out of the whiteness like a mirage out of the desert, flickering in Rob's vision. He knew that he would never know enough to be able to appreciate Jessica's widely-acknowledged impeccable taste, which he reminded himself when he and Alex were escorted to bedrooms that looked like they were out of *Downton Abbey*, with hangings on the beds and fabric on the walls.

Alex was unbearable after being forced back from LA; he never articulated what, exactly, had been the moment of truth with his father, but, whatever it was, he was now stuck in a beautiful apartment in Soho that he complained about constantly, and yet never seemed to leave. He was alternately angry, upset, or rip-roaringly drunk, so after a train journey of upsetedness and a car ride of anger, Rob kind of knew what was coming next.

"Hey," Alex said, throwing down all six-and-a-half feet of himself on Rob's red silk bed cover. "Wanna get drunk?"

There was a part of Rob that knew he should be responsible and go say hello to the bride, find out what the schedule was for the next few days and unpack his stuff so it wasn't wrinkled, but there was a larger part of Rob that was acutely aware of the fact that Will had chosen Alex as his best man. This was laughable, because Alex kind of hated both of them, never did anything for anyone, and was completely untrustworthy when it came to showing up to events sober enough to give a speech. They all knew that Rob was going to do all the work, and they all knew that Alex was going to take all of the credit, and really what they all knew was that Will had crossed a threshold with his bride which he could never uncross. He picked the son of the billionaire for the headline, for the footnote in his life. That was just that. There was no way around it.

So he said, "Sure."

They went down the stairs, through the marble hall with too much carpet, into a library with a bar cart. "You have a weird intuition about houses you've never been in before," Rob said, because Alex did. He always had.

"There's always some kind of bar in the library, and the library's always at the back," he replied, and then he started to pour.

Getting drunk with Alex wasn't like getting drunk with anyone else, and Rob hadn't done it in a long time. These days there were girlfriends and fiancées and swanky bars with marble and too much light. They never seemed to hang out just the three of them; even at Will's birthday party there were so many groomsmen and random stepbrothers and people neither of them had known, despite being Will's best friends for so many years. It was like Jessica handed him an outline of what a bridal party should be, and he filled it in with actors and impersonators.

Making drinks, for Alex, meant mixing up something that felt original, without worrying about how it tasted or if you were going to run out of one of the key ingredients. He pulled out a bottle of Campari. Rob didn't know why anyone kept Campari, which tasted like alcoholic cough syrup, and why it was one of Alex's go-tos in a bar, except that Alex liked the color.

"I hate not having my phone," Rob said. Jessica had insisted that phones were only allowed to be used in their rooms; she wanted the weekend to feel *unplugged.*

"Did you ever think we would end up like this?" Alex asked Rob. He dropped ice into two glasses. He sniffed the top of a bottle.

"What do you mean?"

Alex sprinkled orange peel on top of the ice. "When we were twenty, for example. Did you ever think this was where we would end up?"

Rob knew Alex well enough to know that this wasn't about him being jobless; this wasn't about his inherent lack of purpose or drive. This was something else.

"Like, I remember in high school, all I wanted was to have a more interesting life than my parents did. Not get stuck, the way they did." Alex sighed. Rob tried not to roll his eyes, Alex's parents were billionaires. Rob didn't know what *more* he would want. "You always used to say you didn't want to end up like your dad." Alex accused Rob.

Rob's father was a dentist in Miami. Rob didn't want to end up like him. He wanted to end up like Alex's dad. "I don't," Rob answered.

"Do you feel like you're not? Working long hours at a job you don't care about, dating someone like Ronnie. *Ronnie*. Jesus. Do you really want to spend your life with someone named *Ronnie*?" He poured Campari on top of the rest of the concoction, something brown and heavily alcoholic-smelling. Rob felt like Alex would have put maraschino cherries in if he'd had them.

Rob raised his glass, looking at the swirling liquid in the light. "I don't know," he said honestly, because he didn't. How could you know who you wanted, what you wanted, what you cared about? Other than money. There wasn't anything Rob felt so passionately about, or enjoyed doing so much, that he wanted to devote his career to it. It was the same way with girls, Ronnie was pretty and not super annoying. What else was there? "Maybe you want things that don't exist. Part of growing up is realizing that not everyone is going to be Steve Jobs."

"We're not everyone," Alex said. He clinked his glass to Rob's, then tossed it back in three easy gulps. "Not as bad as it looks." Rob twirled his with a silver drink stirrer. It had a little devil dancing on top.

"The people who live here must be fucking weird," he said. He knew after he said it that Alex wouldn't understand, because the people who kept a mansion in the middle-of-nowhere New Hampshire with devils on the drink stirrers were definitely the same kind of people as Alex's parents, who inexplicably had a ten thousand square-foot house in Pound Ridge that they called a hunting lodge when none of them hunted. It was filled with stuffed animals which no one they knew had killed. The drink was almost undrinkable. Rob debated whether it would be easier to sip it or gulp it and get it over with.

He drained the glass and realized he didn't know what they should talk about next. Alex hadn't had a girlfriend in ten years of knowing him. And Alex's acting-slash-producing career didn't seem to go anywhere, or take up much of his time, so that wasn't really something to discuss. It felt weird asking how his family was; it felt weird having to *think* about what to say, when it had always been so easy between them, the dice falling into three-of-a-kind with ease.

A knock sounded on the door. "Hello?" A voice called, a voice that distinctly belonged to the loud-mouthed loser, Adam, who had somehow wrangled an invitation. "Anyone in there? Is this locked?" he jiggled the door but appeared to be too stupid to figure out how a knob worked. Rob held a finger to his lips and shook his head as Alex opened his mouth. Alex rolled his eyes.

The door opened; Adam came in. "Hey. You guys hear me?"

"We're having a private conversation," Rob said. He sort of yelled it and took a breath to calm himself down. Adam made him angry and the fact that Adam made him angry made him even more angry. It wasn't fair that Rob had been fighting for his place in this group since he'd gained his temporary admittance at age eighteen, and Adam didn't deserve a spot among them. He wanted to shove Adam back through the door, but Adam was taller than Rob, and gave you the impression that behind his blankly idiotic grin he might just break and punch you in the face.

Adam stood in the doorway. Rob stayed in front of him, like a bullfighter.

"We have a lot of stuff to talk about that's personal," Rob explained. "Sorry, man," he said, in a way which made it abundantly clear that he was not actually sorry. "Go find Will. I'm sure he wants to see you."

"You guys going into business together, or something?" Adam asked. "Text me when you're done talking."

"We will," Rob replied, swinging the door closed.

Alex raised an eyebrow. "Really? He's not the end of the world. That was pretty rude."

Rob shook himself a little. "I can't stand him. He's just in your face, all the time."

"Huh." Alex ate an olive. "He's not that bad. He's, like, alone in this random place and doesn't know anyone. Give him a break. Anyway, he reminds me of you. How you used to be, before you became a *trader*."

The word trader could have easily been *traitor* and Rob wanted to say *It's your fault that I'm this way, you who gave me trips on private planes and summers on Broad Beach in Malibu and a lifetime of things to want and need and pine for.* It was Alex's fault, and it wasn't. Rob had always wanted to be one of the rich kids, but he hadn't understood how necessary it was until he became friends with Alex and learned just how superior life was there, at that level. Alex said that Rob had changed when he started working in New York; he had. He finally had the opportunity to make everything he wanted his, and that was and would be Rob's entire focus, for the rest of his life. Alex couldn't understand that because Alex already had it.

"Jessica asked me not to drink at the rehearsal dinner," Alex said. He flashed his wicked smile, a theatrical look that had gotten them into the only bar fight of Rob's life.

Rob licked the edge of his glass, preparing himself for the taste of the drink. "What'd you say?"

"I said I would see how it went. It's a long way off." Rob knew exactly how he had said it, in that condescending tone of voice he reserved for telling Rob to read a book, occasionally, with a little wink at the end that almost seemed menacing. He would have rumbled out of the room with all six-plus feet of swagger, forgetting that Jessica was more than just Jessica.

"Now Will's gonna have to ask you." It would be a weird predicament for Will, who had always subscribed to their silent agreement that Alex had final say. Alex forfeited his right to his dictatorship when he stayed in Neverland; they'd lost their dynamic, or their momentum, or maybe just the pure idiocy that had allowed them to follow almost blindly.

Alex shrugged. "I *will* see how it goes."

"You can drink after the speech." He took a deep drink. The second concoction wasn't as bad as the first. "Ronnie wants to move in together." Sometimes being around Alex pulled this stuff out of you; it was like the magnetic weight of his personality sensed it and drew it towards him. "I haven't told anyone yet," he said, trying to make it sacred.

Alex raised a fat black eyebrow and grabbed a bottle of Scotch from the cart, jerking his head to a couch. They sat. Alex poured the brown liquid into the scarlet stickiness in their glasses. "When?" he asked. That was one of the best things about Alex, he knew what to ask you, not to say stupid things like *are you gonna do it* or *do you think it's time* or *what did you say?* He lined up the facts and knocked them out; in the time before Alex's wastreling, he had been smart and logical and calculating and an asset as a friend for more than his last name.

"Two weeks ago." Rob drank again. The whisky might have made it worse. "I told her I needed to think about it."

"And?"

It reminded Rob irresistibly of the conversation they'd had two years ago, when he visited Alex in LA and told him he wanted to quit his job. Alex was the only one who said he should. Alex said he should more because he wanted to start a fake business with Rob, have someone to hang out with all day, than because he believed in Rob, so Rob didn't quit, and sometimes, when he saw a buddy whose career had rocketed with the success of a startup, he wondered if there was a world in which that would have been him. It could never have been him, because Alex was allergic to work, and Rob didn't have the wherewithal to start something that was entirely his own. Alex would only want a company that was a front for doing nothing, and Rob needed a company that could actually be successful, but lacked completely in entrepreneurial spirit. He just wanted it to happen *for* him.

"What do you think?" Rob asked.

Alex shrugged, poured, bobbed his head right to left, left to right. "Do you want to get married in the next two years?"

"I don't know."

"Do you want to get married to *Ronnie* in the next two years?"

Rob dropped his face against the side of the velvet couch. "There's nothing *wrong* with Ronnie," he reasoned. "I guess I love her as much as I could love anyone."

The big booming chest laugh Rob had all but forgotten about burst into the air in front of them. "Sounds like an endorsement for marriage." Alex rolled his eyes. "First of all, there are *many* things that are wrong with Ronnie. There are many things that are wrong with everyone, but Ronnie's weaknesses are all the same as *your* weaknesses. Which is obviously a problem. She tries too hard," he held up one finger. "She's not funny or even interesting," he held up a second finger. "She's okay-looking," he held up a third finger. "And she's always whining." Four fingers confronted him. "Not to say that those are all your bad points, because you're worth talking to." He laughed. "But if you're gonna pick someone for the sake of having a wife, be smart, like Will. Pick someone who will compensate for all the ways that you fall short. At a minimum."

"I guess," Rob said. It was depressing and mean and that was how Rob knew it was true, because the truest things were always the hardest to hear, the ones your friends skirted around so widely that you thought they were imagined, until Alex broke it down for you honestly. "She does kind of try hard."

"You should do this..." Alex began, and Rob watched a plan clouding across his friend's vision. He topped up their glasses. "Find someone else, someone who checks *one* of the boxes. And sleep with her, and see how you feel then."

"What do you mean?"

"You know, someone who's actually hot, or successful, or... what else would you want?" Alex thought for a moment. "Fun to be around. They just have to have *one* of those things, and own it. And then you sleep with her and see if it makes you, you know, happy. Because all Ronnie does is make you feel... lame. Because she's lame."

He could be horrible and cruel and impossible and tyrannical, but he was still the best friend you could find, the very last of his kind. Maybe the only one of his kind, crushingly truthful and obnoxiously *right*, telling you all the things you already knew but didn't want to.

Will
February 10th, 2017

Will jiggled his feet as Jessica rearranged name cards around a leather thing that was supposed to represent a table. He wanted to peer over her shoulder, but she was getting a blowout, and the Italian guy smoothing her hair into perfection didn't like Will *lurking*, as he put it.

Will didn't like the Italian guy who did Jessica's hair, but no one asked him. "Okay, so, Adam just arrived," his bride-to-be said without turning her head. Will had the idea that she should spend a weekend at the Heathcotes' remote estate and see if she *really* wanted to have her wedding there — it was her wedding, not theirs — and she parlayed it into this strange Valentine's Day house party with *their closest friends*, because she had sixteen bridesmaids, and she didn't want to try to fit in all of them, and all of Will's groomsmen, as they would have to for the actual wedding. "Do you think he'll be ready for drinks at seven thirty? The girls will be on time, even though they're coming later. But he's an unknown quantity." Will checked his watch. It was four fifteen; Alex and Rob were already drinking, which made it way more questionable that *they* would be ready for drinks at seven thirty.

"Definitely," Will told her, watching Gianni wrap Jessica's honey-colored curls around a brush. He still couldn't believe she had brought a hairdresser for the weekend. A hairdresser who got a nicer room than *Yael*, who was Jessica's only real friend of the bunch — the only one who she saw consistently, the only one who actually knew how to be a friend. Maxie was psycho-competitive, Victoria was a swirling mess without a personality and Lulu was coldly selfish in the fakest way possible. Sometimes being around her excuse for friends made him worry about their life together, but he reminded himself that Jessica represented so much more than the people she spent time with. She would build a whole life for them; she was his partner, his equal. He leaned in to kiss her. The brush hit him in the forehead. Jessica acted as if the entire interaction hadn't occurred.

"What do you think?" she presented the table to him. Will was between Lulu and Jessica, undoubtedly for the tags he would rack up sitting next to the girl with 895,000 followers on Instagram. Yael was between Adam and Rob. He still regretted inviting Adam, his one law school friend, the absolute outlier of the group, but Jessica insisted that none of them knew each other anyway, so what did it matter? Except that Will didn't really *know* Adam, and there was an intuitive part of him that knew the small-town kid and Alex would not get along.

"Do I have to be next to Lulu?"

Jessica swiveled in her chair; Gianni pushed her back to face the mirror. "Lulu is the best possible person for you to be next to. You only decided you didn't like her since she got famous."

When Lulu and Jessica first became roommates, she was just this nice girl from the Swanson drugstore family, the daughter of a financial genius and an old school New England debutante, with a full face and shoulder-length hair and a propensity for long, intimate conversations. Will wasn't sure they'd had a real conversation in four or five years; she just had nothing to say. But Jessica shoved everyone at him with both hands until something worked, something stuck. She made things happen where Will hadn't even known there was something to be done. He loved and respected and revered that in his wife-to-be; Lulu just sort of floated around by the edges of her very chic, very important life where she was very busy doing all the things that an Instagram influencer had to do in a day.

His fiancée heaved a sigh to end all sighs. "Do you *really* want me to move her? You know, she's had a terrible time since the plane crash. You should be nicer to her. She was just in emotional rehab."

Emotional rehab was the kind of bullshit thing that made Will dislike Lulu. The plane crash — the ridiculous story around it, which he had trouble believing had actually happened — was a convenient excuse for a break-up and a break from reality. "Sure. I don't know. Move me." He walked to the door and hit the top of the frame with his hand. "I'm gonna go find the guys."

"I'm not moving *you*," Jessica called. Of course not, he had to be next to her. They only had the rest of their lives to be with each other.

The Heathcote house was built like an old English house, or, at least, what Will knew an old English house to be built like from watching *Downton Abbey* with Lulu Swanson, on the couch in their common room seven years ago. There was a guest area, with massive bedrooms draped in six different kinds of silk, and then there was a subtle door that looked like a panel which took you up a narrow flight of stairs and into what were rehabbed servants' rooms. Jessica stuck Yael into one of these. *She's not the kind of person who will even notice her room*, Jessica had said. There were only nine bedrooms in the main part of the house, and Gianni needed one. *Needed.*

Jessica commissioned an Etsy artist to do drawings for each of their doors, so they knew which room was theirs. She put Yael in scrubs. He jiggled the knob and walked in; a fire was burning — probably because the heat didn't extend to this part of the house, he thought darkly — and it *was* very cozy. *Thank you for joining us on this early weekend of #jesswillyou! We love your love. Will + Jessica*, a note on the bureau read. Will dropped it back where it had been and peered into the box of chocolate-covered cherries Jessica had apparently left in each room, resting next to their welcome note. Chocolate-covered cherries were disgusting. They didn't make any sense as a candy. His bride-to-be had also placed a framed picture of herself and Yael on the dresser; he picked it up and sank into the bed.

He hadn't known Yael when she was at Harvard; in his many visits, he encountered plenty of Maxie Steins and Victoria Schwarzes and Lulu Swansons — of Jessica's sixteen bridesmaids, nine were from her Harvard friend group — but Yael emerged after Jessica graduated, when she moved to Philadelphia while he was in law school. She mentioned one day that she was seeing a friend from Harvard, a girl in med school at Penn, and eventually Yael came over for Halloween candy and *The Bachelor* and Chinese take-out dinners on Sundays. She was clean-cut and self-possessed and talked about anything and everything. She was nothing like the teeny-tiny Jessica and her matched set of friends who weighed under a hundred pounds; she looked like a normal person. Usually she came straight from the hospital, in scrubs. They'd tried setting her up with Rob, who, as it turned out, would rather have a cheap knock-off of Jessica than a real person, and then Adam, on Jessica's insistence, and then, about a year and a half ago, Yael brought them Abraham, who worked on a newspaper in Philly and was nice. Normal. Boring.

Yael had been Will's favorite of Jessica's friends from the first time he met her; she felt solid, not molded into a particular shape or color or *thing*. He liked to go out with Jessica and Yael and Abraham; they drank and laughed and took long walks along the river, Jessica and Abraham prattling on about day-to-day lives, Yael discussing capital punishment with him.

In November, they were supposed to meet to do a pub crawl together, a fall-themed thing that Jessica found online. Jessica's train from New York was late and Abraham was stuck at the paper, so it was just the two of them, drinking beer — which Jessica would never touch, sitting on barstools — which Jessica couldn't do because of her platform shoes, and talking about how the election had gone so terribly, terribly awry — which Jessica didn't care about, except for social media purposes. They drank many beers and walked to many pubs and drank many more beers and walked to many more pubs and then somewhere along the Schuylkill River their hands touched, and they touched, and he kissed her and kissed her and kissed her.

Will had been with Jessica for seven years; they'd suffered long distance and shared the heartbreak of their parents' early divorces. Jessica set the table elaborately and roasted Brussels sprouts and paid a maid to change their sheets once a week. She was good at caring about what happened to him on a daily basis. She would be a good wife and an even better mother. She came from a similar, though wealthier, background to his. She was great, and he thought he probably loved her, and kissing Yael standing up outside in the snapping November cold didn't *change* that he probably loved her, or the way he probably loved her — it didn't change anything about her to him, except that sometimes he found her more unbearable, pushing him to ask Alex to be his best man instead of Rob, pouting when things weren't according to her *vision*, Instagramming her ring. The ring she'd picked out herself, because in Jessica's world, there were no surprises. She'd made that abundantly clear, she wanted to pick out the ring and have her hair done for the popping of the question and make sure that there was a videographer to capture everything. Photos were currency to her.

So he kissed Yael. She kissed him back. She was the one who pulled away, but she didn't say any of the things he thought she would; instead, she just said *Will* and looked up into his eyes in a measuring way that maybe no one had ever looked at him. It was more intimate than a kiss and later, when he tried to parse if it was piqued interest or boredom with Jessica or maybe love, he felt a tightness in his chest, a nervousness.

We should go back, she said, and they walked up the stairs and onto the street and she hailed herself a cab and stopped him when he tried to get in it.

When he got home Jessica was watching *Real Housewives* and scrolling through Net-a-Porter for white shoes. She kissed him on the cheek and told him he stank of beer and to shower before getting into bed, please.

That was November and now it was February and between the holidays and her hospital hours Yael had been completely unavailable to hang out. It made his anxiety worse; it made his chest tighten, almost to breaking point.

He'd called her twice, both at night. She'd answered, but he didn't speak, and she didn't speak; they each listened to the other one breathing.

He got up from the bed, put the photo on the bureau and took the stupid note Jessica had left, taking *Will + Jessica* out of Yael's room and dropping it into the first available trashcan along his way.

Yael
February 10th, 2017

There was no one to greet the girls outside the house, but Lulu waltzed in like it was her own home. *Leave the bags*, Maxie commanded, waving a hand through the fast-falling snow, *someone else will deal with them.* She followed Lulu and Maxie and Victoria into the house that looked like it belonged in an updated Agatha Christie, the kind where everyone dies.

"It's so weird to be back here," Lulu said, ominously, and Victoria burst into tears. Victoria had spent much of the car ride either sobbing over her break-up or complaining about how unfair it was that Lulu had this gorgeous romantic end to her relationship, and she, Victoria, had nothing. Yael couldn't get out of the Range Rover quickly enough.

She located a staff member — would it be too much to call him a butler? — who showed her to her room, which was roughly the size of a broom closet but did have a bathtub —and laid, face down, across her silk bedspread.

It was slippery, so she had been slowly inching her way towards the floor for what was probably ten minutes when she heard a soft knock. "Come in," she said.

"Hey." It was Will's low voice. Yael snapped to attention.

"Hey," she said. They both looked around her tiny room.

"Cute room," Will told her. He stood at the door.

"Cozy," Yael said. He looked older, or maybe he looked *aged*, like his hair was beginning to thin and lines etched themselves on either side of his brown eyes.

"That's what I thought when I was in here earlier."

She knew he wanted her to ask why he'd been in there earlier, but she couldn't give him the satisfaction; she couldn't give him a centimeter, because if she did then she would lose it all over again, and she wasn't the kind of girl who kissed boys with fiancées late at night.

She wasn't the kind of girl who betrayed her nice boyfriend and one of her few close friends.

She wasn't the kind of girl who kissed back.

Will lingered.

"Was it hard getting time off?" he asked. "At the hospital."

"I figured you didn't mean time off from Abraham," she said, and smiled a little bit.

He pushed the door shut, looking at the four paces of space between them. She looked at him.

Will crossed to the fireplace and picked up a china dog's head from the mantle, inspecting the bottom. "How have you... *been*?"

His tone was heavy enough to knock her out if she got too close. "Fine," she said. "Busy." She could hear the pattern of his breathing.

He sat down on the bed next to her. "This is weird," he said.

She turned to look at him. "This *is* weird," she laughed. "We're better than this," she told him.

Will bit his thin lip and looked away. He took her hand in his. She wanted to pull his face to look at her, but she didn't want to touch him, and she didn't want to let go of his hands. After a moment, she kissed him. There was the bubbling wellspring of hope within her, and then there was the gulping drain of fear that Will would never leave Jessica. That she didn't *want* Will to leave Jessica and suddenly, she wished she hadn't kissed him.

Jessica was her friend. You couldn't help but enjoy the easy way life was lived with and around Jessica, and Will would never be able to give that up. Will, Yael knew, had been partially seduced by the life Jessica offered him, and Yael couldn't hold it against him, because she had been, too.

"This is nothing," Yael said, slowly, telling him, telling herself. "You're engaged. To my friend. I'm dating someone. This is just... different, so it feels... thrilling, I guess. It's not real." He held her hands more tightly.

"I think this maybe is real," he said, in the measured way they used to talk about religion and books and politics.

Yael shook her head, although she knew exactly what he meant, and when he caught her eye she knew that he knew that she knew exactly what he meant. "I'm gonna take a nap." She dropped his hands and stood up. "I had a twenty-four-hour shift before this, and I didn't get to sleep in the car."

"Yeah," Will said, "of course." He stood, walked the four steps to the door. "I…" He lingered.

"I'll see you in a bit." She opened the door for him. He was standing with his back to her.

"I missed you," he said. She missed him, too. In an aching way that sometimes felt like she was coming down with a cold, except that she had the immune system of a horse after four years in a hospital.

Yael shut the door behind him and collapsed into bed. She was the worst person in the world, and she was also confused, and she was scared. She was scared that she would ruin four lives for nothing and, conversely, scared that she would ruin four lives by *doing* nothing. All of the options were bad. The real option, the grown-up-adult-real-life option, was to do nothing, keep everything the way it was, never ruminate on *what if.* That was the thing to do. That was the quiet life-ruining thing to do. She wondered if they would get divorced, Will and Jessica.

Someone rapped at the door as her eyes had begun to close. She sat up, running a hand through her hair and her tongue over her teeth. "Come in."

Jessica burst through the door with the full force of her tiny body, and Yael physically recoiled in fear that Jessica had run into her fiancée. "I am *so* glad you're here!" She flung herself onto Yael. "It's so weird with the other girls because I just don't see them as much any more. I mean, as much as I see you. They can't understand what it's like to live anywhere except New York." She sighed. Jessica basically *did* live in New York; she was there at least three days a week, and both Maxie and Lulu *didn't* live in New York, but that was Jessica, choosing a reality and stepping into it with complete confidence that it existed.

"They're all nice," Yael said.

It was weird to have Jessica hugging her on the bed that she had just kissed Will on. It was weird to be friends with Jessica at all, to have had this glamorous girl decide that she wanted Yael as one of her inner circle. Yael was easy because Jessica knew her from college and going to Harvard gave you some semblance of a pedigree. Yael was easy because she would go to work-out classes with Jessica and eat breakfasts instead of brunches, and she provided Jessica with the very important accessory of *close friend where you live*. Yael was an easy person to spend time with and so was Jessica, Jessica who liked activities and made friends with random people in coffee shops and was somehow doing ten things at once while also doing nothing. Yael never knew where she stood with Jessica — if it was sincere, the enthusiasm, or if it was all just a temporary front. Being invited made it seem like it was authentic, and that made Yael feel all the more twisted and shredded into bits over what she had done. What stood ahead for her and Will or what didn't.

"You already know them, so that's easier. Much harder with these random outsiders, like Adam. But Will's friends are all lovely, too. How are you doing?" She talked so quickly; Yael's sluggish brain was having trouble feeling out the words. "You look… well, I don't want to say you look tired, but you look tired. You should have stayed home to rest. I'm sorry," Jessica began.

"No, I'm happy to be here," Yael lied. "Just had a long few weeks. I guess no one wants to become a doctor because no one wants to work for twenty-four hours straight." She smile-laughed, the kind of tired laugh that doesn't really emerge from your mouth. For all that she was self-centered and self-serving, Jessica was kind and Yael was probably a bad person, was definitely not the kind of person her family would be proud of. What would she have done if Jessica had waltzed in? Why did someone like Will *matter* so much that nothing else did?

"I'm *so* happy you're here! It's so nice for you to get to know all the other bridesmaids and groomsmen before the wedding. I just have this vision of us in, like, ten years, celebrating our anniversary, and everyone is still friends." Jessica beamed up at the ceiling.

"Or maybe even dating. Aren't some of Will's friends single?" Yael felt herself trying to force the conversation, to act like these things were important when of course they weren't, when of course being this tired made nothing *important* at all. She didn't know how she would go back to work on Monday without having slept the whole weekend. She didn't know how she could believe that hooking up with *Will Christensen* was okay. It was not okay. She was not okay.

"They're not good enough for Lulu. And she's still a mess, anyway, after her whole plane crash disaster. The strangest things always happen to her. It's because she has terrible taste in people," Jessica confided. She didn't seem to see the easy joke about herself, as one of Lulu's best friends, and Yael didn't think it would be funny if she said it. "She *seems* to be all right, but... I don't know. It's like she's dead behind the eyes, now." Jessica paused and waited for a reply.

"She seemed fine," Yael replied. She couldn't speak to Lulu Swanson's mental state or, really, Lulu Swanson's anything. Lulu was an empty vessel with the brightness of an Instagram influencer projected onto her. At Harvard, she hadn't been one of the prettier girls and now that she was she seemed to have lost the flickering personality that once made her so compelling. Where she'd been sarcastic and winning, she was friendly and polite, pretty and well dressed. Yael had never seen makeup and highlights and veneers and a twenty-pound weight loss make such a drastic difference to who someone was; maybe Jessica was right, and the missing spark was due to the traumatic experience that everyone kept referencing, *the plane crash*. "She's always polite."

"She is." Jessica nodded. "She'll be fine. I don't know, I guess she could end up with Alex or something. I mean, they're sort of on the same level, but I don't know that he could pull it together for her, you know? He would be a fine match for Victoria, though. A step up, I guess." Jessica shrugged.

One of Yael's biggest issues with Jessica was how she referred to the obtuse fortunes of people as if they created a ranking system which everyone knew. Yael not only didn't know it, but she didn't believe in its viability. You couldn't measure people against each other that way; she knew it better than anyone else. Rich people in hospitals had private rooms but they were still just as sick as everyone else; they still died. Their family still gathered around them and cried.

"Sorry," Yael told her. "I'm so tired, I'm having trouble processing. How's everything going with the wedding? Do you have your dress?"

Jessica blinked at her, twice in rapid succession. "I ordered it months ago. Remember? I told you. I mean, it doesn't matter. You should probably rest, anyway. I just wanted to catch up. I feel like I never get to see you any more. Has your schedule changed?"

"No," Yael said, and then stopped herself. "Maybe. It's been particularly bad, lately. I don't know why. More people get sick in the winter, flu season, busy ER. I'm sorry," she said, sincerely, trying to infuse it with every kind of meaning she could. "I'm so sorry. About forgetting about the wedding dress, and showing up here so tired, and everything. I'm sorry for everything."

Jessica laughed. She stood up and smoothed her miniature skirt over her legs that were the width of arms and she leaned over to give Yael another hug. "Are you kidding? It means *so much* to me that you're here. Seriously. Sometimes I feel like you're the only one of my friends who really knows me, because you get to see me, you know, in Philly." She shuddered as she said the name of the city. "Anyway, take a nap. It's going to be a really good weekend," she promised.

"I know," Yael assured her, and they both knew that they were both lying. This weekend was Jessica's way of forcing Will to do the wedding here and none of it was going to be fun; it would be too many drinks and forced rounds of shots and, knowing these girls from their Harvard days, lines of cocaine on coffee table books. Yael watched the door shut and wished she had a *do not disturb* sign that she could hang on it for the next two days. When she woke up two hours later she was surprised to find she'd fallen asleep at all.

Alex
February 10th, 2017

Alex was laying on his bed, in his robe, staring at the Gilbert Stuart portrait of a Heathcote, when Rob came barging in. Rob barged in everywhere he went. He didn't know about knocking and taking measured steps. They didn't teach that in Florida.

Rob looked at himself, in his tux with his bow tie untied, and then looked at Alex, on his bed in his robe, and then looked at his phone.

"It's seven fifteen," he said.

Alex sat up. "Is tonight really black tie?"

Rob handed him a printed sheet of paper with the weekend's itinerary, *Dinner, Solarium, Black Tie.* "I can't believe it's only Friday." Alex walked to his suitcase and unzipped it. Rob didn't say *we're definitely gonna be late*. He didn't say anything at all. He sat where Alex had and was uncharacteristically quiet.

"Thinking about Ronnie," Alex told him. Rob nodded. Alex had seen him see Lulu Swanson for the first time, cartoon hearts blossomed into the air around him. "But, seriously, what do you think those three girls would think about you marrying someone named Ronnie?"

"Probably not much," Rob replied. Lulu had gotten a lot prettier than she'd been three years ago, when she'd briefly dated Alex's obviously closeted friend. Alex had kind of forgotten that they were the same person, Lulu Swanson the heiress to the drugstore fortune and Lulu the bleached blonde in mom jeans who thought, for a three-month period, that Henry wasn't gay.

She figured it out pretty quickly, and disappeared, and now here she was, reborn from the dead with golden hair, definitely thinner, looking like a grown up. Looking like she deserved the 900,000 followers Alex just saw she had.

Alex finished getting dressed and went to tie Rob's bow tie, which was why Rob had come in the first place. "It's just like tying a bow,"

Alex told him for the hundredth time in their friendship, but there was something nice about it, like some things really did stay the same in a comforting way, a way that Alex didn't hate.

"I know," Rob said, almost cutting him off. Rob smelled like alcohol and Ivory soap. His cheeks were starting to flush.

"Not used to drinking, Robbie?"

"Not the way we used to."

"The way *you* used to," Alex replied.

They ran into Maxie and Victoria in the hallway. Maxie was showing about six inches of ribby chest in a bright red dress that slit almost down to her belly button.

"Love a black-tie event on a Friday," Alex said, adjusting a cuff.

Maxie and Victoria exchanged decidedly dark looks, they agreed. "Especially when it's such an *intimate* group," Maxie said.

"Where's dinner?" Rob asked.

"The solarium. Didn't you read that piece of printer paper in your room?" Victoria asked.

"He's practically memorized it," Alex replied. They made their way back into the library, then through a glass passageway that was freezing, into a greenhouse with steamed up windows. Blankets were draped artfully across the chairs. The aggressive photographer was taking pictures of Will and his miniature bride by a huge spray of orchids. Alex went to check his seat at the table, only to be waylaid by Will's small-town-lawyer-friend, Adam.

"Some place, huh, buddy?" Adam's gap-toothed smile was distracting.

Alex nodded. "Yep. Sorry — just going to see where I'm sitting."

"You were next to Lulu Swanson," Adam said, smile widening, so much gum and so much *tooth*. "But I got one look at her, and moved you. I thought you wouldn't mind, girlfriend and all." He winked. He was almost seven feet tall and brought to mind the word *bumpkin* before you even knew that he was, actually, a bumpkin. Alex suspected he looked a lot like a young Ichabod Crane. His neck was too long. "I'd take her or the other one. Victoria. But I like blondes. Do you mind?"

"No," Alex said, even though he did mind, and he didn't have a girlfriend. "Not at all, my friend."

Adam smiled. "You're an okay guy, Alex," Adam told him. "I have a good feeling about us, this weekend. Hey, you got any drugs?"

"What kind of drugs?" Alex asked.

"I don't know. I thought these were drug people. Like in *Cruel Intentions*." He lifted his ridiculous shoulders in his cheap suit. He looked so much like a pumpkin that Alex could only see him that way, orange-headed, a Halloween nightmare.

"Do *you* have any drugs?" Alex asked, purely out of curiosity.

"No," Adam replied, disappointed. "I don't know where people *get* drugs, you know? Besides weed. You want weed?"

Alex's sole use for weed was when he had done too much coke and needed to mellow out. "I'm good, thanks," Alex told him. "You know, you should ask Rob. Coke, ketamine, he's there for it, he's got it. And make sure you ask in front of the other girls. You never know, in this group, who'll have them."

"Okay," Adam said, and stood there for a moment longer. "What's ketamine? I haven't heard of it."

Alex sipped his scotch. "Horse tranquilizer," he replied. Adam nodded and started off in the direction of Rob.

Alex grabbed a drink off a passing tray and took three mincing steps over to Lulu. She was wearing a short fur thing and gloves up to her elbows, like she was going to dinner on the *Titanic*.

"You knew it would be freezing," he accused her, tugging on her fur.

"Rooms made of glass don't scream *warm*," she replied.

"Adam moved your place card."

"Who is Adam?"

"Adam. Face like a jack o'lantern?"

"Oh, God." She peered around Alex. "He looks just like the kind of guy who would target me. It's always guys with this ridiculously inflated sense of self."

Alex laughed.

"What?"

"You basically just said you're better than this guy."

"Oh." Lulu shook her hair out of her dark eyes. "I guess it sounds terrible when you put it that way, but it's just kind of a fact. We're expected to pretend that some people aren't just *better* than others. It's the strangest thing. If you asked me to do a cartwheel next to an Olympic gymnast, it would be fine to admit that the gymnast is better than I am. But you put me next to that guy, and I'm supposed to pretend that we *all* don't know that I am me, and he is him."

"Spoken like a true child of Wall Street."

Lulu shrugged. "I would only say these things to you. But that's one of the reasons why I like LA. There's such an honest divide of who is worth what."

"And, yet, here you are, hiding behind me," he said. She was half-concealed by a large banana plant.

"So, Rob," Adam's voice said loudly, on the other side of the plant, "you have any drugs? Coke, ketamine, whatever it is? I heard you're the guy for that."

Lulu arched an eyebrow at Alex. "Why do I suspect that a prank is afoot?" she whispered.

"I have to keep Rob on his toes. He's getting boring. I might have to replace him with the pumpkin soon if he doesn't pull it together," Alex whispered back. "Come on. Play along."

"What the fuck, man. I'm not the guy for *anything*. Don't come up to me and accuse me of shit in front of everyone." Rob's voice raised as he spoke. Peering through the fronds of the tree, Alex could see him looking all around, trying to ascertain who had heard.

"My, my," Lulu said, loud enough for Rob to hear. "One little comment, Rob, and you're off and running. Adam, I'm sure I can find you some cocaine at some point this weekend. I can also absolutely supply you with a dealer, if that's something you'd like to pursue in your life," she said.

Adam looked from Lulu to Alex in confusion. "I don't get it."

"Nothing here except complete sincerity," Lulu replied, and sailed to the table, and switched the place cards.

"Can everyone please take their seats?" Jessica called. Adam and Alex approached the table together.

"Sorry about that, man," Alex told him, reaching up to pat his back. "Not sitting with Lulu, I mean. But she put you next to Victoria, so that's something."

Adam nodded. “Can’t win every time, you know?”

“Isn’t that the truth?” Alex replied, eyes on Rob.

Lulu and Alex took their seats next to one another. “You know what I didn’t even tell you? I’ve been seeing loads of your cousin lately.” She spoke in a theatrically loud voice. Alex didn’t mind sharing dinner with her, watching her carve a piece of artichoke like a Thanksgiving turkey, gossiping about all the people they knew in common and all the people they didn’t like in common.

After their appetizers, Victoria came to share Lulu’s seat. “I can’t take it any more,” she said. Lulu grabbed her arm and held her, tightly, like she was pulling her up. “I cannot sit next to that — *excuse* for a human being.”

“Who?” Lulu asked, swinging her head from one side of the table to the other.

“Adam,” Victoria hissed. Alex tried to swallow his laugh, and failed.

“He’s not that bad. He doesn’t know anything.” Alex finished his wine and started on Lulu’s. “And he’s staring at you,” he told Victoria. All three turned, Adam *was* staring, staring with too much eyeball on view.

“Victoria,” Adam’s voice boomed across the table, and Alex grabbed a waiter by the cuff to order some actual alcohol. Wine was definitely not enough. “Where are you from?”

The conversation around them halted in confusion. Victoria looked to Lulu and then to Alex, as if to say, *Me, Victoria? Are you sure you have the right person?*

Instead Victoria said, “New York.”

“I’m from New York, too,” Adam replied. “Aren’t you gonna ask me what school I went to?” He was already slurring. Maxie, next to him, clucked her tongue.

“Do you want some water?” Maxie asked.

“I wasn’t talking to you,” he said, batting her hand with the water glass away. “I was *talking* to Victoria.”

Victoria closed her eyes and leaned back against Lulu. “I think this is the most uncomfortable dinner conversation I’ve ever had,” she told Will.

“Have you had more uncomfortable lunch conversations?” Alex asked, helpfully.

“He’s not bad,” Will murmured.

Alex, Victoria and Lulu turned to look at Will in tandem.

“He’s not.” Will defended.

“I guess he’s better than Rob, who starts salivating at the sight of a Goldman tote bag,” Alex replied.

“You’re all just brats,” Will said, lightly.

“I’m the nicest person I know,” Alex told him.

“Exactly,” Will said. “You don’t know a lot of people.”

Yael
February 10th, 2017

Alex Sable, as it turned out, did not understand the basic principle of *tired.* Yael learned this when she declined the absinthe bottle, and he tipped back her head and started pouring it down her throat before she could push him away. Then she was coughing, then she was sputtering, then the sticky liquid was dripping down her chin and onto the white blanket she was wearing because *who had a dinner in a greenhouse during a blizzard?* She wrenched herself away from Alex with such force that she tripped; Maxie caught her. Yael wanted to berate him, but her throat was still burning, eyes still streaming, and she couldn't quite catch her breath to form the words.

"Wow. Ever encountered alcohol before?" Alex asked.

Yael pulled out a chair and sat, taking deep breaths. "What is *wrong* with you? Why would you ever do that to another human? If you want to poison yourself, fine, but don't make anyone else suffer." She rested her forehead on her hand and thought she was going to vomit, considered going to make herself vomit — Victoria had already left the table to throw up once, which Maxie assured her was *just an emotional thing* — but the light was shifting and moving in front of heads and faces and arms, and everything was in slow motion, and suddenly she could feel herself becoming very, very drunk.

Alex laughed at her. Directly at her, in her face, like he was five years old and had just tied her shoelaces together.

"It's not funny. You can't — do that to people. You can't treat people like that."

"It's fine," Maxie said, waving it away. Yael wanted to say *yes, because you've been flirting with him all weekend, so it's fine*. "She's fine; Yael, you're fine; this is just fun; this is how people have *fun*. Why don't you have a drink to calm down a bit?" she said, and handed over what turned out to be a Bellini. Yael slurped it down too quickly and wished she had eaten more, slept more, stayed away from this place and these people and long ago decided that whatever strange semblance of a friendship she had with Jessica wasn't worth it. Jessica was inherently a good person and that was what made it so hard to say no to her. Yael should have said no. She reached for a glass of water and found it was vodka and half-swallowed it, half spat it out.

"Oh," Yael said. "No. I did not want to get this drunk on a non-drinking night."

Maxie said, "You're such a *doctor*, sometimes." The light was blurring in her vision. The light was blurring with Maxie's face and her head and Alex's face above that.

"So, doctor," he said, "what was it they used to do in Victorian times to make the absinthe more potent?"

Yael's mouth was sticky and tasted like she'd just used the weird organic toothpaste that Jessica stocked in their bathrooms here. She wondered if she was tasting the toothpaste again, hours later, it was purple and reminded her of candy at Colonial Williamsburg.

"There's a slotted spoon component, I know that," Alex said. She wasn't a violent person, but she wanted to smack his shining, smirking face. "And something with fire."

"And a sugar cube," Maxie said. "This is strong."

"This *is* strong," Yael said, sipping the vodka again even though she knew she shouldn't. Her voice was the only one that sounded normal. "I think I'm going to go upstairs and go to sleep."

"No," Alex said, but Maxie was standing, too, or maybe she had always been standing and Yael was just standing next to her, or maybe they were both sitting. "Come on, stay."

"I have to wash my hair," Yael told him, and it echoed. She couldn't remember the last time she had washed her hair. Where was Jessica? Where was Will? "Where are Jessica and Will?"

"Probably taking photos," Maxie said. "Come on. Lulu? Louie? Louisa?"

Lulu floated into the light. "Oh," she said. "You are drink-drank-drunk *drunk*, aren't you?"

"Your real name's Louisa?" Yael asked. She was not a Louisa.

"Yael has to wash her hair," Maxie said.

"I do," Yael said. Her voice was so clear in all the fuzziness. "I'm going."

A butler helped her find her way to her bedroom, where she drank two liters of water and ate the rest of her bagel from the car ride. When she was sober enough to see straight, she ran herself a bath and let her head dip under the warm water that lapped gently along the sides. Who knew you could get that drunk that quickly? Maybe the Europeans were onto something when they banned absinthe. Yael had never read anything about it; no one had ever shown up in the hospital with absinthe poisoning, at least not while she was on rotation. She let bubbles of air float out of her mouth and up to break the surface of the water; she could almost hear something faintly in the background, some kind of music, or maybe it was just the after effects of the alcohol.

It was loud. Her eyes opened without meaning to; two blurred faces swam above her. She pulled herself up, gasping for air. Lulu laughed, one sparkly hand dangling next to the tub. Maxie smirked. Victoria, leaning on the sink, took a slug directly from the mouth of a champagne bottle.

"Come on," Maxie said.

"We're going out."

Yael hugged her knees into her chest and slicked her hair out of her face. "We're in the middle of nowhere," she said. She was acutely aware of the fact that there were no bubbles to cover her nakedness.

"Yes," Lulu replied. "But I have the keys to the *cast-le*." She opened a painted-nail fist; a skeleton key on a burgundy tassel almost brushed Yael's nose.

"I bet you never do stuff like this," Maxie said, and Lulu's dimples flashed, and Victoria took a step across the miniature bathroom to proffer the champagne bottle.

"It's just us," Victoria said. "It will be fun." Yael took the bottle and took a gulp. She never *did* do stuff like this, because all she saw every day was the unexpected, and drinking brought on the unexpected, and that was why you had to make the conscious, adult decision to go upstairs and sober yourself up.

"We won't pour absinthe down your throat," Lulu said, but she said it in that low, throaty way, with the slightest raise in her brow, with the most intimate smile you'd ever received, and suddenly Yael understood why eyes tracked her across rooms and through dinner courses.

"Okay," she said. "But give me a minute to dry off."

Maxie rolled her eyes. "It's nothing we haven't seen before."

Victoria took the bottle back. "Like, five seconds ago."

Lulu laughed and got up, motioning them with her sparkly hand. "Come on."

Maxie and Victoria followed. Victoria leaned her head back in. "And Yael? Don't do that thing where you *decide* how drunk you're gonna get."

It took her five minutes to get out, dry off, and pluck the robe from the back of the door. When she emerged, the three girls were seated cross-legged on her bed, with cards stuck to their foreheads. They were all in varying degrees of pajamas-plus-coat, Maxie in a floor length down puffer, a black lacy bra, and matching silk shorts; Victoria in an oversized men's shirt, knee socks, and a fur-trimmed jacket; and Lulu, looking like she had dressed for her close-up, in a canary-colored silk slip and a fur coat that trailed off her shoulders.

"You have to wear more than a robe," Maxie told her.

"Two," Victoria said.

"No," Lulu replied. Victoria drank.

"Vigorous movement awaits."

"Hearts," Lulu said.

"You cheat! You always cheat!"

"No I don't. I'm intuitive." Lulu dropped her card and pulled another.

"Spades," Maxie said. Lulu shook her head. Maxie drank.

"Four."

Yael pulled out her own pajamas, a med school T-shirt and Abraham's cotton boxers.

"You pick the numbers because of the lower odds. You're purposefully losing."

"So what?"

"So you can't play a game with someone who's purposefully losing." Maxie clutched the bottle.

"You can't *dictate* how I play."

Lulu unfolded herself and stood up on the bed, bouncing on the balls of her feet. "Come on. Let's get out of Harry Potter's bedroom and *do something*."

Maxie handed Yael the last of the champagne. "Finish it," she commanded, and Yael gasped into the fizzing bubbles.

"Where to?" Yael asked, dropping it into her tiny trash can.

"Get a coat."

She pulled the robe on and followed the rest of the lost girls out of the warren of rooms and down a back staircase she didn't know existed and down and down and through a panel that was actually a door and down another flight and then there, behind a velvet curtain like a magician's act, was a massive safe door.

"Victoria? Care to do the honors?"

"How do I do it?"

"Just twirl the thing. It's unlocked."

"I don't think so."

Maxie rolled her eyes and spun the wheel like she was Vanna White, *step right in*, but the lights were on and the room that was supposed to be empty was heavily occupied.

"*Really*," Lulu muttered, but Maxie was already striding forward, into the poker game, dropping a deck of cards from her pocket onto the table, laughing in her hoarse way.

"How did *you* find this place?" she asked.

"There's always a vault," Alex said. "Please, ladies. Join us." He spread his hands to encompass the four of them, Alex and Rob and Adam and Will, sitting on spindly wooden chairs around a marble table.

Will looked at Yael and Yael refused to look at Will. Instead she asked Maxie, "What are we playing?"

They were playing poker, five-card-stud, which caused an exchange of looks between the other girls. Yael thought about how strange it was to be down here, sans Jessica, with Will, who she definitely had something more than a crush on.

What were you supposed to do when you started to feel the possibility of someone else? When they were taken, and you were taken, and you knew it wasn't right, but he made you *feel* like it could be possible. It was all feeling, no thought. Like you could be the one, the better-than, even the best. Just being chosen by him meant something more about you than you ever could have imagined. For the first time, it made you something.

Rob
February 10th, 2017

Rob was beginning to develop a mild concern over paying his debts at the end of the weekend. Alex always insisted *everyone* pay up, but they had never played poker with Lulu Swanson before. Will's condescending explanation of the game was now silently shaming him from the two thousand dollars of Will's *alone* that sat in messy pile of chips next to Lulu's furry arm.

"How many furs did you bring?" Rob asked her.

"We drove. So I brought whatever I wanted." She was one of those hot-and-cold girls, smiley and twinkling at dinner, cold and unyielding inside the stone-floored vault.

"Rob, come on, pay attention to the game, or stop playing," Alex instructed.

"Don't be rude," Maxie told him, but she smiled as she said it. "He can't *help* being a terrible player."

"I'm not being rude. I'm the one who will pay his debts when he can't," Alex replied. "So I'd like him to at least *try*."

"Why stay in the game if you're bad at it?" Victoria asked. Victoria folded almost every hand.

"I'm not bad at it. It's luck," Rob replied.

"It's not luck." Lulu shifted her long hair over her shoulders. "If it were luck, with this many players and the number of hands we've played, you ought to have won at least once." She gracefully slid her chips onto the mountain in front of her.

"I'll bet you I win this hand," Rob told her, feigning confidence.

"No thanks," Lulu replied.

Rob opened his mouth, but Alex spoke before he could. "I like that. Rob, I'll give you fifty grand if you win this hand. You don't have to win it high. You just have to win it."

Maxie laughed. Lulu yawned delicately behind her hand.

"Well?" Alex prompted.

"What if I lose?"

Alex leaned back in his chair. "*What if you lose*. Then you lose. You don't get the money."

Rob was silent, trying to figure out how Alex was tricking him.

"You're not going to actually pay me fifty thousand dollars," Rob told him.

"Really? You think I back out on my promises? Online banking. All I have to do is hit a button." Alex typed into his phone.

Rob couldn't believe it and he also *could* believe it, which was, really, the problem. Alex would give him fifty thousand dollars over a hand of cards and Alex would not give him fifty thousand dollars over a hand of cards. Fifty thousand dollars would change his life. If you had fifty thousand dollars to give away to your friends, wouldn't you just hand it over?

"What if someone else wins? I mean, not you, and not me. Won't they feel bad for beating me out of the money?" Rob looked around.

"Don't worry about them. They're fine. You're fine, aren't you?" Alex asked.

There were a few nods. Lulu sipped her water. "Just get *on* with it," Maxie said. Alex flashed Rob the screen on his banking app and Will dealt them each five cards.

Lulu's face flickered into a mirror of the Cheshire Cat's and Rob felt suddenly again that he would lose to her, to them, that he shouldn't have said yes, that the stronger thing would have been to say no. That Alex shouldn't have dangled the carrot in front of him in the first place, but that was Alex.

"Fold." Victoria put down her hand.

"Same." Yael's eyes hesitated on Rob's face for a moment too long. She turned to look at Will. She was waiting for him to fold and so was Rob; she was waiting for him to narrow the odds for Rob.

He didn't. Bets were made. Cards were discarded and cards were doled out in their stead. Rob had four assorted diamonds and only needed one more to make a flush. He could do it. He could win. People won things like this all the time. The money would be the kind of padding to his lifestyle that gave you the freedom you needed to be happy. To keep up. To do all the things you always wanted but never quite *could.* His last card was the two of diamonds. Lulu laughed when she flipped hers over. "What?" he asked.

"Nothing," she replied.

"Nothing you would understand," Alex clarified. "Nunc tempus est!" He had a straight.

Rob ignored the Latin that he *didn't* understand and watched a pair of tens appear on the table from Maxie, three sixes from Lulu, and then Will, three twos, two kings. A full house.

"Sorry," Will said, quietly.

"Maybe Lulu will split her winnings with you," Alex said. "What do you need 20k for, Swanson?"

"I always donate it to charity. I'm not a *monster*," Lulu replied.

Rob didn't say anything. He had been so close to winning but he hadn't won and that wasn't his fault; that was the fault of people like Will who should have bowed out from the start. He should have known what the money could do, what it would *mean*. Will didn't need it, because Will was marrying a rich girl who would always take care of them, because Will didn't actually *care* about money or actively believe that it made a difference in life even though they all knew it did.

Alex was still laughing.

"Don't be cruel," Maxie told him. "He's allowed to be disappointed."

"I'm not disappointed. He wouldn't have done it anyway. He would have gotten in trouble with his dad," Rob said.

"You know what? Lulu, what's your charity? I'll transfer the money to *them* right now. I can do whatever I want with my money, Rob. It's mine."

"It's an amazing cause, actually," Lulu began. "It directly funds the medical care of animals who have been abused, with no overhead — it's almost like Kickstarter for these good Samaritans out there saving dogs, for example, on their own."

"Alex typed for a few minutes longer. The silence was protracted. "Why don't we move upstairs?" Lulu asked the group. "It's freezing in here."

"I think I need to throw in the towel," Will said, standing, stretching, peering at Yael. "Anyone want to come up with me?" Alex sent cards flying across the table as he dealt.

"Aren't you just getting into bed with Jessica?" Victoria asked, fanning her hand out in front of her, shifting her fingers around. "Do you need an *escort?*"

"No," Will replied. "But I know Yael worked a twenty-four-hour shift before this, so I thought she might be tired."

"She napped," Maxie put in, helpfully. "She's fine." Lulu dropped her cards onto the table and yawned.

"I did nap," Yael said, even though her eyes were sticking together in a way Rob could see from across the table. "I *am* fine."

"You could take Adam up," Lulu suggested, her head balancing on her palm. Adam had passed out cold in the middle of a hand; Maxie insisted they check his cards (a pair of threes), and let him sleep.

"I don't think I can carry Adam upstairs on my own," Will replied. It was the first time Rob had seen his best friend in close quarters with the bridesmaids, and it was beginning to seem like they didn't actually like him. Which was strange because Will was one of those people *everyone* liked, easygoing, nice, thoughtful. He was just — Will.

"I think she meant wake him up and help him to his room. Unless you want to let him sleep in the vault." Maxie dropped a card from her hand. "Hit me."

"I don't want to deal with that," Will said, turning.

"Well none of *us* are going to deal with it, Will," Maxie told him simply, shifting her cards in her hand. "He's *your* friend."

"It's not late," Alex remarked. "Only midnight."

"Midnight?" Yael sat up properly. "I have to go to bed. Goodnight, everyone."

"Leave your chips and we'll tally at the end," Alex told her.

She shook Adam's shoulder. "Adam? Can you wake up?" He was silent. "I tried," Yael said, shrugging, stepping out of the vault. Will followed.

"Maybe he's dead," Victoria proposed.

"That sounded suspiciously hopeful. Are you a little psychopath and we didn't know it?" Alex asked, hopeful himself. Sometimes he looked at girls in a way that Rob thought was kind of leering, but Rob wasn't a girl and they never seemed to care. The only important thing was that he was the son of a billionaire.

"*You* so utterly fit the profile of a psychopath," Lulu told him, her voice so light and smile so fleeting it was *maybe-just-maybe* a joke. Everything about Lulu was a *maybe* and *either or* a *do you really think so?* Lulu was like the example sentence that taught you how to use grammatical devices, you didn't know you hadn't understood the intricacies of the language until you encountered her.

"Louie. Show 'em," Maxie said.

She had a royal flush.

Alex dropped his hand on the table. "You've got to be kidding me. Do you count cards?"

"We used to play poker at Andover. It was how we exchanged stuff like bottled water and Oreos and cocaine."

Rob laughed. "And cocaine!"

She looked at him so evenly that he had to pretend to lose a card and dive under the table to retrieve it.

"Boarding school is like the Wild, Wild West," Alex said. "Everyone I know who went away has a vital piece or two missing." Lulu surveyed him with those steady eyes. "It makes them all the more fun." She was silent. "I wonder what you have missing. Since Maxie's the fun one."

"I think most of my emotional damage has been inflicted evenly throughout my life," Lulu told him. "With a special emphasis on my most recent break-up."

"What's your most recent break-up?" Rob asked. Victoria sighed so loudly they could all hear it.

"We don't need to talk about it," Lulu said, looking at Victoria across the table.

"What?" Alex asked, head swiveling between the two girls. "What is it? Victoria?"

"Lulu acts like she's the *only* one who's ever had a break-up, and she barely dates guys for ten seconds, and then gets in a plane crash with one and it's the *end of the world*." Victoria hiccupped delicately at the end of her sentence.

"Just because you were with Jason for twelve years doesn't—" Maxie began.

"Yes. Yes, it does. Mine is worse. I invested my entire *life* with him—"

"I'm not saying yours isn't worse! But I may also be allowed to be sad about a break-up too—"

"But you're not allowed, Lulu! You're not. Allowed. You're not allowed because he asked you to marry him and you said *no*." Victoria was crying, quivering sobs that soaked her face.

Lulu got up and walked around the table and hugged Victoria. "Darling, I said no because we weren't happy together. You wouldn't have wanted me to say yes."

"But you *got* to say no. You had the option. I had *nothing*. I have. Nothing."

"You have a life that's worth living with someone who actually loves you—"

"Jason tried to kill me, too. He did it slowly, but he did it. And he succeeded. I'm nothing now. I might as well be him." Victoria flung a hand towards Adam. "They all try to kill you, or own you, or just *have* you. No one wants a real partner. No wants a *shared* relationship. And now I have to try to do it all over again." She wiped her nose on Lulu's exposed shoulder. The skin glistened with a rainbow of snot. "I just don't know if I have the energy."

"You don't have to have the energy now," Maxie said. "I mean—"

"I feel like someone who invested their life savings in Bernie Madoff. Or Enron. Or some stupid start-up." Victoria said, as Lulu dashed tears off her friend's face. Alex watched the pale, dark-haired girl with such intensity that it made Rob nervous. He had never seen a break-up this close; he had never seen this much *damage* this close. "We weren't supposed to play poker," Victoria said, her tears slowing. "We were supposed to have a dance party and get really drunk."

"Is that what you want to do?" Maxie asked. "Or do you want to go to bed? Or have a bath…"

"I wanted to dance," she said. "It's so easy to be sad when you're sitting."

"Okay," Lulu told her. "We'll dance. Let's go upstairs."

They left Adam sleeping on the table without comment.

The library was roasting after sitting in a stone vault; the girls lost their coats and Maxie mixed drinks while Lulu connected her phone to the speakers. Victoria dabbed her face with cocktail napkins behind the bar cart.

"Just out of curiosity," Alex began, sidling up to Lulu. Rob followed.

"What happened with Victoria? Basically just that. She's been dating the same guy since we were fourteen and she gave him an ultimatum, re marriage, and he said no, and a few weeks later he broke up with her, *and* he's the worst person alive." She spoke so rapidly that the words blurred together, completely without punctuation or pause.

"No," Alex replied, half-turning to see if Rob was still there. "What happened in *your* break-up?"

"Oh." She dropped her phone onto a bookshelf. "I mean, basically, you know Carlos Santo Damantia Zissou, right?" She put a hand to her chest, fingertips brushing the hollow of her neck, and lifted them up and down in rapid succession, beating like the wings of a bird.

"Of him."

"Well, basically, we dated for like two years — right after I ended things with Henry, actually. We were together for a while before things started happening for me, in my career, if you will," she rolled her eyes, at herself, at her career. "And, I don't know, there was a shift in the power balance we'd always had. It became this obsession with him that I didn't love him. He kept trying to *bait* me into doing these things for him, to prove that I loved him." She looked up into Alex's face. Her hand was still moving; Rob didn't know why. Her eyes were clear. "And it just kind of escalated to me saying yes all the time to placate him, and one day he decided to fly us to Vegas, because he'd just gotten his pilot's license, and I didn't want him to, and it became this whole *you don't trust me, you didn't want to fly with me,* blah blah, and then he sort of lost it and started screaming about how I loved myself *so much more* than I loved him, and if I loved him, I would let him crash the plane." She paused, and laughed, looking at both of them. The laugh was as quick as her words, as her fluttering hand. "The silliest thing about it is that there was no *let him.* I don't know anything about planes. I couldn't take a plane off of a crashing course if my life depended on it. And I know this, because I thought my life *did* depend on it, he crashed the plane right there in the desert. We both survived, a little beaten up, and then he wheeled himself into my hospital room and proposed to me, because now he had the *ultimate* proof that I loved him. Which, of course, wasn't proof of anything except, I guess, that everyone should have some basic knowledge of how to fly a plane. And that's that." She let her hand rest. She exhaled and reached onto the chair behind her for her fur.

"So — what happened?" Rob asked.

"I heard about this," Alex said, nodding. "I just didn't know it was you."

"We broke up and a few days later he very theatrically sent the ring to my room at the Wynn with a letter about his punctured lung as a metaphor for our relationship." She stuck a hand out, like, *really?* "Anyway, I returned the ring — which was the wrong size, which is an *actual* metaphor for our relationship — and then he started stalking me and I got a restraining order against him. Well, Dad did, but whatever. I never said that what happened between us was *worse* than what happened to Victoria. All I'm saying is that we can talk about how break-ups crush you together. She doesn't have to be so drastically wounded alone. But I guess if she's *not* the only one who's suffering, then what happened to her isn't as significant, and if it's not as significant, then… I don't know. She has even less than she thought, I suppose." Lulu lifted her bony shoulders, Victoria's dried snot making her skin ripple in the light. "Shall we?" She walked over to her friends.

Rob looked to Alex. "So she's out," Alex said.

"Why?" Rob thought that if this was her being vulnerable, she just seemed a lot like Alex on drugs. Or anyone on drugs, but he didn't spend that much time around people on drugs, so he didn't know. Maybe she was high or maybe she was just emotionless and a little unusual. Maybe it was just Adderall which wasn't really a drug.

Alex shrugged. "They're just never as — *good* when they're so damaged. I like them whole."

Yael
February 11th, 2017

There were moments when your life split into two, the decision you made, the decision you didn't. The *yes* you said, the *no* that should have been spoken. Some philosopher or astrophysicist or other doctoral-level genius had a theory that there were multiple universes in existence with all the other choices you *didn't* make, the right instead of left, the heads when you asked for tails, everything that you always wondered about when the floor was quiet, or rounds were done in half the time. Yael thought about it sometimes, about the simplicity of her life, the seconds on the weighty clock of the past ticking past all the times she could have diverged and begun again.

As she stepped out of the bank vault and up the hidden flight of stairs and through the twisty hidden pathways of this creepy house, she felt herself divide into two, the Yael who sat on the uncomfortable wooden chair for another two minutes, until Will was safely gone and she could crawl back to her room, and the Yael who heard the siren' song of *midnight* and walked out of the room with Will Christensen. He was so tall, and she could hear his breathing; maybe she could always hear his breathing, like putting a shell up to your ear and hearing the ocean, and he smelled tangy and dirty, something she would like to bury her nose in for the rest of her life. It was just the scent of something, really, fleeting and already forgotten.

The stairs were narrow and dark, barely enough room for one of them. "I think we went up too high," she said.

"This should come out right by your room." He fumbled with his phone, turning on the flashlight, and shone it up, reaching one arm across her. The smell engulfed her; she tried to hold her breath. "What?" he asked.

"Nothing," she replied, letting it out, and then he dropped his phone and pushed up against her and kissed her. All she could smell and taste and see and feel was him, a symphony of perfection that was all hormones, it was all just serotonin releasing her brain, she *knew* this—it wasn't genuine feeling.

She pushed him away and held his face and took another breath through her mouth, so she couldn't be tricked by his scent. "Will," she breathed, and her hands were shaking, and his hands were shaking, jolting against the flesh of her ribs and trailing up her chest to hold the skin above her heart with one oversized hand.

She was still in both realities, the yes and the no. She could push his hand away and find her room, or she could pull his face to hers and find her room. This universe was waiting on her, to make the decision, give the affirmative nod, live or just *be*, to choose.

She brought his lips to hers. It was a long kiss and not a very comfortable one and she wondered if this was a reminder from her body that he belonged to someone else. This was a release, like anything else people did, but it didn't eat at your brain or deteriorate your liver. Compared to those things, compared to the rest of the people in the vault downstairs, this was like eating a piece of candy and she was almost sainted. You did the things you wanted to because they held meaning for you and kissing Will again and kissing Will again and kissing Will *again* felt like meaning, at least to her.

Will
February 11th, 2017

The fissure that began maybe before he even met her had cracked and dropped him into a gaping chasm of uncertainty. Or certainty. Certainty in what he wanted. Uncertainty in where that was going to place him at the end of the game. Will rolled over on the tiny double bed — of course Jessica had given Yael a room with a double bed — and took a sip of water. The room was warm and full, full from rafters to floor with the roiling fog of *something*. He had been expecting her to drop into the sleep of the dead, but she shifted on his arm. He offered her the glass. She shook her head.

"Actually, I will," she said. When he held it up to her mouth and she sipped, it was strangely ritualistic, an agreement reached that could not be breached. She pushed herself up in bed. "Do you think you should go get in bed with Jessica?" she asked. He liked that she asked and didn't *tell* him.

Will didn't want to compare the two, but he hadn't slept with a normal-sized person in so long that he had almost forgotten what it was to embrace flesh with flesh, to feel muscle and sinew instead of bone, to be reciprocated with substance and weight. "I probably should," he told her, honestly. "But I don't want to."

"What are you going to tell her when she wakes up alone?"

The truth was that Jessica woke up alone all the time. She needed to sleep in a silent, dark, scent-free environment, and as a result, Will often fell asleep on the couch, watching late shows or listening to a podcast, trying to relax. When he went out with Alex and Rob he usually just stayed with one of them; he didn't want to get home at two a.m. and have to get into the shower.

"She'll assume I fell asleep with Alex and Rob."

Yael nodded. Her short hair brushed across her shoulders, and he reached up a hand to feel the fringe against his fingers. "I don't know what's next," she said, and it sounded like a confession, *Forgive me, Father, for I have sinned*. Will's first stepmother had been Catholic. In his twenty-nine years, he'd had four stepfathers, two stepmothers, and too many quasi-siblings to count. They used to go to Mass with her, in her veil, and tell the Father how they had sinned, even though they were Jewish and always had been and, as it turned out, always would be.

The thing Will had learned about marriage was that it was a choice. You could decide to be in it and stay in it, or you could decide to give up. Once you'd given up once, it was exponentially easier to do it again.

He'd always looked down on his parents for their flighty love lives, for faux-families constructed out of homemade paste and colored paper and an elaborate wedding, but now he wasn't sure. There was such a comfort in committing to what you had already agreed to, except that he'd made his agreement when he was so young. Things happened and happened and happened and suddenly there you were naked, in scratchy sheets, with someone else's girlfriend.

"I don't, either." He could say to Yael all the things he couldn't say to Jessica, how her father fought so grotesquely in the pre-nup, how he wouldn't be able to make them half a million dollars in a year, how fucking delusional she was about her fake interior design business. "I don't think I love Jessica."

How could you know what love was? Actually know, in a concrete way that allowed you to make logical decisions? Jessica had a Fitzgerald quote emblazoned on a print in their bathroom, *never the same love twice*. No one *knew* what love was, not in a way that was quantifiable, that could be distilled and taught and learned. There was the way he loved his father, which was sad and grasping at the same time; there was the way he loved his only full brother, which felt like loving himself; there was the way he loved his mother, grateful and always forgiving, which was maybe the way he loved Jessica, out of a sense of prescribed duty and fair appreciation. In the depths of himself that he was terrified to plumb, he knew that Jessica represented the life that could be lived. What Will had learned or decided or telegraphed throughout his life was that he needed someone who checked all the boxes, who would take care of you and push you and drag you to their charity galas which brought you the contacts who propelled you higher in your career, and so on and so forth.

So forth until you met Yael and found you didn't know what you wanted at all, what mattered, what was *important*.

"If this is about Jessica," Yael began, and he realized she had untangled herself from him entirely. "I think that's something you should work out on your own."

"It's not about Jessica specifically," Will said, immediately, because it wasn't. "It's about you, and what you make me *see* about Jessica."

Yael pulled the comforter up around her. "I didn't do this to help you see your relationship with more clarity." She looked directly at him when she spoke.

"That's not what meant." He shook his head. "I'm thinking through the undoing of my life with Jessica. Which I didn't think was an option. Until now."

"I don't know, Will," she said, still looking at him so *evenly*. "I think you shouldn't sleep here, and we should sleep *on* this, and go from there."

"I want to stay with you," his voice was quiet because he was embarrassed to admit it, but he *did*.

"Please don't," she said, and her voice was equally low. "It's important."

He kissed her full on the mouth and pulled on his boxers and suitcoat while she sort of sat there in bed, looking at the empty spot he had just occupied. When he opened the door into the skinny hallway he turned to check on her, but she just shook her head. There was a sadness in it that he thought about as he made his way to Alex's room.

"You're not who I was expecting." Alex greeted Will's knock.

"Who were you expecting?"

"Doesn't Maxie Golden just give you that two a.m. feeling? Even her *name*. It's like a Bond girl."

"It's her married name."

Alex watched pointedly as Will pulled on his socks. "Yes. Because we all *clearly* respect the institution of marriage."

Will dropped back across his friend's bed.

"You can't sleep here," Alex told him.

"Why not?"

"Because I *know* girls like these; I *created* girls like these, and one of them is going to knock on that door, and I don't think the closet will be comfortable."

"Not Yael."

"Not since you've already fucked her."

Will sat up and opened his mouth.

"Come on," Alex said. "You're more subtle with your fiancée than with her."

Will let his head drop into his hands, running them through his hair as Yael just had, wishing he could talk to Alex about things like what love actually felt like and knowing unequivocally that Alex knew even less than he did.

"You know my dad made me come back," Alex said, out of nowhere, and Will turned to look at him. He was scruffy, bowtie undone and beard overgrown, but he still looked like *someone*. Will was always surprised that Alex hadn't made it as an actor, he owned every room he walked into. Sometimes he owned the whole house. "I trashed their Malibu house. He kept saying *how do we find ourselves here, Alex? You're not eighteen any more*. He's disappointed that he thinks I'm failing. I've failed in *his* estimation. Maybe he just got sick of telling people I was an actor and not being able to name a show I'm in. So I get summoned back to the castle, and I have to answer to their every beck and call, like I *am* eighteen again. My life isn't my own any more. I don't know if it ever was, or I just had the *illusion* that it was."

Will looked at Alex from his folded-up position on his knees. He didn't know how this related to him and Yael and everything else, but it was Alex, so maybe it didn't at all. He opened his mouth again.

"That's why you're doing it. It's not love, or fascination, or your annoying fucking wife-to-be, or that nice doctor girl. It's what Jessica represents, which is a lifetime of being eighteen again. Being beholden. Showing up, with your shiny shoes and your tied tie. It's not having anything for yourself. Yael, she's something that belongs to you. She makes you feel your life is yours."

"He *made* you come back?"

Alex stretched. "He was gonna cut me off. What was I supposed to do, get a job? Live on pennies and ramen?"

"You have your trusts," Will pointed out. Alex claimed that all he wanted was freedom, but in reality he reveled in the comforts of being treated like a child. "Your brothers would have helped you out."

He sipped a drink that he produced seemingly from thin air. "We're not a generous bunch, the Sables. Always looking out for people to be taking advantage. Not something *you* would ever do, Will." They were both silent because they both weren't sure if Will was doing it, if that was all that remained of their friendship. "I could have gotten a job. I can *work*," Alex defended himself. Will didn't say anything for the simple reason that it wasn't true. Alex had never worked and would never work. He wasn't capable of it. "But it wouldn't have mattered. My dad would have gotten me home one way or another. You know what he's like. He gets what he wants, or he takes it."

"You get what you want, too," Will pointed out.

"I don't get what I want. If I got what I wanted, I wouldn't be surrounded by people who can't even pretend to take me seriously." He laughed. "But they always need you, in the end."

"Dude, you're drunk." Will stood up too quickly; the room shifted, then righted itself. "None of that even makes sense."

"You know I'm right about Yael," Alex asserted.

"I don't think so," Will replied. Leave it to Alex to provide you not with solace or comfort but with the plain assertion that you were acting like a petulant child. "I really can't sleep here?"

"No. But I'll stay up with you and have a drink. Let's go downstairs."

Will shook his head. "I need to go to bed."

"Once upon a time, this was a group worth being a part of," Alex said. "You didn't used to say *no* every other word. Night, Billy Boy." Alex slapped him on the back.

Will lumbered into his own room, undressing again and sliding beneath the cool sheets.

"Go shower," Jessica said, in a completely normal tone of voice, as if he hadn't just woken her. "Or sleep with Alex."

Will lifted himself out of bed and wondered when it was that your relationship splintered and broke apart like a dead tree, if you participated actively in it or if you just watched it happen and never thought to call the tree people, to see if maybe someone could fix it. It was easier, always easier, to just agree with whatever Jessica wanted and now Will wasn't sure if there was anything he wanted or anything of his own left to him. It was all hers, including Will.

"Will. You're keeping me up just *standing* there."

Will went to Rob's room and knocked and fell into his best friend's bed and dropped into the sleep of an untroubled child.

Maxie
February 11th, 2017

Maxie woke up in between a swath of yellow silk and a Harvard sweatsuit, which undoubtedly belonged to Jason and undoubtedly had been donned by Victoria when she was incredibly wasted and incredibly sad. Victoria had managed to kick the covers off of all three of them, and Lulu shivered in her sleep, arms puckered in goosebumps. Maxie pulled her hands from over her head — she always fell asleep like that when she was overly tired — and shoved a fistful of covers onto Lulu. It wasn't strange not to wake up next to Freddie — they both traveled so much — but sometimes Maxie felt that she lived two quarter lives, one with her husband and his family in Chicago, one with her friends and family in New York.

That left her with one entirely empty half-life.

Lulu stretched, yawning. "I wonder if there's a breakfast-in-bed component to this weekend," she whispered. They both laughed. Jessica hated laziness, staying in bed, anything that was the opposite of *activity* on a weekend. She would never allow them to luxuriate in comfort and coziness. Sometimes, most of the time, Maxie had trouble remembering why they were friends with her, but sometimes, most of the time, Maxie had trouble remembering why she did most of the things she did. Why these things had seemed to matter so very much, things like having a husband, things like owning a house, things like being friends with the society princess everyone loved. People said Jessica was so sweet and adorable and didn't you just love what she'd done for the Boys' Club Gala? They became friends with Jessica because she had been one of the pretty, popular girls at her school just like they were the pretty, popular girls at theirs, and their time at Harvard molded this friend group of lookalikes into a wax tableau worthy of Madame Tussauds. You kept it up because it meant something to be one of Jessica's bridesmaids, to post about her on Instagram on her birthday, to be *one of those people*, the ones you *wanted* to be.

Victoria let out a particularly loud snore. "Maybe that's why it didn't work out with Jason," Maxie said, voice hushed. The bed shook with their idiotic giggling. Maxie sighed and fell back into the European pillows. "Let's get up." Maxie knew they should, because that was what you did at a house party; that was what you did when you were a guest, and an adult, and a real person. "Dazzle our hostess with our excellence as guests."

Victoria slept through the racket of them getting ready; Maxie and Victoria had never even moved their suitcases out of Lulu's room. Lulu Instagrammed while Maxie showered; Maxie dried her hair while Lulu showered, and in ten minutes Lulu was kicking her leather-clad shins on the side of the bathtub while Maxie applied mascara. "It's so LA of you to wear leather pants as loungewear," Maxie commented.

Lulu looked down at the cuff of her oversized, off-one-shoulder sweater, like that was what Maxie had been talking about. "Is it? They're just warm." She wore fur-lined combat boots and had her hair back in a high bun and looked like she was suffering from some minor, long-lasting illness.

Maxie brushed mascara onto her eyelashes. "Alex Sable is kind of hot."

"Meh." Lulu shrugged. "You know he must just run through girls."

Maxie reached for her blush. "*Does* he, though? He's not in our friend group," (the born-and-raised New Yorkers who went to Ivies) "and he's not really in either of yours," (Lulu's boarding school friends or her shiny European socialite crew) "so who does he hang out with?"

"Other random outcasts, like Henry." *Other random rich kid outcasts* was what Lulu meant, but the half-Yankee in her DNA wouldn't say it. They tiptoed through the bedroom, as if they'd been remotely quiet while getting ready, and into the hallway.

A door opened and Will, half-dressed, emerged. "That's not your room," Lulu said. It was uncharacteristic of the Lulu Maxie had grown up with and she suddenly appreciated this Lulu, standing there with confrontation rippling across her face.

"I slept with Rob. You know how Jessica is about sleep." Will walked towards them, stopping a little too close.

"But you went up before Rob. Were you like, waiting there for him when he went to sleep?" Maxie asked him, hand on her hip.

Will smelled like alcohol and sweat and something else, something that Maxie very distinctly recognized.

"Are you guys headed down to breakfast?" Will asked, dodging the question. A little well of redness flashed as he spoke.

"Are you bleeding?" Lulu asked. She touched her own bottom lip, standing on tiptoe to peer into his mouth. "Oh. You are."

Will wouldn't put a hand to his mouth and Maxie knew *exactly* why, it was an admission of guilt. "Maybe just this weather," he said.

"We should get down to breakfast," Maxie told him, pulling Lulu behind her.

The bottom of the stairs yielded a very loud, middle-aged woman named Carol who had a clipboard and *a lot* of questions, along with Jessica, who needed to show them the plans for the wedding so far. This necessitated a tour of the bottom floor with the accompanying details of what kind of flowers would go where and the color of the trays for the hors d'oeuvres and how long she should keep her veil on after the ceremony. Lulu excused herself to the bathroom and came back with a chocolate croissant.

"What?" Lulu asked, scattering crumbs across the carpet.

"Where'd you get that?"

"This is *my* friend's house. I know where the kitchen is. And, like, I can't starve."

"Why didn't you get me one?"

"You never eat carbs!"

"Neither do you." Maxie snorted.

"That's *so* not true. I eat all my vegan healthy carbs like brown rice and nuts like every *day*."

"Nuts aren't a carb."

"What do you guys think?" Jessica asked, turning to them, looking pointedly at nothing.

"It's really about what *you* think. What are you leaning towards?" Lulu asked, wiping flakes off of her chin.

"I think the damask," Jessica said. "Max, what did you do for your wedding again?"

Maxie had zero idea what she was talking about. "Oh, the damask, *definitely*." Jessica nodded and stepped back to the window. "At least *share* your croissant with me," Maxie said to Lulu.

"It's a pain au chocolat," Lulu said. "But okay."

"Goes to Paris Fashion Week once," Maxie mumbled through a mouthful.

"Try twice a year for three years, you ungrateful minx."

After an hour, Jessica released them to the buffet brunch in the dining room, borrowing Victoria instead. "See you guys later," Victoria said, tonelessly, wiping sleep from her eyes.

Maxie waved and shoved Lulu towards the dining room door. "Ow! What are you doing?"

"Have you completely forgotten about the fact that we *basically* caught Will sleeping with Yael?"

Lulu pushed the door to the dining room open two inches and squinted at the sideboard. "It all looks cold," she said. "And where did you come up with *that?*" She let the door swing closed.

"Oh, my God, do you even pay attention to *anything?* Her perfume was wafting off of him in waves strong enough to kill someone. He and Yael left the vault together *hours* before Rob went to sleep. And his lip was bleeding!"

"I don't know," Lulu said. She pushed the door a little again; Will, Alex and Rob took up one end of the table. "Would one call that *leaving together*? They just kind of ambled out at the same time. And neither of them are really stay-late people. I mean, maybe Yael is, who knows, but she doesn't *seem* like it, and Will *definitely* isn't."

"You're just hungry." Maxie sighed. "Go on."

Maxie watched Lulu weigh her plate down with French toast and sliced avocados and one Benedict egg, then made herself a bowl of yogurt and fruit. She knew that Lulu would eat two bites of each thing and complain endlessly about how full she was. They both watched Rob staring at her; Lulu crossed her eyes at him. He blushed.

"Sorry," she said. "Couldn't resist."

"Sorry," he blundered in reply. "I was just… staring off into space."

"The space of Lulu's face?" Maxie asked. Alex snorted.

"Has anyone seen Adam?" Will asked.

"Hard to miss, isn't he?" Alex replied. "Like an extra from *The Walking Dead.*"

"What time did he go up?" Will took a bite of French toast.

"As if we know," Maxie replied. "We left him at the table."

Will looked up from his syrupy plate, from face to face. "Ha, ha. Very funny."

"Oh," Lulu said. Alex whuffled in quiet laughter. Rob's cheeks got redder. Lulu looked to Maxie.

"We did," Alex said.

Will shoved back from the table. "What the *fuck*, you guys. He could be frozen to death!"

"What were we supposed to do?" Alex asked. "He's *your* liability. You should have dealt with him before you *went upstairs*." Maxie wasn't sure if she heard a particular emphasis on the last two words because she wanted to or because it was actually there.

"Jesus *Christ*." Will ran a hand through his hair.

"Maybe you should call Yael, take her to check on him," Maxie suggested, chewing a raspberry. Will's head whipped in her direction. "Since she's a *doctor*, and all."

"Yeah," he said. "Maybe I will."

Jessica and Victoria entered the dining room, trailing staff.

"Will, Adam isn't feeling well; he said he's going to try to sleep off his hangover," Jessica told him, easily.

Will stood up. He took a step towards the door and a step back. "Should we take him to the hospital? Is it serious?"

"It's a hangover, not the plague," Jessica said, rearranging a candlestick on the table. "Apparently he woke up alone at like four a.m. and threw up on the floor in the vault, then took himself to bed. Poor Carol is dealing with the vomit." She seated herself. "Will. Sit down. So. What's everyone's plan for the day?" She took Will's limp hand in hers.

"Oh, my God," Lulu said. "I *completely* forgot to thank you, Alex. The dog charity emailed me this morning saying you'd given them fifty-grand in my name! That was so thoughtful of you. You have no idea how many dogs you've just saved. I mean, truly, that helps them so much."

Alex waved her aside. Maxie wasn't sorry for Rob, it wasn't as though Rob was *destitute*. The money was better off going to abused animals than to his fund for bottle service and a decent button-down. "Happy to help the dogs, Lulu. Sorry it didn't work out for Rob, but, you know, that's gambling." He winked at Rob. Rob's face didn't move. "What's your plan, Jessica?" Alex asked. "I thought we were all hanging out together."

"I have so much to go over with the wedding planner," Jessica said, a note of apology lacquering her hoarse tones. "It's really the only time we get into the house until we get married."

"I thought… we were waiting… until we — decided." Will dropped her hand and cut himself a bite of what was definitely cold French toast.

"Decided on what?" Victoria asked.

"Deciding if we were having the wedding here for sure," Will said, and Victoria dropped her fork with a clang.

"Oh, we can talk about it later, babe," Jessica assured him, kissing his cheek and standing up. "Carol has a whole list of activities, if you guys need suggestions!"

"I have a feeling we'll be *just* fine." Alex winked at Maxie.

She took a heaping bite of yogurt and swallowed it with renewed appetite.

Lulu
February 11th, 2017

A game of sardines was proposed, Victoria and Maxie dispatched to check on Yael, Lulu given the assignment of hiding while Rob trailed Alex, asking for another explanation of the rules. Lulu slipped into an out-of-the-way attic bathroom; she wanted a hiding place that allowed her the luxury of reclining, instead of hunching over in a dark wardrobe. She felt bad that they had spent almost no time with the bride; she liked Jessica more than maybe any of them did. There was a quality of fascination to watching Jessica push through life with such force that things broke into the shape she demanded. Jessica was a person, and it was easy to forget that, because Jessica was perfection personified.

Lulu slid into the bathtub and pulled the curtain across it. The inside of the empty tub was cold through her sweater. Her bra poked into every inch of rib and sinew; she hated the unfamiliar feeling. No one wore bras in LA; sometimes she forgot how unacceptable it was to show your nipples through your shirt on the East Coast. It was an entirely different world, here.

She sank deeper. If the tub were full, she would be in past her chin. Lulu closed her eyes into the imaginary bubbles. She decided not to see the plane, not to see the desert and Carlos' neat face. Everything on his face was laid out like an architect had planned it. He made it untidy with stubble that she hated. She'd maybe loved him, but she'd probably never know. How could you feel love in a way that allowed you to identify it? It was like going from house to house, feeling out what was acceptable, inching through unfamiliar hallways, searching for a light switch.

House parties, like bras, used to be a mainstay of her life. She spent eight years traveling to houses up and down the Eastern seaboard, getting to know Cape Cod and Maine and Rhode Island the same way she brought friends to Amagansett, making your bed every morning out of politeness even though you knew the maid would do it over again in an hour, driving strange cars into tiny towns with people you often never saw again, people who followed you on Facebook and later Instagram and claimed some kind of connection with you, who thought that sitting on a beach watching the sparks of the fire fade into the sparks of the stars was something special or even different. The guys who thought running out of gas on the Merritt was a distinct and important memory; the girls who thought being naked together in the sauna was something *unbelievable*.

At a certain point, you reached a threshold of human experience that made almost nothing significant. You lost all your shame after monthly trips to the Korean spa; bonfires on the beach became par for the course on Malibu Sundays. You left the East because you'd already done it all, had it all, met everyone there was to meet, and after four years in the vast and gaping West, the place where young sons went to find their fortune, you found your own fortune, and then you found that your past had happened all over again, in half the time, you'd done it all, you *had* it all, you'd met everyone there was to meet, and the things that were supposed to be different and special were beginning to blend into one another so seamlessly you couldn't remember what it was you were supposed to care about in the first place.

Lulu kept finding herself stuck in this chasm of repeating time, reliving the exact things she'd done ten years ago, or five years ago, or six months ago. She laid in this very tub the first time she ever played sardines in this house, when she was fourteen years old and wracked with homesickness and excited about the beginning of the rest of her life. It was like the universe was trying so desperately to show her something, illuminate the Christmas lights to correspond with each letter on the wall, and she didn't even know that a little boy was lost, that there was an Upside Down, that something was wrong in Hawkins, Indiana.

She heard the creak of the opening door and restrained herself from sliding lower into the tub. There was a pause, then the running of water in the sink; Lulu peeked around the heavy curtain. Will leaned heavily on the bowl of the sink, water dripping off of his face, eyes slitted.

"Hey," Lulu whispered. He jumped and gasped simultaneously; she held a finger to her lips. "We're playing sardines. Don't give me away."

He pulled the curtain back and stared at her, her combat boots stacked on top of one another, her sweater pooling around her, the dark circles Maxie told her to hide.

"I'm not playing." His wide mouth pinched. Lulu felt his dislike for her undulating off of him in waves. They had never been alone before, she realized, and here, in this small place, it permeated every atom around her. She couldn't comprehend *why* Will disliked her, he wasn't jealous, the way so many girls seemed to be; he wasn't secretly attracted to her, and ashamed of it, like most men who were openly cold to her were; he just had some *issue* with her that she thought even he probably wouldn't have been able to identify, if she'd bothered to ask.

"I know," she said. "Are you okay? You don't look… well." It was something her mother said, *you don't look well*, a polite method of inquiry. "I did recently return from rehab for non-addicts. So, if something *is* wrong, I'm not the most embarrassing person to talk to about this stuff. I am, essentially, certifiable." Lulu didn't know why she was still talking; she thought she'd outgrown her nervous tic of needing to get everyone to like her, but maybe she hadn't changed at all, maybe people had just started liking her more. She pulled her legs into her chest and rolled so that her back was up against the wall of the tub, making room for him.

He dropped the seat of the toilet and sat down. "I think I'm having some kind of — quarter-life crisis."

"Okay," Lulu said. "Does it feel like a life crisis or a nervous breakdown?"

"What's the difference?"

"Well, a life crisis is more of a recalibration. It's having some huge realization that feels like it changes your entire future, and trying to figure out how to move the pieces of your life around to make the adjustments you've realized you need, which is scary and hard and you're not even sure you're *right* about it."

"I think it's that," Will said, head tilted up to the ceiling.

"A nervous breakdown is when everything is wrong. Every *single* thing is broken and shattered and something like bumping your head on the side of a table because you dropped a pen throws you into chaotic sobs and abject terror and a spinning feeling, like you're spinning into darkness, because there's nothing left for you." Lulu sighed. She shouldn't have left Lanserhof Lans. She needed more time there or maybe she'd spent *too* much time there or maybe all the things that everyone said would fix you actually didn't *do* anything. The only thing that could fix you was you.

"It could become that," Will said. Lulu shifted her boots around in the tub. "Which one did you have?"

"I don't know, both." Lulu directed another sigh through her nostrils. "It's different for everyone. It's sort of a level-of-reaction thing. And sometimes it's not even about what you think it's about. It's usually a lot more about *you* figuring out what kind of person you are than it is about your boyfriend breaking up with you, or having a bad meeting, or whatever."

She could sense his waning attention; Lulu supposed that if you somehow managed to live in this world *without anxiety and mental health problems*, which seemed impossible, you wouldn't care about this kind of thing, which was probably why Will didn't care. There was a level of empathy that some people seemed to intrinsically lack, an inability to feel as deeply as you did, and talking to those people was like speaking to someone who didn't know your language. They could never quite *get* there with you, grasp the idioms and metaphors and humor.

"Thanks," he said, staring at his feet.

"Is this about Yael?" she asked. He turned his head too quickly and she supposed she should have done the polite thing and pretended that she didn't know, but the truth was that she *didn't* know, and she wanted to see the truth written across his unremarkable face.

"What did she tell you?"

"Some lawyer *you* are. She didn't tell me."

He nodded his head a little from side to side, measuring. "I'm impressed. I would have thought you were too self-centered to pick up on that."

It was meant to wound, but Lulu was used to it. She spent her life having her photo taken for an app. A dose of self-absorption came with the territory. And he was right, she hadn't noticed. Maxie had. "So. What's the crisis?"

"Are you going to tell Jessica?" He pronounced the *going to* instead of gonna, like he was in court.

"No," she said, because it was none of her business. Telling Jessica wouldn't change anything; Jessica would find a way to fix it and lead Will down the aisle herself if she had to. "I'm not that good of a friend."

"You're not. That's why I never liked you." He stood up and got into the bath, sliding down the marble wall to sit next to her.

"Well, you're not that good of a fiancé."

"That's why I got into the tub."

"So here we are." Lulu wrapped her arms around her knees and balanced her ear on one. "What now?"

"I don't know." He closed his eyes. "I don't know." He opened his eyes. "What would you do?"

"I honestly don't know." Lulu lifted her cheek off of her knee, and let her chin drop back onto it. "I am sorry, though. It all seems kind of unnecessarily unpleasant."

The door flew open and Rob burst in. "Hah! Found you!"

"Oh," Lulu said. "Is anyone still even looking?"

Rob
February 11th, 2017

Rob accompanied Will and Lulu to the library, where Alex was pawing around the bar with an occasional growl.

"You look positively bearish," Lulu said to Alex, flinging herself onto a couch. "What's wrong?"

"Nothing's wrong. Do we have anything decent in this house?"

"Isn't there enough alcohol?" Will sat in a chair with his eyes closed.

"Not alcohol. Lulu?"

She stretched her arms over her head and reached for the *Vogue* on the coffee table. "Landon will have. We could go over and swim."

Sometimes Rob felt like they were communicating at a level that he would never be able to understand, no matter how many odd, specific, rich-people things he learned, like where Pound Ridge was, and that Round Swamp was a fancy grocery store and William Greenberg was the *only* place to get a black and white cookie and the importance of a Yura pinwheel. It was as though Alex and Lulu, growing up four years apart on different streets in different schools, still shared a life together, had a secret code that they could speak in fluently, despite barely knowing each other. Rob would never be able to translate; they didn't sell this Rosetta Stone to people like him, who had the mortifying luck of landing a dentist for a father, who didn't boast symmetrical features and a low way of talking that made you lean in to listen. He had always wanted to have someone say *he comes from a nice family* and no dentist would ever be a *nice* family — *nice*, the euphemism that all rich kids used for *rich, just like us*. Money made people care about you and respect you and talk to you in a low way that made you lean in to listen. Rob had always wanted it and they could sniff that out with their pedigreed noses that were born to find a user or a phony or a wannabe. Rob didn't want to be a wannabe, but he did *want* to be one of them. Rob got to be in the game because Alex let him. He knew that and he hated Alex for it, and he loved Alex for it and somewhere along the way he lost what had made them friends. Wasn't sure they had ever *been* friends.

"I will not have any *drug use* on my record," Will stated, over-emphatically. How was it that Will, whose background of upper-middle-class average affluence was not so very different from Rob's, could understand them, was understood by them, was accepted as one of them where Rob was shunned and mocked? It made Rob itchy with self-consciousness, like it was *personal*, this separation of *them* vs. him, like it was about who he was as a person instead of the invisible boundaries of class that Rob chose to blame.

"Then don't do drugs, Billy boy," Alex said. "But don't stop the rest of us. Is this Landon Heathcote?"

"No. The many *other* Landon's you know."

"I don't know him. I mean, I've met him. A long time ago. I know *of* him." Alex zigzagged a hand through his hair. Rob had never seen him like this, he was either desperate for a drug fix, or nervous.

"Oh, right," Lulu said. "The Chris thing. He testified, right? Wasn't it a whole thing? I remember his parents were in a panic over him coming to the defense of a rapist. But I suppose they were childhood friends. I mean, you would probably come to Rob's defense if he were accused of being a rapist." Lulu bared a flash of teeth.

"I — yeah. I met him then." Alex started pacing. "Can't you just go over there and get it? Why do we have to go?"

"They're *your* drugs. I don't want them. Go yourself," Lulu said, but she was looking at Rob, just barely edging up part of an eyebrow. He didn't mean to stare; he really didn't even feel like he *was* staring, it was simply that his eyes seemed to find her and rest there. Looking at her was a respite from the rest of the world, especially when she wasn't speaking.

"Why is he even out here? No one's out here." Alex took a drink of someone else's drink. Rob wasn't sure it was even alcoholic.

"Obviously since we're in his house this weekend,—'—he's staying at his cousin's. Next door," she explained, inclining her head to the windows. "I already told him we wanted to come swim." She typed rapidly on her phone.

"Swim?" Rob asked. "It's twenty-five degrees out."

"It's an indoor pool," Alex said of the house he'd never been to. He leaned over the top of the couch, reading Lulu's messages. "Don't say we want to ski. No one wants to ski."

"You can't ski here. It's too flat. Ski," Lulu held one finger to a nostril. "Come on. Are you still calling it nose candy?"

Alex gathered the rest of the girls, and Will grudgingly agreed to drive one of the two cars across a back lane that Lulu knew, and somehow navigated in the fast-falling snow, a dirt road that dipped suddenly to reveal a garage door in the act of opening, like it had sensed them coming.

Lulu flung her car door open and walked straight into the arms of a tall, thin guy whose hair was almost the same color as his pale skin, he looked like a member of the Malfoy family.

"I wish you would ever call me," she said, and laced her arms around his neck.

"I wish you would ever answer the phone," he replied. Lulu kept her face turned into the guy, who held her like a toddler and appraised the group with eerie, silent eyes that were almost too light to be blue.

"Landon!" Maxie smacked him with a kiss on his cheek.

"Hello, darling." He took her hand with one long-fingered pale one, grasping it briefly, not a handshake but not a hand squeeze, something in between. "Hi, Vic."

"Hello." Victoria touched her cheek to his.

"This is Landon," Lulu said. "This is Will, Alex, Rob, and Yael."

"I know Alex, of course," Landon said, reaching out a hand to take Alex's in a manner that was decidedly more adult than any of the rest of them. "Nice to see you again. I'm actually glad to run into you like this. I've been trying to get in touch with you for a while," Landon explained, smiling his white smile with his white lips on his white face.

"Yeah. You too," Alex told him, pulling his arm away.

"Nice to meet you all! Shall we go get warm?" Landon snaked an arm around Lulu's ribs and led her down the hall, Rob behind them. He wanted to be the first one to ask Lulu if she was okay; he wanted to be *there*, right there, in case this maybe-Voldemort decided to suck the life out of her.

"You look horrible," Landon told her, cheerfully.

“I know,” Lulu replied, just as pleasant.

“I hope you give up on that godforsaken place, and come home, already.” Landon turned suddenly. “You are… ?”

“Rob.”

Landon held out a hand. “Nice to meet you.”

“Thank you for having us, darling.” Lulu swept a curtain of hair back over her shoulders. “I missed your beautiful manners. I used to have beautiful manners, and then I went away, and now I’m just another Instagram influencer with incorrect grammar.”

“You still have beautiful manners, Lulu. Carlos didn’t chew you up and spit you out as some sort of monster. You’re still exactly the same.” He turned the brass handle of a door, and suddenly they were in another faux-manor house, with stone walls and marble floors. “How do you know Lulu?” he asked Rob.

“This wedding,” Rob told him. Landon blinked, nodded, led them to a descending staircase.

“Weddings are such an imposition, aren’t they? But I suppose your life is much improved for having this one in it.” He gave Lulu’s waist a squeeze and she took a long, wavering breath. “Lulu?” Landon asked.

“I’m fine.” Her face was taut and pulled. “It’s harder when I’m not, you know. Putting on my party face.”

“You’ll be fine. You *are* fine. Shall we swim?”

“I’m going to the kitchen to make myself tea. Do you want some?” Lulu touched a hand to her temple. It was strange to see Alex nervous and Lulu vulnerable, like seeing your teacher outside of school.

Landon shook his head, arms wrapped around the banister. “I suppose I’ll lead the others.”

“They’re not so terribly dull,” Lulu promised him, as she slid through a closed door and out of sight. Part of Rob wondered if she would bother coming back, if he would see her again or she had only ever been an illusion, a trick of the light that made you believe you saw something which was never really there.

Will
February 11th, 2017

No one wanted to swim. Maxie applied lotion to her legs like they were actually sunning themselves, and Lulu dangled her tanned feet in the water, but the rest of them scattered around the edges of the artificially blue pool, unsure of what to do. Yael and Rob had congregated by the sauna; Victoria laid behind Maxie, and Alex paced, sucking down the gin martinis Landon had made a pitcher of like they were water.

"Why don't you just drink them directly out of the shaker?" Maxie suggested when Alex went to pour another.

"You promised me party favors," he said.

"Ask Landon," Maxie replied. Alex had shied away from three of Landon Heathcote's quiet-voiced attempts at a conversation; Will almost felt bad for his friend. It was always awkward, anything to do with Chris Newman. Alex avoided it like a bad case of pinkeye, and so Will did, too. Rob was too stupid to remember the little nuances like this, which was why Rob spent half of his time moaning about being disliked and excluded. Which made you want to dislike and exclude him even more.

"It's fine," Alex muttered. "I don't want to be rude."

"Landon," Maxie called across the pool, underneath the sand-colored marble ceiling, echoing in the emptiness. "Do you have any cocaine? Alex wants to ask, but he doesn't want to be *rude.*"

These were the things he didn't like about Maxie. It was like she *enjoyed* calling them out on their manners and decorum, which was so ridiculous, because she was from the same place the others were. She acted as though growing up in a penthouse on Fifth Avenue instead of on Park made her more of a real human than the rest of them, made it okay for her to say the word *cocaine* like she'd asked for a ginger ale.

"Of course," Landon removed a bag from the pocket of his robe and jiggled it.

"There you go," Maxie extended her hand.

"Aren't you going to do any?" Alex asked.

Maxie raised a brow. "Do you need company for such an endeavor?"

Alex walked along the edge of the pool toward Landon.

"It's not really a cocaine-and-tea kind of afternoon," Landon said mildly. "But I'm sure someone will join you."

Alex shrugged. "Anyone else?"

"I've never done it," Yael said, quietly, arms wrapped around her knees. "Drugs change your brain forever."

"Prescription drugs change your brain, too," Maxie said. "There's no point in being high and mighty about it. Prozac is just as bad as cocaine." No one bothered to reply to this.

"*High* and mighty," Landon smirked. "You want a bump, Max?"

"Alex, get straws from the drink cart, please," she said.

"I'm getting in the sauna," Lulu said, sighing. "Come on, Yael."

Yael got up to go with her, so Will followed. "How does everyone know each other?" Yael asked.

"Oh, from growing up." Lulu yawned. "Maxie knows Landon through me. His brother, Phillip, is one of my best friends. I brought Maxie and Victoria up here a few times freshman year of college."

Will couldn't stop looking at Yael's fingernails, which were short and unpolished, the complete opposite of Jessica's. Jessica had her nails done once a week. Sometimes Will joked that Jessica loved her nails more than she loved him. Once, on a trip to Iceland, she threw such a fit about being unable to find a salon that he sincerely considered booking flights home. She ended up texting Lulu, who had a friend doing a shoot in Reykjavik with a manicurist, and the manicurist appeared at their hotel in under an hour.

Things always worked out when you were Jessica because you *made* them work; you tried every possible outlet until a solution appeared. She planned her manicures around their trips now. He wondered what she would do for their two-week honeymoon in the Seychelles. He wondered what they would do for fourteen days by themselves, with no one else to fill the space.

"Do you miss Carlos?" Will asked.

"Not as much as I thought I would." She blinked up at him in that defeated Disney princess way, like she was unspooling right in front of him. "I just *loathe* how people react when I tell them I'm single, as if I've told them I'm suffering from some minor illness. I guess I miss having him more than I miss *him*. There's such a… comfort in that other half. And you come to know them so intimately that eventually you can't even tell if you dislike them." She tilted her head back against the wall and smiled a little.

"I know what you mean," Will said, slowly. That was almost what he felt about Jessica; that, along with her intoxicating way of making everything happen, was probably why they were still together. Without her, he wouldn't be enough. He had landed Jessica purely through the luck of pertinent timing and now he wasn't sure that he could do it on his own, build the life he wanted, live as one of them.

Lulu half-stacked her legs on Yael's and let them tangle together. Yael didn't move. "I don't understand why anyone would do coke at three in the afternoon on a day like today."

"Alex gets like this after he talks to his dad," Will said.

Yael laughed. "If only *that* were the basis for a tough day."

One of the things Will liked most about Yael was her picture of perspective. He supposed when you spent your days around people who were sick and dying, the things that mattered *so much* to everyone else really didn't matter at all. Things like getting a manicure in Iceland and the color of the flowers on the banister; things like your father telling you exactly what to do and you having to do it; things like deciding if you wanted to marry your fiancée or hang her out to dry.

"What is that?" Yael turned her head to the door. "I think someone's yelling."

Lulu flipped over onto her stomach. "I'm sure it's just a game of Marco Polo, or something."

"No one plays Marco Polo any more." Will got up and opened the door. It was definitely Alex, and he was *definitely* yelling. Yael followed Will out to the pool.

"Can you shut the door, please?" Lulu asked, and Will swung it closed.

Alex and Landon stood six feet apart, Alex holding Landon's drugs and a bottle of Ketel One, breathing heavily. Rob loitered behind Alex, waiting to be called into action. Maxie and Victoria sat in a ring of towels, unconcerned.

"If you want to accuse me of something, say it," Alex spat.

"No one's *accusing* you of anything." Landon's voice was obnoxiously calm, the worst possible answer to Alex's temper. "I'm just saying, there could have been other… answers. There was no physical evidence. Only your testimony. Maybe you walked in at a bad time—"

"That girl was scared," Alex said."

"Chris Newman is not the kind of guy to rape a girl."

"You never know, do you, Landon? You never know who's going to hurt someone. You can't know." He shook his head. "You weren't there. Don't talk about things you don't understand."

"He was my friend," Landon said, simply. "I went to see him in prison, a few months before he died. He told me a very different version of the story."

"Well, he was my fucking friend, too, and how do you think I feel about him being *dead?* How do you think *I* felt that he had to go to jail, for what? A girl with a big nose and fat legs. He wasn't a bad guy, but he couldn't help himself." Alex shook his head.

Landon shook his. "When it happened, he was too scared to explain it, to even talk about it, but once time passed and he came to understand that your family isn't everywhere, Sable — they don't matter in prison — well, then, he was able to finally say everything he couldn't. I'm just asking you—"

Alex swung his hand into Landon's face as easily as he would take a water bottle from the refrigerator. It happened exceedingly quickly, Landon dropping into the water, blood curling up above him, Will diving in after him, feeling his dead weight and pulling him out, Yael saying *he's breathing* and cleaning the blood off his face with the sleeve of her robe.

"Did you need to hit him?" Will asked.

"Did you need to hit him *that hard?*" Yael dabbed at his eyelid.

Rob muttered something.

Alex laughed. "It's called the gym, man."

Landon opened his eyes. Lulu appeared next to Will; he didn't know how she'd gotten there so quickly.

"I don't know if that was the reaction I was looking for," Landon commented. "But it certainly does clarify a few things."

"I'm leaving," Alex declared. "Rob. Get the car." He walked out, unfurling his hand as he went. Rob scurried after him.

"I should go, too," Will told them. He wasn't sure what had happened, if he needed to apologize because he felt like he should, or if Landon was the one who should be apologizing because he didn't want to believe what the police and a jury and a judge had all declared. It must have been hard, impossible even, to learn that your friend was a violent offender, but it was against the unspoken code of this group to question Alex's authority, his final word. To even acknowledge that such a thing was an option.

"Is that his normal state, Will?" Landon asked, sitting up.

"Probably just the drugs," Will replied. "He doesn't — like to talk about Chris. I think he feels guilty about it. You know, putting his friend behind bars."

"Funny thing to feel guilty about." Landon's pale eyes riveted on Will. "It's the kind of thing I think you feel *sad* about. One of those horrible things that happens and shows you how horrible people can be. A maudlin hero. That's what I would expect Alex to be."

Will shrugged. He didn't know how he had become the focal point of this conversation that he didn't want to be in. "Sad and guilty, it's basically the same thing, isn't it?"

"No," Landon replied. "It's not at all."

Rob
February 11th, 2017

Alex shoveled ice violently into a glass.

"If you're trying to break that, just do it," Will said from his reclining position on the couch.

"Cute mood, Billy. Your girlfriend tell your wife about that late-night tryst?" Alex poured vodka to the top of the glass, then took a swig directly out of the bottle.

"What are you talking about?" Rob asked, taking the shot Alex pushed at him and warming it in his hand. He didn't want to drink again. He didn't want to do anything except go home and break up with Ronnie and ask Lulu Swanson to go out with him.

"Will had sex with Yael last night," Alex said.

"Alex! Jesus *Christ*. Jessica is here!" Will hissed.

"She's not *here,*" Alex answered.

Rob turned from Will to Alex and back again. "*What?*"

"I know," Alex replied, downing Rob's shot and pouring them each another. "Will regrew his personality. I didn't think it was possible."

"Are you gonna tell your wife?" Rob asked.

Will sat up. "She's not my wife."

"Not yet." Alex drew a line of cocaine on the top of a dark green leather book.

"Where'd you get that? Did Landon give it to you?" Rob looked from one to the other.

"Will had sex with a bridesmaid, and your question is *where did you get coke?*" Alex shook his head. "You're an epic disappointment, Rob." Alex dropped the bill he was rolling and took a key bump instead, snorting and shaking his head like a horse in a Western, white powder dusting the bottom half of his face. "No, you really are. Going after Lulu like that. I could *see* the dollar signs in your eyes. Like you just figured out that gold-digging is a two-way street."

Lulu chose that moment to swan into the room, wearing a dress that made her look like she'd been mummified by a hundred scraps of bright yellow fabric. "What a fun conversation to walk in on. Will, Adam's looking for you."

"Okay," Will snapped.

"Wow. Did someone tell your wife about your mistress?"

"Late on that one. I said it two minutes ago." Alex slid a glass of cherries across the counter to her.

Will got up and stormed out of the room, slamming the door behind him.

"Kind of a subpar storming-out," Lulu commented, sitting down at the bar, one seat away from Rob. Rob looked at the empty stool and looked at Lulu and wished he were bold enough to say something about how rude it was that she hadn't just sat next to him.

Alex proffered an empty glass.

"Ice," Lulu told him. She gathered her hair into a knot at the base of her neck. "Do you really think Rob's a gold digger?" she asked, conversationally, like she was asking if it would rain later.

"I—" Rob opened his mouth.

"I don't know," Alex interrupted. "Only time will tell."

"Hm," she replied. "I suppose the only one worth anything out of the entire despicable lot is this angelic drunkard." She tilted her head at Alex.

Alex raised his glass. "I'll drink to that. What did Adam want?"

"To look less like *The Nightmare Before Christmas*, I would assume."

They laughed together; a cruel sound that made Rob hate them all the more. If Adam weren't there, he would have been the Adam of the weekend, the subject of mockery, of derision.

"Jessica told me slept all day. He didn't even drink that much," Alex remarked.

"In fairness to Adam, I did give him a bar of those really good chocolate mushrooms. I *told* him only to eat a square, but I guess he ate the whole thing." Lulu inspected her nails.

"Lulu," Alex let out a booming laugh, shaking his head. "I underestimated you."

"He said he wanted drugs. It's harmless. Plant medicine, as they say in LA." Lulu motioned for a large glass bottle of water.

"*He's* harmless," Alex replied. "Just annoying."

"Better to be annoying than *grasping*." Lulu dropped a cherry into her glass.

"If only they could all understand that." Alex poured himself another shot.

Rob could feel himself missing it, this important concept that, like everything else, he couldn't *quite* grasp. He was always just a few seconds late, a few meters short, a few words off. He would never be a part of the *them* that he had spent his life trying to melt into — he would always be like Adam, studiously ignored, harmless but annoying, there to fill space, accused of money-grubbing by his own best friend.

Maybe he was money-grubbing. Maybe there was money in her too-big eyes and her shiny hair and the way her hands fluttered when she spoke. She looked expensive, like something in a shop window you knew you needed immediately, something that would make you everything you thought you wanted to be. Maybe that was just what money looked like, and she was the embodiment of it, wrapped in yellow gauze, diamonds twinkling on her neck and her wrists and her fingers and all the way up her ears. He wanted her to melt into him; he wanted to absorb that impossible luster into every pore and particle, until, like Lulu, he glowed of his own accord.

Will
February 11th, 2017

The table in the dining room was too big for the nine of them, so they had to get up to pass each other the Brussels sprouts, the salt, the Parker House rolls. Yael wouldn't look at him when he was looking at her but then she looked at him too much and it made him feel sick, dramatically sick, and wildly emotional, like he was sixteen again.

Jessica got up to bring him the salad. It had pomegranate seeds in it; he didn't want it. "I don't want it," he told her. "Don't get up," but she dropped it next to his hand like he hadn't spoken at all.

"Alex is *wasted*," she said. "What did you guys *do* today?"

What Will wanted to say was, *nothing, because there's nothing to do here.*

What Will said was, "Who knows. It's not like this is the rehearsal dinner."

"Well, we won't be able to get any good photos."

"We can move your chairs closer," Adam volunteered. "Or you two could get a *roo-oo-oom*."

"That would actually be great," Rob said, through a too-big bite of mashed potatoes. "Then I would finally get a bed to myself." He stole a look at Lulu, he was showing off for her, doing his best impression of one of Maxie's uncomfortable call-outs, except that Maxie would never have said something so boring.

"This," Lulu interrupted, voice a little too loud, "is a *beautiful* house for a wedding."

"Gorgeous," Maxie said, nodding. She'd been drinking her dinner and her eyes were starting to stick on one thing or another.

"*Beautiful*," Victoria said, and hiccupped quietly. Jessica returned to her seat and spread her napkin across her lap like a queen taking up her scepter again.

"I know," Jessica said. "Imagine it in June."

"June is the best month to get married," Lulu asserted.

"It is," Victoria agreed.

"I wish I'd gotten married in June," Maxie added.

"Me too," Alex said, and four of the five girls, including Jessica, burst out laughing.

"You must hate him," Adam said to Rob.

"He's easy to hate," Maxie emptied her wine glass.

"He *did* punch our host today." Lulu smirked.

"I've never punched someone and had it go so well." Alex took a sip of champagne.

"I've never *seen* someone punched," Maxie put in. "So thank you for that."

"I've seen a lot of people who have *been* punched," Yael told them. "But never the actual punching."

"I've always wanted to punch someone," Victoria commented. "I think you would feel so *free*. Like you'd done something for yourself."

"A life lesson," Alex declared. "Stay away from the pretty ones. They'll eat you alive if you let them." Alex winked at Maxie.

"Lulu practically eats men for breakfast," Victoria remarked. "She finishes off the leftovers at afternoon tea."

"There aren't leftovers," Lulu replied. "I'm like Sylvia Plath, from the ashes I rise with my blonde hair, and I eat men like air."

"I'd like to watch that," Adam told her, so overtly suggestively that Will was embarrassed.

"Why don't we take dessert in the living room?" Jessica interrupted. "You guys could play bridge, or something."

Yael agreed, nodding. "Very *Downton Abbey*."

Maxie pushed her chair back and stood immediately. Jessica looped her arm in Lulu's. "Come on. It's pavlova. I know you love meringue."

Will grabbed Adam's shoulder as he went to leave. "Hey. Can you tone it down a little? Lulu's talking about poetry, so drop the innuendo. She's not gonna hook up with you."

"How do you know?" Adam asked.

Will knew because Lulu opened her mouth and inhaled the vapor of what had been a man just by the way she returned a gaze. She anticipated it, anticipated *them*, what they wanted from her, what they needed from her, and she used it to reduce them to nothingness. Will thought it was the result of *becoming* beautiful instead of being it. She assumed the worst of men because she knew it well, knew it from too many slights over too many years. Lulu was a monster of their own making.

By the time they got to the living room, it was half-empty, Victoria and Jessica flipping through a coffee table book, Yael sitting silently across from them.

"Where is everyone?" Will asked.

"Alex and Maxie went to find a book, and Lulu went to check her phone," Victoria reported.

"Will," Jessica began, not looking up from the book of Tim Walker's photographs. "Can you go get Lulu? I want to remind her that she said she would get my approval before she posted anything."

"Sure." Will wanted to shake Rob off of him like a wet dog.

"I'll go with you." Yael stood. "I know where they went."

"That's okay," Will told her, because he didn't know what he wanted and he didn't want to be tested, not right now, when he was exhausted and desperate for tomorrow.

"Why don't you all go?" Victoria suggested, and Will wanted to murder her. It was like, in the absence of her mistresses, she had to sprinkle a little mischief around.

"Yes," Jessica said. "But Will, check on Lulu alone, okay? Or — just don't bring Rob in with you."

"Sure," Will shrugged.

Will felt Yael's steadiness next to him, felt her waves of confusion that he didn't want to be alone and maybe her hurt and maybe her own misgivings about what they were doing. What they had done.

"So," Rob said, "I'm popular tonight."

"Where are we going?" Will asked Yael.

"I don't know. Alex suggested they go to the smaller library on the second floor to check some piece of poetry they were arguing about, but Lulu's probably in her room."

"That was always Alex's move." Rob hit the side of the paneling with his heavy class ring. "Get a girl alone on some random dispute. When we were in college," Rob added. "I know Maxie's married."

“I wouldn’t be surprised by anything Maxie did,” Will said. Maxie was much more likely to be a cheater than he was. Maxie lived off of admiration and miso soup; that was how she kept her six-pack. And, if Will was a cheater, who wasn’t? Other than the venerable Lulu Swanson, of course. Will needed to get out of this house. “Let’s go find them,” Will said, suddenly. He wasn’t his girlfriend’s lackey, and he wasn’t a fan of Lulu Swanson and for the first time in a long time he wanted to get really, really good and drunk in a way that only Alex could get you.

“Jessica told you to get Lulu,” Rob reminded him, and Will thought that in another life, Rob and Victoria could have worked out as a couple.

“I know,” he said. “But I don’t want to. Where’s the smaller library?”

“We’ll pass Lulu’s room anyway,” Yael said. “See? It’s that door.”

Lulu’s door was partially open, lights blazing, and Will spotted her phone on the ground a few feet in front of them. He scooped it up; *of course* she had the giant phone. “Weird.”

“I think we turn down here.” Yael pushed another door left ajar, a darkened hallway, and, at the end of it, Will caught sight of a yellow scrap whipping around the corner.

“Come on,” he said, and quickened his pace, and he could hear it, then, something muffled and undistinguishable but *there* nonetheless, like elevator music, a moaning or maybe a screaming and then Lulu Swanson was kneeling at a heavy oak door with something in her hand, trying to pick the lock.

“Something’s wrong,” she said. “I heard Maxie screaming.”

“I’m sure they’re just having sex,” Rob said, and then Will heard it, the noise, one word, stifled but intelligible nonetheless, *help.*

Yael
February 11th, 2017

Yael didn't know why they didn't start knocking and banging and yelling, in retrospect. Lulu was calm in a manic way, twisting those bobby pins, Rob unhelpfully in the background saying to just leave them alone and when had bobby pins ever opened a door? The lock clicked, and she shoved the door open, and Will pushed in behind her so that Lulu fell onto hands and knees and that was what Yael saw first, those floating pieces of yellow across the carpet, and then Maxie, with her face shoved into Alex Sable's elbow and his hand around her throat, enclosing her neck entirely, holding Maxie so closely in front of him it reminded her of a shoot-out from an old Western, or something, except that Maxie Stein-Golden had never been a hostage in her life.

Alex must have loosened his grip upon their entry because Maxie twisted out and away from him — his arm was bleeding, Yael noticed as he pulled himself out of her and zipped up his pants.

"They don't teach you how to knock on Park Avenue?" he asked Lulu, who picked herself up and inched towards Maxie like he had a gun.

"Should we go?" Rob asked Alex. Rob was incontrovertibly stupid, Yael thought, and then she wondered at the fact that her mind was capable of thoughts like this.

"Alex," Will said, and his face pinched in on itself, and he looked like he was about to cry. "I think you should come with us."

"Maxie and I were just having a little fun," he said, and Lulu was holding onto Maxie, holding her up with her own shaking hands, staring at Alex in a kind of fixated horror that Yael wasn't sure she'd ever seen outside of a movie. "It's not like I single-handedly brought down the institution of marriage," Alex said. "She wanted it."

Maxie said nothing at all.

"Alex." Will's voice was his litigator voice, his courtroom voice. "Come with us."

Will threw Alex into the hallway—"*Ow*," Alex said, rubbing his elbow — slamming the door behind him. Yael looked from Rob to Lulu to Maxie and wanted to ask, *What now?* but she knew no one would answer her.

"We need to call the police," Lulu said, in a voice that was calm and controlled even though Yael could still see her shaking. "You need to get a rape kit."

"Rape?" Rob said. "That's not a word to throw around. That ruins lives."

Maxie moved her dress aside, exposing her missing underwear and swipes of fluid on the inside of her thighs. Lulu started ripping pieces of her dress off, handing them to Maxie, who looked at the yellow scraps like she couldn't recognize them, who looked at her legs, at the shiny, wet evidence of Alex Sable.

"A rape kit and the morning after pill," Yael said. She found Maxie's torn underwear on the oriental rug, a smear of hot pink against the muted colors.

"Rape…" Rob began.

"Rob," Lulu replied, in a voice with no feeling. "Get a grip on reality, or get out of this room."

Yael didn't know why Rob hadn't gone with his friends, why he had chosen to stay with them except that maybe he didn't know what else to do. Maybe on some level he knew that what they'd just seen was the word that ruins lives and he didn't want to follow his best friend, the rapist, off into the sunset.

"But—" Rob began.

"We can't," Maxie interrupted. "It would — I mean — everyone would know. *Everyone*. I would always be that girl. I would be — and no one would believe me, anyway. Even if they pretended to. They would say I made it up. For attention."

She wasn't wrong. On some level, a small, sad part of Yael had almost thought that herself, when she saw Lulu half-splayed on the floor, scrabbling at the door, *God, these girls just LIVE for drama.*

"So what do you propose we do?" Lulu asked, and there was a

fierceness to her tone that frightened Yael. They were silent, cowed Rob, broken Maxie, scared Yael. “There has to be something. We can’t just… live like this.”

Part II
Tyler
June 2017

Tyler spent two days with Sean, sniffing around the Heathcote estate, before the family appealed to the chief of police for their privacy. On Sunday, the remnants of dinner still remained, knives stuck into the tree, folding tables and chairs assembled in a ghostly charade of the last supper. There were three knives in the tree, only one of which Tyler and Sean's combined strength could remove and enter into evidence. The rest were stuck, Tyler supposed, for time immemorial

Alex's room was already scrubbed clean; the only evidence that something had happened was the absence of a rug. The butler, who ran the house, showed them the bed and bath that looked of hotel-quality, with little to say. He let them paw through Alex's remaining things, waiting to be shipped to the family, which were primarily black-tie shoes and Brunello Cucinelli sweaters. Someone had folded them neatly into the monogrammed suitcase in which they'd arrived, but Tyler would have guessed Alex was the kind of person who just threw his clothes in. They found three bags of cocaine in his Dopp kit, no Valium, nothing else, and when Tyler asked about anything that might have been found in the room or bathroom the butler looked suspicious of *him*.

"We wouldn't leave anything of Mr Sable's behind. My employers are very eager to move on from this incident. The new mattress and sheets arrive on Monday," he told them.

"He didn't die in bed," Sean replied. "You replacing the bathtub, too?"

"Yes, as a matter of fact," the butler told them. "But that had to be custom ordered from England, so we won't have it for weeks."

"Did you go in there, before the police came? Did you see a bracelet like this, anywhere in the room?" Tyler showed him the photo.

"I did not go into the room until it was ready to be cleaned," he said, stiffly.

"Can I ask you a question? You seem like a man who knows about watches, especially nice ones." Tyler brought up a photo on his phone. "Do you think that a watch like this could break if it hit the bottom of that tub?"

"Ah. A beautiful Patek Philippe." He looked at Tyler approvingly, as if the watch belonged to him. "It's possible. I couldn't say. But the watch would stop soon after it was submerged in water. This isn't a waterproof model." He handed the phone back.

Tyler and Sean thanked him and went on their less-than-merry way. Tyler turned around on the driveway, watching the palatial home retreat into the distance behind him. When the gates shut, he knew it was the last time they would be there.

Armie, the county medical examiner, was waiting for them when they got back, sitting in the windowless vault that was his office, next to the table which usually held a body. "First death in weeks that wasn't an overdose. Kind of a relief to look at a healthy body." He greeted them.

"A healthy dead body," Tyler said. "Ironic." *Death is full of the oddest ironies, isn't it,* Lulu Swanson had asked them. Tyler lifted the tape recorder; like Sean, he'd worked with Armie extensively on his first case. "Okay?"

Armie nodded, waving him on. "Some kidney damage for someone his age, definitely a drinker. He had a good amount of cocaine in his system, some OxyContin, and so much Valium I'm amazed he managed to make the lacerations which killed him. All the drugs do account for the differing depths in the cuts on his arms, although they're almost all the same length, which is surprising, again, considering everything he was on. We've got to assume he had a decent tolerance for the drugs, otherwise he just would have passed out."

"Wouldn't cocaine counteract that, and keep him awake?" Tyler asked.

"The cocaine was probably first, done a few hours before the rest. Based on what Strickland told me you found, I'd guess he does that the most. Probably took the Oxy and Valium because he was afraid of the pain, or he thought he'd have to watch himself bleed out slowly." Armie looked at the empty table where the body usually rested for these conversations. Tyler had to hand it to the Sables, they got what they wanted quickly.

"How many cuts? How deep?" Sean asked.

"Only two on each side. Probably would have been a slow bleed out, with only two, but he was too out of it, from the drugs, to do more. I'm impressed he did these. He was left-handed, but severed the artery on the left side. That was the first one, I would guess. The second cut on the left side was only about half as deep as the first. On the right side, which should have the more significant damage, because he was left-handed, the cut closest to his hand was shallow, just opening the skin. The second one is deeper, carefully done, almost looks surgical. Must be handy with a knife," Armie said.

"Time of death?" Tyler asked.

"I would guess around one thirty a.m."

"The watch is stopped at four," Tyler said. He knew that Sean thought he was focusing too much on the watch, but Sean hadn't spent his vacations reading Agatha Christies, where a stopped watch was the first sign of foul play.

There were a lot of podcasts on the opioid epidemic, and Tyler's weeks in New Hampshire hadn't shed any new light on how to fix it, how to help. He'd pitched the Alex Sable story to his producer on the basis of expanding information about mental health and urging people to get the help they needed, but Tyler wasn't sure that this *was* that story, yet, or that that was a story he wanted to tell. He liked the idea of laying out a death before the public, letting them see what it looked like through the eyes of the people who removed the body and measured the incisions and asked the questions about a person they'd known only in death. He liked the idea of painting a picture of this person, everything he'd had and the vital pieces he'd been lacking to keep himself alive.

And he believed, in some small part, in the strangeness of the scene, of the two girls he'd met in their ethereal costumes, of the lawyer swooping in just at the moment Maxie wanted to say something. Maxie had something to say; Tyler knew that much. He'd been interviewing people long enough to watch it flicker across her face.

"I pulled his medical records, like you asked," Armie told them, handing Sean a sheaf of printer paper. "A few hospital trips for stitches from *accidental* cuts, the most recent one just a few months ago, in Philly, where the doctor sent him up for a psych eval afterwards. Looks like a pattern of behavior."

Sean handed a page to Tyler. *I recommend Mr Sable for an immediate psychological examination. He exhibits violent behavior not simply towards himself, but to others with him. He fits the profile of drug-seeking behavior. The wound on his hand was self-inflicted. Sable refused to tell me that he had been drinking or taken any drugs that day other than Adderall, although his pupils were dilated. I recommend keeping him overnight for observation and drug testing.*

"Not a shocker," Sean commented, flipping through a few pages. He handed the stack of paper to Tyler, knowing that Tyler would want to review every inch of it, and sighed. "So, whaddaya think, Armie? Definitely a suicide?"

"Hoping it's a homicide?" Armie asked, smiling again. "Could be. Likely. Based on the profile," he indicated the papers in Tyler's hands. "What did the friends and family say?"

"Family's so rich it got the chief to ask us to shut up. Friends didn't really know him. I'm hoping Tyler can use his podcast magic and get a little more info." Sean took out a pack of cinnamon Trident, offered it around, chewed his own piece thoughtfully. "I want to believe that it's a suicide. I guess you can never tell with these people, can you?"

"He cut deeply. Deeper than a usual cutter. That's why he had to keep getting stitches," Armie told them.

"What are you going to do?" Tyler asked Sean.

Sean shrugged. "Decide it was a suicide, I guess. Go back to chasing Fentanyl. I thought there was something here."

Lulu Swanson was easy to find on Instagram. She had over a million followers and, to Tyler's surprise, she responded to his message within a week. *Hi! I don't want to be recorded, even off-the-record. I'm happy to talk to you, though, on background.*

Tyler asked if he could meet with her and with Maxie as soon as they were free; Lulu invited him over for the following week. *I thought that Alex's case had been — closed? Not sure if that's the terminology,* she wrote in her reply.

He came to Lulu's apartment at eight p.m. on a Friday, almost two weeks after Alex's death. It was either a bid to be discreet or sheer laziness; Tyler wasn't sure which. She lived in a fancy building with two doormen and a Calder in the lobby; since Tyler was early, he waited outside in the fading cold and watched the light shift from natural to manufactured until a low glow scattered across the cobblestones and onto his shoes. Some quick Googling a few days ago had revealed that Lulu Swanson was heiress to the Swanson drugstores, as commonplace as CVS, of which her father had sold a controlling stake to Amazon in 2011. She was half-Jewish, went to Harvard with the rest of her fellow bridesmaids, and in the past three years had become something akin to *famous*.

"You're early," Lulu said. She was carrying a thin cardboard box under one arm. "I wanted to get something for us to eat, but I never know what other people eat. I have, like, salad and eggs ninety times a day, or, some days, just chocolate. Anyway, I got pastries from La Mercerie. Do you know that place?"

"I don't. I live in Brooklyn."

"Of course you do." She glanced at the empty front desk. "I never know where the doormen are," she said, as if this were a universal issue to which anyone could easily relate. Tyler followed her inside, offering to take the box she was carrying and the two shopping bags on her arm. "You can take the Chloe one," she told him. "I find myself strolling by Chloe and suddenly I'm inside. I don't know how it happens. Anyway, I hope you like pastries. I ordered cheese and everything earlier but I'm sure it's not very nice because it's all just from Max Delivery. Murray's and Balthazar." She rolled her eyes at this, at herself, at eighteen-dollar cheese from Murray's and seven-dollar baguettes from Balthazar.

"I'm sure it's great," Tyler replied, as the elevator cruised up to her floor.

"How's it going, by the way? Your… should I call it an investigation? What does one call such a thing?" Lulu asked, opening her door. The apartment was white and *big*; it looked like a hotel, like it had been professionally decorated. It smelled like candles and Tyler was almost astounded that someone who was so near to his own age lived in a place like this; it reeked of overpriced home goods and rent that could serve as a down payment on a car. "Sorry," she told him. "I just moved, so it's a mess." There was no evidence of moving, no boxes, no piles of clothing, not even an errant pair of scissors for cutting tape. "Can I get you anything?" she asked. Tyler shook his head. "Please, have a seat."

Tyler sat. The couch was soft and warm. She had Hermes pillows on it. He knew they were Hermes from a story he'd helped research in his early days, about the Hermes factory, where they hand-feed their sheep. Lulu appeared, handing him a glass of water that he hadn't asked for. "Nothing else? Tea? Coffee? Wine?" He shook his head. She left again and returned with a platter of cheese and grapes and sliced pears and fig preserves and three kinds of expensive crackers and two kinds of bread from Balthazar and even cornichons. She caught him looking at them and said, "I don't know what people like on a cheese plate. So, anyway," she said, and inclined a hand out.

"It's going fine. I'm not sure… what there is to investigate, and what there isn't," he told her, honestly. "I thought you would be a good jumping off point. I'd like to ask you to put me in touch with the groomsmen; I've reached out, but no one… will answer my calls." He had a feeling that if Lulu asked, she would get what she wanted. "Is Maxie Stein-Golden coming?"

"No. She wasn't feeling well. I'll give you her number. I can put you in touch with people, but most of them won't want to talk to you. His family won't, certainly. I think Theo would be furious if he even knew I was speaking to you." She drank her water and looked at the cheese. "You won't eat *anything*?" she asked. "I have a whole *box* of pastries you're going to have to take home, because I can't have them in the house."

Tyler smiled and sipped his drink. It had the distinctly mineral taste of bottled water. "In a minute," he said. "It would really help if I could record."

"It's like the pastries," Lulu told him. "It has to be an unequivocal no, at least for now."

"I'll change the name," Tyler offered. "Disguise your voice."

"If I let you record now, and I change my mind later, will you promise you won't use any of it?" She tapped her foot, tapped her water glass.

Tyler hesitated. "Okay," he said. "I think you're going to come around to it."

Lulu laughed.

The talk was easy, she launched into the story seamlessly. Alex had always been a big drinker, yes, there had probably been some drugs that night; there was a mention of Oxy, she remembered, to do with Rob. There had been a drinking game, and Alex cut his hand. Lulu had gone upstairs by then, so this was all, she informed Tyler, what she'd learned later. She woke up in the middle of the night but didn't see Alex. The next morning, she and Theo went in Alex's room when they heard the scream. She fainted and hit her head and Yael said she might have a concussion. She still thought about it. She would always think about it.

"Did it make sense to you?" Tyler asked her. "His suicide?"

"*Making sense* is only a part of it. You have to be able to piece it apart in a hundred different ways, to begin processing it. I don't know. It's impossible to think of Alex as anything but alive." She picked up a piece of cheese, looked at it, put it back. "Sometimes even in death Alex looms so much larger than his compatriots do in life."

"What do you mean?"

She offered Tyler the tray, pushing it on him until he helped himself. "I don't know. The more I got to know him, the more I came to understand how difficult he was to know. I never would have expected him to do any of what he did." She sighed, pulling a corner off her Balthazar bread, chewing it slowly. "Parts of it feel very much like Alex. Picking Jessica's wedding. Wearing his untied bowtie in the tub. He *was* an untied bowtie. And then, of course, parts of it make no sense to me at all. I can't—" she shook her head. "I cannot express to you the horror of what I saw that morning. I can't believe a single person has that much blood. Anyway," she said, standing. "I don't know how much more I can talk about this. It's fresher than I thought. I suppose the more you talk about something the more real it becomes."

Tyler nodded. "I understand," he said. "Thank you. Can I ask you one more thing? What did you know about Chris Newman?"

"Just what everyone else does. You know, he raped a bunch of girls; Alex caught him, whatever. I didn't know him."

"Did Alex ever bring it up?" Tyler asked.

"No. It was years ago. I do want to help you, to the best of my limited ability," she assured him. "Now, tell me everything about podcasting," she said, leaning forward, and before he knew it he had eaten two plates worth of cheese and three pastries and forgotten to turn off the tape recorder. "In the last one you did. The five episode one. He told you, didn't he? He told you that his brother did it. That's when he asked you to stop recording. And then you basically ended the podcast. Why didn't you, I don't know, sort of insinuate it, more, to your listeners?"

"I can't say whether or not that's true," Tyler replied. "But there are some things that you want to know more than... sharing with your listeners. I put a year of my life into those five episodes. Whatever it is that he told me, that's mine. It belongs to me and to him. The rest is just an interesting story, and a commentary on justice. I wanted people to turn it off and ask themselves what qualifies as murder. If someone's killed five people, maybe more, and someone else kills him. Does it justify the death, the murder? If it saved lives. Was it worth it?"

"Was it?" she asked him.

Maxie Stein-Golden met him a few days later in a park in Tribeca and told him he could *of course* record. She had two coffees with her and drank them both herself, but she offered him a croissant, which he declined. She interrupted to tell Tyler that she remembered him very well, even though she didn't listen to podcasts. Tyler suggested she might now that she was about to be on one.

"No," she said calmly. "There are podcast people, and then there are people who never listen to podcasts; you're an either/or. You can't be both."

She was comfortable talking about Alex's death, answering Tyler's questions evenly, that night; she'd gone to bed first of anyone, with Victoria. She'd seen Alex later, when she heard yelling and went in to check on them; her husband, of course, wasn't even back at the house yet. "Out playing some stupid game. That was how Alex cut his hand, playing with knives. Idiotic. So I went in, and Yael was trying to stitch

Alex up; he wouldn't sit still, even though Rob and Will were holding him down. He was flailing everywhere, throwing things, going crazy. I *told* them to just leave him; who knows what they did. I went to bed and the next morning one of the boys screamed like a girl and we all went in there and of course no one thought to stop us, so we saw it. And that was that."

"Around what time did you go to bed, and what time did you go to check on Alex?" Tyler asked her.

"Bed… I have no idea. Maybe eleven, ten thirty. I'm not sure when I went to check on them, or even when Freddie came up. I think around one; I know I looked at my phone and checked Instagram, but I just can't remember." Maxie looked up at him from beneath her sunglasses, studying his face.

"Were you surprised? That he committed suicide?"

Maxie paused, finished one coffee, started on the next. "No one wants to talk about death after it's happened. I don't know why it's one of those stigmatized things, like periods, but it is. I suppose it's a way of telling someone you feel sorry for them, and that's awkward. Of course it's very different for me than it is for Will or Rob. I didn't know Alex at all; none of us did, really. It's funny because people seem to think that following someone on Instagram is an indication of *knowing* someone, but I think it's so difficult to know anyone. I've known Will for, what, like six years now? I don't think I could tell you anything about him. That his parents are divorced, I guess. I know that. That's it. I can't even tell you if he likes sparkling water or still."

"Aren't you guys friends, though?" Tyler asked.

"No. We don't speak at all." She had a way of looking at you *within* a look. "He was having an affair. This stays between us, by the way. He was sleeping with Yael. Isn't it horrible? You would never think she had that kind of betrayal in her. Or even Will. He seems like such a straight-and-narrow person. You can never really know anyone; that's what I mean." "She sighed, leaning back into the bench, putting a hand to her stomach. "It's the people with a little flimflam in their souls who you can trust. It's the rigid, serious, rule-followers you have to be afraid of. When you're so inflexible, it makes you more hypocritical, and the more hypocritical you become, the more filled with self-loathing you are. I suppose that's what happened to Alex."

"Alex doesn't sound like he was inflexible, though," Tyler said.

"No. But he lied to himself about the kind of person he was and the kind of life he lived. And, eventually, it caught up to him. It always does."

"Did you know Chris Newman?"

"*Everyone* knew *about* Chris Newman. It was the *biggest* deal when we were in high school. Alex was the hero. Everyone wanted to know who the girls were, but no one ever found out." Maxie looked up into a tree.

"Did Alex talk about it? Talk about Chris?"

"Not to me," Maxie said, eyes still fixed on the sky.

They said their goodbyes at the entrance to the park. He found himself turning around to look at her retreating back, and, as he did, she stopped herself to wave at him, a dramatic wave that he thought about for three blocks.

Will talked to Tyler on Lulu's insistence, or that was the impression he gave off. He wanted to do it over the phone, but Tyler coaxed him into coffee at a Joe and the Juice in Flatiron.

Before they sat down, Will said *no recording, none* and he didn't order a drink at all. When Tyler asked him how he was doing, he gave Tyler a withering look. "Let's get to the point. To the questions. I don't see why this matters, or why it's *important* that we do this," Will said.

"I appreciate you doing this," Tyler told him. "Let's start with when you found him. That morning. What time was it?"

"I don't know. My alarm went off. I woke Rob up. Rob's room had an adjoining door to Alex's."

"Why were you in his room?" Tyler asked.

"Jessica doesn't like me to sleep in her bed when I've been drinking."

"So you woke Rob up…"

"And then Alex. His room was empty, and we'd left him in the bathroom. It's not unusual for him to sleep wherever he lays down when he's drunk. I opened the bathroom door." A pause. "He was in the tub. His face was so white. I think I felt for a pulse in his neck. I must have pulled him out of the water, or tried to. Maybe I did that first. Then everyone was in the room. Both the doors were open. Both of the doors to the bathroom." It was such a dramatic place, almost perfectly chosen as the backdrop of his death, Tyler remembered thinking. "I remember seeing Lulu hit her head. Then I was sitting on the bed."

"What was Alex like, on his last night? Can you walk me through the events before you all parted ways?"

"He was… like Alex. Everything seemed normal. He got drunk, and cut his hand. We carried him up to his room…" Will let himself trail off.

"Who is *we*? What time did you carry him up?"

"Maybe midnight. It was me, Rob, Yael followed. She wanted to bandage his hand."

"Did you know anything about Chris Newman?" Tyler asked.

Will paused before he spoke. "Everyone knew about it. Even out in Westchester, we knew. It was a big deal. Alex got upset when people talked about it, especially after Chris died."

"Why did he get upset?"

Will looked at Tyler for a beat too long. "I don't know. I always thought Chris Newman would be a good case for someone like you. Just one witness, Alex, and he was probably drunk. Seems like an easy way to get confused about what happens."

"I didn't know there was any question over who did it," Tyler replied.

"I don't think there is," Will answered.

He met Rob at The Smith in Midtown during what was obviously his lunch break. Rob was much like the defeated-looking photo Lulu had shown him on her phone, hair curling over his ears, certainly not one of these groomed and trained elites.

They chatted, the uneasy small talk of two people with only one thing to talk about, and Rob told him immediately that he didn't want to be recorded.

"Afraid of the Sables?" Tyler asked. Rob gave a half-lift of a shoulder that wasn't a *yes* but certainly wasn't a *no.*

"Let's get to it," he said. "I don't have time for more than a drink." He did drink, a liquid, Don Draper lunch of one martini and several handfuls of peanuts, while Tyler asked him the same questions he'd asked Will, beginning with the finding of the body. "I heard Will yell. I thought he might have stepped on broken glass, because the night before Alex kept throwing stuff, and there was glass all over. I didn't know whether it was Will or Alex. I thought *Alex* might have stepped on glass, or something. I walked in—"

"You didn't run?"

"Alex has... *accidents* a lot. Cuts... always, you know, mistakes. Accidental." Rob repeated himself. "It's... something you get used to."

"So you went into the bathroom," Tyler prompted.

"Will was trying to drag him out of the tub, and his head was rolled back. I think I noticed that before I noticed the blood, and then I kind of saw it all at once. We had so much trouble getting him out of the bath."

"Do you remember anything else?" Tyler asked.

"Yael checked his pulse, and said *he's dead.*"

"Did you know he was dead, when you first saw him?"

"I don't think I knew what was happening." There was a sudden tightness in Rob's voice."

"Did Alex strike you as the type to commit suicide?"

Rob sighed. "How can you know? If someone's really serious. What they actually mean. Alex is impossible to read. We could never have known."

"Did you know anything about Chris Newman?" Tyler asked.

"Vaguely. I know the basics of the story, I think, from Google. Alex doesn't like to talk about it."

Both Will and Rob spoke of him in the present tense, as Maxie and Lulu had. Rob paid for lunch in cash, counting out bills onto the table.

"I've got this," Tyler said, reaching for the check. "You don't have to pay."

Rob shook his head. "Lulu told me I did." He handed the leather folder to a waiter and got up, not looking at Tyler.

"Thank you," Tyler told him. Rob shrugged again and put on his suit coat and walked out as if he'd said goodbye. He hadn't.

Tyler took a train to Philadelphia to meet with Yael in the cafeteria at the hospital. "I'm sorry," she told him, sitting down, immediately beginning on her tuna salad sandwich. “I don’t have long for lunch, and I’m starving.”

She couldn’t let him record, because of doctor-patient confidentiality. Her story was as simple as the rest of theirs, her assessment of Alex coldly damning. She started talking before he asked his questions, clearly in a hurry. Her life was in such stark contrast to the rest of the people he’d spoken to that it was hard to reconcile. “Alex cut his hand playing some camp game with a bunch of the other guys. He was obviously high out of his mind on some cocktail of things that no one should mix, and he wouldn’t let me touch him, other than wrapping a napkin around his hand. We got him upstairs to his room, Rob and Will and I, and he went crazy, throwing things, yelling. At one point I went to look for a first aid kit, but I gave up. I left Rob and Will to deal with him and went to bed’.”

“The next morning, I knew he was dead before I checked his pulse; he had been dead for hours. The boys pulled him out of the tub — I think that’s why Lulu fainted, seeing those cuts on his arms. And the blood in the bath, the blood on the floor, the blood in the broken glass. Maxie asked if we should bandage him up, and I was like no, he’s dead. Maxie’s husband insisted they put Alex down on the rug — he was holding Alex up, too — and Jessica told them not to put him on the rug, but they did it anyway. The ambulance arrived. It turned out Rob and Will both had glass in their feet. They were all cut up because they’d been barefoot. And then, hours later, we got to go home.”

“You saw Alex in the past, as a patient.”

“Doctor-patient confidentiality.”

“Do you know anything about Chris Newman?” Tyler asked.

Yael shook her head. “Just what the girls have mentioned. I don’t know the details. And Alex didn’t talk about it at all.”

Part III
Alex
February 12th, 2017

Alex expected to be woken by Will, or even Rob, prodding him and insisting he join them at breakfast, but he slept the disturbed sleep of the drugged — ten milligrams of Valium would do that to you — waking in confusion that no one had come to check on him.

He woke at one p.m., which never would have happened if someone had come to *get* him. It was pitch black in his room, the curtains drawn and the lights off and he was suddenly *angry*. He broke a lamp getting out of bed and cut his finger, was still in the dark, was still pissed. He banged a knee making his way across the room to the light switch, and then what? Then his room was illuminated, pointlessly, just some mess and no one there to cajole him into gracing the table.

Maybe it was the hangover — Valium always left you a little defeated — or maybe it was the feeling he had that things had changed. Maybe he was particularly paying attention to what they did this morning, because he was still unclear on how they parted ways last night. Will hustled him off to bed and demanded he go to sleep; Rob looked unconcerned. They knew girls like Maxie — they hadn't seen anything too embarrassing — it was *fine*. They knew girls like Maxie, and he knew girls like Maxie, and Maxie knew him, knew who he was and what she'd gotten herself entangled in when she flipped her extensions and laughed her hoarse laugh up into his eyes.

He needed to quiet his rampant anxiety and remember that everything would always be fine for him. Things were always *fine* for people like him, no matter what happened, because he could retreat back into the safety of his family, of his money, of knowing that he would always have everything he wanted. If you did as Alex did, and deliberately befriended people who were impressed by your stature in life, everything would always be swept under the rug; there was nothing that couldn't be forgiven. Jessica wanted that line in her wedding write-up, *the best man, Alex Sable, son of Wall Street scion Cornelius Sable*, the same way she wanted a wedding at this ridiculous faux-Versailles, the same way she wanted a husband with a decent pedigree, whether he loved her or not. Alex respected someone like Jessica, who was satiated by the excellence of appearance; she lived in what it looked like to the outside world, and she was happy there.

Those were the kind of people Alex wanted to surround himself with. Those were the kinds of people Alex had *chosen* to surround himself with. Life was easier when you were guaranteed an even-keeled state of *it's fine*.

In some distant part of Alex's past, he knew that he had cared, once. He'd had more bells and whistles, props that reminded him how important it was to be liked, to be respected. Eventually he came to understand that there was no respect for him. No matter what he did or said or wanted, he would always be a consummate wastrel in everyone's mind, the person who would never *do* anything because he didn't need to. There was nothing left for him from anyone now that he understood that. Before, when he was young and fresh and the habit of being with girls still felt foreign, every detail was vital to the operation. Now, it was an old game, one that sometimes ended in phone calls with lawyers and small settlements, nothing, really, because when you asked for nothing, that was what you got.

People said change was good because there was no alternative. You couldn't exist in stasis forever, much as you might try. Much as Alex had tried. He was safer in stasis, happier there. They never should have made him come home. They never should have made him into what he was. When you always knew you would *be* something it was so much harder to *become* that. Sometimes he didn't know if he ever would. He wished he could still be as he was at eighteen and twenty-one, maintaining a base level of belief in… everyone. It was the *everyone* who had ruined him, taken and taken and taken until there wasn't even a crumb left in the icebox; they were greedier than the Grinch. What was left to give away?

He wrapped a towel around his bleeding thumb, shrugged into his robe and slippers, and made his way downstairs. Jessica was at the bottom, with her coterie of wedding minions and a clipboard.

"Oh no! What happened to your hand?"

"I broke a lamp. Accidentally," he clarified.

"That looks bad." It was still wrapped in the towel. She couldn't see it. "Should we have someone clean it and bandage it?"

He shook his head. "Later. Where is everyone?"

"The boys are having breakfast in the dining room, and the girls left early this morning, because Yael had to get to the hospital immediately, and Maxie was sick."

"Maxie was sick?"

"Don't worry," Jessica said, holding up a piece of white silk to the banister. "It's not contagious. I'm sure she's just pregnant."

Alex felt something like Nickelodeon slime slipping down his neck. "Pregnant?"

"She's been wanting kids forever. Freddie doesn't, but Maxie always gets what she wants. God, I can't imagine her walking down the aisle *pregnant*. Go join the boys. I'll be in soon," Jessica instructed him.

He walked to the dining room and decided that Maxie couldn't be pregnant, because she'd been drinking for two. Maxie was the kind of person who wouldn't eat a Cheeto when pregnant, let alone polish off a bottle of wine on her own. Even if Maxie was pregnant, so what? She was already pregnant. 'What was he talking about? She wasn't pregnant.

"Hey," Rob said. He looked strikingly like Mr Potato Head.

"Dreading going back to Ronnie?" Alex helped himself to the buffet, two chocolate croissants and four pieces of bacon, a scoop of hash browns and eggs that looked cold. He would go back for fruit and yogurt after.

"How did you know?" Rob asked, and it was a genuine question, like he was surprised that Alex had deduced this from one glance at his pathetic basset hound face.

"Your face."

Will didn't say anything; his face didn't glower or mope or look heroically maudlin, which was becoming less and less heroic as he lost his hair. Alex wondered hazily if this was Will trying to express his disapproval for Alex having sex with Maxie. Well, fine. Alex was angry that Will had burst in and interrupted them, that he hadn't just left him and Maxie, that he'd had acted as if something was *wrong*.

"What's up with you?" Alex shook his napkin onto his lap.

"He's been quiet all morning," Adam said, and Alex actually started, he genuinely hadn't noticed the grinning pumpkin moonshine who was sitting, inexplicably, a foot back from the table. His shirt was the same light blue as the dining room walls.

"Jesus. Where did you come from?"

Adam laughed his idiotic laugh, and Alex wondered if this was what it was like in the tenth circle of hell, where you were condemned for being tragically, lethally boring.

"Thinking about a potential case," Will said, staring at him from under his eyebrows. Alex wondered vaguely if this was supposed to be some Maxie-related guilt-trip, except he knew that Will would never be able to be mad at him, not really. Anyway, Will was the one cheating on his fiancée *with a bridesmaid*; who was he to give Alex a hard time for having a little fun?

"The girls left," Rob offered.

Alex nodded. "They told me." It was such an easy lie, such a simple thing that would solve all of it.

"They told you?" Will asked, picking himself up a little.

"Yup." Alex wanted to laugh at him. They were all predictable, every last one of them, even Will, Supreme Court justine-wannabe, was fine with Alex if everyone else was. Maybe Maxie hadn't shown her interest in him *obviously*, but Alex knew what she wanted and had given it to her. No one could hold that against him.

"What did they say?"

"Just came to say goodbye. Said we would catch up in the city. Lulu's moving, Maxie felt sick."

"That was some dress she had on last night," Adam said.

Alex stood up. "What time are we leaving?"

Will shrugged. "Whenever."

"He coming with us?"

"Yup." It was a challenge, said in the same intonation as Alex's.

"I should have gone with the girls," he said, picking up his plate, taking his juice. "I'm gonna eat and get dressed. Then let's go."

“Fine,” Will said, like the petulant child he was, the boy who had lost. It wasn’t Alex’s fault he had a child-sized almost-wife who he didn’t love and maybe never had.

“We’re leaving?” Adam asked. Alex resisted the urge to smack the back of his buzzed head, just because.

It was cold in his room, cold and half-dark, curtains still drawn, bed still unmade. If the girls were here, or anyone fun, today would have been an excuse for *more*, more debauchery and silliness and more *something*, anything to make you feel like today was yours, it belonged to and was owned by you, Trademark Alexander Sable, 2017, and you weren’t the property of your father or your family or the vast wealth that kept you safe when you did something that you had to do to prove you belonged to you. Maybe that was the tenth circle of hell, maybe this was.

Maxie
February 15th, 2017

Maxie flew across the country with Lulu; half-asleep with her head lolling on her friend's shoulder, waking as Lulu's hand reached up to steady her, *don't worry, I've got you.* Three thousand miles to the place Lulu called home and now couldn't stand to be in, to the Spanish house with big windows and vines growing up the front, the tiny, blue-tiled pool and the sun pouring on to you even in February. She took Maxie to private yoga classes and kombucha tastings, and on their third night, an influencer dinner at a far-away Italian restaurant and jazz club. Maxie sat among bleached blonde bobs and cascades of brunette locks and a thousand photos of napkins and flowers and pasta. The other girls were surprisingly nice, nicer than Maxie's friends would have been to an outsider, chatting and tagging Maxie for no reason and asking her things like *what is it like to be married* even though most of them were older than she was.

"What are you doing while you're here?" a lavender-haired girl asked her. "Like, anything particularly *California?*"

Maxie shrugged. "I was just going to tag along to Lulu's stuff." She stabbed a piece of penne.

"No," the girl told her, like some kind of violet fairy sitting across the red-checked table, telling her how to live her life. "You have to do something just for *you.* That's what I did when I came out here to see a friend, and I haven't left since."

"Like what?" She couldn't bring herself to eat the pasta. She just didn't care enough, or she felt sick, or something was off. Maxie wasn't good at being damaged; she'd never been damaged before. To a certain degree, everything in her life had been controllable by her or her parents or her husband, and since she did a decent job of getting what she wanted from her parents and husband, she had always been the ultimate authority in her own life. The biggest compromise she'd made was just that, a wedding for a move to Chicago — transactional, meaningful. When you wanted the big things, things like Harvard and Freddie, you had to give up pieces of your life — the time spent studying, hours at tennis matches, moving to the Middle West — in return for a worthwhile change.

You didn't have to give up pieces of *yourself.* That was what she wasn't sure of, any more — if she still had all of herself. It felt like something was missing — but it wasn't lost, it had been taken from her.

"You know in *Practical Magic,* when Nicole Kidman is driving from, like, Arizona to Maine, or whatever?" The violet girl had violet glitter running underneath her brown eyes and above her cheeks and along the edge of her collarbone even though she wore a white cashmere bandeau and matching sweatpants. In the shifting lights she really *did* look like some kind of LA fairy, winking at you a little, promising you gems and rubies to emerge from your mouth if you just let her touch a sparkly acrylic nail to your throat. Your slim throat, which had never felt small until Alex Sable had one hand around it and suddenly there was no substance at all, it was just skin and sinew, not enough to hold your head up, not enough to keep you alive.

"I've never seen it," Maxie told her, and the fairy traced lines in the air in front of Maxie.

"I read energy, you know," she touched a palm to Maxie's forehead. "And you need a restorative journey." Everyone in LA read energy and believed in some kind of cosmic plan and burnt white sage in their dining room and smoked Marlboros out of their Teslas while subsisting solely on coffee and Moon Dust. Everyone in LA needed a goddamn restorative journey and no wonder Lulu had grown into this ethereal half-human version of herself. Yuval Harari was right, the next species of human was *homo deus* and these God-like creatures were evolving first in this land of almond milk and local rooftop honey.

Lulu drove them home at midnight, west through places with names Maxie didn't recognize, *Eagle Rock* and *Glendale* and *Toluca Lake,* blurring neon signs and strip malls with sushi. Lulu talked about things that Maxie didn't want to hear, things like seeing a doctor, things like filing a report. Maxie didn't know how this person who she'd grown up with had fallen so far away from their shared reality that she could no longer understand how impossible this was. Maxie tried to explain it in manageable, digestible pieces, it would ruin her, *it will ruin me*, no one would ever speak to her or look at her or regard her as human; she would be a victim. Men would avoid eye contact with her, would skip out on cheek-touches and fake hugs. Women would murmur about her at every lunch and charity event and black-tie wedding, murmurs that became conversation that became a reputation. She was already the girl who'd had to move to Chicago to get the useless engagement ring on her finger. She had always been the girl people hate-followed. She had always worn dresses that were too short and too low-cut, and she knew what these people would say, that she was the girl who cried rape, that she'd flirted with him, that she was just doing it for attention. It would dog her steps like a shadow; her children would go for playdates and the other mothers would look at her piteously. New York, her New York, had a long memory. And what did it say about her? That she was someone who could be had, be possessed, be taken. That they were right, she was a victim. A dirty husk of a word which made her feel like he'd taken more than she'd even realized; he'd walked away with her strength.

But Lulu couldn't understand, because Lulu had disappeared in this strange hinterland where nothing stuck to you. Here, in LA, you could be anyone. No one cared about your story or about you. They were here-and-now people, this moment and the next, residents of a new frontier where the past didn't exist. Lulu had lost every sense of what Maxie's world was like; she was California apathetic. She didn't care about people like Alex or what snubs you received and what invitations you didn't, about the horrible things people said about her behind her back and on her Instagram's and sometimes, passive-aggressively, to her face. She was missing that, the *caring,* the necessary piece that made her human. Maxie supposed she'd actively discarded it, which was probably what they should all do.

"Do you ever think you sold a little bit of your soul, for all of this?" Maxie asked. Everyone was so nice and maybe it didn't matter whether it was genuine or not, wasn't it better just to feel *good* after you'd interacted with other people? Instead of clawing your way into a group or a social setting, leaving exhausted and a little vindicated, wasn't it *easier* this way? Did you lose yourself in the process, give up something that felt like authenticity but was maybe just insecurity? Did it matter either way? Maybe these girls who made money from living out their best lives on social media just had less to lose by being nice. They had so much so easily that it didn't cost them to treat people well, or maybe that was why they were successful in the first place, how they'd cracked the inexplicable code of what made someone worth following.

"I don't know," Lulu held the wheel with one hand, eyes on the road ahead of her. Maxie still couldn't believe Lulu had learned how to drive; she'd been trying since they moved to Chicago, and it was still utterly foreign, like learning how to operate a rocket. "Maybe I did. Some days I feel like a lost a piece of myself. Some days I just feel like me. You know what I mean?"

"No." Maxie pulled a leopard coat out of Lulu's backseat and draped it over her knees.

"What part is *no?*"

"I don't have days where I just feel like me."

"Of course you don't. You just suffered a major trauma. You need to go to therapy—"

"*Drop it,* with the therapy."

"But you—"

"*Nothing* is going to fix me. There is no solution for this… this… *this*. There is no prescription that can help the way I feel. Raw from the inside out. Like someone's — like I'm still just red and purple and bruised and bloody, like something was taken from me but I can't give it a name. If I could, I would just get a new one. But I can't."

She found herself crying even though she didn't want to be. Lulu pulled over. Maxie shook her head and covered her face with one hand and motioned to go on with the other. She couldn't stand this, the pity, the sadness, the shame she saw flicking across the face of everyone she encountered, like they already knew, knew that she was blemished and mangled, battered and left in a basket that promised it was half-off for day-old sandwiches. She hated him and she hated herself and she wasn't sure, from day to day, that she would ever be able to think around the dark malevolence that seemed to grow inside her with every passing hour. It was eating her up, one vast, starved bite at a time, and it smelled like Alex Sable, acrid and alcoholic.

"I think I need to go for a drive tomorrow," Maxie said.

"Okay," Lulu replied. "You can take this car, and I'll drive the old one."

She woke up at four a.m. to find Lulu sitting in her yard, pretending to smoke. It smelled like eucalyptus and fall and the water from the fountains in the blue tiled pool splashed music into the air.

Maxie sat down next to her on the green cushioned couch, folding her legs into her chest and her hands into her legs. "You're thinking about it, aren't you?"

Lulu nodded. "Just wondering how we all got here." She looked up at Maxie with her molten eyes and Maxie watched them stretch and drip down those evenly sliced cheek bones and into the hollows that were getting worse and then seep onto the neck that Alex Sable could fit in a fist. "If it was us, our generation, or if it's a part of American culture, or if it's something bigger than all of that."

"No." Maxie tipped her head back. She couldn't see the moon. "I think it's something within him." Something that was twisted and mangled and unnatural. Unnatural to Dinah and Bathsheba and Susanna. Natural to Absalom. Natural to Amnon. Or maybe it was more than that, a legacy begun by the legend of Eve, the first weak woman, beguiled by the serpent, *and she did eat*. It was easy to blame Eve and Pandora and the faceless witches of Salem. It was easy to move from blame to the lapping temptation of dark water. Who were men to question what they were taught, what was telegraphed to them through hundreds of years of conditioning? Who were men to listen to women, to *believe* them? After all, witchcraft, like being born a woman, was an invisible crime.

They sat on the outdoor couch for another hour. Maxie was sad for her friend and sad for herself and most of all just *sad* that this was what they'd become, the girls who had always been the aspirational ones, the group you stalked on Facebook and fought for entrance to. They'd had all the best clothes and the greatest parties and the boys who mattered, but none of *that* mattered. The things that mattered to you in the space before adulthood were only the ones that you could somehow absorb into the porous fiber of your soul, and Maxie was beginning to realize she'd missed all of it. What was left to matter when everything you'd been told and taught and coached was important actually wasn't significant at all? What was there?

Maxie took the keys and put on Uggs and shakily drove back the way they had come last night, back East, through Laurel Canyon and Glendale and Eagle Rock, like she was driving all the way home. She had to focus on the movement of her ankle, brake to accelerator, the way her hands caressed the wheel, the cars in front of her. She listened to the *Practical Magic* soundtrack even though she hadn't seen the movie and when she pulled over at a gas station in Pasadena to get water, she Googled *best road trips in California*.

The shortest one was three and a half hours from where she was, so she got back in the car and maneuvered onto the highway and put *A Case of You* on repeat and drove through the sun rising above the mountains, slashing the sky into uneven layers. She drove through the sun and the sky and the mountains, always the mountains, not real mountains like the ones you skied on but something that felt different, nonetheless. There weren't mountains in her part of the world; people didn't paint their eyes and hair with lavender glitter and touch a chord to the center of your heart. She drove through the sun and the sky and the piles of strip malls and eventually scrubland that looked like Italy, orange trees and little bushes pruned onto lines. She drove to where her phone dropped service and she could see the shape of the sand-colored cliffs. She drove through the barrier after she'd paid her thirty dollars, up and up and up twisting roads that made her slow to a crawl.

Eventually, she stopped, looking down into a valley obscured by fog that rolled over gnarled branches, over greenery and ground, over the prehistoric, untouched land. It was empty and cold and felt like moving in time, maybe backwards or maybe forwards, to this last virgin place. A furry spider bigger than her hand scuttled underneath the car. She got back in and drove up and up and up, for an hour or maybe forty-five minutes or maybe no time at all, until they were everywhere around her, stretching their leafy arms straight into the sky, twisting their trunks around each other, twirling gracefully towards the ground.

Maxie parked in what might not have been a space and got out in her Uggs and sweatpants and the *Swanson's* shirt she'd borrowed from Lulu. It was cold so she put the leopard coat on even though she was sure she looked insane, but it didn't matter because there wasn't anyone there to see her. She hadn't even bothered washing her face. When she closed her eyes, she could still smell him, sour and heady, surrounding her, feel his fingers everywhere on her body, phantom hands that swept across her whenever she had the audacity to blink.

She opened her eyes and took the deepest breath she could hold, down into the bottom edge of her lungs. It smelled like Christmas and being little again and Southampton in the early summer and the playground at Horace Mann. The chill wrapped itself around her, dogged her steps as she walked among the giants, feeling their fuzzy orangey-red bark with the pads of her fingertips and then her palm and then she just sank into the tree, curled up and waited to let it absorb her and all of the past, the small apartment they'd lived in until she was nine, the one with the funny bathroom next to her parents' room, the dressing rooms in the Intermix on Madison, the black eyes and matching lashes of the first boy who really broke her heart. His name was Alex, too. She hadn't admitted to anyone how deeply it stung that he was engaged to the girl he'd dated after her, a prettier version of Maxie. She even invited them to her wedding, *see how happy I am?*

And what was the point of it? What was the *point* of being one oozing wound, barely healed, always able to crack open and bleed all over again? What was the point of letting someone break your heart — break *you?* There was so much they could take from you if you *let* them, your safety and your courage and your dignity and your *joy*. They would take it all, if you gave it up, Alex Sable was the son of a billionaire. He took what he wanted and let his father foot the bill and maybe that was fine for him, but no part of Maxie was there to be taken. She hadn't surrendered the pieces of her shattered self-esteem when the other Alex chose someone else, because he didn't deserve them. *No one* deserved any little bit of her, not a drop. She would fight you tooth and nail for it; she would fight you to the last ounce of her strength.

She would keep it all. She stood in the famous forest of redwood sequoias, in the empty National Park that time forgot, and decided that she would restore what had been taken from her.

Yael
February 28th, 2017

It took two weeks to disentangle her life from Abraham's, to divide up books and sheets and silverware. They had lived together so briefly that it felt, at times, like they were roommates parting on awkward terms. She wasn't sure how well you could ever know someone, even after a year and a half; he didn't know that the real reason why she'd broken up with him was sitting in an office in downtown Philly, filing injunctions and claims and doing exhaustive research on *precedent*, and she didn't know why Abraham had taken it so quietly, so easily. Like he'd almost known, all along, that they were just playing pretend, setting up house, deliberately choosing each other instead of being alone.

That was exactly what they had done; it seemed special to Yael because he was her first real boyfriend. He was the first one who said *yes* to the potential of spending at least a *piece* of his life with her, and that made everything different. Suddenly she was someone worth loving, worth being loved, worth *another person*. She wasn't the outcast at weddings and lunches and casual catch-up coffees; she was *someone*, because she *had* someone. And — oh! — how people were nicer to her, how invitations from colleagues were suddenly extended, how much it legitimized her in the eyes of society. Everyone had thought she would be a sad, single, cat-less cat-lady, and, for one glorious eighteen month stretch, they were proven wrong by the existence of this middling-height, temple-for-religious-holidays-only, nice-enough boy who wanted to settle down with a middling-height, temple-for-religious-holidays-only, nice-enough girl.

For Yael, that was enough to build a life upon, so they did, went to Stephen Starr restaurants and for walks along the river, caught screenings of old movies at the theater in the historic district and did things like pub crawls, things that Yael didn't care about and Abraham probably didn't care about, but they were the things you did when you were a couple.

There was a degree of satisfaction, until there wasn't. Until Will infected her with his late-onset millennial apathy.

The strange thing about Will was that he was a man of her generation — a man pretending to be a boy, a procrastinator masquerading as a busy control freak, the child of a helicopter parent who just wanted everything done *for* him — but he had flashes of being a real person, someone Yael could love. She believed, when he stood next to her on the banks of the Schuylkill, when he ran his hands through her hair in the darkened stairway, when he curled up into her in the quiet of her warm room, that Will *was* real, by nature. It was the *nurture* that caused him to contract this disease, to exhibit these symptoms. If he could treat it, battle it back into remission, there was someone kind and smart and funny and loving and thoughtful waiting right there for Yael, *right there*, except that he was engaged to her friend and her hypothesis was utterly, humiliatingly, incorrect.

The text came, as texts from boys you've slept with and then been ditched by usually do, because he needed something. *Are you working tonight? Alex needs stitches.*

Her response took twenty-three minutes and the help of her sister in Ohio. *I am. He can come by and ask for me on the 11th floor.* She thought the *he*, not a *you guys,* was strong enough to convey her personal view of Will, but she also secretly hoped that Will would appear anyway, and went to her locker to put on a little bit of concealer, a little bit of blush, and a little bit of mascara. Then she went back to her charting, conveniently out of sight of the front desk but with a view of the hallway, so she would see them before they saw her.

Will's hair was thinner than she remembered it, plastered awkwardly to his forehead, Rob's face overly pale in the bright lights. She hadn't seen Alex since he'd held Maxie's throat in one thick-knuckled hand. He was red and unsmiling, scarier than she remembered, but she knew that was just her own psychological response to knowing what he could do.

"We're looking for Yael," Will told a nurse.

"Doctor Tarrance," Yael told them, stepping out from her hiding place. "We don't use first names at the hospital."

Will nodded weakly. "Of course."

Alex didn't smile. He picked up a paw bandaged with a bloody dishtowel and growled at her. Rob hovered too closely behind him. "Can't you *do* something about this?" Alex demanded.

"Sure," she said. "But we have to admit you. As a patient."

"Do we have to bother with that? I'm in *pain.*"

"Everyone here is in pain," Yael told him, in her calm, doctor voice. "But we can't treat a patient who hasn't been admitted to the hospital. It's illegal."

"So can't you leave and sew me up at Will's apartment?"

"No," Yael explained, keeping her tone even. "I'm on a shift. I can't *leave*."

"What if you had an emergency? They would let you leave then."

"This isn't an emergency."

"It is for me!"

Rob took the clipboard Yael held and began filling in Alex's information. Yael escorted them to an empty room and started her usual line of questioning.

"I was slicing lemons and the knife moved and gouged out my hand."

You couldn't gouge out a hand, but Yael didn't bother to correct him. "The knife moved?"

"It slipped," Will said.

She ignored him, eyes still on Alex.

"It *moved*," Alex told her. "It jumped."

Is that the hand you used to strangle Maxie? She wanted to ask. "Is that your dominant hand?"

"Yeah."

"What medications are you taking?"

"Valium. Sometimes Adderall. Vicodin to sleep."

"Do you take those on a consistent basis?"

"No."

"What have you taken today?"

"Adderall."

"And how much have you had to drink?"

Alex glanced down at the dishtowel. "A drink. Nothing."

He looked at her for too long; they both knew it was a lie, a stupid lie because it was only going to be a problem for *him*. "Let's take a look," she said, like he hadn't lied, and he hadn't strangled Maxie Stein-Golden with the hand she was slowly curling open, untying the blood-soaked towel and staring at the wound there. It was clearly self-inflicted, and Yael tilted her head up to look at him, trying to decide if he was doing it for the high or the attention, or if this was simply an extension of his lack of respect for the sanctity of the human body. She should have recognized it from the moment he poured absinthe down her throat and maybe that was the problem with all of them, everyone she knew, everyone who didn't speak up, that they should have recognized it but didn't. That they didn't want to. Maxie had ranted at her and begged her and cried to her when Yael said they had to report it; they had to tell someone. *Please get a rape kit. Please, please, get a rape kit*, Yael had said in the car the next day, until Maxie screamed that if she heard *that word* one more time she was throwing herself onto the road.

Yael cleaned the cut slowly, letting the alcohol seep into the wound and sting.

"Fuck. Jesus. Is it supposed to sting like that?" Alex breathed heavily through his nostrils. "Fuck! Yael, what are you doing to me?"

"Cleaning your cut," she replied, calmly. It was enough to break her heart, how much Maxie didn't want anyone to know. *Is it his family?* Yael had asked. No, it wasn't *just* his family, but of course they were a part of it, of course you would never want to be on the bad side of the Sables. It was that it would ruin her. *Don't you understand that, Yael?* It would ruin her, socially, everywhere, to everyone. She would never be the same. She would always be *that girl*.

She couldn't bring herself to say *the girl who was raped*.

"Can I please have a little anesthesia, or something? Maybe some fentanyl? Are you *trying* to hurt me?" Alex grabbed his hand back as she prodded.

"Do you want help, or not? Because you can go wait for three hours in the emergency room with *everyone else*, or you can thank God that I'm here doing this for you in the middle of my shift when I have *sick people* to take care of." She waited for him to hand over his hand. He did. She blotted it as hard as she could, right in the middle.

"Thanks," he murmured.

"Don't joke about fentanyl," she replied.

They were silent. She wondered for the hundredth time or maybe the thousandth if she *should* just go file a report with the police about Alex. If it would help to have that, maybe, someday, down the line. If Maxie would ever let it get to that. If Maxie could understand that it would help her, that it would help the others, the ones who would come after her, because that was what people like Alex did, they preyed on others. There were always others.

"It looks like the stigmata," Alex said.

"What's the stigmata?" Rob asked.

Alex dropped his head back, eyes on the ceiling. "Didn't you go to private school?" Yael poked the lanced center of his palm with a gloved finger. He pulled away once more.

"The stigmata are the wounds of Jesus Christ." Will told Rob. "Give him a break; he's Jewish," Will told Alex.

Alex crossed himself, incorrectly. "*We're* Jewish. And we know." Yael continued to clean it. "But, in all seriousness, don't I get pain killers?"

"I'll give you some once I stitch it up."

"Surely our lord and savior doesn't need painkillers," Rob commented.

"Says the guy who doesn't know what *crucified* means." Alex tapped the fingers of his uninjured hand against his jeans. "So, what's the deal? How long is it gonna take to heal?"

"They're self-dissolving stitches, but you should go have it checked in a week. You'll need to apply a basic dressing, which I'll show you, for the next five days; then you can use a lighter bandage."

"Robbie," Alex commanded. "You be in charge of the dressings."

Rob didn't say anything. Yael looked up at Alex from her stool, his hand in hers. He shrugged the littlest bit.

Yael made her stitches too loose, so it would heal sloppily, so he couldn't hold another neck in that hand for at least a month. She worked silently, moving in measured strokes while the boys bickered, and Alex shifted around too much. He asked for a prescription for Percocet, and she dropped ten ibuprofen into a plastic bag. “Don’t tell anyone,” she told him. “I could get into trouble.”

“Thank you,” he whispered, utterly placated, gracefully grateful, extending his hand to her like he was *our lord and savior*, thanking her for the pills that weren’t strong enough to kill a real headache.

“Before we can discharge you, I have to send you upstairs quickly,” Yael said, scribbling onto his chart, handing it to a passing nurse. “Can you please show Mr Sable the way to the fifth floor?”

Will
March 15th, 2017

Landon Heathcote met Will at Brookfield Place; an ugly mall adjacent to Goldman Sachs. Will privately thought that the developers probably overshot it, building a mall that was, essentially, solely for Goldman employees and Tribeca's yummy mummies, because it was half empty and there wasn't even a Momofuku to get a cookie at. Landon offered Will a slim-fingered hand. Everything about him was long and drawn out, pointed, almost old-fashioned looking, chin, face, nose, hands aristocratic and out of place.

"I haven't been here since it opened," Landon said, sitting down on a bench in the forest of fake indoor trees.

"I've never been," Will told him. "I was hoping there would be somewhere more… private that we could sit." He had chosen this mall out of deference to Landon, trying to be polite and pick somewhere near his office, and he already regretted it. He should have just asked Landon where he wanted to go. Will had always been bad at stuff like this, reaching out to people, cold calling, picking a restaurant.

"There's nothing here," Landon replied. "Not even a decent bakery."

"I know," Will nodded emphatically. He could feel that he was nodding too much but he couldn't stop himself. "I was hoping for a decent cookie." He hadn't meant to say *decent* after Landon had but now it was done, and he couldn't fix it.

"We should have gone to Locanda." Landon watched a woman with a double stroller stroll by.

"Next time," Will told him.

Landon arched one eyebrow. He was too polite to ask *will there be a next time?* to someone he barely knew, but the sentiment was there.

"I mean — sorry," Will said. He wanted to tell Landon he was nervous, but Landon wasn't the kind of person who would empathize and put you at ease. Will was surprised Landon met with him in the first place.

"In your message, you said you wanted to talk about Chris," Landon reminded Will.

"I did. I do." Will had DMed Landon, something he'd never done before. "I didn't know Chris."

"No," Landon said. "Westchester, right?"

Will nodded too much again. Growing up in Westchester was like being from Iowa to an old school, fifth-generation born-and-bred New Yorker like Landon. Landon was one of a dying breed, Will wasn't sure who else was left, from a wealthy and storied family.

"He wasn't like most of the people I grew up with," Landon said. "He didn't live uptown. I only went to middle school with him. We stayed friends, though, after I went to boarding school."

"So didn't you go to school with Alex?"

Landon shook his head. "I went to Allen Stevenson, then Andover. Chris was one of our scholarship kids. He was on the baseball team with all of us. He was a nice guy. He wouldn't hurt a spider, and I mean that, whenever there were spiders in the classroom, he was one of those people who would catch them and let them outside."

Will wasn't sure if this was creepy or kind. "What else?"

"I could never imagine him raping anyone. I've thought about it a lot, obviously. I was the only one who would serve as a character witness; not that it mattered. No one cares who any of us are, any more. Which is probably how it should be." He squinted out ahead of him. He was so unlike Alex it made Will desperate to be his friend, to gain some validation that he, Will, wasn't a bad person for allowing someone like Alex to be a part of his life. For not knowing what Alex was even though, on some level, he should have understood it. "At the time, he just kept saying, *I didn't do it. I just walked outside. That's all. I just walked outside.* I went to see him in prison a few years ago. He told me that he hadn't done it, and—" Landon stopped himself. "I always wanted to ask Alex what happened that night, so when I had the opportunity, I did. I wasn't trying to goad him, or set off the famous Sable family retribution. I just question if the story Alex told was *right*."

"So you don't think he could have done it."

Landon spread his long-fingered hands. "How can I know, or you, or anyone except Chris? It's just something to wonder about. I hoped… to find out if what I'd done was right. Not that it made a difference. Or at least to see if Alex questioned it at all. What he'd seen. What he thought he'd seen. Part of me always wondered if it was just one of those things, a freak accident that everyone interpreted wrong. After I saw Chris, I thought maybe it was something more deliberate than that. The answer I got from Alex… doesn't really matter. It's all just down to believing one versus the other, and there's nothing in that, is there?"

"There's a way to find out," Will told him, because this was what Will did, what his *job* was, to listen to the he-said-she-said and discover what actually happened. "If the case wasn't still sealed, I would have a better idea."

Landon shook his head. "Sorry I couldn't be of more help," he said, unfolding himself and reaching out to shake Will's hand. It was an oddly formal gesture, old-fashioned and out of place in the glass-walled, white-floored mall that looked like it was from a 1980s vision of the future. Will played it out in his head so many times it began to warp, like a VCR tape that had been improperly rewound, until he started to wonder why he'd asked to see Landon in the first place, why he thought anyone who wasn't Alex would have answers to questions that no one else seemed to care about.

He wouldn't ask Alex. Alex wouldn't tell him the truth. There had been and always would be the things they didn't confront each other about, the things that you just couldn't *say*. If he did speak them into being, it would only be shrugged off, Will placed into the deepest corner of the freezer, made to repent for his sins. It should have been a relief, the idea of being banished by Alex, but there was some part of him that couldn't understand or fathom a world in which Alex existed and their friendship did not. Will would become a footnote in Alex's memoir, another friend dropped, another story about how Alex was betrayed, and Will would spend a lifetime being gently jostled out of rings of conversations at cocktail parties. None of that should have mattered, but it all did, or maybe it just mattered that Alex was a liar and Will was a coward. Did it make you a coward if you didn't want to ask questions you already knew the answer to? Did it make you a fool if you asked?

There was nothing to be gained from the conversation they would never have, only something to be lost, and Will didn't have enough left to lose anything else.

April 15th, 2017
Lulu

Lulu had never left behind a phase of life with such little fanfare, no broken champagne glasses or barefoot dancing on the beach. She woke before the sun rose and watched it from her balcony at Chateau, then left her key at the desk and flew back home for good.

Nothing was different except for her. It was a change that had been taking place since she graduated from Harvard, a dusty sparkle that she acquired in LA which looked like a particularly glamorous Instagram and felt like a key bump of cocaine. The Lulu she'd left behind on the East Coast had been the physical manifestation of a lifetime of ease and love from her family and the opposite from everyone else. What she'd known was men who thought she wasn't pretty enough or was too smart or *intensely uppity*, as one put it. What she'd known was anti-Semitism from the WASPs and a polite turning of the cheeks from the Jews because her mother wasn't Jewish. What she'd known was the overwhelming love of her parents; what she'd learned was how that could keep you whole. What she learned was that, sometimes, that was the last thing keeping you together. What she learned was that your physical appearance came to reflect your interior until you *were* the Facetuned photo. What she learned was that eventually it stopped choking you, the things people said about what you weighed or how you looked or your nose or your last name. *That's Jewish, isn't it?* People said that girls were mean, but Lulu had found men to be the cruelest, the harshest. Girls responded to the kindness you tried to suffocate them with. Men were superficial to the point of persecution, at least her generation of men.

What she learned eventually was that men, these millennial men, were so heavily entrenched in their own self-consciousness that it was easier to hate, to hate, to hate. It was a thousand times easier to hate what you didn't understand and what scared you. What she learned was that she scared men, because she was smart and independently wealthy and wanted something for herself more than to be someone's rich wife, the person paying the bills while her other half did exactly what he wanted with *her* money. What she learned was that the confidence her parents had drilled into her made her incapable of acquiescing to all of the *less* that these men wanted. They wanted to cheat, to say the things no one ever should, to make you feel their disrespect through every atom, to teach you that *you weren't worth it*. They wanted you to submit, and submit, and submit again, and to that, Lulu said *fuck you very much.* Lulu knew real men, ones like her father, like his friends, ones with accomplishments to their name and a reverence for the opposite sex, she knew it was possible, and she wouldn't take what was being offered to her in their stead.

Old Lulu had believed for a long time that *she* was the problem. That they were right, that she wasn't *enough*, that she wasn't worth it, that she was lucky to have them, all of them, even the girls who weren't very nice, even the men who called a hundred-thirty-pounds *fat*. Old Lulu obsessed over her arms in photos and thought constantly about exactly what she had eaten and was embarrassed to be so smart, so smart it was intimidating. Was embarrassed to care about people so much, to feel everything so deeply, to be such an utter failure when it came to dating and men, to be such an utter failure when it came to her career. In 2014, the term *Instagram influencer* carried a hefty dose of disdain with it. Old Lulu was Maxie and Jessica and Victoria and all of these girls who acted on what everyone told them they were supposed to want, who made other people's opinions their lives. Old Lulu cared just as much as they did about what people could say about you; maybe that Lulu would have done what Maxie did, and buried a rape deep inside of her out of a crippling fear of *what people would think*.

Success in your own right would cure you. Someone trying to kill you because they wanted you *that much* would cure you. Lulu's astrologer in LA said that she was apathetic by nature, but she thought she was apathetic by nurture. To have a real relationship she'd had to become numb to the hope that used to spring eternal when she met someone great. To demand respect she had to wave those million people who tuned in for her content every single day in the faces of the people who said that she couldn't sit there because she was too Jewish, not Jewish enough, too smart, not smart enough, too fat, too thin, too rich, not rich enough, because they couldn't see around the hulking nose on her face, because she just intrinsically didn't deserve a seat at the table. She was, in the mind of these tried-and-true cultures, the consummate outsider. The only safe space was her home, with her parents, or LA, where people didn't care whether you were a bastard or an immigrant or had the audacity to come from parents of differing religions.

Eventually, out of the twisting shadows that she had allowed her peers to impose on her, Lulu emerged, victorious, new Lulu, the shiny sparkly Mattel version that came with a collectable stand. This Lulu made her own money and had her own impressive boyfriend and used a different last name on Instagram as the ultimate proof that these people were here for *her*, not for who she was. Barbie Lulu said *Fuck you very much!* in swirling pink cursive on the box and decided a long time ago that the only person who mattered was her. That was how she'd walked away from Carlos' 6.5 carats and that was how she'd left Los Angeles, the conquering hero, to return to her home and spit her venom at anyone who asked her to be less than all of the *everything* she was.

Lulu walked out the door at Newark and into a cab line; she watched the scenery change as they crossed from New Jersey into New York, as they crawled from Tribeca uptown, as they pulled up outside the stone house she'd spent half her life in. It reminded her irresistibly of being twenty, and coming home from a ski trip in Switzerland after Hunter broke up with her. Their last conversation was on the curb at the Geneva airport, her begging him frantically *please don't do this; I can't get on a flight for eight hours and get off thinking I'll never see you again,* and he had calmed her down, and said it would be fine, and he would be there, and they would talk.

When she landed in the States, he wasn't there. He wasn't waiting after baggage claim or parking in the ugly three-story structure or standing at the curb, he wasn't *there*. She'd stepped out onto the sidewalk and motioned to a cab and felt a hazy, dreamlike mist descend over her and all around them, this wasn't real. This wasn't the way things happened, not in her life.

Then-Lulu, twenty-year-old Lulu, had taken the cab uptown and walked into her parents' empty house and ordered a peanut butter milkshake and a tuna salad sandwich from EJ's and eaten them in the silence of the library, sitting on the floor in front of the ottoman with eyes glazed and a strange, creeping feeling of detachment, like she wasn't her any more, like *she* wasn't there, like she was someone else's idea of a girl named Lulu Swanson. It was prophetic, or maybe it was just then that Lulu decided she wouldn't be that person any longer. She was done. She would change herself until she was *more, better, best*.

Maxie showed up a few hours in, ringing the doorbell of the dark house three times before Lulu came to enough to turn on some lights and answer it. She took one look at Lulu — ten pounds heavier Lulu, bleached blonde Lulu, bright-young-thing Lulu, and Lulu broke, folding herself up into a ball in the entry hall, with the front door open and the cool March air floating in, caressing her hands on her eyes as she sobbed, real sobs, the can't-breathe-can't-think-can't-speak kind of sobs, which, Lulu thought now, unlocking the door to her parents' empty house, she wasn't sure she'd cried since.

That was so long ago. She'd been so sparkly and shiny and *fun*; this Lulu, the one staring back at her from the antique mirror in the hall, felt a thousand years old in comparison, and it didn't matter that she'd become the person she'd been pretending to be since that day, so long ago, when she'd decided on some subconscious level that she would never be the kind of girl who let herself bend over and break, die the slow death of a torn heart.

The joke was on her. Being thin and beautiful and famous and all the hours and hours of her life that she had devoted to these pursuits was irrelevant to whether or not your heart would break or could break. She had shattered, and the person who came to replace her, the girl with the low voice and California eyes, had nothing to do with the fact that some kind of film had grown across her mind, one that congealed and hardened until she didn't have the emotion left to love someone enough that they could break her heart. When the only person who mattered to you was you, you still had to fight tooth and nail to wake up every single day and claim to be some semblance of *okay*.

"Staring at yourself again?" Maxie held a hot pink Mr Chow's bag in one hand and towed Lulu's suitcase in the other. "You left the door wide open."

"I was right here."

"You're such an LA kid, now."

Lulu tried a smile that felt sad on her face. "Don't say that."

"Are you being maudlin about wasting your life?"

"Who knew it was so easy?"

"I could teach a class on it."

Lulu took her suitcase from Maxie and shut the front door. "Chinese?"

"I was in the mood."

"You've never been in the mood for Chinese food, in the entire time I've known you." Lulu pushed into the kitchen.

Maxie shrugged, following behind her. "I'm giving up, I guess."

"On what?" Lulu pulled down two plates.

"Victoria's coming," Maxie said from the wine cooler below the fridge.

Lulu took out a third plate. "What are you giving up on?"

"All the stuff that I thought mattered."

"What do you mean?" Lulu carried the plates, silverware, and napkins to the upstairs den where they'd played endless games of Guitar Hero in high school, Maxie following with two bottles of Veuve.

"I thought it all mattered. If you were a good person, if you were thin, if you did all the things you were supposed to do. I thought that if you wanted something enough, you got it."

Lulu unwrapped the intricate dumpling flower and broke one off with her fingers. "No. It only matters to us."

"It doesn't *matter*, that's the thing. It's all just the trappings of a life. But it doesn't make a life."

"No," Lulu said, hollowly. "It doesn't."

They ate Chinese and watched *The Ides of March* and then Victoria showed up with cookies from William Greenberg and a bottle of gin. "How old are we, fifteen?" Lulu asked, but Maxie drank directly from the bottle, chasing with Veuve. If they had been fifteen or even eighteen, they would have put on her mother's jewelry, the necklace that belonged to Elizabeth Taylor and the pair of emerald rings from a trip to India and the strands of pearls that Lulu could assign back to her many-greats grandmother, who came to America in 1676. They would have eaten ice cream out of the pint and watched Gilmore Girls in bed, fallen asleep in sugar comas, hair tangled in tiaras.

Maxie's father gave her a diamond bracelet for her wedding, but it was tragic, with the wedding date and Freddie's name in sparkling diamond script. Maxie left it next to the sink in the hotel suite, hating the bracelet and hating her father's ways. When Mr Stein grabbed her hand to walk her down the aisle he shook her empty wrist and said she wouldn't be walking down the aisle if she weren't wearing twenty thousand dollars in diamonds.

It was a different lifetime, when Maxie got married, when they were nineteen and home from Harvard, when the things you were sad about were things like not getting a text back and missing out on a shoe sale at Bergdorfs. The most significant things that had collectively happened to them were deaths of dogs and friends being sent to rehab. They sat in bathrooms in dorms and hotel suites and each other's childhood homes and later their own apartments in Cambridge and then New York. They always ended up in a bathroom, Maxie and Victoria and Lulu, getting ready or taking a breath or ending the night or beginning a day. They always stayed at Lulu's parents' when they could and slept in the master bedroom when the Swansons were out of town. It had nine windows, three on each side, and Maxie insisted they leave the shades open, because you never got to sleep with that much light in New York.

Something shifted when Maxie moved. Maxie following her husband to Chicago was the first adult thing that any of them had maybe ever done, and after that, nothing was quite as light and bright.

They ended up in Lulu's parents' massive bathroom, Maxie in the empty tub, swigging from a bottle of champagne, Victoria sitting on the side of her father's sink in a yellow facemask that left smears on her glass, Lulu patting oil into her face. She was starting to age, to look tired and worn, like she'd lived too much already. Maxie talked about needing to move back to New York and dropped empty bottles onto the marble. They didn't shatter. Victoria passed out on a bathmat, after no crying and very few words; she'd just prodded her porcelain skin and asked if she was getting thinner. Maxie vomited her heart out into Lulu's parents' toilet while Lulu held her head, brushed strands of dark hair back, patted her friend's bony shoulders and handed her glasses of water.

When she was done, they sat with their backs to the white marble tub, to the Keith Haring hung above it, facing Victoria, who twitched lightly in her sleep.

"I'm pregnant," Maxie said, calmly, as calmly as if she were telling Lulu she was hungry.

The lights in the bathroom were so bright they started to smear across Lulu's vision. "Are you sure?" She couldn't imagine Maxie drinking while pregnant.

"Pretty sure." Maxie took a mouthful of gin.

"You're drinking."

"It's Alex's."

Lulu pressed her cold palms to the cold floor. "Like, definitely?"

"Pretty sure." She mushed the words together and strung them out, *pritt-ee-shh-ore*, so they sounded like something in a song that you heard but weren't sure you understood.

"But it must be too early to take a paternity test—"

"In terms of how far along the baby is," Maxie said. "According to the doctors."

"Oh," Lulu said, quietly.

"Freddie and I have both been traveling so much, and ever since—"

"I know," Lulu said. "I understand."

"I just thought that this stuff, you know, these things, these things that make you small and cold and broken, these things that tear you from top to toe, these things don't happen to people like — us." Maxie raised her head. Lulu was sitting close enough to see the freckles on her nose, almost washed away by a sunless winter. "Because what can you gain from it? What does it do for you? What do you get, to take something that belongs to someone else. To take it by force. You can't hold it in your hand. They get nothing from it. They get nothing for it." Her eyes were liquid, viscous and unsteady. "But they do it." She wiped her nose with the back of her hand. "They do it, and it's done, and then I guess they get to know that they're men, or something. They do it, and it's done, and it will never not be done, never stop playing. It plays on a loop in my head so constantly I think I could tell you which of his fingernails had dirt under them, and the pattern on the carpet, and the subtitles of the books in the shelves." Maxie raised her head to Lulu's. "I wonder if he remembers it. I wonder if he remembers it, or if he just goes out and does it again."

"I'm sure if this were a regular occurrence, he would be, you know, in jail."

Maxie laughed. Her eyes were swollen fat and puffy, and her lips were chapped and red. "So at least I'm special," she whisper-said, and her voice splintered. Her face was wet while her mouth stretched open in the laugh, in the white, white light on the white, white marble in this beautiful bathroom in this beautiful house where bad things didn't happen to beautiful people. That was what they had been promised and told and assured and now that Maxie sat across from Lulu with the evidence to the contrary growing inside her there was a fear in Lulu that felt like nothing else, like the clouds of soot blowing uptown on September eleventh and Carlos with his hand on the console of the plane. It felt personal and *real* and breathed smoke into every crown-molded edge of her mind until she saw it sitting in front of her, bloody-raw-cracked from edge to edge, promising her that they would never be safe again. That they had never been safe, it was all just an illusion, sleight of hand and tricks of the light, misdirection at its finest.

Part IV
July and August 2017
Tyler

Doctor Sue knew the podcast. Tyler wasn't sure he would ever get used to it, going to talk to people — only to find that they had an opinion on whether Josh's brother had done it and if he should have turned Mrs Carrington into the police. Dr Sue had opinions on both, which he told Tyler.

"So, working on a new case. Opioid epidemic?" Dr Sue asked, as if they were old friends.

"Not yet. I may come back to you for that episode," Tyler told him. "I'm here about a suicide case from about a month ago. You might have read about it. Alex Sable?"

Dr Sue shook his head. "You think it was an overdose?"

"No, but our medical examiner mentioned the amount of drugs in his system — how hard it would be for him to cut his wrists, based on what he'd taken. He was six feet two inches, around two hundred pounds, and, over the course of a night, had sixty milligrams of Diazepam and thirty of OxyContin, plus cocaine, and alcohol."

"How much cocaine?" Dr Sue asked.

"The medical examiner didn't give me a number. But we found one of those empty drug bags in his room."

Dr Sue nodded, thinking. "Do you know what his day-to-day drug usage looked like?"

"His drug of choice was cocaine," Tyler explained. "But his friends say that he often took Valium, although I haven't been able to track down the doctor who prescribed it to him."

"His family?" Dr Sue asked.

"They're not willing to talk to me," Tyler replied. Tyler had already received three cease-and-desist letters from one Mr Khan, esq., in the month he'd been quietly working on the case.

"Ah. Well, in that case, we can only speculate. For most men of his size, yes, this would be enough to knock him out for hours — sixteen to eighteen hours, I would say. Assuming he's using the Valium to cope when he comes down from cocaine, or just to sleep, he could be averaging thirty to forty milligrams a night. Valium is a drug that you build up a tolerance to. You would have to assume that Mr Sable was abusing it continuously, over a period of months, until his daily dosage got high. That would either mean a prescription in conjunction with buying it off the street, which '*is* possible, or multiple prescriptions that he was paying out of pocket for. No doctor would prescribe him that amount."

Tyler nodded.

"Now, OxyContin… again, we can't say how much or how often he takes it, and that's not a shocking dose. For a normal person, any normal person, I would look at just the Valium and say there was no way they could be conscious, let alone functioning, but we don't know at what level he *was* functioning. However," Dr Sue spread his hands. "Drugs are a difficult thing to guess. Especially because of the cocaine, I've had patients come in here who should be dead from the cocktail of drugs they've taken, but cocaine is keeping their heart going," Dr Sue said. "It depends on the purity of the cocaine. Was he the kind of guy who would spend money on drugs?"

Tyler nodded.

"Drugs are a difficult science because everyone reacts to them differently. Maybe he took the Valium in shifts throughout the night. I would guess, and this is purely speculation, that he took thirty to forty milligrams to sleep, gave into his suicidal thoughts, took twenty more, perhaps in an effort to numb the physical pain, perhaps to overdose, perhaps to go to sleep, and then went through the process in the twenty or so minutes it takes the drug to hit your system. I've had patients who find themselves waiting forty minutes for Valium to work; it's different for everyone."

Tyler nodded. It wasn't the answer he wanted, but it was *an* answer. "So it's possible, but with a lot of *if*s around it," he said.

"Yes," Dr Sue agreed. "Well put. I always find myself surprised at what the human body is capable of, with the right drugs. It's possible that this combination of drugs in his system *caused* him to be suicidal. You can't know how they reacted together, in conjunction with his body chemistry. At the end of the day, it all comes down to his tolerance. People can be horses if their tolerance is high enough. You'd be shocked to see what I have."

Mr Milwee was a delicate old man who moved with the fluttering grace of a dove. He had looked, he said, carefully at the photos Tyler sent him, and was excited to see the watch. It was a *beautiful* watch, he said again, when Tyler entered, after Mr Milwee had offered him tea and taken him through the greatest hits of his watch collection.

"I don't have it with me; I'm sorry," Tyler said. "It's in evidence, with the police," he explained.

"Oh," Mr Milwee said, concealing his disappointment well. "Then I'm afraid it may be hard to tell which happened first, the water or the crack. And which broke the watch." *Of course it is,* Tyler wanted to say, because this was starting to feel like his conversation with Dr Sue, a lot of qualifiers to get to no conclusion. "Now, I believe you wanted to know if this break was deliberate. Of course, this is a fragile watch; most of the Patek Philippes that aren't in the sport or waterproof collections are. If he was a careless man, likely banging it against a sink would have caused this. I've repaired many a Patek that way; someone goes like this on a marble ledge," Mr Milwee lifted an arm to demonstrate hitting his wrist on the counter. "And the face cracks, and sometimes stops the watch movement all together. Those are usually antique models, though. This watch looks like it just had one good break."

"And that would have stopped it working?"

"That we can't say, because we don't have the watch. We don't know *why* the watch stopped working, if it was water damage, which would have happened slowly, or the break, which would have happened as soon as the watch was cracked. But we *do* know that watch was likely broken before the water inundated it. Because of the way the water droplets are fanning out across the face, do you see? That means that the majority of the water was sucked in through this big fissure," Mr Milwee traced the largest crack. "Not through the gears of the watch. At least the water in the face. The gears would soak in water, too, but at a much slower pace. But, without seeing the movement, I can't say for certain that the watch was broken and *then* waterlogged."

"Because the water damage would start through the back of the watch," Tyler clarified.

"Yes, exactly," Mr Milwee said, clasping his hands together. "It's a shame. A beautiful, beautiful watch. What an end for it to have," he said.

"I know what you mean," Tyler replied.

"Hey," Tyler said, on the phone outside of Mr Milwee's shop. "I know you said you would help me, and I have a favor to ask. Call me back when you can."

Lulu texted him ten seconds later, *oh my god, are you dead? You just called me AND left a voicemail?*

No, Tyler wrote back, laughing in spite of himself. *I thought it would be easier to talk on the phone*.

She called him. "Hi. I'm in hair and makeup so you're on speakerphone. Say hi to everyone! Sorry, my AirPods are dead," she explained.

"They're charging!" someone called in the background.

"I'm calling because I'm having trouble getting people to talk to me," Tyler told her.

"I mean, I don't want to say *I told you so*, but I also *always* want to say *I told you so,*" Lulu replied. "No one wants to come crosswise of the Sables, and they've made it, like, abundantly clear that they don't want anyone talking about it. I mean, it's horrible, I get it; we all get it. I don't *want* to talk about it, but I am also totally seduced by the fact that you're my favorite podcast reporter and I've probably spent thirty-plus hours listening to you."

Tyler couldn't help but like her; where she was loquacious she was funny; where she was self-centered, she was self-aware. Half of what she said was ringingly true, and the other half eased you into what you didn't want to hear. "And, to a certain degree, what else is there to say? But I get the impression that *you*, at least, think there's more here than meets the eye." She waited for his reply.

"I'm not sure yet. I've spent hours researching everyone as best I can, researching the Heathcote mansion, trying to get any insight into the

Chris Newman case, but I keep running up against dead ends. And the people who I *do* find don't want to talk to me. But I got the impression that you convinced Rob and Will to talk to me—"

"God, Rob literally has no social graces; he might as well just shout uncomfortable things from the roof of a building for a living," she interrupted.

"And you did offer to help," Tyler asked. "So I'm calling in the favor."

"Who do you want to talk to?" Lulu asked.

"Landon Heathcote."

There was a pause. "Huh. Why?" she asked, which was a shorter response than he was expecting.

"He seems to be the link between Chris and Alex," Tyler told her.

"The link between Chris and Alex is their school," Lulu said. "Landon and Alex didn't actually spend time together until we were at Landon's cousin's house, in February. And their interaction was pretty much the once, when Alex hit him in the face for asking about Chris, and then at the wedding, when they played that stupid game together."

"Why did he hit him? What happened?"

"I mean, as I said, Landon brought up Chris Newman. Landon and Chris were friends; Landon was actually the only one who, like, went to court for Chris. He testified as a character witness; all of our parents were freaking out about it. My parents and Landon's are friends; I grew up with him," she explained. "And went to boarding school with his brother. I've been going to that house my entire life. Although now I'm not sure I ever want to go back. We always used to fight over who got that room, obviously, because it's the nicest. I was so pissed when I found out Jessica had given it to him, *twice*. It was such a blatant suck-up thing to do, but everyone was always sucking up to Alex."

"Because of his family?" Tyler asked.

"That was a huge part of it. *Strictly* between you and I, even *Theo*, his own *cousin*, sucks up to that branch of the family. They always defer to them; they give them the better seats at baseball games, even though Theo's family owns the team. Alex's family is the reason they have any money; he set them up with a satellite branch of the firm, but they'll never have half as much money as Cornelius. Anyway, it doesn't matter;

I'm getting off topic. We went over to Landon's cousin's house — because Alex wanted coke, and Landon's one of those people who always has drugs because he never does them, you know the type," she paused, she waited for him to say he knew the type.

"I don't know the type," Tyler replied.

"Well, it's a type——'." She sighed. "They seemed fine at the wedding, though. As if nothing had ever happened."

"Did they see each other between February and the wedding?" Tyler asked.

"Not that I know of. I'll see if he'll talk to you. He's polite," she said, almost defensively. "So, if you do talk to him, just… know that."

Landon, when he agreed to meet Tyler at a quiet Swedish coffee place a few blocks from Goldman, was certainly nice. Easy-going, but opaque. Tyler made an effort not to just launch into questions, but Landon sat back, in his suit at seven thirty a.m., and said, "I'm sure you're busy, and Lulu told me you had a few questions for me," and inclined a hand out as if to say, *proceed.*

"I'm trying to get a little more information on this whole Chris Newman thing. On his relationship to Alex, why Alex was so sensitive about it… I'm still trying to get a handle on who Alex *was*. And this seems like an important part of that," Tyler explained. Landon was pale, with shifting green eyes that made him look almost reptilian. His features were too long on a thin face, and he looked like some lost member of a royal European family, regal and elegant.

"I didn't know Alex, really, at all. We knew of each other — same age, same groups of people, I suppose, who knew one another — but we didn't have much interaction. I knew Chris well; we went to school together for years and stayed friends. I thought he was a genuine person, honest and open. I asked Alex about what happened because I wanted to know; he hit me, and why he did that I couldn't tell you."

"What was Chris like?"

"Quiet. Nice. Hard-working, in school and in sports. Easy to be around. I wouldn't have gone to court for him if I hadn't believed him anything but incapable of the crimes he was standing against."

It was something like a quintuple negative, and it took Tyler a moment to untangle it. "You never would have testified for him if you hadn't believed he was innocent," Tyler clarified. Landon nodded, slowly. "Why did you think that? What made you *believe* that?"

Landon opened his hands, this time both of them, revealing tapering fingers and long palms. "I'd like to think you just know a person."

"Nothing more specific than that," Tyler said.

"Nothing more specific than that," Landon replied.

"Will said something similar to me. You two are friends?" Tyler asked.

"Not at all. He invited me to his wedding, I assume, because it's my family home. Whatever Will may think has no bearing on my opinion," Landon told him. He even drank his coffee neatly, like it wasn't liquid. It was all very formal, in this very informal place, all very *out* of place.

"Anything else to say about Chris? Anything you might know about his relationship with Alex?"

"I'm sorry, no," Landon said. Tyler knew that the answer was yes, but Tyler also knew that Landon probably hadn't wanted to talk to him at all. Which was strange, because if you really believed that your dead friend was innocent, wasn't Tyler precisely the kind of person you *would* want to win to your case? Someone with an investigative background and a national platform?

"And… what did you think of Alex?" Tyler asked.

"Very little, I'm afraid to say. I didn't know him well."

"Was there anything unusual you noticed that night, with him or any of them? Anything at all that struck you as out of place?"

Landon tilted his head back a little and allowed himself to think for a moment. "The only notable thing was how they'd divvied up the rooms, which surprised me. Will and his best friend, the one with the curly hair, I'm afraid I don't know his name—"

"Rob."

"They had a room to themselves, I assume because the bride wanted them to sleep separately the night before the wedding, and get ready separately. But I did think it was odd that they shared a room, when Rob's girlfriend was there. She was in the room next to mine. When I asked her about it, she said the boys always had sleepovers. Which struck me as out of place. I don't know a lot of men who do that. But I don't know many men who are as close as that trio, I suppose." Landon stood up. He dusted off of his pants, even though there was nothing to dust, and took Tyler's hand. "Thank you," he said, although he had nothing to thank him for. "Lovely to meet you."

Part V
Maxie
April 26th, 2017

Lulu showed up in Chicago in a coat that was too thin and a pair of suede boots that would be destroyed by the salt. *It's April*, she said. *Not here, it's not,* Maxie told her. She brought things that she thought would *help* embroidered pillowcases, bagels from Sadelle's, a list of appointments in her Smythson diary. "You have time to decide," she said, in that confident way she said basically everything, like she really believed it. Maxie knew that she didn't, which made it harder, but Lulu was the only person she could ask to do this.

"Did you make the appointment?" Maxie asked. Lulu had dyed her hair a golden, bright blonde that undulated in waves underneath the deceptive morning light.

"Not exactly." Lulu leaned forward, into the front seat, looking at the driver. "Jim? Did Maxie mention we're dropping my luggage at Soho House?" Maxie heard her voice in the silent, black-and-white film that was her new life. Everything that happened to Maxie was being viewed on a screen in front of her; she couldn't experience anything firsthand any more. *Why would we be going to Soho House?*

Lulu watched the sad, shabby houses out of her window. "It's awfully depressing here, isn't it?"

Maxie didn't say anything. She waited for the camera to pan over the lack of tears gumming her eyes. She had nothing left to feel. "I wasn't going to stay with you. I didn't want to be in Freddie's way." Maxie didn't bother to tell her that Freddie wasn't home — Freddie was never home, which seemed ironic, since they had moved there *for his job*.

"I thought you were driving," Lulu said, quietly, so Jim couldn't hear.

"I gave up," Maxie replied. She had given up on any semblance of being *normal*, and fallen back into the lukewarm comfort of her parents' money. She didn't take Ubers because she was scared, and she didn't drive herself because on the walk from Whole Foods to her car she thought a man followed her. She didn't go anywhere by herself; she could afford not to, so that was why she had Jim, the nice chauffeur who picked her up every day that she was in Chicago. "It's not safe here," Maxie told her. *You wouldn't understand.* It wasn't safe anywhere. She would never be safe again; it was only at night, with the security system armed and the bedroom door double-locked and Freddie asleep next to her that she felt like maybe it wouldn't happen again, at least for the next eight hours. Maxie pressed her forehead to the cold glass and swallowed a wave of nausea. "Did you make the appointment?" She asked again because she hadn't liked the answer.

"I made *appointments*," Lulu told her, and snapped a photo of a park.

"Just always be Instagramming," Maxie said.

"Do you want me to pull over, Miss?" Jim asked. Jim could be trusted. Jim could be trusted because Jim had a photo of his three daughters on his dashboard, which was very unprofessional, but made Maxie feel something like *safe*. They had dark hair and bright blue eyes and she thought of them as her three fairy godmothers, there to watch over her.

"Don't bother," Maxie told him. Lulu reached for Maxie's hand. Lulu's hand was bony and very soft, and her nails were too long, an affectation she picked up in LA. Maxie wondered what Mrs Swanson, the Connecticut debutante, must think of those shiny, oval, Kardashian nails. Maxie wondered what her own mother would think of the fact that she had a baby inside of her, temporarily, a baby that belonged to someone else. She wanted to tell her, but she also knew that her mother wasn't strong enough, or empathetic enough, or enough of a grown up. Her mother hadn't grown up with money, and that made her grotesquely self-conscious, always trying just the littlest bit *too* hard, always talking just one octave *too* loudly, holding on to things she could control, things like the ladies from temple and Maxie, just a smidge *too* tightly.

"I wonder what my mother would say, if she knew," Maxie said.

"At least he's Jewish?" Lulu suggested, in a pitch-perfect rendition of Rachel Stein's Long Island accent. Maxie laughed without meaning to.

"Maxie?" Lulu's voice cut across the screen, set it alight with her too-long fingernails pressing into Maxie's hard palm. Maxie turned. She waited for Lulu to ask if she was okay, but she knew already that Lulu wasn't going to ask it because Lulu knew that she wasn't okay.

"Where are we?" They were parked outside of a too-tall building in the financial district.

Lulu closed her stupid Smythson diary. "This is a woman I want you to meet with—"

"About what?"

"About — everything. I'll come with you—"

"No." Maxie turned her face away from the window. "No."

"You—"

"No. Lulu, *no*. Why can't anyone understand me when I say *no?*" She was yelling. Jim and Lulu exchanged looks in the rearview mirror and Maxie caught them.

"Okay," Lulu said. "Why don't we go to the spa?"

"I don't want anyone to touch me." Maxie pulled her knees into her chest and rocked a little on the seat.

"What *do* you want to do?"

"Go home."

"Okay. Jim, could we go home, please?"

"No! I want to go *home*." Maxie could feel the tears tracing sticky trails down her face. She was rocking and crying, and she didn't know how she would ever be able to go *home* again, what *home* meant or where it even was or if it was just some piece of the past that she would never be able to regain, never, not ever, and wasn't it time to just give up? Completely and totally, collapse and give in. Be done with all of *them* and all of *this*. There was no one left but her. She would never be safe, and she would never be *home*. She had the demon spawn squirming inside of her, the physical manifestation of what he had done. She had what had been done to her, the way it felt, the hand on her neck, the way she felt. Maxie didn't know if there was a word for it, or words, that could ever explain it; it was the blue-tinged white of the city's sky on the thousandth day of January, an eerie, high-pitched keening that you could never stop hearing, the taste of something sour and hot that you couldn't spit out. It wasn't any of those things on its own; it was more and more and more. It was so much it had taken root inside of her and begun to grow, squirming, twisting, scrambling her interior, until she knew she would never be the same. He wouldn't let her.

Yael
May 6th, 2017

Maxie melted into sobs on Lulu's bed, fat black tears that stained the custom pillow cases. Lulu ripped her dress from vigorous movement while she comforted her friend, while she held her and rocked her and let her cry mascara tears onto the *Valentino Runway* confection she had been so excited to wear. Yael stood two feet away from them, watching their spindly arms in a symphony of movement, Maxie's pressing up against her face, Lulu's trying to hold her, all of her.

"You don't have to go."

"I can't not go. It's Jessica's *engagement* party."

"That's idiotic. Just don't go."

"If I don't go, does he win?"

"Do you *want* to go? If he weren't there, would you want to go?"

Maxie closed her eyes. "I can't do this."

"So don't do it."

"Jessica will never forgive me."

"We don't even *like* Jessica."

"What will you tell her?"

"I'll tell her you started vomiting violently and we left you with a nurse and that I should get back to you, sooner rather than later."

"What will I do?"

"You'll stay here, and I'll get Fletcher to come, and it will be fine."

"I can't be alone."

"I know. Fletch will be here." Lulu smoothed the hair on Maxie's temples.

"I don't know. Can I have a Valium?"

"No."

There was a moment that passed between them, a long look, and Yael immediately understood the extra inch around Maxie's middle, the shine to her skin and her suddenly thick hair.

"It's going to be fine. We won't leave until Fletcher gets here." Lulu got up and motioned for Yael to sit down in her place. Yael sat, putting an arm around Maxie. "I'm going to change and call him. You two stay here," Lulu said, like she was leaving them alone in the house where Maxie had been raped, not a five-room apartment.

"Who's Fletcher?" Yael asked.

"Lulu's friend from boarding school who does assistanting." Lulu was sending her *assistant* to sit with Maxie. Jesus Christ.

"It's going to be okay," Yael told Maxie. "I promise you."

"You couldn't understand."

"You're pregnant." Yael counted in her head. "There's a decent chance it's Alex's."

Maxie sat up so quickly she fell backwards into the pillows. "Is it that obvious?"

"No. I'm a doctor, so I notice this stuff. And, in the six or seven years I've known you, you've never gained an ounce."

Maxie put a hand to her uterus, almost exactly where it was, which surprised Yael. Most newly pregnant women touched the bottom of their ribcage.

"Are you keeping it?"

Maxie nodded. "I don't know. I haven't decided yet." But Yael knew that she had. "Sometimes I think it's *my* baby. It doesn't belong to anyone else. Only me. But what if it's like him?"

Yael shrugged. "What if it's not?"

"What if it's a girl, and what happened to me happens to her? What if it's a curse, a family curse, and she's cursed, too? What if it's a boy, and he does to girls what *he* did to me? What if I don't have it, and I can never have a baby again? What if Freddie finds out? What if Freddie doesn't? What if I hate Freddie and he's useless and I don't love him any more?"

Yael nodded. "Assuming it's done properly, you shouldn't have any trouble conceiving after an abortion."

"It's all like this. If I don't have the baby, does he win? If I don't go to the party, does he win? If I do have the baby, does he win? If I do go to the party, does he win?"

"If you don't do what you want, he wins."

"I don't want anything." Maxie shook her head. "I want to go back in time and not walk into that stupid room, not giggle with him all weekend, not develop… whatever rapport I let happen between us. I feel like I have worms growing inside of me, eating me alive, and no one can see, and I'll just become this *thing*, like the girl in *Nightmare Before Christmas*. I want to throw up all the time. I am twisted. Everything is twisted up inside of me, broken and sick. I say my mantras and I go to the therapy and read the books and try to release him from me, but he dogs my every step. He is with me always. Everywhere. Like a ghost no one else I can see. But I can see him. I can see him and feel him, up against me, every single waking moment, sometimes every sleeping moment."

Yael nodded. "I think that's fairly common." She had to stop herself from saying *among rape victims*. Maxie couldn't tolerate the word *rape*; she was deathly allergic to it. "Have you gone to a support group? Studies have shown it really helps, in situations like this, to understand that you're not alone in your experience."

Maxie's eyes drew together in confusion. "Of course not. I don't want anyone to *know*. God forbid. The only people who will ever know are the ones who saw it. It would — ruin me. No one would *ever* look at me the same way. You already don't."

"I see rape victims at least once every two weeks." Yael got up and brushed off the long skirt of the dress she borrowed from Lulu. "Last month, one was beaten so badly she died on the table. I look at everyone differently, after things like that."

It took Maxie twenty-five minutes to fix herself back up, during which time Fletcher appeared with a suit in a garment bag, because Lulu had somehow known that maybe Maxie would want to go to the party, at least if she had an escort.

"Where's Freddie?" Fletcher whispered. Lulu slid a hot pink dress over her head and pulled her hair down. It hung in a golden curtain to her waist.

"Traveling for work. Always traveling. One would think he was Willy Loman." Lulu fixed a massive diamond bracelet around her wrist.

"So, darling, stick with her like you're a bodyguard. Not a moment alone. Not a second. Not a *step*."

"Got it."

"Max? Ready?"

Maxie's hair waved thickly around her ears; her face had one-third of its usual make up, but she looked better, Yael thought. Pregnancy suited her. The dress she'd borrowed from Lulu boasted an empire waist and the entire picture was utterly un-Maxie; it was quieter, calmer, kind of *lovely* and old-fashioned. "Ready," she said, and she looked steadily at Lulu for too long, and Lulu looked steadily back at her.

Alex arrived after they did, an hour late. Yael occupied herself entirely with Maxie, trailing Fletcher like she was attached to him. Will hadn't bothered to say hello, which was what Yael was trying not to think about when she saw Alex, broad-shouldered and blue eyed, flashing teeth that were too white.

"LULU!" He roared, dipping into their group, reaching for the blonde girl who stood, feet planted firmly, grasping Maxie's wrist in one small hand, like she was watching an incoming airstrike. Fletcher pinned himself to Maxie's side and Yael pinned herself to Fletcher. "Why isn't my cousin here with you?"

Lulu rolled her eyes and, Maxie in hand, excused herself to *get a glass of water.*

"Five minutes in New York, and she's icy cold again," Alex said, shaking his head. His dark hair was long, and his stubble overgrown to cover the bottom half of his face.

There was an acute horror to it, staring at the man who had raped the girl who less than an hour before cried into Yael's arms. There was a horror to the baby inside Maxie and a horror to the way that Alex watched her walk away. There was a horror to his hand stretching out in front of her *good as new* and closing around her wine glass and taking a sip, to the flicking of his eyes as they roved across the room too quickly and to the crocodile smile when he saw Maxie emerging from the kitchen.

Lulu
May 6th, 2017

It was too cold to be outside on the balcony, but Lulu couldn't be inside for a minute longer. Lulu's hand couldn't stop shaking long enough to hold a drink, or even her purse. She'd noticed Rob staring at it as she tried to accept a glass of water from Victoria, who sat outside with her in the unseasonal chill. Lulu couldn't watch Alex in a room or look into his wasted face, that devilish, debonair charm he doled out on bridesmaids and friends of friends and one red-headed waitress who smiled at him from the edges of her eyes. She didn't know how Will swallowed around the bile and sat across from him, pretended to be his friend, *indulged* him in believing that he could get away with all of it. He *was* getting away with all of it.

Lulu knew that if she seriously dated Theo, she would have to spend time with Alex. They were cousins, and they were close cousins — they were planning a ski trip in a week — and sometimes Lulu wondered if there was any future with someone who was related to Alex Sable. It was some kind of tangled joke being played by the universe that Lulu started to see Theo a month before she walked into a room with lights too bright and acrid air that weighed on your lungs.

Victoria clinked the ice cubes in her glass. "I cannot tell another person about my break-up," she said, reaching for the champagne bottle cradled in her fur. "I cannot continue to do this." She popped the top without spilling a drop and gulped thirstily. "I always think champagne is going to make me feel better. You know, you can't be sad if you have good champagne and chocolate croissants around, except you can." She took another sip. "I just don't know what the way forward is. If there is a way forward."

"There's only forward," Lulu said. She was suddenly exhausted and maybe starting to get a cold. Sometimes she felt like she spent her all of her time lounging around, waiting for life to actually start; at some point, after Andover and Harvard and the early LA jobs that failed and the accidental Instagrammer life, you just lost whatever was supposed to propel you forward. You burnt it up too early, and now it was only ashes at your feet. Ashes and ashes and a little bit of dust.

"The prodigal son returns," Alex drawled. Lulu found her back had starched itself into straightness and she was holding Victoria's champagne-sticky hand. "How does it feel to be back? Was there a welcoming gala at the airport?" She could barely identify the lines of his profile against the darkest part of the brick, melting into covered lawn furniture. There was a humming in her heart, and she wished suddenly that she could spend the night at her parents' house instead of her own.

"No welcoming gala," she told Alex.

Victoria slurped. "I think he's joking, because you've been on the host committee of, like, every event since you got back."

"I know," Lulu murmured. Alex slid out of the shadows, lolling against the rungs of the balcony. He offered them cigarettes from a red and white box and the lights of Park Avenue ran red and white behind him, blurring in stripes across her eyes and his face and the memory of what once was. Chris Newman was caught on a balcony like this one, an Upper East Side apartment on a night so unseasonably cold no one bothered to venture outside. Places came to hold special meaning for you, the way Maxie and Lulu and Victoria always ended up in the bathroom, spent their lives sitting on the edges of sunken tubs and cracked marble and worn bath mats. It was funny how you thought you could know someone just through the people they knew and the schools they'd gone to and their families and their Instagram, funny how you thought you could establish their character by hints and clues that had nothing to do with who they actually were.

"You know that part in *Gatsby*, where the narrator says they were all children of the West, and they couldn't make it in the East?" Alex was halfway down his cigarette.

" 'I see now this has been a story of the West, after all — Tom and Gatsby, Daisy and Jordan and I, were all Westerners, and perhaps we possessed some deficiency in common which made us subtly unadaptable to Eastern life."

"God. Why do you know that by heart?"

Lulu shrugged. She knew it by heart because she'd thought it so often about herself, at the end of her time in LA, the city where *anyone* could survive and thrive, and she, a child of the East, had found herself so very wanting, so very incapable of just sinking into the artificial blue of the pool at Sunset Tower.

"Theo was talking to me about us moving back, and it made me think of that. A hundred years on. Easterners are unadaptable to Western life."

It made her sickly clammy and nervous that her mind could move along the same strokes as Alex's, Alex, a rapist of at least one, maybe multiple, girls she sort of knew; Alex who was a level of psychopath that should have scared them off of the empty balcony the moment he announced himself, or maybe he wasn't a psychopath at all, which made him all the more terrifying.

Alex gazed out onto the street below. "I wonder if they still build apartments like this. With a balcony twenty floors up." His glass rested on the edge, and he twirled it a little, a little too close, almost losing its balance. "What?" he asked, looking up at Lulu.

She thought if she told him not to do it he would be all the more likely to. She thought that on some deep, energetic, soul level she must have developed an intuition for his choices and his thoughts. She thought, standing there, looking back at him, that he really didn't believe he'd *done* anything — or, if he had, he had no remorse at all. Maybe both, even though the two were contradictory. When he flicked the glass over the lip of the balcony and into the street below he kept his eyes on her, waiting for her to flinch or betray a flicker of emotion. She stayed like stone and thought about what a silly gamble something like that was, assuming you could or would beat the odds. They didn't hear it fall or shatter and she didn't know if they would have, all the way up there.

"We should go," Lulu told him, standing. Alex lit another cigarette. She brushed flecks of ash that didn't exist off of her purple brocade skirt.

"We should," Victoria replied, rising. Her small hand choked the neck of the bottle.

"Hey," Alex said. He stood so close to the edge of the railing. If they both pushed, he would just topple. End-over-end, end of it all, just like the glass. Sometimes Lulu thought the worst part of the whole thing was not being able to talk about it. It was one of those things, one of those few things, that you had to deal with yourself. "Be nice to my cousin. Don't — break his heart. He's a good kid." She couldn't see his dark face in the dark night, no moon, too high up for streetlights, just dashes of traffic illuminating the background and the distinct shine of those eyes, texture against the sky. His eyes were too shiny, too shiny and too aware, a human trapped in the skin of an animal.

"Goodnight," Lulu told him. The redheaded waitress was walking out as they ducked inside, balancing a tray of caviar new potatoes in one hand.

"There's no one out there," Lulu told her.

"I thought I saw someone," she replied.

"There isn't," Lulu said flatly, and a few guests looked at them, pumpkin-headed Adam, Jessica's mom, the hostess. "And we shouldn't be letting the cold air in." She shut the door and stood there, arms crossed, barring the way.

"Okay," the redhead replied, taking a step back, and Lulu knew that later, when she followed Alex into a stairwell or shared the elevator with him, she would bring it up, the pretty blonde girl who hadn't wanted her to go outside.

Victoria said goodbye to Jessica while Lulu rummaged through a wallpapered closet for their coats. Her mother would have commented, *no one for coat check?* but her mother would have been able to pick apart the entire party, inch by paper-napkinned inch. This world of hers, this world of theirs, was dead and dying, slowly and gracelessly, a hand carefully closing around a neck, letting *just enough* air come and go, so you could feel it, too, the gasping, the grasping, the fear, the *terror*.

When she closed her eyes in the car home she could see that lustrous gloss against the matte sky, how it gleamed black and blue like a fallen star, those shiny eyes that she would maybe never stop seeing in pockets of suspended darkness.

Rob
May 10th, 2017

Rob kicked his shoes off in Alex's hallway and hung his jacket on a pair of skis. "Hey," he called. "Alex?" The gummy, thick toes of Rob's socks caught a splinter as he crept down the darkened hall, into the wide-windowed living room. It was empty. "Hello?" he said, but it dropped out like a whisper, and Rob felt coldness leaking into his chest. Something was wrong; something was very, very off. "Alex?" But he wasn't sure if he said it, or it existed only in his throat.

"AHHHHHHHHHHHH!" Alex dropped out of a closet like a dead body, sending Rob toppling back onto the floor, screaming. "I forgot how you screamed," Alex said, mouth stretched out like the Cheshire Cat. "That was *so* much better than I was expecting."

Rob sat on the floor, breathing too shallowly, trying to come down from the adrenaline. "I was about to call the cops."

"And say what? 'My friend just buzzed me up, but his apartment is empty. Emergency'!"

"Have you ever heard of the boy who cried wolf?"

"Have you ever heard of paranoia?" Alex took a long draught out of a bottle of red wine.

Rob got to his feet, still shaken, and poured himself a large glass of vodka. "You have any orange juice?"

"Are you a forty-five-year-old man at a Florida racetrack in 1998?"

The fridge had only leftover take-out containers and water, sparkling and still, in glass bottles. Rob flung open a cabinet, found some blue Gatorade, and topped his glass off with it.

Alex shook his head, sinking into the couch. "The stuff you drink is depressing," he said. "It makes me worry about your future."

"Not all of us have a basement we can steal thousand-dollar bottles of wine from."

"It's a cellar. And you can *have* some hundred-point wine."

“I don’t drink screwdrivers in public.” The fastest way for Rob to get drunk was with alcohol that didn’t taste or look like alcohol. He didn’t like wine and he didn’t like the taste of scotch, and when he’d just had a nine-hour work day, all he wanted was something palatable.

“That’s what’s so sad about it,” Alex replied, stretching out to fill the couch with his six-foot-plus frame. Rob drooped into a chair. “How’s Veronica?” Alex had taken to calling Ronnie Veronica. He claimed that if she was going to be in his life he had to at least *try* to improve her, and Veronica was a step up from *Ronnie*.

Rob privately kind of agreed about her name, but he still found the entire thing extremely annoying. Ronnie sucked up to Alex in person — she wasn’t stupid — and abused him roundly the moment she could. Which was also extremely annoying. Rob lived his life either working or being extremely annoyed by the people he had chosen to surround himself with, and sometimes he wondered if people ever actually *did* just run away and start their lives over, *begin again.* Could you do that? Did it work? “She’s fine.”

“Please. Stop all of this scintillating conversation. *I can’t take it!*” Alex’s phone rang. Rob let his head fall back and rolled his eyes to the ceiling. “I’m just bringing my skis. You want to borrow a board? I can show you what I have. FaceTime me.” Alex hit his screen. “Hey. Rob’s here.” He aimed the phone at Rob.

Alex’s cousin Theo waved. “Hey! Rob, how are you?” Rob waved.

“He’s very apathetic right now. He moved in with his girlfriend,” Alex told him confidently.

“That’s a bad thing?” Theo asked.

“I’m just tired,” Rob called. “Some of us work for a living.”

“He sounds like a downtrodden dad in a nineteen-fifties sitcom,” Alex told his cousin. “Come on, Robbie, why don’t you and I start a little business up? No more nine-to-five, no more boss. Just us.”

“What kind of business are *you* going to start?” Theo asked. “Rob, don’t leave your job. This will never happen.”

“You know what? Rob, you leave your job, and I’ll make sure we have a million in capital to start… whatever enterprise we want. We can even call it *Starship Enterprise.*” Alex laughed at his own joke, at how he knew Rob would never leave his job.

"Don't be a dick," Theo instructed. "Ignoring him is the right thing!" he called, raising his voice.

"I know. He's been saying this for years. Can't take someone seriously when they never *actually do anything*," Rob replied.

"And he's *back* in the game!" Alex yelled; voice too loud in the apartment. "Batter up!"

"Can we talk about packing for a second?" Theo asked, and Alex redirected his attention to his phone screen.

"What's behind you? Did you get new art?" Alex asked his cousin.

"No, man. I'm at Lulu's. Haven't you been over here?" Theo's voice tilted up in surprise.

"No one invites me anywhere," Alex replied.

"Because you're annoying," Rob yelled. He wondered if Lulu could hear him.

"Just trying to improve you, Robbie. You deserve better. Don't you think he deserves better in his life, Theo?"

"You're like a Jewish mother. Let him live. Can I see my snowboard options?"

"Then I have to get up."

"Get up!"

"Hold on." Alex dropped the phone on his chest. "Rob, will you go to the hall closet and show Theo the boards in there?"

"No."

"Come on. I'll give you two bottles of wine!"

"You can't bribe me!"

"Just bring the board," a lovely, low voice said from Alex's chest, and he picked up his phone again. "You're not flying commercially, you have plenty of room." Rob got up and leaned onto the back of the couch, so he could see the screen. It was just Theo's rodent-like face, a less attractive, smaller version of Alex, and he was so *young*. Rob couldn't believe that Theo and Lulu were the same age.

"Hi, Lulu," Alex said. "Where is she?"

"Putting on shoes," she called.

"When are you guys going skiing?" Rob asked. He sometimes forgot that Lulu lived in the same city he did. He felt like they were on a long-distance call, from her life to his, except that she and Rob were just the background people in this particular interaction, adding color and commentary.

"Tomorrow night," Alex told him. "Whistler."

"Didn't Will want to borrow poles? Should I bring an extra pair?" Theo asked.

"Will's going?" Rob asked. Theo nodded. Alex didn't say anything. "I'm surprised you guys aren't going to your house in Vail," Rob heard himself saying, but really what he was saying was *I'm surprised you guys didn't invite me*.

"Lulu's right. Just bring everything."

"We should go, darling," Lulu's disembodied voice said again. Rob thought she would make a good AI companion, like in *Her*.

"Where are you guys going? It's like eight o'clock at night."

"UNICEF party, or something," Theo replied.

"AmfAR," Lulu said.

Theo shrugged into the camera. "She's on the board of so many of these things. They're fun. You should come to one."

"Invite me!" Alex said, flipping over onto his back. Rob sat in another uncomfortable chair.

"We will. See you tomorrow."

The call ended; they were silent. Rob didn't know how to say that he couldn't believe he hadn't been invited and *Will* had — Will, whose loathing of Alex scared Rob, showed a complexity of character that Rob hadn't even known existed within Will.

"What's good Italian here? That we can Postmates from." Alex still didn't know his way around downtown, still acted like he lived in LA and couldn't leave his house to get dinner, still only used Postmates like it was the single delivery service in existence.

"I don't know," Rob said.

"Is Serafina still around?" Alex asked.

"So Will's going skiing, too?" Rob asked.

Alex scrolled through options on his phone. "Yeah. You know, he's a serious skier."

The implication was that Rob was not a serious skier.

"Like, Olympic-level? I didn't know that." Rob tried to keep the sarcasm out of his voice.

"You know what I mean." Alex sat up. "You want pasta?"

Rob shrugged. "What do you mean?"

"You don't really ski. You don't like it. You always complain the whole time. And we couldn't invite you and assume you would do the right thing, and sit this one out. Because you always come."

"Okay." Rob *wasn't* a great skier; he'd only been doing it since he met Alex and Will, and he didn't really *get* it. It was cold and you got hurt easily and it didn't seem to have any purpose. Skiing, to Rob, was like horseback riding, mildly uncomfortable and something people did for the photos. Which he'd once said to Alex, who said *not if you know what you're doing.* As if he needed further emphasis on the fact that he, Rob, did not know what he was doing. In skiing and in life.

"Don't be weird about this," Alex instructed him. "It's just a weekend."

Nothing was *just a weekend* with Alex; didn't Rob know that better than anyone? One weekend with Alex could change your life, change your friendship, change his life, change — everything. Anything. There would be the jokes Rob could never understand and the pressing, poignant moments that caused a long exchange of thoughtful looks; there would be the wall that grew, ever higher and ever thicker, up between him and the people who were supposed to be his friends.

"It's just us and Gabriel." Rob looked at him. "Theo's roommate." There were at least eight seats on the private plane they were taking. Seats they probably needed for all of those extra snowboards and poles that Lulu told them to just throw in the plane, because what did she care? What did *they* care? They were all such careless people that something as deliberate as a purposeful exclusion was the deepest kind of a cut. Rob couldn't show up at the hospital and expect to be stitched up by Yael, pay the out-of-pocket charge of a thousand dollars without blinking, hire a town car to take them back to New York because it was *impossible* to travel with a hand injury.

Sometimes Rob wondered if Alex actually did improve him, make him a better version of himself, make him want more and try harder. Sometimes Rob wondered if Alex undermined him psychologically at every turn, if Alex had thrown off his confidence, if Alex had changed the course of his life. Sometimes Rob wondered — if they hadn't shared a dorm room if he hadn't known Alex past a hello on the street outside the Racquet Club. If he would have belonged to the Racquet Club, if it weren't for Alex. If he even would have recognized Alex walking down Fifth Avenue, swinging a Sherry-Lehman bag with a bottle of Louis Roederer Cristal Rose Vinotheque. If he would have known what that was, been able to identify that some champagnes *mattered more* than others, just like some people *mattered more* than others, just like some *things* mattered more than others, things like being a good skier and not mixing your vodka with orange juice. Things that Rob would never be able to entirely erase away because he wasn't educated enough or quick enough or even smart enough to learn it all and commit it to memory, to make it a part of his everyday living breathing character, and even if he *did*, he would always just be Rob-from-Miami, the son of a dentist, raised in the two-bedroom house that Alex had never even bothered to go to, a marked pretender on every count.

They sat in silence for twenty minutes, thirty, silence for Rob but nothing to Alex, who watched *The Office* like he'd never seen it before. The buzzer rang; Alex answered it. He didn't ask Rob to get the door, which was his silent gesture of apology, but answering the door at your own apartment for the food you ordered didn't feel like a massive *sacrifice* on Alex's part. The truth was that there were four extra seats on the plane, and Rob wasn't being offered one, and Rob was never going to be offered one, because Rob wasn't Freddie Miles, he was Tom Ripley, no matter how long he'd been around, no matter the drunken nights and blurred photos and private jokes that these days none of them remembered. None of it mattered to someone like Alex; if Rob pushed him, he would just hear more about how inadequate he was for a trip like this, for invitations to amfAR — whatever that was — for the intrinsic *belonging* that he simply couldn't participate in.

Rob found himself standing, blue Gatorade glass on the marble-topped coffee table, slinking his shoulders into his coat.

"I got it. Don't need to go outside," Alex told him, holding two heaping Serafina bags.

"I'm going," Rob replied.

"Rob." Alex lifted his hands. "You're not gonna make me eat all of this alone." It smelled like garlic and pizza and the mushroomy cream sauce Alex loved.

"I didn't want pasta. I'm going home."

Alex dropped the bags onto the floor. "Seriously. You're leaving?"

"Sorry," Rob said, looking at the floor, looking away from him, because Alex would pull you in, if you let him, beat you down into it if he couldn't convince you of it. Rob skirted around him.

"This is embarrassing, Robbie," Alex picked up the bags of pasta and pizza, too much food for two people. "Even for you. Come on. Sit down, grab a fork. Everything is the same. Nothing's different because you can't ski. You've never been able to ski. This isn't a big shock. Or, at least, it shouldn't be."

"Nothing is the same," Rob told him. He could pretend and pretend and pretend and Alex could play an imaginary game of life where what had happened hadn't happened, but it had happened, it had *happened* to all of them. Alex had done it. *Alex* had done it. Alex had committed the act and it didn't matter if Rob had spent the better part of three months constructing an elaborate delusion for himself wherein Alex hadn't done anything. Like everything Rob created, it failed, and he didn't know or care if Maxie had *asked for it* or hadn't. What he knew was that *nothing* was the same, nothing would ever be the same, and it was Alex who had done this to all of them, who had taken something from every single one of them. Rob was angry at Alex for doing this to them, for creating this world in which things no longer moved according to their easy rhythm. Everything had been shaded through the tinted lens of *what he did.*

Rob waved without turning around. In all the years of loyalty and devotion to Alex Sable, all of the heated defenses and insincere laughs, Rob thought he had proven himself to be above the wage gap that separated them. *Of course* he wasn't; *of course* it still mattered. If you couldn't ski, what use were you to someone like Alex? That was the only thing that really meant something, what you contributed toward the grand pursuit of all things *fun*. Why should it be anything else, for someone like Alex? It shouldn't. Rob was a fool to have thought anything else.

He was too angry to go back to Ronnie, and without Alex there wasn't another place for him, so he bought vodka and orange juice from the bodega across from Alex's and gulped it in the conference room of his office, until he was stinking drunk and full of the kind of deep loathing that takes a lifetime to build.

Will
May 11th, 2017

It took two flights to get to Vancouver, Will missed the plane, maybe on purpose. He connected in Salt Lake, where the sky was a blaze of reds and oranges. He wanted to leave the airport and drive through Utah, the craggy cliffs and canyons that made you contend with some *part* of you.

Will he watched the mountains from above and thought about Yael. He wondered if he'd actually loved her for a moment or if she'd simply been the catalyst to inform him that he couldn't marry Jessica. It was happening and yet it wasn't going to happen, and he nerved up with every passing day. If there was one thing Lulu taught him, it was to let the bridges you burn light the way to your happiness. If only he could, watch them burn and burn and burn, ashes swirling into his eyes and throat and nose, choking him with the acrid smell of freedom.

Will landed too soon. Alex told him not to come to the hangar, they were at the Fairmont on the water. There were, it turned out, at least six Fairmont's in Vancouver, and Will's cab driver took him to the wrong one twice before they actually got where they were supposed to be going. He wasn't happy with Will and Will wasn't happy with him and he wasn't sure why he'd said yes to this weekend in the first place, why it was such a staple of adult life that you were obligated to do all of the things you didn't want to, and required to try to eke out happiness from them.

Alex and his cousin were seated at the bar of an empty restaurant, eating burgers with blue cheese and talking to a third kid who introduced himself as Gabriel.

"It's a good burger," Theo admitted.

"I told you so."

Will sat and ordered a beer. "What are we doing here?"

"No snow," Theo told him, and Gabriel nodded.

"It was supposed to snow," Alex said. Alex was drinking beer as water and whisky as beer.

"No, it wasn't," Theo replied. "It's too late in the season."

"No skiing," Alex explained, as if this weren't obvious.

"Maybe we should just go home," Gabriel said, twirling his empty glass, and Will liked him immediately.

"We're not going *home*. Will lives a depressing life. Don't make him go home."

"I'm fine to go home," Will sipped his beer.

"I'll call Louie. I'm sure she has a suggestion." Theo unlocked his phone and hit her name in his favorites. *Favorites*. Favorites was like bringing her to meet your family, in Victorian times.

"Put her on speakerphone. I want to hear her being mushy," Alex commanded.

"Please don't," Gabriel put in. "We're good."

"You know what I mean," Alex turned to Will, looking at him for the first time. "She doesn't have any emotions."

"You know who's emotionless? Landon Heathcote." Will picked up a menu. "I've been seeing a lot of him, and he is *cold*." It was a lie, but Will wanted to watch Alex react.

"Why are you *seeing* him?"

Theo ate one of Alex's fries. "Well, Lulu says there's a magical little island an hour away. Her friend has a house, and she's seeing if we can stay." Theo and Gabriel looked like a different generation, even though they were only Jessica's age; they exuded a kind of youthful ease, like no one had told them yet how hard and unpleasant it would be. That they would get less attractive and less interesting, that their metabolisms would slow until they had a hefty ring around their middle, that the girls available to them would narrow and narrow until it was just a pool of people either desperate or money-grubbing. They didn't know any of that yet.

"What do we *do* on the island?" Alex batted his cousin's hand away.

Theo shrugged, motioned for the waiter, ordered more fries, and asked if Will wanted anything. Will ordered a burger.

"So I guess we can take the plane out there tonight." Theo yawned into his water.

Gabriel checked his watch. "We already booked the room for tonight. Let's stay here and fly in the morning."

"At least we can have one good night," Alex groused.

"I made us a reservation at the best restaurant," Theo began.

"For Vancouver," Alex put in.

"Are you okay?" Theo asked him, suddenly, hands in front of him in confrontation. "You've been a pissy little brat this entire trip. What's up?"

"I'm fine." Alex shook himself like a horse shaking off flies. "I'm sick of everyone yelling at me."

"We're not yelling at you," Will told him, evenly, and he felt like he was talking to a child, explaining the nuances of human behavior. "Everyone just wants to have a good weekend."

Alex swept up the check.

"Hurry up. We're eating again at eight," he said, slapping the blubber around Will's belly button. "Is Jessica freaking out that you're gonna be fat for your wedding and the rest of your lives?"

"Jessica just wants to get married," Will told him.

Will and Alex's suite overlooked a beautiful harbor with silver mountains reflected in its boat-skimmed surface.

"Send up a bottle of Macallan 81, please."

Sometimes when he looked at Alex he could see the boy he'd known, cheeks over-red and face fleshy. Now he had lost weight and was starting to age, skin sagging around his bright eyes and heroic jaw.

"Cheer up, William. You're not dead yet."

They got too drunk. They got too drunk to go to dinner, to leave the hotel, to make any actual sense. The night fell to pieces in Will's already fractured mind, a bottle of scotch and then a bottle of vodka and scuttling down long hallways in their hotel robes and someone else's bachelor party, blonde Southerners with accents. Theo and Gabriel slung their arms around the groom, and they sang *The House of the Rising Sun* together, dropping words and dissolving into giggles. Someone brought out cocaine and Alex had a crusty white ring around his nose that no one bothered to tell him about. They ate another round of burgers in their robes in the hotel bar, burgers which Will vomited up in someone else's bathroom, or maybe in their bathtub. Strippers appeared at one point, strippers who Alex chortled were too fat to make it in New York. Theo cried and so did Alex and when Will woke up with his hand in a melted ice cream sundae and Gabriel next to him on the floor of a room that almost certainly was not either of theirs, he figured this was a minimal amount of damage, all things considered.

He went to check his phone for drunk dials, but he didn't have it; he poked Gabriel with a sugar-sticky hand and the boy rolled over, moaning quietly.

"Gabriel," Will hissed. "Get up."

The room belonged to Bob, Bob the bachelor, a room with two beds that were occupied by five sets of sprawled limbs. Will swung himself to his feet, grabbed Gabriel, and snuck into the hallway, trying to remember their room number and feeling his pockets for a key.

"I don't think I've ever been that drunk," Gabriel said.

Will nodded. "Do you have a key?" Gabriel shook his head. "Phone?"

He removed a phone from his robe pocket, sent a text, turned back to Will. "Breakfast?"

Theo met them in the restaurant, also in his robe, shoeless and sporting one sock, one slipper. He ordered French fries and pancakes and doughnuts and ate steadily while Will swallowed around his nausea.

"I lost my phone," Will said.

"I think we all lost something, last night," Theo told him, smirking. "You put it in the minibar in our room." Gabriel got up from the table. "I wonder if they can make me tacos." He looked around for the waiter. Will thought one of them should be worried about where Alex was, but since they hadn't left the hotel, he wasn't sure it really mattered. "Your wife mad about last night?"

Will shrugged. He hated that everyone referred to Jessica as his wife and he was sure that she would be mad if she knew anything about it. Probably she didn't and she wouldn't until Alex slipped up with a story about it at the worst possible time, her hands tightening on his arm as she said *and* when *was this?* "Hopefully, she'll never know," he said, leaning back in his chair, sighing.

Theo nodded. "You know, what you said about her last night — I don't think I'll ever forget it."

"I forgot. What did I say?" Will asked.

"It doesn't matter. Do you mind if I call Lulu?"

Will shook his head. The tacos came and Theo recounted his phone with stories of the night, doing the can-can with the strippers, eating onion rings at 4 AM. Will could hear her trilling laughter through the phone. Theo smiled too much for his hangover. When he hung up Will put down his fork.

"Lulu's messed up," he told Theo, because he felt guilty, suddenly, letting this innocent involve himself with someone who was so deeply damaged, or maybe because he wanted Theo to have a reality check, or maybe because he wanted to remind himself that he wasn't the only one who was borderline hopeless. "That's not the kind of person you want to settle down with."

Theo shrugged at him, still smiling that Cheshire Cat grin which looked too much like Alex. "Maybe she is. I don't know. It doesn't matter, anyway, because I fell in love with her the way you fall into a ditch. One minute you're on the road, the next, you're in the ditch.." He grabbed a handful of fries. "I'm in it. I'm in the ditch."

It made him sad, sad for Theo, because he was too young to understand what he was giving up by pursuing the beautiful and the damned; sad for Lulu, because she was fatally flawed and would never settle into happiness; sad for himself, because he didn't love Jessica and he wasn't sure he loved Yael and he definitely didn't even *like* himself. Sad for how self-conscious he was about his unhappiness.

In the end, they didn't go to the magical island that was only an hour flight. In the end, the hotel manager knocked on their door to speak to Alex about a complaint from the girl who brought their late-night room service. He was upset and Alex was apologetic, and Will turned his face away from the monetary exchange that he was certain took place, so that he would have plausible deniability. He wished he could remember the girl's face but part of him was glad he couldn't. Part of him only saw Maxie and part of him wondered if Alex was getting worse or Will was just finally paying attention.

Part VI
Tyler
August 2017

Lulu was true to her word, she and Maxie met Tyler on several occasions to talk about what they knew of Alex's mental state, and they let him record, although Lulu insisted *both* of their names be changed, because *one* name would *give up the game*, as she put it. After they'd set him up with Landon, they gave him Victoria's phone number, who talked for five minutes flat and said she knew nothing and no one, basically. 'Tyler dug up Alex's piano teacher and the guy he'd been producing a short with, who talked about Alex's potential and smoking weed with Alex, respectively, and when Maxie begged to go with Tyler, he let her sit next to him. She seemed bored and a little lonely and he wondered for the hundredth time where her husband was while his pregnant wife was here, alone. Neither interview proved fruitful — the producing partner hadn't known Alex did more than drink and smoke weed, and said *who?* when Tyler asked about Chris Newman — but it was nice not to sit there alone. Nice to have someone else to listen.

Maxie helped him set up meetings with girls who'd known Alex since dance lessons in the 4th grade and boys who'd had cubbies next to him, K-12, people who she and Lulu knew personally. Most of the interviews took place with either or both of the girls present, Lulu usually responding to emails or sketching out complicated schedules, Maxie listening like a child, eyes wide. Some people said that Alex was talented and genius-level-smart, but most of them told Tyler what he already knew, that Alex made anything a party, that he never said no, that he was always there with a mocking smile and a half-insult, half-joke. Over the course of three weeks, no one Tyler met seemed to know Alex well enough to be able to comment on his mental fitness, his deep-seated emotions', what he was actually thinking.

So Tyler made lists of people to talk to, and, when he couldn't get phone numbers or addresses or responses, Maxie and Lulu, who *knew everyone*, put him in touch. He thought it was fair game to let Maxie, at least, who wanted to sit in on *everything*, join him.

Often, after an interview, Maxie would ask *Tyler* questions, what kind of picture of Alex was he building? Did he think Alex was a good person? Did he pity Alex?

"I'm just trying to ascertain what kind of person you think he is. If you weighed his soul against a feather. You know what I mean." Maxie flicked a handful of long hair over her shoulder.

He didn't know what she meant; it was from the Ancient Egyptian Book of the Dead.

"You know it, Tyler," Lulu assured him.

"Everyone knows it. *On this day of great reckoning, behold me, I come to you, without sin, without guilt, without evil, without a witness against me, without one whom I have wronged. I am one pure of mouth, pure of hands.* It's, like, very famously paraphrased in the Bible. It's one of those things people always refer back to."

He didn't know it. He didn't think you could weigh anyone's soul against a feather. He certainly didn't know anyone who could call themselves *pure of mouth, pure of hands.*

The girls shrugged and ordered milkshakes. Two days later, Maxie gave him a book on Ancient Egypt.

In his line of work, there was support; there was a team around him, but, when you came down to it, he was really out there on his own, finding connections, asking strangers if he could stick a tape recorder in their face and talk about something deeply personal, for all the world to hear. There was a kind of comfort in having the girls flanking him, not just because their knowledge of Alex's network — and easy connection to them — made his job much simpler, but also because the creeping loneliness that often set in in projects like these, that moment where he knew he wasn't a part of the story, in fact he was the outsider trying to pry his way in, had completely disappeared under the weight of Lulu's healthy cookies and green juices and big bowls of oats. Tribeca became a second home; in between interviews, while they *debriefed*, as Maxie termed it, he found himself telling them the kind of personal things he never told anyone.

"Don't you have a wife? I found her in a photo of you on Google Images."

"Maxie!" Lulu said.

"Oh, it's fine. We can ask personal questions," Maxie told her. "Can't we?"

They were divorcing, he told them.

"Aaaah," Maxie replied. "I know divorce well. I know all the good lawyers."

"Are you and your husband divorced?" Tyler asked Maxie.

"No," the girls replied, together. They often replied to the same question with the same answer at the same time.

"We're separated," Maxie explained. "We'll probably start the divorce proceedings around next October."

"Specific date," He commented.

"I just don't know what to do about my Instagram handle. If I drop Freddie's last name."

"It's such a good last name," Lulu said, wistfully.

"Did you guys have a prenup?" Maxie asked.

He shook his head.

"Tyler," they both said.

Maxie's focused heavily on the interviews of two people. She wanted Tyler to talk to Henry Frod, who Lulu had dated briefly, and Mckenna Dishery, who was, according to Maxie, Alex's best friend. Lulu was cold to both ideas from the start. Over her *dead* body would she ask Henry for any kind of favor, and, anyway, they weren't that close. '

"They weren't that good of friends," Lulu told Maxie for the hundredth time, as they circled through a fancy interior shop where the girls were buying linen dish towels and $300 cutting boards. "I've *told* you; they fell out ages ago. Henry's family doesn't have any real money, and he's, oh, what's that phrase, Tyler?"

Tyler didn't know.

"You know. Like, a swindler. On-the-something. I don't know. He's one of those people who's from a supposedly nice family but they're on the last legs of the last trusts, you know what I mean?"

"Oh, everyone knows that, Louisa." Maxie always called Lulu *Louisa* when she was harried. "Who *cares*. Tyler doesn't *care* about his family. You're just bitter because he dumped you—"

"The point is, he — Henry, I mean — completely used Alex to get in with another group of kids — the Tim Hennessy group, Max—"

"They're such losers. No way is anyone trying to get in with them."

"Henry is! He wants to befriend them so that he can convince them to finance his ridiculous *film* projects. That's why he befriended *Alex* in the first place."

"Hm." Maxie put the down a wooden spoon that she'd been appraising. "That's actually kind of genius."

"Yes. Exactly. Thank you. Anyway," Lulu turned to Tyler, a little breathless. "As you can see, he's a dead end."

"Fine." Maxie appeared in front of them, wielding a large slab of white marble that looked like it would be too heavy for her to hold so comfortably. "Then you have to get Mckenna. That's the deal."

"I would rather die than ask *Mckenna Dishery* for a *favor*."

"If you don't, I will."

Mckenna was the only daughter of a famous 1980's country singer. She had known Lulu, she told Tyler as he began the recording, on and off since they were two.

"And I've never liked her," she said, exhaling smoke into the air of the Soho House rooftop. She wasn't a member, but she suggested meeting there, so Lulu did some kind of magic and got him in in two days. "She's, like, all of the worst things about where we grew up. When we were in school, she had this little clique, and they were obsessed with Bergdorfs. In the *fifth* grade. And she cares so much about her appearance. I mean, she's an Instagram influencer. Is there a lower form of life? She doesn't need to be. She doesn't *need* to work at all."

Mckenna, it transpired, worked *when she was inspired*. She had a mustache lining her upper lip, which she sometimes jutted outside so purposefully he wondered if she wanted him to notice it. She was sloppy, hair a bushy nest of knots, and her yellowing teeth spat bits of chewed carrots his way as she ate, as she talked. Her work was "poetic film," which he didn't ask about because it sounded made up. Tyler didn't know if it was his loyalty to Lulu that made him dislike Mckenna, or the entire strange interaction — why would anyone insist on meeting at a members-only club *of which you were not a member?* — but something was so off-putting about it all that it gave him another dimension into Alex. Mckenna was, the girls assured Tyler, Alex's favorite person. He gushed about her; he worked with her; he called her his best friend. They went on trips together, which Instagram confirmed, photos of them on cobbled European streets or at Burning Man showed a strange kind of dynamic that Tyler couldn't entirely grasp. Will and Rob even follow her on Instagram.

Tyler explained what initially brought him to the subject of Alex's death, the inference of foul play.

"No," Mckenna told him, somehow managing to smoke and eat at the same time. "Alex killed himself. He and I talked about this stuff. He used to get really, really low. That's why I hate all of his friends, you know, because none of them *cared.* I understand it, it's a lot of pressure, coming from successful parents. Everyone expects *you* to be successful, and everyone wants to be friends with you. You have to weed out the people who are actually fun and the people who just want to say they went to your house in Palm Springs."

Tyler nodded. "Why do you think, so definitively, that he killed himself?"

She blinked. "Tyler," she said, putting down a piece of celery, ashing her cigarette. "I just told you. I feel the *same way*, sometimes. It's like, honestly, it's like when rock stars commit suicide. It's the pressure. It's everyone else always putting *their stuff* on you. And you don't understand. In our little community, people like me and Alex, we *are* the rock stars."

She didn't have anything else to say about Alex, except that she'd caught him trying to drown himself in her parents' pool two years ago. "Can you imagine what *The Daily Mail* would have said about that?" When she exited, she left Tyler with the check, which he was unused to among this group of people, he couldn't get a credit card out in time to pay for so much as a piece of gum around Lulu and Maxie. He'd had a glass of water, Mckenna had sucked down half a bottle of rose and eaten a crudité plate by herself. Tyler paid the $122 and walked back to Tribeca.

He was disappointed by her. He'd been hoping that he would find some missing part of Alex in this cherished friendship; what he discovered was vulgarity and deep-seated narcissism. Tyler wondered what they talked about, Alex and Mckenna, why he thought she was so special and different and *amazing*, this girl who made his skin crawl.

"Because she *is* different," Lulu said, handing Tyler a bowl of brown rice and seared tuna. "I mean, think about how different she is from everyone you've met on this project. She's from the same place we are. Her parents' house is on the same street as mine. How do you think I know her so well?" Lulu set her own bowl down on the dining room table and fetched chopsticks. "She's one of those people who got so deeply into her persona at such a young age that she was too embarrassed to do anything about it. And now she's stuck with it." Lulu handed Tyler chopsticks and a cloth napkin, always cloth napkins in her house, cloth napkins and linen dishtowels; paper products didn't exist there. "Alex liked her because, to him, she was honest, and refreshing. Mckenna thinks she's the only person with money in the entire *world*, and it makes her special. Some of us are smart enough to understand that being born lucky doesn't make you anything other than *lucky*; you have to work for everything else."

The nuances of their world were like catnip. Tyler understood how you could get caught up in all of it, wanting it and wanting to be a part of it, in a way he hadn't before. Mckenna and Alex were both the children of billionaires, and, yet, as he ascertained through over a hundred interviews and his own personal research, they were never in one of the three revolving inner circles of *cool kids* from the very place they'd grown up. More than anything, he thought what brought them together was probably the shared camaraderie of being outcasts when everyone believed you should be the belle of the ball.

They'd hit the end of people who were willing to talk to Tyler; Maxie wanted "grown-ups," but Lulu was leaving in a week for a trip with a bunch of other influencers that basically involved them being photographed as collateral for an online retailer, and she maintained that they'd gone as far as they could.

"Anyway, we've spent barely any time in the Hamptons this summer. And I don't think Tyler would want to come. Maybe to your house. But you know my mother doesn't like strangers," she told them from inside her dressing room at Jeffrey's. She peeked her head around the curtain. "Sorry. Not that we're strangers. My mother considers, like, people I've known for five years strangers."

Tyler laughed. "I'm good. You two have done… so much to help me. I would love to get an interview from someone in the family. And I have a few questions about a few things from you… but, maybe tomorrow."

"Don't you want to hear more about Alex? What Alex was *like*? Get a real picture of him for the reader?" Maxie always called Tyler's podcast listeners *the reader*.

"I think he *has* a real picture. Tyler, weren't you just saying you have 98 interviews?"

"I was."

"We should get two more. An even hundred."

Lulu emerged. "What do you think?" She did a twirl. Tyler was fairly sure she was wearing exactly what she'd been wearing before, a white silk slip dress, just without the long sweater and cowboy boots.

"It looks exactly like what you were wearing before," Maxie said.

"It does," he agreed.

She sighed and flopped down into Maxie's chair. "There's still Theo. Maybe 99 is the lucky number. Anyway, Tyler, you tell us, do you have enough?"

Though he had a colorful picture of Alex, it wasn't actually *enough*. The story had always been about an average boy born to an extraordinary family, crumbling under the weight of mental illness. The crime was the rampant disease that ran untreated across America, even in someone as privileged as Alex. The question was what they could do about it, in *theory*. In actuality, the question was what exactly had happened that night, the pieces that didn't fit into place, no matter which way you put them.

He wasn't sure what there was about it all that felt so roughly unfinished, like he'd missed some vital clue to who Alex was and why he'd done it. Tyler said this to the girls as they walked back to their apartment building, Lulu texting the whole way.

"Come by tomorrow morning," Lulu said, rounding on him. "Theo will be waiting." Maxie raised an eyebrow.

Lulu held up her left hand. "Since neither of you have noticed."

A diamond the size of a dime sparkled on her ring finger.

"Oh, my God."

"Congratulations," Tyler told her.

"I never expected you to say yes," Maxie said.

"Me neither."

"Why did you?"

Lulu shrugged, pausing outside of the door to their building. "I feel safe, with him. Like he could protect me against anything. He would never hurt me. And I'm sick of feeling unsafe."

"I know what you mean." They waved to the doormen. "Want to come up?" Maxie asked Tyler.

"I'd actually… like to talk to both of you," he said. "Somewhere private."

"This is fine," Maxie said, motioning to where they stood outside of the elevator. "Go ahead."

"There are a few things from the night of Alex's death that don't line up," Tyler began. They got into the elevator. "Maxie, a diamond bracelet that was identified as belonging to you is in the photos in the bathroom. But it wasn't there when *we* looked."

"Yes, it was," she replied, tartly. "I picked it up right in front of your face, and put it on."

"You've never mentioned it," Tyler said, surprised at her candor.

"Of course not. What is there to say about it? I was in the bathroom; I've said that to you a hundred times. So has everyone else." She shrugged. "The clasp was broken — I've always hated it; I'm always fiddling with it — and when I saw it in the bathroom I just took it. I assumed someone from the police, who came to clean up, would take it, and even though it's horrible it is, like, 4 carats of diamonds. Now I'll probably have it remade into something better. I should think of what."

"You were sitting in an active crime scene, and you took a piece of evidence, with no concern about it at all?" Tyler asked her. The elevator doors opened, and they got out. Lulu let them into the apartment, silent.

"*An active crime scene?* There wasn't anyone there! Not even a real policeman! I mean, Tyler, I love you, but you're not the police. Should *you* have been in there? You were only there because you're, like, best friends with that detective; you said so yourself. And I thought if I wasn't supposed to take it, one of you would have said something to me. You were all in the bathroom with me. I mean, really, if I'd left it there, don't you think *someone* would have taken it?"

"No," Tyler said. "It would have been entered into evidence."

"And then *someone* would have taken it," Maxie said, again. "Plus — it's mine. I can't fathom thinking that I *wouldn't* take it."

"So it ended up over by the toilet because you were walking around on broken glass, when you said your feet were hurting, and the clasp came undone, and the bracelet fell off, and you didn't notice until the next day."

"He hadn't broken *all* of the glass, at that point. I went to sit down on the toilet because my feet *were* hurting, and I was still wearing my shoes. I came in in the first place because Alex was making such a racket, and I was on my way back from Victoria's room to my own. We'd fallen asleep watching Elizabeth Taylor movies, and I was avoiding alone time with Freddie. I heard Alex and went in, and they were all totally useless, well, Yael wasn't useless, she was blathering on about the stitches on his hand. He was acting crazy; I don't think he even recognized any of us. I've *told* you this, Tyler," she said, although she hadn't, not at this level of detail. "And Will and Rob were telling me I should just go. *Then* he broke a big thing of bath salts in a crystal decanter — such a waste, it was probably a hundred years old — and I was like, ugh, I have to go." She sighed. "I can't believe you've been sitting on this for *months*, thinking I had some sinister purpose in all of this. You have a dark mind, Tyler, I'll tell you that. You wouldn't trust anyone, I suppose. That's probably what happened to your marriage," she added, easily, not meant to hurt but to inform.

"Maxie," Lulu admonished.

“That explains why Maxie was out of her room,” Tyler began. “But why were you?” he turned to Lulu.

“I wasn’t. At least, not that I remember.”

It was a hedge. “Adam, one of the groomsmen, saw you entering Alex’s room.”

“Adam wouldn’t be able to pick me out of a line up if I had a nametag on,” Lulu answered. ’

“He also saw you having an argument with Alex in the kitchen earlier that day—”

“Yeah, we were fighting over who got the regular Tate’s and who had to take the gluten free.” Lulu laughed. “*Sinister* certainly is the word for that. I do feel bad that I took the regular ones. The gluten free leave stickiness in your mouth.”

“Adam said that he saw Alex getting violent with you,” Tyler pressed.

“Oh, my God, doesn’t Will have a single friend in the world besides that walking Jack Skellington? Adam is an idiot. ’You *know*, you know, right, that Adam didn’t like Alex. He tried to sue the Sables over *Adam* passing out drunk. I wouldn’t rely on him as a credible source.” Lulu shook her head again.

“What else?” Maxie asked. “What have you been holding back? Honestly, I’m flattered that you thought we were capable of it.”

“I am, too,” Lulu murmured. “It’s almost like calling us courageous.”

“I don’t think murder is courageous,” Tyler replied. “The other things… I don’t know if you could answer them. How his watch broke before the water got in, three hours *after* he was dead. How he took enough drugs to knock out anyone of his weight, but he was still awake to cut his wrists. Why the cuts were the deepest on the left side, even though he was left-handed. Why you hesitated, that first day, when I asked you about the Valium. And why some of you say Rob gave Alex the Oxy and some of you say Alex gave it to Rob.”

“I was weird about the Valium because I was worried Yael might have prescribed it to him, and I didn’t want to get her in trouble,” Maxie told Tyler. “He could be pretty convincing. I asked her about it later and she said *of course* she hadn’t, so that was just me being overly-cautious.

I don't know for sure who gave who the Oxy, and I doubt Lulu does, but Alex had a tendency to tell different people he'd gotten drugs from other people, so that he wouldn't have to share, which is probably why the stories aren't the same; we never heard them the same."

"And the cuts?"

"That's more your wheelhouse than ours," Lulu said. "Look, if you really think it was a murder, *go* to Mr Sable. I'll set you up with him. He'll spend endless time and money helping you pursue this."

"His lawyer swooped in the first day we met you. Got all of you out of there before we could even talk to you," Tyler said. "I don't think he would help."

"I'm sure Mr Sable would listen to someone who had real evidence of a murder. The question is if you *do*. Because if that's all there is…" Maxie spread her hands, her gigantic engagement ring winking in the light.

"I've got to change for dinner," Lulu said, apologetically. "But, seriously, Tyler, we're happy to answer whatever you want to ask us. I would think you would have figured it out by now, but… we want to help you. I wouldn't have done… *all of this* to help you if I didn't actually care about what you're doing." She got up.

"We should go," Maxie said. "Want to come upstairs? Magda made dinner." Magda was the nanny that Maxie had prematurely employed. "I want to talk to you about doing a podcast. Talking to victims of sexual harassment and abuse."

They went out into the hallway, got on the elevator.

"You don't listen to podcasts," Tyler said. "Why sexual harassment and abuse?"

"Why not?" Maxie asked, and her eyes on his face were even and still. "I can't believe Lulu's engaged," Maxie said. "To *Theo!* Of all people. He's so much more boring than everyone else she's ever dated."

"I understand," Tyler said. He did. Lulu turned heads every single place they went, even when he was sure no one knew who she was. Men stared, sometimes looking at him like *how can a guy like* you *get a girl like* that*?*

"I do, too," Maxie replied, quietly. She shoved a key into her door. "I just never thought they would get Lulu, too. The eternal optimist. Scared out of her mind to the point of marriage."

He opened his mouth to reply; Maxie's brow furrowed, the door was unlocked. She swung it open.

"Hello, lovely wife of mine," Freddie Golden said. "Thought I'd come to see you and the offspring." He reached out for her stomach.

Tyler was expecting a dramatic reply, but Maxie simply dropped her keys on the counter and moved away from him. "Magda let me in."

"Tyler, this is my husband. Freddie, this is Tyler."

Freddie Golden shook Tyler's hand. His name was fitting, muddy hazel eyes stared out from under a mop of golden curls.

"I'm a huge fan," Freddie said. "That episode about the judge? I think about it, still."

"Thanks," Tyler replied. "I should go."

"No," they said, at the same time.

"If you go, Maxie'll probably kill me."

"I still might," Maxie told him. "But this way Tyler can report it live for *Crime and Question*."

Tyler left the Stein-Goldens after a very uncomfortable early dinner. Freddie walked out with him, he was staying at the Greenwich Hotel, despite his wife's three-bedroom apartment.

"I hate this. Everyone tells you not to get married young. Everyone's right."

Tyler nodded. "Believe me, I know." Maxie had revealed his own romantic situation over the burrata and breadstick portion of the meal. "Are you here to work things out?"

Freddie shook his cherubic head. He was short and particularly boyish-looking; Tyler couldn't imagine that he was the same age as Maxie. "No. I'm here to try to make a deal with her. She won't divorce me until she can get a good chunk of money from the pre-nup. That's almost a year from now. I want to be able to live my life, you know? I started seeing someone, and I can't meet her parents until I can say *I'm divorced.* We've gotta work this out."

"What will you do about the baby?"

Freddie looked up at the entrance to his hotel. "You know, she didn't even tell me she was pregnant until she was like halfway along. And, I don't know. My mom keeps suggesting it's not even mine; that Maxie had an affair, and that's why she's been acting like a lunatic since February. You want a drink?" he asked. Tyler shook his head.

"I don't think Maxie's the type for an affair," he told Freddie. "Based on the past month, she seems to spend most of her time with Lulu, and other pregnant moms in her building."

"Whatever she's going through, she's made it very clear that it's not my problem, and I'm fine with that. I would've been happy for her to work, or whatever. Whatever she wanted to do. I just didn't think it would matter so much, living in Chicago versus living in New York. I still don't think it does; I guess it just does to her. You sure you don't want a drink? I've got an hour to kill."

Tyler shook his head and left Freddie there with his killable hour, with the girl whose parents he wanted to meet, with the baby he didn't care about. There was something about the rolling, arrogant way that he walked, and the fact that he was already dating someone else that made you know he was never right for Maxie. It seemed so stupid that something like a city was breaking them up, but then it seemed so stupid that they hadn't figured it out before they got married. It seemed so stupid that you picked someone to be your forever person and agreed to live their life with yours when you could never imagine what their life would turn out to be.

Tyler

Theo, like Freddie, looked prematurely youthful, like he was too young to vote, let alone be sliding a massive diamond ring onto the finger of his beloved. He was short, shorter than Maxie's husband, blue-eyed and black-haired. When he excused himself to take a call, Tyler turned to Lulu.

"I know," she said, immediately. "He looks like a smaller version of Alex."

"A lot like Alex."

"They *are* cousins." She'd made flax seed waffles for the occasion. "He's very different. A lot more controlled."

Theo emerged from the guest room and slid into his seat. "So. What can I tell you about my cousin? From what Louie's told me, you already know a lot about him."

"I'll leave you to it," Lulu said, giving Theo a kiss. "I'm gonna go see Maxie." She smiled her reassuring smile at Tyler, like a mother to a child about to give a school presentation, and closed the door gently behind her.

"If you can talk a little bit about what he was like, growing up with him, if you saw any signs of depression, any indication that he would do something like this…"

Theo nodded as he chewed, chewed as he nodded. It was clear that he didn't want to talk to Tyler, but Lulu had cajoled him into it, and now here he was, trying to kill time with his cardboard waffles.

"Did you ever meet Alex?"

Tyler shook his head.

"He was an… up-and-down person. A person of extremes, I guess. I'm the oldest of my family, so Alex was like an older brother to me. I saw him get seriously fucked up, like, at a level that I think most people don't even approach in their lifetime. And that's probably not a sign that everything is great with someone. But he was never an emotional person.

He never talked to — any of us, I guess, about what he was feeling. Or even what he was thinking." Theo took another bite of his waffle, dunking it twice in the cacao chip syrup. "When I was little, Alex was always getting in trouble in school. I have the most distinct memory of my parents talking about it one night, when they thought I was asleep. My mom told me that Alex was all the worst parts of his father, all of the dark corners. You know, we didn't grow up like this. It wasn't until I was nine or ten and Alex was about to start high school that our parents started making real money. I think that changes you, too. That was when Alex started to cause trouble. Almost like he knew he could get away with it."

"What kind of trouble?" Tyler asked.

"He was always getting into fights with people, or having weird things with girls."

"How were the girls causing him trouble?"

"Just — talking about him, saying he'd done less-than-polite things to them, that kind of thing. I honestly don't know, and I don't want to talk about it. I don't even know how I got on that subject," Theo told him.

Tyler nodded. "So… did you feel like he was emotionally troubled, towards the end? Was his behavior abnormal? Did he ever speak about suicide with you?"

"No. He wouldn't have, even if he'd been planning this for years.' He always seemed like Alex to me, although I don't think Alex was ever normal."

Tyler nodded again. "What's your last memory of him?"

"He was standing on the other side of the table, by the edge of the trees. He'd taken off his jacket, and his bow tie was untied. He was playing with the sparklers they'd brought out with the cake, letting them burn to his fingertips and then dropping them in the grass and stomping them out. When we were walking up to the house, I turned around and I could see his blurry outline against the trees, his white shirt and the sparklers moving through the air. There were trailing lights that I thought were fireflies, but Maxie said it was too early in the summer." When Theo looked up at Tyler his eyes were full. He was the first person who'd even begun to shed a tear over Alex's death in front of Tyler, and he suddenly felt sorry that he'd asked Theo to do this.

Tyler opened his mouth to say something, but Theo stopped him. "I think that's the most I can talk about this."

"Thank you," Tyler said. "I'm sorry about Alex. From everything I've learned about him, losing him seems like a real loss."

"It's the strangest thing," Theo said, "but I almost wasn't surprised. When it happened."

He should have felt a release, a relief, some kind of closure, *finally*, his questions answered, the story explained. How easy and simple it all seemed when you had a picture of who Alex was. How easy it could be if you could let it.

Part VII
Maxie
May 15th, 2017

Maxie's total weight gain, thirteen weeks in, was four pounds. The doctor said it was unhealthy. Maxie said *the whole thing is unhealthy*. She thought it would be one of those things, like moving to Chicago, that you decided on, and that made it okay. She thought once she decided it was okay, the feeling of what he'd done to her would go away. It didn't go away; none of it went away. The only thing that went away was her goddamn husband, who she was starting to suspect was having an affair. She hadn't told Freddie she was pregnant yet; she was going to have to, sooner rather than later, and tell everyone else, too, and pretend to be excited about it, and take the Instagram holding her stomach, and let people throw her a shower, and do all of the things you were supposed to do.

Maxie met with a lawyer in Chicago, the city her husband made her move to so that they could spend no time together. She wasn't even sure what Freddie actually did. She wasn't even sure it mattered.

The pre-nup they'd signed fell into her favor now that she was pregnant. It used old-fashioned language like *give Frederic a child, or children.* It never specified that she had to give her husband his own child. If she could hold on for a year after the baby was born, she was entitled to enough money that she wouldn't be entirely reliant on her parents again. She would be free.

Maxie could hold on for a year after the baby. Maxie could do anything. That was one thing Alex Sable had taught her, Maxie had the ability to withstand *anything*. She was going to get what she wanted; she was going to have her own money; she was going to do whatever she wanted. Freddie would have to deal with it. Freddie would have to divorce *her*. She sat in the uncomfortable leather chair across from Michael Greenstein, Esq., and felt a smirk unfurling across her face. Rich parents gave their sons drawing accounts to live their lives and their daughters credit cards to monitor their lives. Maxie would finally have her own money, her own life, no more waiting for her father to fall over and die, already, and leave her the trust she'd felt like she'd earned from being the child of her parents.

Freddie was home when Maxie got there, home hugging her in a way that said *I notice you've gotten fat* and asking what was for dinner. She told him she'd already ordered food even though she hadn't; her pregnancy dinner was a container of cottage cheese, which she'd never eaten before, consumed with an ice cream spoon while watching *Law and Order, SVU.*

She ordered Thai food because Freddie didn't like it. She set the table with the silver they'd gotten for their wedding and the plates that cost $300 each and the crystal candlesticks from Tiffany's. She gave herself a sharper knife and poured Freddie a big glass of wine and watched while he tasted things and shook his head. She took too big of a bite of a spring roll and dabbed the grease delicately away from her face and smiled at him.

"Freddie," she said.

"I'm gonna order something else," he told her. "I don't like Thai."

Obviously, she knew he didn't like Thai. She'd been with him for so long she knew what he liked and disliked better than she knew what *she* liked and disliked. She'd forgotten, in all the years of living life *for* Freddie, of making sure that Freddie had what *Freddie wanted* so that Freddie would slap the giant rock on her finger and make her a *Mrs*, what Maxie Stein wanted to eat or do or wear or be.

Now she remembered. Now she knew. Alex Sable made her remember, shoved it down her throat and inside of her until she couldn't breathe or sleep or think. This baby made her remember. She had a choice, her therapist told her. She could make the baby her own, or she could let the baby be Alex's.

Nothing was Alex's. Nothing was Freddie's. It all belonged Maxie. It was hers. She would take it back until she was taking what didn't belong to her but what she knew was her due, for what she had earned.

"I know," Maxie said.

"Then why did you order it?" Freddie asked. He didn't look at her; he was already scrolling through Postmates.

"Freddie," she began again, "you've basically spent the entire first year of our marriage traveling."

"We haven't been married a year, yet. It's a year in September."

Yes, thank you. I was there, too.

"No, but—"

"We had that month-long honeymoon."

"Since then. You're barely home."

Freddie shrugged and bit into a spring roll, taking his time to answer. "You're never here, either. I didn't think it bothered you."

"*I'm* never here because *you're* never here. I want to live with my husband."

"Maxie," he said, calmly, putting his napkin down on the table. "I don't know how we could live together more than we do."

"You could live in this godforsaken place that you forced me to move to!"

Freddie shoved his chair back. "Well you could spend some fucking time with my *family* while you're here."

Freddie's family was irrelevant, other than them choosing to live in a cultural desert in the middle of the country. Maxie was never going to spend any time with them, because they were bumpkins who bragged about their country club and lived, much to her horror, *in the suburbs.*

"Your family isn't you. I didn't move here for your family," she told him, calmly.

"Well, I did."

Maxie stood up from the table. "Okay. Let me put this to you in terms you understand. I am taking my baby," she put a hand on her stomach, "and my*self* to New York. Where we are going to live. You're welcome to join us there, but I'm not spending one more second here."

"Is this seriously your way of telling me you're pregnant?"

"Yes," she said, taking the keys to the car she never drove out of the bowl. "It is."

She picked up her purse from the front hall and she and the baby walked out of the door. Freddie didn't try to stop her, probably because he was busy figuring out what he was going to order for dinner, or making plans with his family, or working *so hard* for his *father*, or having the affair she assumed he must be embroiled in, or just generally being one of the top five most selfish people known to man.

Maxie very shakily drove herself to the Four Seasons, where she ordered herself and her baby a bacon cheeseburger and watched *Nocturnal Animals*. It was violent and cruel, and she felt better after seeing it, less guilty and less angry and less sad and most of all less alone, because she wasn't alone, there in her hotel room; she had the baby. She would never be alone again.

The next morning, they left the car for Freddie at the valet, landed at Newark, and moved into Lulu's second bedroom. She went up to her parents' to get all the documents she could find about her trust, withdrawing from it, how it worked, which she'd asked about but never bothered to actually learn. Her mother dithered over her clothes and her split ends and the smattering of pimples across her nose, asked what was *wrong* with her, told her not to take anything from her father's study. Maxie walked out with four huge folders and told her mother that she was pregnant as she got into the waiting cab. Everything seemed so impossibly hard until you actually did it. Once it was done you couldn't imagine that life was anything different, before.

Yael
April and May 2017

Will's case in New York closed, and suddenly he was here. Knocking on Yael's door at 10 PM and 2 AM and 9 AM on weekends. He complained about Philadelphia. He complained about having no friends and getting his tux altered. Yael's mother used to describe the women in their neighborhood as *going to seed*; Will had gone to seed. There were dark hollows under his eyes that seemed emphasized by the fleshiness around his neck. He was suddenly losing his hair, or maybe it was just that he seemed so defeated, it gave him the appearance of hair loss. 'He ate guacamole from Trader Joe's out of the tub in her fridge with a spoon.

He didn't talk about Jessica. He didn't ask about Yael. He didn't want to know about her family or her friends; he was surprised that she had friends in Philadelphia. *Who has friends in Philadelphia?* He asked her. *People who live here*, she told him. It was strange because Jessica and Will were no longer a connected entity in Yael's mind, and maybe also in reality. She wanted to ask if Jessica wondered where he was and where Jessica was but most of the time Instagram stories told her that Jessica was in New York or Palm Beach.

Yael diagnosed his constant consumption — of content, of food — as unhappiness. She diagnosed his need to be with her as loneliness. She was starting to feel like she was dating a shade of Will's former self, a version of him who somehow got pushed off onto the wrong path and stayed there. He wanted to move from corporate law into criminal law. He didn't just want to sleep with her, he wanted to talk to her, but he didn't want to talk about anything that could belong to either of them. They talked about the president and Russia and advances in medical technology and the cases Will was working and the patients Yael was seeing. They talked loops around their real lives; they talked like the only people they knew in common were Maxie and Lulu. One night, Yael mentioned Victoria and he shuddered like he'd swallowed something cold and slimy and got up out of bed to splash water on his face. Sometimes she could see edges of the person she thought she'd fallen in love with, this person who was idealistic and smart and serious and straightforward, but usually those slipped out of sight, sinking back into the churning sea of who he currently was.

She didn't know what to do or who to tell. She started keeping cookies in her apartment, and Babybel cheese, and dried fruit, the things he liked to snack on no matter time or place. Some nights she woke up to find him awake and staring at his screen, eyes blurring together in the blue light, reading about rapists or Chris Newman or annulments. He never drank in front of her, but she suspected that on nights when they didn't see each other he drank enough to make up for it.

Some days Yael began to feel as though he really was her boyfriend, they really *did* live together, and they had been together for so long that what was left between them was monotonous and disheartening. She had been happier sharing a space with Abraham, who she didn't love, than experiencing Will fall apart in front of her. She wanted him to slide back into his skin, find his soul again and inhabit his body once more, but as she watched him watching the news obsessively or errantly finishing a box of Triscuits, she felt a realization dawning that maybe this had always been Will, and she had missed it. You could never really know someone past what they let you know.

One night, Yael ordered in pasta and took a shower and changed out of her scrubs into real clothes instead of pajamas. She locked the door so that he had to knock and opened it for him in a way that reminded him that this 700 square-foot apartment was hers, not the palatial two-bedroom place he lived in with Jessica. His eyebrows contracted when he saw her, but he didn't say anything other than *pasta.* She watched him eye the plates and the take-out containers neatly spread across the table; she watched him inhale a little bit of strength for whatever she was about to set out before him. He pulled his chair out and sat down. She poured him a glass of wine.

"How was your day?" Yael asked, serving herself penne with a pair of salad tongs.

Will was already chewing. He nodded. "Good." He swallowed. "Yael," he began, then waited for her to interrupt him. This was something he did a lot; she assumed Jessica interrupted him all the time, so he never had to speak. She waited. He waited. "If this is going to be the night when you confront me about leaving Jessica, I'm really not ready for that."

"It's not," she told him. "This is going to be the night when I decide if I want to continue having a relationship with you that mirrors what an unhappy couple of several years would have."

He absorbed it in pieces, eating, listening, nodding once. "You think that you don't want this."

"I think that I don't want whatever this has been."

"That's surprising," he said, and put down his fork. "I thought, considering you broke up with your boyfriend for me, that you would be happy with whatever I could give you."

"I broke up with Abraham because I cheated on him." Yael ripped a piece of garlic bread in half. "What is it that you think you're giving me?"

"Companionship," he said, so immediately that she knew he'd thought it himself, many a time.

"Companionship," she repeated. The word was too simple and rounded at its edges. He nodded, picked up his fork, ate three pieces of penne. There was a break that indicated the end of the conversation. "I don't want companionship," she said, simply, and she knew immediately he was more annoyed that she had continued talking about this than he was about what she was actually saying. "I don't want companionship from you. I suspended my morals for you because I thought that you were someone I could maybe love. Now I don't think we're compatible enough even for companionship."

Will put his head in his hands. "This isn't happening," he told his palms.

Yael had nothing to say. She speared a piece of mozzarella.

"*You* are not breaking up with *me*," he said.

She looked straight at him until he met her eyes. "I'm sorry," she said.

"This is too weird." He looked around her apartment and back at her. She shrugged at him and tried a little smile. Will dropped his fork again and pushed himself away from the table, standing. "I'm sorry," he said, suddenly, abruptly, looking out of her apartment windows. "I'm sorry I couldn't be better. It's me, isn't it? Something's wrong with me."

"I think you're having trouble making a cohesive picture out of all the pieces of your life," Yael told him. It was a line she'd wanted to say to him for so long that it rolled off of her tongue too quickly, overly-rehearsed. "I think… you may be having a reaction to witnessing what happened to Maxie. It was traumatizing, and Alex is your friend—"

"I'm sorry I couldn't give you companionship," he interrupted, which was a strange thing to say, and then he sort of shrugged at her and walked out the door. She could hear him standing in the hallway, not moving towards the elevator. She hadn't planned to break up with him until he'd sprung it on her and then she knew he wasn't right for her, at least right now. If there were an alternate reality in which he actually left Jessica; if there were an alternate reality in which he hadn't seen what she had seen in New Hampshire; if there were an alternate reality in which he pulled himself together instead of falling apart, maybe they could have been. She could imagine herself as the wife of the man who was marrying Jessica last November; now all she saw was the chalk outline of who he had been.

What he said to her wounded so deeply that she couldn't even feel it; she wondered if she'd gone into shock. She wondered if she'd spent too much time with people like Maxie and Lulu and even Alex Sable, people who laughed at the cruel things that were said to them, at the cruel things *they* said. How lovely it would be to hear someone say *I thought, considering you broke up with your boyfriend for me, that you would be happy with whatever I could give you* and laugh right at them, openly, right into their closing mouth. How daring it would be to live securely within the religious fervor of your own entitlement, to know unequivocally that you were better than everyone else, to be able to laugh at the things people said that were meant to leave blood on the floor.

Whatever I could give you. What could he give her? When they were peers, mere months ago, he had given her something like hope, a belief that there was more to love than the kindly camaraderie that existed between her and Abraham. Now he was damaged beyond repair, which was his own fault, really, for picking up shiny things without knowing what they might do. They all spent so much time dismissing Rob that they skated right over Will and his average background, did a double axel around the fact that *he* was friends with Alex for a reason, a reason that certainly wasn't friendship, at least not by the time they had congregated at the house in New Hampshire. Call it nostalgia or loyalty or maybe call it what it was, the naked fact that someone like Alex could be a useful friend, that someone like Jessica could be a useful wife. These people were terrified of being used because it was the first instinct of anyone beneath them, even if they couldn't admit it to themselves. Even if, like Will, they couldn't admit anything at all.

Will had sat there in her very kitchen, at this very table, saying *that you would be happy with whatever I could give you*. What he had given her was a courtside seat to his own disillusionment with everything he cared about, his friends, his fiancée, the law, justice, right vs. wrong. He'd watched it shatter within his own actions and then there was nothing left for him.

Will
May 2017

Yael met him in the Starbucks across the street from her hospital. Will couldn't remember the last time he'd been in a coffee place like this, one that didn't have the faux-local vibe of a La Colombe. As he ordered his coffee and didn't drink it and thought about this, it grew on him that this mattered, this was the evidence he'd been searching for while he sifted through the sands of his life to find out how it had happened that he was no longer the person he'd always believed himself to be. Jessica had changed him. Jessica would only go to a place like Starbucks, a place that was too dull to Instagram, under greatest duress. Alex had probably never been to a Starbucks. People like Alex and Jessica had invaded his day-to-day life, his habits, and he'd let them change him. He'd actively changed with them. He'd thought that they were the kind of people he wanted to be with and to be. He thought that where their lives were better his could be better, too. He was adaptable; he always had been, that was why he fit where Rob never could. He had fit. He had found himself snugly in place and then watched it all fade away around him under the light of the rising sun. When he opened the door to that room and saw Alex behind Maxie.

That was what had made him this way, that was what was *making* him this way. The lack of accountability. The complete absence of justice. Finding out that none of it mattered, that people like Will, lawyers in pursuit of fairness, were irrelevant. There was nothing Will could do because Maxie didn't want anything to be done. There was nothing Will could do because Lulu was right, in the dream world that they took down Alex Sable, he would serve, what, two years? Two years in jail, and, in turn, they would destroy their own reputations, because they had all roped themselves to the masthead of this iceberg-bound vessel. They would make an enemy out of Alex, who would return reborn, to haunt them again.

Yael walked up to the table and let out a short bark-laugh, something she'd definitely picked up from Maxie.

"What?" he asked.

"Nothing," she sat.

"Don't you want a coffee?" Will asked.

Yael shook her head. "I don't have time to wait in line, and talk to you. I texted you asking you to get me one," she explained.

"I didn't see it," he explained.

"You replied to it," she crossed her arms. "What's going on?"

Will wanted to put his head into his hands and collapse. Collapse into the kind of shaking, broken tears that seemed to help you, that seemed to help people. Yael was his equal and could have been a person he'd loved and maybe he had loved her, in some mutated way that he thought was worth something. It wasn't worth anything and he wasn't worth anything and what he'd always been afraid of, that he wasn't as good or as special or as smart or as worthwhile as he'd pretended to be, was true. Yael, this girl sitting across from him, staring at his coffee, was proof of that. She'd told him herself.

"I wanted to say… that I'm sorry. For what I said to you. And. For everything that happened. Since I brought you into my life." He wanted to say *I'm not better than you are,* but he couldn't form the words. "I'm sorry," he said again because he was. Sorry for her and sorry for him and sorry for all of them, for this shared sorrow.

"I know," she said, and it was an act of kindness that they both knew he didn't deserve. "I know myself well enough to know what's true and what's not," she assured him. "But I do appreciate you…saying that. I know that it's been difficult for you. This…secret."

Will hadn't known or understood, or maybe just realized that it would eat at you until you couldn't see yourself any more. "I didn't know that it would be like this," he said. Yael looked at him in her hard, clear way and nodded. She had known that it would be like this because she knew about things like rape and abuse and things like dying and death. She knew, she saw them, she understood them, she *fixed* them, but they couldn't really be fixed.

"This is trauma. This is hard. It's hard on everyone. I really encourage you to seek help," she said, in such a bland way that he wanted to put his fork down on her dining room table and leave her apartment all over again. She had broken up with him. Not over Jessica or some moral objection but because he wasn't enough for her, which was the ultimate irony. Once upon a time he thought that she wasn't enough for *him*. Sometimes when his mind scrawled rapid spirals across its surface like this he wondered if this fear of not being enough had been lurking inside of him, or if it was newly realized with adulthood. If you could be an adult when you didn't do the things that you were supposed to, the things that mattered. When people told you that you weren't enough and you believed them, you knew they were right. He knew that she was right.

"It will all be over soon," Yael said. "Everything, even trauma, fades away."

She patted his hand like a doctor. The whole thing was so clinical and condescending that it made him feel worse than he had before and he wished he'd never texted her, never walked into the Starbucks, never bought the coffee he wasn't going to drink but wasn't going to offer her. He had apologized so that she would apologize. So that she would ask for him back and make him understand that they were the same, Will and Yael, they *were* equals, they *did* deserve each other. He deserved someone like her. He was *enough* for someone like her. He felt like he'd been lucky to be with her and he was crushed by the wasted time he'd spent on her couch, moments next to her instead of with her. If he hadn't been a coward it would have been different. If he hadn't been a coward Alex wouldn't be poisoning him, what Alex did to Maxie, what Alex did to all of them. If he hadn't been a coward he would have left Jessica and been with Yael and if he weren't a coward he would leave them both because he didn't deserve them, because he wasn't *enough*, because in the end nothing that he did held any weight, and once you knew that, once you comprehended it, there was no forward for you. There was nowhere for you.

Lulu
May 2017

Max came back from three weeks in the Middle East. He had two good stories, and he was almost too excited to write. He wanted to see Lulu, but really he wanted her to prepare a feast for him while he wrote his vital *New Yorker* pieces. She felt like Grace Kelly at the beginning of *Rear Window*, right down to the shitty apartment. Sometimes Lulu derided herself for wondering how much money Max's family *actually* had left, because it was none of her business. Even if Max had no money, her parents would take care of them. Her trusts would take care of them. The money she made from collabs and sponsored posts and Revolve trips would take care of them. Except that Max gambled in a way that made her a little nervous. But she hadn't *decided* on Max, and, moreover, he hadn't exactly decided on *her*. He'd met a fat-faced blonde girl on assignment, and Lulu stalked their every Instagram interaction with Maxie leaning over her shoulder, pointing out her flaws *thin hair, face that already isn't aging well, weird body — look at that*, the way she dressed *so that you'd be uncomfortable to look at her, but not at all fashionable*, the lack of information about what school she'd gone to, the fact that she claimed to be an actress/producer but had 3200 followers and only shorts on her IMDB. Maxie's exquisite picking apart of this girl made Lulu more nervous than anything else, it meant that Maxie thought she was *worth* taking to pieces. She was a threat.

But Lulu, as Maxie reminded her, was marriage material. Lulu had the money and the fame and the pedigree, except that it was her parents' money and Instagram fame, and the pedigree didn't do too well with low-key anti-Semitic Europeans. At one dinner, Lulu heard some of Max's friends hissing that it was so embarrassing to call diapers and diarrhea medicine your fortune. They whispered it in their lovely, dulcet, English-boarding-school-educated tones, and Lulu turned around to smile at them happily. *I do get such a good discount on diarrhea medicine, though*, she told them, and Max had been embarrassed, spiriting her off to stand with him while he smoked his pretentious hand-rolled cigarettes.

Lulu made Max the beautiful dinner, accepted his invitation to a wedding in three days which they both knew he should have asked her to months ago, went and *bought* a dress instead of asking someone to dress her for free. She got her hair and makeup done and they all knew she was the prettiest one in the room, which was why Max puffed up and held her arm in his, which was why the horse-faced girls called her a *kike* within earshot, which was why she smiled at the men when they stared at her. It should have been one of those golden nights, twirling into the fallen confetti, dancing every dance, eating the spongey cake that tasted too much of lemon. Maybe it was; Lulu wasn't sure, her head lolling on Max's shoulder in the car, that he would be enough for her. *Just him.* It was always going to be just him, because she was never going to crack through the frozen exteriors of these old, beak-nosed Brits and Germans and their half-snubs, and the worst part of it all was that she didn't want to. She wanted Max to wave goodbye to them from the deck of the *S.S. Reality*, and come into *her* world, where people could be snotty and rude, but they were never mean.

"We're going to my apartment, you know," he told her.

She nodded. "Maxie's still at mine."

Max made a noise. Lulu lifted her head. "What?"

"I don't like Maxie very much," he told her, looking out of the window. Max thought he could say anything to her because of his accent. That was probably why he'd chosen an American. That and the money. "She's just a bit — selfish and grasping, I suppose. The whole way she's done this move, for one thing." He was wearing his ridiculous Clark Kent glasses that he didn't need.

"I think we're all *a bit selfish and grasping.* I certainly don't know anyone our age who isn't selfish."

"Well, that's an awfully depressing thing to say, Louisa. I hope you have some unselfish friends."

"Maxie's had a really hard year—"

"Everyone's had a hard year. It's 2017. No one's had an *easy* year."

"Well—"

"What's a hard year for Maxie? They sold out of bronzer at Barneys?"

Lulu sat up properly. "That's a disappointingly close-minded thing to say. You never can know what someone's been through."

"Maxie hasn't *been through* anything. She's more sheltered than you are."

"Because *you* live the life of an average person. Half of your close friends will barely shake my hand because I'm Jewish."

"Half Jewish," he said, sharply, raising his eyebrows.

"Winston Churchill was half Jewish. Maybe I should remind them of that, next time."

"Well, so was Hitler."

Lulu drew back in surprise. "So the reason these people dismiss me for my half-Jewish birth is because it likens me to *Hitler?*"

"Don't be absurd. They don't dismiss you."

"It's not absurd, Max. It's the truth, whether you choose to see it or not."

"And you don't *choose* to see the truth about Maxie. What's the worst possible thing that could happen to her? Her parents would somehow lose all their money, and her husband, and her husband's parents, and she'd have to — *gasp!* — get a *job?*" Max chortled. "I hope one day that something actually bad happens to her, so she can know how it feels. Honestly, Lulu, you live such a small life it's terrifying. I'm going to take you on a tour of your Deep South, and then you'll understand."

"Stop the car," Lulu told the Uber driver. "Sir. Stop the car. Pull over, please."

"And now, for the dramatic touch."

"I'm done with you," Lulu told him, opening her door.

Max let his head roll back against the seat. "Honestly, Lulu, I'm too tired for this. Shut the door and let's go."

"Goodbye, Max." Lulu hated that she'd bought a dress for this night. *Why is this night different from all other nights?*

"Suit yourself. See you tomorrow when you calm the fuck down."

Lulu shut the door and walked half a block in the wrong direction, to get away from Max and catch a cab. She was shaking when she got in and she wished for once in her life that she could keep it under control when she got upset. Her phone buzzed, Max. She dropped it into her feathered bag. The strange thing about PTSD or whatever you wanted to call it, this mental virus inside of her that was aroused by the most mundane things, was that it didn't kick into action when you wanted it to. It would have been so nice to feel her body spiraling out of control, here and now, evidence that something significant had just happened to her, but of course Lulu's mind betrayed her. Sometimes she felt like Carlos had existed in another dimension, and her hazy memories of him couldn't be revisited, any more. Since Maxie had been pressed up against Alex Sable nothing else had mattered as muchany more.

Maxie was awake when she got home, sitting up on the couch in dim light, sipping ginger ale and watching *The Postman Always Rings Twice*.

"You're up late," Lulu said, dropping her purse on the kitchen island.

"I thought I felt the baby kicking," Maxie said, hand on her stomach. "But I think it was just me *wanting* to feel the baby kicking."

"That's better than not wanting," Lulu replied.

"So we're moving out, but we're moving in. There's an apartment coming up in the building next month."

"That's the best thing I've heard all night." Lulu laid down on the other side of the couch. "Max and I broke up," she said.

"Good. I never liked him." Maxie took a long sip. "Why?"

"I think I always kind of suspected that he was a disappointing person. I just finally had my nose shoved in it."

Maxie shrugged. "Everyone's disappointing."

They fell asleep to the rising sun. Lulu received two large bouquets of flowers the next day, the ridiculous hatbox roses that last a year. She gave them to the doormen to give to their wives and went to buy an egg-shaped crib with Maxie. There was a part of her that felt crazy but knew unequivocally that he really wanted the fat-faced blonde girl with the hero worship complex who said *fuck* too much and felt like something different and exciting. There was a part of her that had always suspected his family was on the last legs of their money and her family was a good solution, just like it was 1901 and you married to save the roof of your estate. It wasn't 1901 and that was the real problem, for him and for her.

She didn't need to get married, and he had to be calculating about how he dug for dividends in someone else's yard. The worst thing about all of it was that she'd almost suspected it from the start, had this funny loose-tooth feeling that something wasn't quite right. He'd been disappointed by her lack of daring and adventure and excitement. Her life looked so glamorous and large on Instagram, and he'd been led astray just like everyone else. You could make anything look good online; Lulu had parlayed it into a profession.

Rob
May 18th, 2017

The Sables lived on an entire floor of a building on Park Avenue. Rob had spent a decent part of his college life in their apartment, with its fancy art and faceless staff, but he'd never really been comfortable there, something he felt forcibly as he waited while the doorman called up. The apartment door was unlocked, and Rob walked through the silent, cream-colored rooms until he came across a maid who screamed and dropped her basket of laundry.

"Donde esta Alex?"

"I speak English," she said, her voice unaccented. "They're in the family room."

The innards of the apartment were dark, windowless hallways that intersected and sometimes spat you out in the wrong place. It took him two tries to find his way to the family room, where Will and Alex were throwing darts at Will's wedding invitation in silence. No one acknowledged that Rob was there.

"Hey," Rob prodded the emptiness.

Will threw a dart; it pierced Jessica's name. "Hey."

"How's that whole wedding thing going?" Rob asked.

"He has two weeks," Alex said.

"Three," Will corrected him, dropping onto the couch. Alex tossed another dart. Rob loitered in the doorway.

"You're still doing it." Rob said it like a statement. They both knew it was a question.

"I'm still doing it." Will didn't look at him.

"All of it. You're going to go through with it." Rob meant it to be weighty and attention-grabbing.

Will looked up at him, his brown eyes a yellow color that looked reptilian. "All of it."

"When do you get the marriage license?" Rob genuinely couldn't believe that Will would do this, any of it. All of it.

"Tuesday. When I'm supposed to be in court, so I don't know how that's gonna work." Will twirled a dart between his fingers. Alex didn't look at either of them. "She's the kind of person who could change your life. Who *will* change your life. She's the kind of person you would think you would want to be your wife. I don't know if I could find another one of those."

"You mean, if you could bamboozle another unsuspecting girl with decent connections to marry you," Alex said, and laughed. Rob had come to understand that Alex didn't *bamboozle* anyone; he took them by force. He took everything that way.

Rob took a few steps into the room, taking a seat on an ottoman. "I guess you have until Tuesday, then."

"He has until whenever," Alex said, turning to glance at Rob for the first time, rolling his eyes without actually rolling them. "There's this amazing new institution called *divorce*."

No one said anything. Rob was surprised that Alex didn't have a bottle of something pressed between his knees. The darts had all been thrown and there was nothing to say between the three of them except for the obvious admission that they were no longer friends. Whatever it was that kept them together for ten years had rotted beyond repair. Maybe it was loyalty or a sense of duty or a misplaced love, because Rob believed that these people he had chosen at eighteen to eat bad sushi with and cheat on Econ homework together and talk about all the things that matter to you when you're young but think you're old would be the people he did the real-world things with, too. He trusted that the people he picked as his family, his brothers, would be there when everyone else had abandoned him. That he would want them to be there. That having them there would mean something, would be a comfort instead of an endless, slow torment.

They'd run past the expiration date on the side of the carton and were trying to drink the milk anyway. Rob had anticipated some kind of fight or argument or final explosion, a symbol of what they had together, but it was only a dim quiet that mirrored the setting sun.

They ate tenderloin and olive oil mashed potatoes in the relative hush of each other's company. Alex talked enough only to hurl his usual insults at Rob, Rob who wasn't funny or attractive or interesting or fun or at all worth being around. Rob who dated someone so beneath Alex that the mere mention of her was grotesque; Rob who would never be really successful because he didn't have it in him, that feral instinct of kill-or-be-killed. *Robbie'll just be killed*, Alex said in response to a random comment Rob made about a promotion in his office. Rob considered having a fight with him, throwing down the stupid cloth napkin on the table in protest, but he'd done that before, and they both knew it didn't work. *Rob probably won't even be killed. He'll just be run over by a truck, or something.*

"Probably," Rob said, and took a bite of his mashed potatoes. It was funny how he'd believed all of these things had mattered, once, things like being Alex's anointed ones and having someone like Lulu Swanson think you were special. That they could change your life, the way Will thought Jessica could change his life. They were all the same, Lulu and Alex and Jessica, the real anointed ones, the people who lived life with the careless belief that everything would always be fine. They would always have money and people would always be nice and they would always get what they wanted. Rob still wanted to be One of Them in an aching way that made him wonder where the evolutionary need to belong stemmed from. You put your soul up for auction in trade for a place in the pack. It was high-risk, high-return, and he'd been losing at it his entire life.

Will
May 23rd, 2017

Will wasn't sure when it happened that his home was no longer his home, or if it had always been Jessica's home and he was just beginning to notice, but, either way, it wasn't his, any more. It wasn't just Philadelphia, which they both hated and Will stayed in out of a deep resentment toward his bride — a move which began as passive-aggressive, and was slowly morphing into a cause for deep self-loathing. It wasn't just the high-rise apartment, which was so grotesquely anonymous that sometimes Will found himself getting off on the wrong floor and trying the door of an apartment that wasn't his. It wasn't just the careful decorating scheme by Jessica, most of which came from a place called Jonathan Adler that seemed to specialize in bright pops of color and velvet on every surface and lots of lacquer. It was his fiancée. Somewhere in accidentally dating Yael and not coming clean to his wife, somewhere in losing all of his friends and finding himself with only Lulu Swanson to talk to, somewhere in the pornographic viewing of Alex and Maxie, he and Jessica had come to define the term *estranged.* They were an estranged engaged couple getting married in a week.

The day he missed their appointment to get a marriage license, because a hearing ran over and he'd known all long he wasn't going to make it, he was afraid to come home. He loitered at the office; he ate dinner by himself at the hotel bar across the street. He went back to his desk and read *Harry Potter and the Goblet of Fire* on his iPad. He dithered and dallied until he hoped it was late enough that she would be asleep, or too tired to fight, or, maybe, knowing his ingenious wife-to-be, she had figured out a way to get a marriage license without him, because that was just the kind of thing she would do. It used to be the kind of thing he loved her for, the taking care of everything, the never-leaving-anything-to-him, but now he resented it in a way that filled him with the bubbling anger that scared you after it left you.

He walked into the building he didn't like and took the elevator up to the apartment he hadn't picked. She was awake, scrolling through Instagram in long john pajamas that it was too warm for. The lights were very bright, very bright and very white in the living room full of shiny things. She didn't say anything and he didn't say anything and for a moment, while he stood there with the door open and Jessica pretending she hadn't noticed him come in, he had the urge to walk right back out of it and keep walking and walking and walking until he was completely gone. Why hadn't modern life created an app for an easy out from the life you didn't like? An automatic service that completed your break-up and found you a new apartment and quit your job and sent you listings of new positions, that changed your name and your phone number and your email so no one from your past could ever find you again.

"I go to New York tomorrow, and New Hampshire this weekend," she said, bursting through the quiet, and he shut the door. "So I've made an appointment for us to go the Monday after the wedding."

He nodded, which she couldn't see. She didn't turn around. He took a step. "Jessica," he said, and when she did look at him he was surprised to see she hadn't been crying and she didn't look mad. Her face was open and calm, and he realized that this was just what they were, this hushed stillness was simply the state of the union between them. It felt impossible that he had ever loved her for the possibilities she represented to him, a can-opener twisting and leveraging until it achieved results. She was easy to love if you were an easy person, if you wanted what that she did, the trappings of a life instead of the life. He had fallen in love with the idea of what their life could be. It was before Alex hacked into Maxie Stein-Golden's interior and forced him to ask all the questions that he would never be able to unthink and maybe that wasn't even the problem, what had happened, this epic emphasis of his lack of judgment in terms of the people he surrounded himself with. Maybe they had always been two puzzle pieces that you forced together but didn't actually fit, and he was starting to strain where she'd clamped him into place.

"What?" she sighed.

"I have to tell you something." He stayed standing where he was, behind the navy-blue velvet couch that was too uncomfortable to sit on.

"What?" She asked, too innocently, and it occurred to him that she already knew; of *course* she already knew. She was so much smarter than he was — she went to Harvard, for God's sake — and always had been. She'd probably known the night he kissed Yael by the river. She probably knew it was Yael.

"I've been cheating on you," he said, and his voice didn't shake even though he felt like it should.

Her face didn't move at all; she had no reaction. "I think you need to get on a weight loss plan, after the wedding. 'Hypertension runs in your family."

"Jessica," he said again, and he felt like they were having two different conversations, which of course was what she wanted, she *was* having a different conversation; she didn't want to have his. "We're unhappy. We don't love each other. We can't get married." The heft of what he said hit him in the chest, reverberating through his lungs and making him suddenly fearful of what not getting married meant to everyone else.

"Will," she told him, dropping her phone onto the couch, twisting to face him properly, with the almost-annoyed air of a mother who's been disturbed one time too many. "*You're* unhappy. I am not unhappy. I'm unhappy with the way you've *dealt* with your unhappiness, but while we're in Philadelphia, I don't really care. No one here knows or is going to know, and when we move home, you'll get it together."

"I don't love you any more," he said it slowly. "I don't know if I ever did. I don't know if *you* ever loved *me*."

"We love each other as much as anyone can love someone else. And we are getting married in two weeks, and joining our lives together permanently."

Will ran his hands through his hair. "I'm not marrying you."

She stood up, phone in hand, and he'd almost forgotten what a miniature person she was, how diminutive and childlike. "You will not *ruin* my life, the ten years I've wasted on you, embarrass me in front of *everyone,* make me the center of malicious gossip. I have *killed* myself for this life. I have killed myself for *our* life, for us, for *you.* We are getting married in two weeks if I have to drag your cold, dead body down the aisle. I'm done with this conversation."

Jessica walked into their bedroom and shut the door, leaving him in all that bright, white light, looking at his own reflection in the glossy windows. He didn't know what to do next and he didn't have the strength to do whatever it was, so he laid on the uncomfortable couch and closed his eyes. When he woke up two hours later he couldn't believe he'd fallen asleep at all.

Part VIII
Tyler
November 2017

It was the nicest hospital he'd ever been to. Maxie was in a private room that was roughly the size of Tyler's apartment. Lulu sat on a chair, Theo fed the baby from a bottle, and Maxie reclined in bed. She greeted him with too much energy for a woman who had given birth in the last twenty-four-hours. "Tyler! We've missed you!"

He smiled, gave her a kiss on the cheek which he was nervous to dispense, asked where everyone was.

"I sent my parents' home, like, an hour after the baby was born. Freddie isn't here; we had a little confusion on the due date," she said, and Tyler had the distinct impression that the *confusion* was deliberately created by Maxie. "My friends are dropping in all day. Which is why I told Lulu to call you. You spent so much time with pregnant me."

"I did," Tyler murmured, circling over to Theo in the rocker. "Can I see the baby?" Theo held it up for Tyler as best he could.

"Say *hi, Uncle Tyler*," Theo cooed. They looked up at him together, Theo and the baby. Tyler took a step back without realizing it, hitting into the edge of Maxie's bed. The baby could have been Theo's own, dark hair, dark blue eyes, the same exaggerated, handsome features of Alex Sable.

Tyler looked from the child to Theo to Lulu and the moment he saw her face he knew.

It felt like an anvil smacking him over the head, what Theo had said about Alex's trouble with girls, Maxie wanting to do a podcast about the abused and harassed. The way Maxie listened when people spoke about Alex, almost hopeful, like there were good parts of him that made it into their child. How Freddie didn't care about the baby, and she didn't care about Freddie caring about the baby. The change Freddie said had come over her, *acting like a lunatic since February*.

"Theo?" Maxie asked. Theo got up and returned the baby to her.

"Time for coffee?" he asked. "Tyler, what can I get you?"

Tyler said he was fine. The girls put in their orders and Theo strode out the door and after a beat of silence Tyler spoke again. "I want to talk to you," he began. He allowed himself to appreciate the fact that he was treating Maxie more delicately than he would anyone else; he oscillated between needing to assert his journalistic integrity and wanting to proceed with caution. "I know," he told them.

"You know…?" Maxie sipped some water from a straw.

"*I. Know.*"

Neither of them said anything.

"I'm not recording," Tyler said.

"Fine." Maxie sat up as best as she could. "What do you *think* you know?"

"Maxie," he said, and when her face remained still he decided to shock the truth out of her. "That's Alex's baby," he didn't say it as calmly as he wanted to.

Lulu edged closer to the bed, to the baby. Lulu looked at Maxie and Maxie looked at Lulu and he could have sworn he saw Lulu give the tiniest nod. "Can I trust you, Tyler? Can *we* trust you? Trust you in a forever-and-always way."

Tyler hesitated. There was an implication underneath her words of an accord being struck that he wasn't sure he was ready to make.

"Yes," he said, simply.

"Yes," she said, simply.

Tyler dropped into a chair. "From what Theo said, Alex had problems with girls. I thought …" They were a few weeks outside of the Harvey Weinstein revelations, and he didn't know how to phrase it without sounding like he was pushing her to share something personal and painful. Maxie looked at him in a knowing way that was too old on her youthful face. "Can I ask?"

Maxie nodded. "If it was consensual? It wasn't."

"So Will thought Alex did it. Alex was the rapist, all those years ago, not Chris Newman," Tyler clarified. "That's why he said that to me, planted that little seed about Chris maybe not being guilty."

"We'll never know what really happened. None of us. And now the only two people who would know are dead," Lulu said.

"It doesn't matter, though," Maxie told him, shifting the baby in her arms, "because, in the end, even if it was Alex, he kind of got what he deserved, don't you think?"

"Why did you help me with this, then?" Tyler asked them, still seated. "After what he did. To you."

Maxie's eyes were bright and shiny. "A lot of different reasons that you couldn't understand," she said. "Primarily because I thought it would make me feel better. To know that my child's father wasn't *just* a monster."

"Did it help? All of this." He had to ask.

"Of course it helped," Maxie told him. "It helped just being around someone like you."

He stood up slowly. Theo came in and Lulu ushered him out immediately, murmuring into his ear.

Tyler looked at the empty room, at the space between him and Maxie. "It was funny," Tyler began, walking towards Maxie, just a step. "Theo told me that Rob gave Alex the Oxy. No one ever mentioned to me how it was that Alex was practically carried up to his room under the supervision of three people, but he managed to take a knife from the table."

"He probably dropped it into a pocket," Maxie replied.

"Even Yael said she was surprised he had been lucid enough to slit his wrists."

"I'm surprised Alex lived as long as he did," Maxie told him, evenly, unmoving.

"No one ever mentioned that Rob was in *Will's* room; they referred to it as *Rob's* room. Everything had an answer, although I never got a real solution to how he had enough drugs in his system to sedate someone who weighed 100 pounds more than he did, but he still cut his wrists, cut his left arm so deeply he severed the artery, even though he was left-handed. Even you couldn't explain that," Tyler said, looking down at the baby's face.

"It would be too neat, if you could explain *everything*, wouldn't it?" Maxie asked him.

"It would be funny if, all along, I was right. If this *was* a murder, and you and Lulu swooped in so helpfully to throw me off the scent." Tyler tried to peer into her face.

"Does Lulu strike you as the murdering type?" Maxie asked.

"There were only four cuts. Jagged, uneven cuts."

"Anyone could make four cuts. Including Alex."

"But anyone isn't holding Alex's baby," Tyler replied.

"When the Puritans came to New England, they killed rapists. Funny, for a society that declared women the obedient servants of their husbands. Only if there were witnesses, of course. *Of course* you had to have witnesses. Who would trust the word of a woman?"

"Plenty of people," Tyler said, quietly.

He waited. She watched his face for a reaction, wasn't sure she saw one, opened her mouth again. "Not enough people," she told him, her voice low. "It doesn't matter. Nobody needs to know. Nobody ever will, now." She looked up at Tyler."

They were quiet for a moment. The baby was quiet. Tyler expected her to look different but of course she was the same. He wasn't sure if she was telling him what had happened or something else. He wasn't sure he could ask her to clarify, and he wasn't sure he wanted to know, either way. "No," he agreed, finally. "Nobody ever will."

Tyler

It always happened after Tyler finished a case that he slept. Not average, every-night sleep, he fell into the slumber of someone returned home after an odyssey. It wasn't the end of a case, but it felt like *something*, something true, which was a real end to the story he'd cued up from his listeners, who would only hear the version he'd given them, a sad tale of a bright young man who took his own life.

Tyler woke 22 hours later to his half-empty apartment with the gaps in the dust to remind him of what stood there once, the bar cart of his soon-to-be ex-wife, her record player, her coffee table books. He steeped in the coldness and the whiteness of the walls, and when he tried to turn his thoughts to something else, they came back to his divorce, which brought him right back to Maxie. Divorce, as it turned out, was easy if you weren't rich and you didn't have anything to divide except for the Ikea furniture you'd bought together. His wife couldn't have what she wanted back, the hours he spent in the studio or researching a story, forgetting, almost, that he had his own life to live, and no number of Billy bookshelves, extra-large, was going to make up for the person she became when he found his semblance of success, cold and empty, like the apartment.

He didn't know whether Maxie had done it the right way, building a new life for herself instead of living alone in the old one, or if there wasn't a right way because Maxie was still claiming that her pre-nup had been signed *under duress* to get the money to never have to ask anyone for anything again. Either way, Tyler supposed that the right way was to find someone you knew how to love no matter the circumstances of each other's lives.

The worst part about all of it wasn't the divorce. The divorce was an afterthought in a life lived in pursuit of other people's stories. It didn't matter whether you had spent five years with someone you loved or someone you thought you loved. It didn't matter that you woke up knowing you had to start again, find a new lead, hit the record button, go to parties with people you didn't know, ask for phone numbers, *begin again*. It didn't matter because Tyler couldn't or maybe just wouldn't start over. There was a part of him that came into being with *the girls*, with Alex Sable, a part that he could not cut out of himself, leave in a box for Goodwill, drop into the trash can on the corner. These people now existed in the knotted strings of his thoughts in a way that felt unshakable. They clung to his consciousness like seaweed matted onto your feet in the ocean, tangled in your toes and tugged you down, into the sea.

He went to a picnic one of his co-workers had invited him to, an event based around some artist's water show near the Brooklyn Bridge. When he arrived, he regretted being there and regretted being divorced and regretted that he still wasn't back to being him. It was very hot, and the grass was dismally scraggy and everyone near him seemed to be milling around the tables with buzzing excitement that Tyler didn't think was necessary for a Saturday afternoon.

When he saw Theo, he felt himself exhale a little, and when he saw Lulu, he almost relaxed completely.

She laughed. "I told Theo that the only person I knew in Brooklyn was you," she said, and he felt people staring at them again, which he had somehow forgotten in their few days apart. She gave him a real hug and said something about him being a horrible texter, now that they were done with the story, and he sort of shrugged at her and looked away.

"Tyler," Lulu said, and it was a serious *Tyler*, weighted and deliberate. "What's wrong?" She took his arm and towed him to an empty table and sat up on the top of it, facing the water. He knew her well enough to know that she was doing this to have their backs to everyone else, to find a margin of privacy and so that she wouldn't have to see them looking at her.

"I still don't know… if there was something more."

She smiled. She watched the water like something was happening. "I guess you have to decide that it doesn't matter. You know us, and we know you. Everything that's happened between us is real. Isn't that what's important?"

"You don't—"

"Do you know that John Dos Passos quote, the one about sleeping in all the beds? I think about it a lot. Sometimes I run through my own version, I'll go to all the parties and run all the yellow lights and climb all the hiking trails and sleep in all the beds. One life is not enough." She looked up at him, leaning on her palms and tilting her chin. "One' life is not enough, or three, or five. What you do is important. You sleep in all the beds. But you need one life for yourself." She stopped. Tyler waited but she didn't say anything. Theo called her name. She turned and waved a lavender-painted hand, sliding the chain of her purse onto her shoulder. She slithered onto the seat part of the bench and then into standing.

When he thought she was gone he turned to check and she turned, too, from the edge of the park, and waved like an old-fashioned film star, like she was genuinely sorry to say goodbye.

One life was not enough for him, and it never had been; that was why he spent his in pursuit of truth and facts and stories and information that maybe, for three forty-minute episodes, would make someone else feel like they'd slept in a different bed.

Part IX
Lulu
June 9th, 2017

They hadn't aired out the house properly; it smelled like dust and cigar smoke. Lulu took the back way down to the butler's pantry. She opened the cabinets she remembered from her youth, the ones that had Annie's Cheddar Bunnies and Ritter Alpine Sport and Tate's, always Tate's, although they only had the kind with walnuts. Lulu dropped them on top of one of the trays of silver for tonight's rehearsal dinner and climbed onto the counter, craning her neck to see the other snacks. They had a Pepperidge Farm sampler, which she knew Maxie could do some serious damage to, and the LU jam cookies that Lulu associated with winter, and an expired box of Petite Écolier. She took the Pepperidge Farm cookies along with the Tate's — who could say no to a good Chessman? Or a Milano? — and looked behind her to check where to put her feet.

Alex stood there, silent, hyaline eyes steady on her in the tiny space. He'd closed the door and suddenly she wished she'd asked Theo to come with her. Lulu jumped off the counter and landed, a bit wobbly, on the side of her foot.

"Fancy meeting you here," he said. He didn't stink of alcohol and that frightened her even more. She stacked the Tate's on top of the Pepperidge Farm sampler and tucked them confidently under her left arm, her right hand resting casually on the tray of Japanese steak knives.

"I was just getting cookies for Maxie. Do you mind if I slip by?" She felt her teeth trying to form into a smile.

"So tell me," he said, and he smelled like cigarettes and Listerine, "how pregnant is Maxie?" He leaned forward so that she was forced to lean backwards against the wooden counter.

"What does it matter?"

Alex hit the cabinet next to her head with the flat of his hand; she heard the quiet rustle of cookies rearranging themselves. "Why won't you tell me? Why won't you reply to my texts? This is important, Lulu. This isn't a sample sale at Intermix."

"Thanks for the update," Lulu said, heart beating too fast. "Maxie's pregnant, everyone knows that; if you want more information, ask her yourself."

"As if she'd talk to me." He framed her head with his arms, pushing his body up against hers.

"I would remind you that I am dating your *cousin*."

"*How* pregnant?"

"I don't know." She looked to the door. "A few months, I guess. Can I get by, please?"

"Lulu," he said, turning her face to face him. "If you want to get serious with Theo, you need to change the way you've been acting towards me."

Lulu arched an eyebrow. "Really. *You* are the determining factor in my relationship."

"Why can't you just be like you were before?" Alex whined.

"Because I have no respect for you. Like all of your family, so—"

She felt it happen instead of seeing it, he smashed her head into the cabinet door and all she could see were stripes of whiteness across his face. She pulled a knife out of the tray and held it up to his nose. "Let. Me. By."

"That doesn't scare me at all," he said, but he shifted his weight. She pushed through, throwing the door open, bringing the knife upstairs with her.

Rob
June 9th, 2017

Rob left cocktails to check on Alex, or so he told Ronnie. In actuality, Rob left cocktails with a stolen bottle of absinthe and a few Oxy's that he'd taken from Alex's mom's medicine cabinet when they had dinner, and wound his way up the grand staircase to Alex's room. Rob knocked twice and opened the door before Alex said *come in*.

"They don't teach knocking in Florida," Alex, in his undone bowtie, remarked. "Your tie looks like the work of a five-year-old. Ronnie do it?"

"Yep. Wanna drink?" He lifted the green bottle.

"Yep."

Alex poured the lurid emerald liquid into two-bathroom glasses, leaving the bottle next to the tub; they cheersed. Rob flopped onto the bench at the end of his friend's bed. "This is hell."

"Which part?"

"All of it." Rob swirled his drink in his glass. "When we were here in February, I thought *maybe I'll break up with Ronnie, and end up with someone like Lulu.*"

Alex held out his wrist and a cufflink to Rob. "And here you are, with Ronnie."

There was a pause of air-conditioned awkwardness.

"You were never serious about Lulu, though," Alex said, looking up at Rob as he buckled on his watch. "I mean, you knew she was always going to end up with someone like my cousin." Scrubbed and freshly showered, with his wild hair combed back and his face beardless, he looked like the sultan of the Upper East Side that he had once been, the kind of person you wanted to know, the kind of person you wanted to be friends with. He looked like the Alex Sable Rob met in their dorm at USC. His dimples matched his eyes and when he smiled they winked at you.

"When did you shave?" Rob couldn't remember the last time he'd seen Alex's clean jawline.

"Just now." Alex tipped back his drink. "We should finish at least half the bottle, before we go down."

"Have you ever taken Oxy?" Rob asked.

Alex laughed. "Yeah." *Yeah. Duh. Who hasn't?*

"A guy at work gave me some, to get through the weekend. He said it feels like you're floating up above everyone, and nothing can pull you down." Rob reached into his pocket and held up a bag of four pills.

Alex's brightest grin unfurled itself across his face. "Robert, I'd underestimated you," he said, holding out his hand. "What's the dosage?"

Rob shrugged. "I don't know. Low." That was a question for a serious drug user, and Rob wasn't even a semi-serious drug user. Alex plucked a pill from his palm and slurped it down with absinthe.

"Sometimes I think you have no taste buds," Rob said. Alex drank alcohol like it was room temperature water." Rob was still holding the pills in his hand and the bag in between his fingers. He dropped the Oxy back into his jacket pocket.

"Come on," Alex replied, flinging the door of his room open.

"Alex," Rob said, rocking onto the toes of his shiny shoes, watching them gleam in the light. "We're friends, right? Real friends. The way we were in college."

"Did the drugs hit you already?" Alex asked.

"Come on," Rob said. His shoes looked too shiny, almost burnished. "I'm serious."

Alex looked from the hallway back into his room, back at Rob. "Sure, Robbie. We're friends."

They both knew it wasn't true and Rob was abruptly grateful that he hadn't taken the Oxy after all. Alex's eyes were all pupil, holographic dark holes that could devour you whole. By the time they got to cocktails everyone was filtering out to the lawn to find their seats on the long table underneath the trees. It was covered in snarls of flowers and twigs and leaves, calligraphed place cards denoting your dining partners for the evening. Maxie's husband, who Rob was morbidly curious about, sat with Landon, Victoria, and Jessica, talking loudly about summer camp, his chair tipped back on two legs. Will was flanked on either side by Lulu and Maxie, all three of them murmuring together and giggling occasionally, while Alex's cousin chatted with Jessica's parents. Yael nodded, long, taffy pulls of disinterest at Adam. The rehearsal dinner had to be at least forty people; Rob wondered vaguely how big the wedding was going to be.

Ronnie was pouting. "We're not seated next to each other," she hissed.

"It's customary not to seat couples together," Maxie told her, politely. "Since you get to see your significant other all the time."

"I've been to a lot of weddings, and they *always* seat couples together," Ronnie replied.

"That sounds like something they would do in the Middle West," Victoria remarked in her bland way. "Are you from the Middle West?"

"It's kind of an institution, at most dinner parties," Lulu put in. "So that you can meet new people, and, if you're not with a partner, you're still included in the conversation, and so on. I'm sure Jessica can move you if you'd like." She smiled. "Although you *are* next to my boyfriend, and I can promise you that he's an excellent dinner partner."

"I *am* an excellent dinner partner," Theo said, ducking into his seat. "I think even the groom can attest to that. I also do well at breakfasts and lunches. But dinner is my specialty."

Ronnie wasn't sure where to look, and Rob was suddenly uncomfortable for her. "Lulu, can you trade with Ronnie?"

"I wanted Lulu to sit next to me," Will said, churlishly. The real wedding party was assembled around him, Maxie and Lulu on either side, Alex across from him with Victoria closing him in, the bride down the table by Theo and Landon, Rob and Ronnie shoved in random places, like stopgaps, next to Adam-the-random-groomsman and Maxie's exiled husband.

"I'll move," Theo volunteered. "No problem."

"Hey! hey!" Maxie's husband cheered. "Camp Ivanhoe reunion!"

"We all went to the same camp," Landon explained, as they fanned out across the table and took their places. "Me, Freddie, and Theo. Although I think Theo was starting his first year there when I had my last."

“I can’t *believe* you went to camp, Landon,” Lulu trilled.

“I always thought camp was for people who had no friends. So they could have summer friends,” Alex said.

“And on *that* note,” Maxie said, standing, raising a glass that could have been a mixed drink or could have just been sparkling water, “let’s toast the beautiful bride and her wonderful husband-to-be. Thank you for bringing us all together to celebrate such a special night.”

Alex got up from his seat and walked over to Rob. “Give me another one,” he whispered, reaching into Rob’s pocket. “I haven’t gotten there, yet.” He popped one or maybe two more pills in his mouth, and Rob wondered vaguely if he should have checked the dosage. “Up, up and away.”

Rob felt a stabbing of something in between his ribs, but it was a phantom sensation.

Will
June 9th, 2017

Will didn't feel like he was at his own wedding. As the setting sun coated the long tables in a dusty violet sheen, as the tinkle of champagne glasses and the light clanging of forks promised that they were making their way through the courses, Will felt himself pulling further and further away. Victoria and Yael played a drinking game with Alex, something complicated that involved place cards and state capitals, which seemed to result in two of them getting very plastered.

It was strange and almost impossible that five months ago they'd sat in the greenhouse, yards away, and argued about who would sit with Adam. Will's mind had focused completely on Yael, and Maxie didn't eat because she wasn't pregnant. Lulu had seemed borderline something and Victoria cried at every meal. Alex and Rob were worse, now, the worst versions of themselves, or perhaps they had stayed the same, after all, and it was Will who'd changed. Will and his cold-blooded bride, who somehow managed to shock him with her calm refusal to break their engagement, who acted like everything was *normal*, who'd planned their honeymoon like they enjoyed spending time together.

Toasts were made; Alex slurred a little, held himself up by holding onto his chair. Lulu Instagrammed dutifully, hashtagging to her many followers, asking other people to text her their photos. After the steak was served, Adam came to say hi to Will and ended up lunging at Victoria in a mortifying manner that resulted in him face down in the grass. They sloshed their way through dessert, the table breaking up and re-forming into smaller groups, as Victoria talked loudly to Will about how much better she was post-break-up.

"But she did say they would always come back, and he *hasn't* come back. I mean, he's dating a 20-year-old. She's still in college. She has to use a fake ID. It doesn't matter, of course, because I'm great. *I'm* great. I-am-great. In the end you know we'll get them all," Victoria told Will conversationally, but it came out as one long string, in-the-end-you-know-we'll-get-them-all.

"Who?" Will asked.

"Men," Yael replied. "She's talking about men."

"This won't be *The Handmaid's Tale,*" Victoria told him. "That's what Jason wanted."

"I don't think that's what Jason wanted," Will replied. Alex swayed in his chair.

"You're right," Victoria said, gulping at her water. "I guess he just didn't want *me*. Isn't that the most impossible thing in the world to accept? That it comes down to you. To *you*, and not the other person. To them not wanting *you*. But it doesn't matter. All those wasted years, he wasted them, too. And I loved him. He *really* wasted them." She hiccupped delicately. "Because he didn't love me."

"Come on," Maxie plucked at the strap of Victoria's pink dress. "I'm exhausted, and you need about a gallon of water."

"What are we going to do?" Victoria asked, twisting her neck up to stare, mouth open, at her friend.

"Eat Toblerone and watch old movies," Maxie told her. Her eyes flicked to Yael's for half a second.

"Can we watch *BUtterfield 8?*"

"I don't know why you like that movie; it's so depressing. But sure."

"Because it's like normal people who have everything in the world they could want and are still unhappy. It's very relatable. That's why it won all the Oscars," Victoria explained, breathlessly.

"I don't think it's relatable for most people," Yael commented.

"We'll come with you," Lulu said, standing up, spilling her purse across the table, French mints and three different lipsticks rolling onto Alex's empty placemat. She gathered it up one-handed, calling for Theo.

"You should stay," Maxie told her. "Don't feel like you have to leave because of me."

"It's late, and we have to be in hair and makeup by 8,30. I'm ready for bed," Lulu replied. She glanced around the table. "Will, will you ask Carol to look out for my little pill box? It's silver and has my initials on it. I think it's fallen into one of these arrangements and I can't be bothered to take the whole table apart to find it."

“I’ll ask,” Yael promised.

“Let’s just look now,” Theo suggested, taking his place at Lulu’s side. “If they don’t find it, and it’s lost forever, you’ll be annoyed.”

Lulu twined her hand in his. “If they don’t find it, I’ll get another one. Goodnight, all,” she blew a kiss to the table.

“Good luck tomorrow,” Theo added, waving widely, like a he was seeing off a steamer.

Will watched their pale figures retreating into the sanctuary of the heavily fallen night. It felt like the end of something, but it wasn’t the beginning of anything else, and that was the most confusing part.

Alex
June 9th, 2017

The surprise of the evening was that Rob, who Alex had lately harkened to Benjy Compson in the internal narration of his life, was correct, he was floating. Just a few inches off the ground, skimming the grass so lightly that no one else would catch on, watching his own head blow up like a hot air balloon and carry him above the softly undulating party dresses and table cloths and fallen flower petals.

Theo waved to him, a pin pricking at the edge of his vision. Alex shook his cousin out of his eyes and watched the moon-faced Icabod Crane leering above him, asking him something. Even through the billowing clouds of Oxy and alcohol, Alex couldn't help but notice that Jessica had seated Adam at the far end of the table, out by Ronnie and the other riffraff who she didn't want *Vogue* to catch a glimpse of. It made him laugh. Maxie was nowhere to be found all evening, always a second or two out of sight, keeping him from what was his, rightfully so, from what he'd created, and he was going to *do* something about it.

"Wanna play?" Adam asked. "They're a team," he pointed to Landon Heathcote and Maxie's husband. Alex laughed and laughed and laughed a little more, until the laughter was fizzing up, up, up out of his ears and eyes and the top of his head. Landon Heathcote, who strongly resembled a young Voldemort, stood with Maxie's husband, who was disappointingly short and oddly immature-looking. He wore sneakers with his tux, and when Alex asked about them he said *you collect, too?* Like sneakers were something worth collecting.

Alex did *not* collect, nor had he gone to *Camp Ivanhoe*, and he resented his aunt and uncle for sending Theo there and making a traitor out of him. "Sure," Alex told the walking jack o'lantern. "What's the game? Stake?"

"No stake," Maxie's husband said, approaching Alex with a handful of the steak knives that Jessica had specifically flown over *from Japan*, which Alex heard her tell someone at dinner. "Just an old Ivanhoe game we used to play. They banned it by the time Theo came along." He had this swinging swing swing swing-ing way of walking, like he was some great outdoorsman at the impressive height of 5'7", and Alex tried counting the months again. No one seemed to know how pregnant Maxie was, but considering that she had no perceivable belly on her, he was pretty sure this baby belonged to her husband, and not to him, which infuriated Alex even more. He hadn't known he'd wanted a baby until the option had been presented and then taken away. He didn't know why he wanted it any more than he knew how he was gliding seamlessly through the air, but he knew it. He did.

"Come on," Landon said, and it echoed slowly through the chambers of Alex's head, come on come-on-come-on-come-On-ON-On?

"Did you get that, Alex? The scores, and everything?" Adam asked.

"Of course. This isn't just a *Camp Ivanhoe* game," Alex told them, although of course it was, and he had no idea how to play. It appeared to involve throwing steak knives at pre-marked notches in the trees. "Who set this up?" Alex asked.

"It's my house," Landon explained. "We all play." Lest they forget! Lest they forget that these blurred stars and the gently revolving table and the swimming green grass and the Japanese steak knives all belonged to Landon Heathcote. Alex watched the sky tilt above him, air breaking gently over his face in cool waves, and took a drink from the nearest glass. Maxie's husband threw a knife and it embedded itself in the middle of the tree and Alex wondered why they were all stabbing trees. Jack from *The Nightmare Before Christmas* threw a knife and it hit the root, split it open, stained the grass with blood from the tree. Alex hadn't known that trees bled but now that he did he didn't want to play the knife game any more, except of course he'd never wanted to play. The drink he was drinking tasted like passionfruit and sloshed onto his pants, spreading the same way the blood had from the tree. Landon Heathcote's white, white hands and his long, long fingers threw a Japanese knife at the highest mark.

"It's your turn," he said, and Alex put the pink drink down into the grass, where it spilled like the splashed tears, and started to pull the from-Japan knife out of the tree. "Leave it," Landon instructed him, but Alex wanted to save the tree, this tree that Landon was trying to kill, to murder in cold blood in front of God and everybody, what was that from, *in front of God and everybody*, except God and almost everybody had gone to sleep.

Someone was tugging at his hand, it was Will. "We've gotta get Yael to stitch you up." He looked down at his hand, which was bleeding; it had started bleeding just like the tree, redness seeping down into the white of his shirt and green of the land. He had caught the tree's contagion directly from Landon Heathcote, who released the poison into the air and waited to watch them all fall.

"I can't until I get this knife," Alex explained, obviously, because it was unfathomable that Will wouldn't understand such a thing.

"I have a knife for you. It's right at your place at the table."

"Not *the knife*."

"It is *the knife*."

"The one he threw?"

"The one he threw."

He sat Alex down in a seat that somehow had his jacket on the back of it. Yael tied his hand up in napkins and he picked up a gleaming silver pillbox from the garlands of broken flowers.

"What is this?" he muttered, flicking it open to reveal many tiny white pills. It felt like fate or fame or maybe fortune; maybe all three.

"That's Lulu's. Will, will you put that in my purse, please?"

"What kind of pills?" Alex asked, but Yael didn't hear him, or maybe didn't understand him, and Will was standing behind her with white, white, white napkins, napkins that hadn't been bloodied yet. "What kind of pills?"

"Anti-anxiety." Yael saw it open in his hand and peered down at it. "Valium, it looks like. Hold on. Stay there."

He *held on* and *stayed there* while she disappeared, and Will bounced up and down across from him and Alex dropped the contents of the silver box into his mouth. They didn't all make it in, but some definitely did and when he swallowed them with a warm glass of vodka it felt like slime running down his throat.

"We've got to take him up to the house to get him stitched up properly," Yael said.

“I’m *here*,” Alex told them. “I can *hear*. You.”

But they couldn’t hear him. They towed him up to the house like he wasn’t floating, and he let the waves that only he could feel crash up and over all of them, jumping just at the break.

Yael
June 10th, 2017

Yael watched Alex scoop up six Valium into one paw and down them like Winnie the Pooh scooping up honey. They were going to kick in soon and they needed to get Alex into his room before they couldn't move him. She glanced at Will, and he stood up immediately.

"Time for bed," Will said. "Rob, help us out." Rob and Will each took him by an arm and Rob snuffled a little bit about the good old days, didn't this *remind* you of the *good old days*? Will didn't say much of anything. It was a long walk to the house, and she wished they could have asked for help. Almost everyone else, except for the *Camp Ivanhoe* boys, had gone to bed, Jessica included, which meant there would be no one to help her, find the sewing kit, get the antiseptic, be a sober adult. She wasn't sure that she needed to sew up his hand, but she needed to create the appearance of trying. The lawn was long and drifted against her bare ankles, her shoes dangling from one hand. You always expected nights like this to be better, to be special and meaningful, to be worth the purchase of the dress and the price of the professional makeup artist, but those were the nights that invariably ended with a billionaire's son, high off his face, trying to pull a steak knife out of a tree.

They were quiet upon entry into the house, the doors creaking too loudly when opened, Rob tripping three times on the stairs and Will hissing at him to pull it together. Yael told them to take Alex into the bathroom because she knew Jessica and she knew that if there was blood on the ten-million-year-old rug which belonged to Aladdin, or something, she would absolutely lose it. Alex swayed and wavered, almost falling onto the marble floor.

"Guys! Hold him up!"

"I need a glass of water," Rob told her. She and Will exchanged glances. Rob was so useless sometimes that it was truly astounding.

"I'm going to get the first aid kit," she looked from one to the other. "Keep him upright." She left the three boys and went in search of everything she would need, none of which she found. The kitchen was dark and empty, the kind of dark that's illuminated by the light from the outside and makes you feel like someone is watching you even though there's no one to see you.

She gave up and went back to Alex's palatial bathroom, with its four windows and double doors on the bathroom, never mind that she didn't even have a shower in her room.

"There's only gauze and tape," Yael said, blinking in the blazing lights. Too much light after too much darkness, and she was seeing spots across her vision. She needed to get it through her head that this was the end for him, he didn't need stitches because he didn't need anything. There was broken glass scattered around him, green liquid seeping into every porous surface. Yael reached for his injured hand, uncurling it with care.

He didn't moan.

"What should we do?" Rob asked. "I mean, does the hand mean it's off?"

"Of course not," Yael replied, and took over, like they were at the hospital. "Get him in the tub, and, Rob, fill it with *warm* water. Not too hot. A normal temperature. Like we talked about. Will, did Lulu give you the knife?"

Will nodded. "He's out," Will said. "It's now or never."

"Yes, thank you," Yael replied, because they all knew it; he didn't need to say it.

"Those drugs really worked. I mean, it wasn't a lot of drugs. To knock him out," Rob said, as he arranged Alex in the tub, as the water lapped over Alex's waist.

"Don't forget to keep his arms out of the water. What's with all the broken glass?"

"Rob freaked out and knocked like three things over." Will looked around. "We should fully trash this place. To make it look like Alex was out of his mind."

Maxie swished in, still in her black-tie dress, right down to her platforms. "So here we are," she murmured. She walked into the bathroom without worrying about the glass or Will making more of a mess or Yael monitoring Alex's pulse with her hand. Maxie tilted his unconscious face up to hers and put her lips almost to his.

"You will never touch me again," she told him. She took his watch from his arm, reset it, and hit it against the top of the bathtub, so hard Yael was surprised it didn't shatter. "Time of death," she murmured.

No one said anything. Maxie put the watch back on his wrist and took the knife from Will's hand without asking for it. The bath was almost full. She made the first cut, on his left wrist, so deep that Yael was almost worried she'd severed an artery. *Almost worried.* As if that wasn't what they all wanted. It was hard to expel the habit of healing. Will did the next cut, then handed the knife to Rob, who moved with excruciating slowness to the other wrist. Yael took it after him and wielded it like a scalpel. His left wrist unspooled blood into the tub; he moaned once, then was silent. Yael placed his right hand gently in the warm water. Maxie, sitting on the toilet, watched in fascination.

"Is that all?" Will asked.

"I'll stay and monitor his pulse," Yael said.

"Isn't Lulu coming?" Rob looked around the bathroom, the closed door.

"Soon," Maxie whispered. "I'll stay with you."

"That watch thing may not work," Will said.

"It wi'll be fine, one way or another," Maxie replied, evenly. "You two should go." She looked up at them from the bottom edges of her glimmering eyes.

Will paused. He stood at the door to the bathroom, at the already-red tub, at his soon-to-be dead friend. "We didn't do anything to him that he hadn't done to someone else," he said, finally.

When Yael looked at Rob, he was crying. "I can't believe tomorrow I'll be free of him," he whispered, and then they were gone.

Lulu slid into Alex's room a few minutes later, shaking and nervous, and Maxie wouldn't let her in the bathroom. Yael watched them through an inch of open door. "It's done. He's already dead," Maxie lied.

"I can't be that much of a coward," Lulu whispered.

"You helped. You did everything. I couldn't have done it alone," Maxie's voice was quiet. "You're not a coward. You've always been... delicate."

Lulu snorted and maybe hiccupped; she sounded like she was crying. "I'm sorry," she told Maxie.

"You have nothing to be sorry for. Come on," Maxie led her out of the room and came back into the bathroom, shutting the door behind her. "I never wanted her to have to do it," she explained to Yael. "I never thought she *would* do it. She did everything else. She brought all of us together."

He was dead before two. Yael felt nothing when she touched her hand to his still neck and Maxie, who hadn't looked away from his face, turned in surprise at the little noise that emerged from Yael's mouth.

"Is he—" she didn't let herself finish the sentence.

Yael nodded. "Did you wipe off the knife, and drop it in the tub?"

"Yes, but we'll all come in here tomorrow morning, so we don't have to worry about it."

Yael nodded again. She sat with her elbows on her knees and her chin on her hands, and Maxie mirrored her.

"I thought it would feel more... hopeless," Maxie said.

"No," Yael replied. "Maybe even the opposite."

She never did look at his hand properly; part of her couldn't believe he'd injured the same hand in the space of a few months. It took her a few minutes to check the room for anything they'd left behind, and she found herself in his bedroom, staring out of Alex's windows onto the remains of their feast, the ruined party they'd abandoned so easily. She wondered who would clean it up, and when, it seemed dangerous to leave it out overnight, knives in the trees and half-eaten macarons heaped along table. Yael had never spent so much time around broken glass in her life, but these people seemed to shatter something no matter where they went.

Maxie
June 10th, 2017

Maxie was awake, and hungry. She wanted some of yesterday's Tate's, but she was worried that the sound would rouse Freddie from his slumber — they were annoyingly loud to eat — and, since she was interested in spending zero point zero zero time alone with her husband, she figured she could be hungry. She could wait; she was supposed to wait. It wasn't *over* until it was over, done and dusted. She stretched up, slowly, languidly, and walked to her window. It was very luxurious to look out over this kind of land, with no nearby houses; they didn't have that in the Hamptons, unless you had a house in the middle of nowhere, like Lulu's in Amagansett. Maxie supposed she could move into her parents' Southampton house and have it to herself for at least two weeks before the vultures descended, wanting an Instagram at Pierre's or Surf Lodge.

A funny kind of yell, or maybe a scream, perforated the air, and Freddie sat straight up in bed.

"What was that?"

Maxie shrugged. "I don't know."

"Will!" Someone yelled.

Freddie was up and out of the room before she was. He scurried down the hall and across it, Theo following steps behind. Lulu paused to look at Maxie, and then they heard Victoria's scream.

Of course the first thing she saw was so strange it took her a moment to unpack it all, Theo holding a hand out, *stop*, Lulu dissolving back into a perfect faint. The room was already full; Yael said *he's dead* and then Maxie saw it, the body, fat with the bloat of the water and slashed with a red-black she couldn't believe was blood. She made sure to go into the bathroom with Yael, to stand there, to involve herself. Will and Rob held him up, this ruined corpse. He didn't look anything like he had last night; he looked like the monster he was.

"Maybe we should cover his arms," she said.

"He's dead," Yael replied.

Maxie watched Rob and Will lift Alex out of the tub with the help of her handy-dandy husband. Her handy-dandy husband returned to her, spraying blood and bathwater, to ask too late if she was okay. Maxie shrugged him away and sat down next to Lulu. He would never know if she was okay. There were parents and paramedics, or whatever the ambulance people were called, and Jessica and Will on Alex's bed. The police asked them to empty the room and took photos of everything, including her husband in his wet clothes. Maxie sat in Lulu's room while Theo paced on the balcony on the phone.' At some point she felt her empty wrist and realized the bracelet was missing, that at some point she or someone else would have to go find it, but it felt irrelevant. '

When Maxie put hands to her cheeks they were wet. "Are you okay?" Lulu asked her. They were still in their pajamas, silk slips that Jessica had given them as bridesmaid's gifts.

It was always going to be fatherless but there was something very final about the whole business that made her spew blistering tears of relief. The windows were open, a bee buzzing against the heavy curtains. Maxie looked out on the rolling green land before them and thought how lucky it was to have such an unobstructed view. They didn't even have that in the Hamptons.

Part X
Maxie
June 12th, 2017

She didn't go to the funeral; she and Victoria went to the spa at the Greenwich Hotel instead. When Lulu called her, she was eating oranges in a robe, trying so hard to relax that her head was starting to hurt.

"Mr Sable asked me for your number," she whispered.

"Who's Mr Sable?"

"Cornelius Sable. Alex's dad. He came up me and was like *can I ask you for Maxine Stein-Golden's information? Specifically, her phone number?* And I was like why, sir? I can pass along a message for you. And he was like *she and I have some business to attend to. Incidentally, how is her pregnancy coming along?* It was so, so creepy. Like, scary movie creepy."

Maxie sat up. "Did you give it to him?"

"*Of course* I gave it to him! What was I supposed to do!"

"I wonder why he wanted it."

"I don't know." Maxie could hear Lulu chewing on her cuticles.

"Stop chewing on your hang nails. You're going to get MRSA, or something."

"Maybe Alex told him."

"Why would Alex tell him?"

"I don't know. I'm sure his father's had a lifetime of cleaning up his messes."

"Well, no longer."

"Obviously."

They paused.

"Where *are* you right now?"

"On the balcony outside of the shiva. Is it shiva, after the memorial service? Whatever the thing is with all the food."

"Pretending to smoke." It already felt like such a long time ago that she'd known someone, anyone, named Alex Sable.

"Basically, yes. I guess I have to go back in."

"I love you. Don't worry about this." It was unnecessary because they both knew Lulu was going to worry about it more than Maxie was.

"I love you. You either."

Cornelius Sable called her that night, from a private number. "Maxine?"

"This is Maxie. Who is this?" She said, formally, even though she already knew it was him.

"It's Cornelius Sable."

For some reason, she imagined him on the phone in Richard Gilmore's study in Connecticut, the one with the globe and the bar cart and the huge portrait of Rory holding a book. "Hi, Mr Sable." They paused. "You can call me Maxie."

"Hello, Maxie," he said. '

"What can I help you with?"

"I was hoping you could come by my office tomorrow. There's something I'd like to talk over with you."

"I'm happy to talk to you about it now," Maxie said.

"I would prefer to talk in person. How's three o'clock?"

There was a part of Maxie that was genuinely curious. "All right."

"My assistant will send you the info. Goodbye, Maxie." He pronounced her nickname with care.

"Bye," she said, vaguely, hanging up and going to her closet to try to figure out what was appropriate to wear to something this strange. This would be the kind of thing that she dreaded and feared, that riddled her with anxiety, that she dressed up for and put make up on for, and then it would be nothing. He would ask her to put together some group of nice Jewish kids to make a donation in Jerusalem in Alex's name, or something. It would be five minutes that she didn't need to dress for, five minutes they could have done over the phone.

There was such a calmness inside her that even this didn't scare her the way it should have. She had drunk the cool ambrosia of relief, and its healing quality was beyond any expectation.

Mr Sable's building was in midtown, like everyone's father's office was. Maxie supposed she should go see her mother after she was done, or go to Bergdorfs and buy a fur stole even though it was 80 degrees outside. There was the usual checking in, the copying of the license, the complicated instructions to the elevator. They directed her to the 48th floor and on the 48th floor they didn't ask her name, just took her back to a big office with a decent view of grey buildings against grey sky. Maxie thought if she had an office uptown she would want a view of the park, but that was just her.

A short man in a suit sat her on a couch in an office and shut the door. A few minutes later, Cornelius appeared through a different door. She stood and watched him walk across the room. He was a salt-and-pepper version of Alex, and Maxie had forgotten how physically imposing he could be, tall and broad and filling a space until it belonged to him.

"Hello, Maxine," he said, and she decided he was deliberately calling her by her full name, which was the kind of thing you did in a negotiation to throw someone off.

"Hello, Cornelius," she replied, even though they both knew she should have called him Mr Sable. She reached out a hand. He took it.

"Please, have a seat. Can I get you anything?"

"No, thank you."

He nodded. "Maxine, I'm going to do you the credit of speaking to you directly. Can I trust that what is said here stays in the privacy of this office?"

Maxie didn't want to say yes, but there wasn't really a polite way to say no. She couldn't go with *it depends on what you say*, even though that flickered in her mind. She wondered if verbal contracts were binding in the state of New York. She nodded.

"Parenting changes, over time. You have to change with it; you have to change with your children. Suss out how to handle them. Try to ascertain the kinds of people they're becoming. You'll understand, in a few years." He nodded at her stomach.

"I think I understand now."

He laughed. He had a low laugh that was like a bark. Maxie didn't remember Alex's laugh. She didn't want to. Mr Sable — he was still Mr

Sable to her, even though she'd had the guts to call him Cornelius — steepled his fingers, elbows on his knees.

"I can't honestly tell you, Maxine, that I was proud of the person Alex became. I can't honestly tell you that I did my part, as a parent, to keep him from *becoming* that person. Suffice to say, if I could do it all again, I would do it differently."

"Most of us would."

"You're too young to think that."

She looked at him from the very bottom of her eyes.

"I think you'll understand me, then, when I tell you that sometimes a problem has to be contained instead of dismissed. I think one of my greatest challenges in life has been trying to learn how to contend with my children. How to talk to them. At the end of a long day, I often find myself struggling to put up with what seems like entitled snobbery from my offspring."

Maxie laughed.

"From what I've found out about you, your parents don't feel that way."

Maxie felt that way about her parents, but she certainly wasn't going to tell *Alex's dad* that. "I'm sure all parents feel that way, in some form or fashion."

He nodded even though he clearly wasn't listening. "What I'm trying to tell you, Maxine, is that I know what kind of person Alex was." She cocked her head, *did you? Did you* know *him?* "I'm not proud of it. Any part of it, really, but there are… measures I had to take, as the head of this family, to keep us all protected. To keep Alex protected. I don't think he ever understood that there were consequences to his actions."

"I find when you keep fixing problems for people, they keep believing there aren't consequences," Maxie told him.

He barked another short laugh. "It's hard to run a family. Run a family, run a business, keep everyone believing in your…fitness. As a person."

Maxie wanted him to come out and say it. She wasn't sure that he would, but she wasn't sure that *she* could.

"I never knew what really happened with that kid, Chris, when Alex was in high school. If Alex did it and blamed him or if Alex just got the idea from him. What came to us later were usually staff with claims that I wouldn't want to repeat to my wife. Or someone like you."

You wouldn't have to repeat them to someone like me. I lived them.

"He tended towards people whose mouths could be stopped up with money. I told him every time that this was the last time, but he knew I would never put myself in the position of being the father of someone... like that. It would have been a liability."

Maxie sat there, spine straight, looking at him with her face composed in utter neutrality. He was waiting for her to jump in, but she had nothing to say, not to him.

"Alex came to me a few weeks before his death. He thought that you might be pregnant with his child. He told me that you were married, and he wanted me to find a way to get you to take a paternity test. If it was his child, he said, he wanted to be able to see it."

Maxie dug her fingernails into her palm to stop herself from crossing her arms over her stomach.

"I was surprised that this was something he cared about," Mr Sable said, carefully. "It was the first time in a long time that he'd expressed real interest in, well, anything. I told him to wait until the baby was born." His eyes were kind of glinty, like you couldn't look into them properly. Cold and hard and glinty. "Of course, he died shortly after that."

Maxie kept her face completely still.

"Is it his child?"

"It's my child."

"If it is — if it isn't — I hope it wasn't — something you didn't agree to."

"Mr Sable, you know as well as I do that I wouldn't tell someone my child may be related to them, and risk having any measure of legal power over that child taken away from me."

"We would never do that to you."

Maxie stood up. "I've learned that you really can't trust anyone. No matter what you know of them. Or what you think you know of their family." She reached out her hand.

"We want to help you — we want to help the baby — it's our first grandchild," he said, and for a moment he sounded like a parent instead of a businessman. "We wouldn't do anything you didn't agree to—"

Maxie let her hand drop. "I've been forced against my will by your son. I would never be so *stupid* as to trust his parents." She spat the word *stupid*, walked to the door she'd come in through.

"I'm sorrier for all those girls you paid into silence. I'm sure it was a pittance, nothing to you, and they had to spend every penny remembering how it was earned.'."

Mr Sable stood. She didn't shrink into the door.

"If you come near me — if you come near my child — if you touch a fingertip to any of my family or friends, I will make sure that your *silent complicity* is seen and heard by everyone who gets a copy of *The New York Times*. Alex left big tracks. Once you find one, it's just a matter of time. Right?"

"Maxine—" He put a hand to hers, shoving an envelope into it.

"I'm sorry for your loss," Maxie said. The door closed so quickly it almost caught the edge of her dress. She walked up to Bergdorfs and opened the envelope on the way, tearing into it. Inside there was a card with a handwritten phone number but she knew she would never call it, so she dropped it into a trash can on Fifth Avenue. Then she walked into Bergdorfs, directly downstairs to a brownie a la mode in the empty basement café. It was bright and white and very clean. They used to eat here after school and ruin their dinners, or on Saturdays when Lulu was back from New England. Of course no one told you that the only consistency you would have in life was a menu of sandwiches and an orange iced tea. Of course no one told you how horrible it was to grow up, or you wouldn't want to do it at all.

She drank the iced tea and ate the brownie with the ice cream, the whole thing even though it was meant for two people. She got Lulu a sandwich to go, because it was her favorite, and stopped to buy herself a new purse on the first floor. In the cab on the way home she supposed that in the end the only thing that mattered was that he was dead. If he was dead he was done, and she was his no longer.

Will
June 28th, 2017

Jessica came to confront him at the over-decorated hotel a block from the Liberty Bell. When he looked through the keyhole and saw her, he wondered how she'd found him in the first place, if she'd called multiple hotels or somehow gotten on with Amex and rung the details out of them. He opened the door.

"How'd you find me?" he asked, which he thought was a decent way of starting off this meeting on his terms. '

Jessica held her locked phone screen up to his face. "I have your location, you moron." She swept in, which wasn't very impressive because she was so petite, and stood with her hands on her hips, looking pissed in a way that he almost wanted to laugh at, it was all so cartoonish. She looked from his rumpled bed to his clothes on the floor and shook her head. "I don't even know where to start."

"Do you want to stay in the apartment? The lease isn't up until November. I can talk to your dad about splitting up the rent fairly, after I move out…"

Her eyes sort of bugged and crossed at the same time. "What. Are you *talking*. About."

"I thought you'd want to go back to New York."

"I want to re-plan my *wedding*."

"Jessica," he said, taking a step towards her, taking his hand in hers. "We're not getting married." He slipped the engagement ring off her finger. It had always been too big, and she'd never been willing to take it off long enough to get it sized.

"Will," she said, trying to open his fist with her sharp little nails. "I am not wasting *eight years* of my life to *not* get married."

"Do you want to get married just so we can get divorced?"

"No. I want to get married to you. Which is what you *promised* me. You promised me that you would marry me. And now, just because you have some stupid out, you're running for the door."

"Some stupid out? Jessica. My best friend *killed himself* in the house we were supposed to get married in, the night before our wedding. And you stood in his bedroom, with his dead body on the floor, and told me we were still getting married." Will dropped onto the edge of his bed. "How can you think that… that would happen?"

"Because you couldn't be cruel enough to do this to me."

"It would be cruel for me to marry you. It would be cruel for you to marry me. I can't believe we're even having this conversation."

She shook her head. He wasn't sure how she couldn't understand this, this basic, fundamental fact, that if they didn't love each other, they shouldn't get married. "I didn't want to live here," she said, starting to sniff. He couldn't remember the last time he'd see her cry. "I didn't want to sink into utter *irrelevancy* here. I didn't want to have to fight so fucking hard to keep up with everyone else, everyone who got to stay in New York. I did that for you. I loved you."

At some hazy point in the past, he might have loved her, too. They'd just gotten too far away from it, so far that he couldn't see it with any real certainty. Maybe he'd loved her as much as he thought you could love anyone. Maybe she'd been there, and it had been easy and comfortable, and she'd made a life for him. Maybe he'd loved that. It didn't matter what it was because he knew that he didn't love her now.

Will opened his palm. "I'm not marrying you."

"I'm not going to be with you if you won't marry me," she told him.

"We're not going to be together," he said. "We're breaking up." He wanted to keep the ring, because he didn't trust her not to tell people that they were just re-planning the wedding, or something. He didn't trust her to do the right thing. She wasn't capable of it.

She walked back to the door. He knew she was thinking that this was such a tiny room, such a tiny room in such a shitty hotel. Such an ugly hotel. She would never stay in a place like this, let alone in a room whose bed was three feet from the door. There was a kind of disgust lurking behind her pinned-together lips that made him hate her, a little bit.

"I will find a way to ruin you," she said, slowly, clearly. "When it all comes crashing down around you, I want you to know I did this to you. In thanks for what you've done to me."

She let the door slam behind her. He didn't know whether she'd somehow managed to get the ring out of his hand or he just lost it in the course of the day, but when he got back to the hotel after work, it was gone. It wasn't his to keep, anyway. None of it was.

Rob
July 2017

Nothing was hard, after Alex. There was a creeping uneasiness that slipped into bed with you, perched on your shoulder and curled up next to you on cold nights, but everything *else* was easy. He broke up with Ronnie. He got the promotion. Things happened that he thought he could never make happen, things that he *did*. For a period of time, he became convinced that Alex was possessing him. He studied it and went to St Patrick's to talk to a priest and paid $40 for a fortune teller on 23rd Street to sprinkle him with holy water.

None of it worked. Eventually he decided it didn't matter if Alex was possessing him, because he preferred his life that way. He thought it would change him, what they had done to Alex, what he had done to his best friend. In the end, it didn't matter what he had done or why he'd done it, only that he finally understood that they would never accept him.

Will wanted to get an apartment together in September, which meant that life would be the way it was always supposed to have been after graduation, if Alex had stayed in LA, and Will had moved in with Rob instead of Jessica. Most of the time, Rob forgot that Alex was dead. Sometimes he dreamt about him, dreamt that he sat in the Ikea chair in the corner of Rob's bedroom and drank directly out of a bottle of Scotch. Sometimes Rob thought he saw Alex out of the edges of his vision, walking down Fifth Avenue with all the confidence of a purposeless errand.

It was never Alex. He was still dead. When the reporter came around asking questions, months later, Will assured Rob that Maxie would take care of it. He never saw any of them, the wedding party, as they would always be in his mind, like they'd melted out of his reality. He ran into Ronnie and his mother's favorite cousin and a guy who lived down the hall from them at USC, but he didn't see Maxie or Lulu or Victoria or Yael or Jessica, even though his office was near Bergdorfs. He always expected to catch Lulu twirling through the door of Barneys, but he never did. Rob watched their lives unfold on Instagram, Victoria found a new boyfriend, Jessica moved to Tribeca, Lulu ate gummy vitamins, Maxie took her baby bump for walks around their neighborhood.

On empty Saturdays, when Will wasn't in town and he couldn't jolly his co-workers into an afternoon of drinking, Rob wandered down to the little cobblestone streets where they all lived. Tribeca was so small, so small and so clean and so anonymous, like living in a city that wasn't New York. There were sleek concept stores and fluffy restaurant awnings and the most mainstream thing they had was a Sweetgreen. Rob's overpriced apartment on Park Avenue South spat him out next to Pret-a-Manger and Chase Bank and four hundred subway stations with a thousand people. He wasn't sure the subway even ran to Tribeca.

He figured they all lived there because it was the Upper East Side of downtown, with clean streets and doormen behind every window. He saw Taylor Swift twice, but he never encountered his former partners-in-crime, not even when he loitered across the street from the building that Maxie and Lulu called home. He didn't know *why* he needed to see them so much, except that he wanted some kind of confirmation that it had all been real. It happened. It wasn't imagined, even though most days it felt like that. Most days it felt like he'd imagined them all.

He did catch sight of Theo, one day, walking towards him on Fifth Avenue with the same confidence Alex always had. He looked so much like his cousin that it was hard *to* look at him; Rob had to steel himself for the run-in, swallow around the anxiety blossoming in his throat.

Theo didn't overtake him. He turned on his heel and swung open the door of Harry Winston. Rob wanted to watch him from the window, but he went right on 55th Street instead. When he got back to his office he unfollowed them on Instagram. It was safer to believe they existed in Narnia than to live his life as a ghost of one of them. He wouldn't go back to Tribeca, not even for dinner. He ordered vodka and orange juice in public and hit on normal-sized girls in red lipstick and jean jackets. They were safe, 'they weren't so out of reach that he was a disappointment waiting to happen. In time, he couldn't even remember that night, the clean lines of their bony faces, the color of the marble in the bathroom, the smell of grenadine poured into an undrinkable drink, the sound of Alex's slow exhale as he tied Rob's bowtie.

Yael
August 11th, 2017

It took Yael approximately twenty minutes to figure out that this car ride to Amagansett was a set up. The only reason it had taken her so long, she thought, texting Maxie and Lulu from the passenger seat, was because the heavy similarity between this weekend and the one in February made her almost, oddly, nostalgic.

"Yael," Victoria hissed from the backseat. "Noah asked you a *question*."

"Sorry," Yael told her, forcing herself to smile at Noah. "So, how was your week?"

Noah *was* nice, as Maxie and Lulu assured her via text, *he's so nice. He comes from a nice family. Give him a chance!* He had a job (in finance); he'd grown up in Maxie's building, but, Maxie claimed, he wasn't a snot. Yael spent the trip oscillating between being touched that the girls were trying to set her up, and feeling genuinely impressed by the guy they'd picked.

"He's definitely husband material," Maxie informed her, laying across Lulu's bed while Lulu drew cheekbones onto Victoria's face.

"So why don't *you* date him?" Victoria asked.

"I'm not dating." Maxie replied, stretching her ankles.

"Well, obviously not when you're *huge*. But you could have saved him. For later."

Maxie got up. "First of all, I think it's stupid to save people. Secondly, I'm not dating again. I'm never getting married again. I'm just going to have my baby. And that's that."

She said it with such a finality that none of them challenged it. Victoria left to get dressed and Lulu suggested they swim after dinner.

Noah *was* husband material. He was nice and easy to be around and polite to a fault, quietly funny, maybe a little bit of a snot. He sat next to her at dinner and floated near her in the pool that was the temperature of bathwater. Theo said it was *too warm* but when Lulu said she liked it he agreed, *you're right, it's nice*. Maxie fell asleep on an outdoor chaise and Victoria clung to her new boyfriend with both hands around his neck, so tightly Yael thought she might hurt him. It was the beginning of a different universe, and she didn't mind it.

Theo's friends arrived the next morning, crumbling muffins across the big outdoor table and talking too loudly. They weren't particularly interested in Yael, but they were perfectly cordial, asking questions while she smiled to herself at their lurid pastel swim trunks. Noah's, to her relief, were navy blue, and unpatterned. She was relieved that he wasn't wearing a bathing suit with pineapples, which meant that he was already something to her, even if that *something* was just a good prospect.

They lolled in the sun for most of the day, eating guacamole and chips from the bottomless kitchen, filling two recycling bins with bottles of Domaines Ott. Landon Heathcote came by with his brother and said hello to Yael in an empty way. Later he asked her if she wanted to *get up a game of croquet*.

"I've never played."

"It's not really worth it. I don't know why we do."

But they played anyway, mallets cracking loudly through the blue air, the smell of broken grass wafting over them in heady drifts, too much use of the word *wicket*. Noah stayed near Yael, rolling his eyes at the right moments and talking to Maxie about her little sister. When they were done, Landon suggested badminton, but Theo told them they had to get dressed for Surf Lodge.

Surf Lodge was too loud and kind of dirty. Maxie held court at one table, where beaming acquaintances touched her stomach. Lulu and Theo danced underneath the strings of lights and Landon *got up* a drinking game that Victoria's boyfriend ultimately won.

When Yael was on her way back from the bathroom, she walked directly into Will.

"What are you doing here?" he asked her.

"What are *you* doing here?" she countered.

"Here with some buddies from high school," he replied.

"I'm staying at Lulu's for the weekend." She motioned to the table.

He turned to look. Landon inexplicably stood on a bench, a pale beacon in the dark night. "Oh. I'm surprised you're still friends with them."

She shrugged. He'd been surprised that she wanted to help exact Maxie's invisible justice, surprised and disappointed, just like he was now. Of course it meant he hadn't known her at all. She'd done it for every mangled woman who laid on the cold table before her, never to be the same again.

"Because I'm not," he said. It was a funny thing that they cared so much about the way he'd broken up with Yael, with Jessica, but, to them, it had been the ultimate sign of his *true character*, as Maxie put it. *He kept the ring. What, is he going to use it on someone else?* Was he? She didn't want him to find anyone else, but she also didn't want *him*. Which was of course how it was. How it always was. *Whatever I could give you. You should be happy with whatever I could give you*, he had told her. In the end it was such a waste, that Alex had destroyed some vital part of him, and Will wouldn't bother to fix himself. He was maybe more broken than the rest of them. "They don't forgive. These people. *Those* people. I don't know if you heard about what happened at the firm."

She shook her head. "Your firm?"

"No room for me there, any more. Friend of a friend of Jessica's dad. Their arms are longer than you could believe," he looked up at the lights, shiny lights, shiny eyes. "Trying to look for a job now. It's hard. With Jessica out for blood. When you leave them, you realize how much easier it was, with them. On the inside of things."

Yael felt like she should apologize even though she had nothing to apologize for. Her heart was beating too fast, that stupid push of adrenaline that she wished she could control or contain. She shook her head. She didn't know what to say so she turned to squint in Noah's direction. She wondered if Noah was watching and wondering who Will was.

Maxie moseyed up behind Will, peering around him. "Is there a line for the bathroom? I hate coming to places like this. All you do is run into people you don't want to see. Oh, hello, Will. I didn't recognize you from behind'. But you're here, too."

Will pulled his sticky gaze to Maxie, then let it fall back to Yael. "Yep."

"That's nice. I'm fine, thanks for asking. The baby's fine. You look well. Are you well?"

He was forced to turn to her. "I'm well."

"Well! We're all well. Isn't that swell? Yael, I think Noah's looking for you. And the line's cleared up. Goodnight, Will. I hope you stay *well.*"

She padded away through the sand.

"She's so pregnant."

"I should go," Yael said. She had the sudden urge to put a hand to his shoulder and assure him that it would be okay, but she didn't. "Goodnight, Will."

When they got back to the house she let Noah kiss her. You could see the stars and the moon was very bright and deep in the grass she could hear the quiet symphony of cicadas playing out the night.

Lulu
November 2017

There's a place uptown where the steps drop down into the park, after the zoo and before the Met, that's reliably empty. If you find the spot between the edge of the fieldstone building and the opening into Central Park, you can probably sit there, undisturbed, for at least half an hour. Maybe longer if you don't go at lunchtime.

It's a long way to go if you live in Tribeca, but there was always something to be done uptown, Lulu reasoned. If only to buy some cashmere socks at Bergdorfs and give her mother a kiss. Lulu took a cab to Grand Central and walked from there. It was the kind of fall day that's reassuring and exciting at the same time, a chill descending over the city after five, the leaves falling down around you in glorious piles of color and crispness.

It was after school had let out but before people started to leave work. Sometimes when she was back home — because this was home, her real home — she felt like she could almost catch herself walking up the numbers in her uniform kilt and 'Prada loafers. Full cheeks and shiny eyes. You got hollow as you grew, as people pulled things out of you and didn't give them back, until you were so empty you had to go fill yourself up again. It wasn't easy to do. Once you got started it wasn't hard, either. Lulu spent the early part of the day sitting through hours of testimony in Maxie's apartment, while Tyler took notes and Maxie asked questions, three hours with six influencers who all had at least one story to tell. It was hard to listen to and harder not to. Afterward Lulu wanted a Linzer cookie from Sarabeth's, but only the Sarabeth's on 92nd, by her grandparents' old apartment. Maxie's face was alight with the fire of a zealot when Lulu hugged her goodbye.

It was a relief to be uptown. It was a relief to be home. It was comfort and the smell of street cart chestnuts and the way you felt sitting on a green bench, looking up at the sky underneath the frame of your eyelashes, wondering when it would snow. Thinking about sometime when it snowed, and you and Maxie went to get sundaes at Serendipity after midnight. How giggly you were and how vivid it all was, radiant and shimmering white walls as you climbed the stairs. Lulu wondered if Serendipity was still even there.

Everyone was surprised that she was marrying Theo. He wasn't handsome or dashing or even particularly charming. He wasn't successful in his own right, and he wasn't some society figure who gave you status. He loved her a lot and she loved him back because he reminded her of her family, like she could trust in his love, believe in it. She had learned over the summer that what she'd always suspected was true, she was a coward. Maxie didn't even let her in the bathroom. Sometimes when she closed her eyes she could still see the light coming from beneath the door, spilling out onto the silk carpet in slashes. It could have been any dark room. It could have been any night. She was a coward, and she was afraid, and Theo made her safe. Theo was safe. Theo would keep her safe. Probably if none of it had happened, she would still be with Max. Probably if none of it had happened she would be someone she didn't like at all. It was such a delicate thing, really. It all turned on a hair.

When Maxie had the baby she only let Lulu in the room. They stood there with the doctor and the baby and held it, this tiny thing with its silly mop of dark hair. "She looks like Alex," Maxie said.

"She looks like you, too."

"It's all right. She'll make his life worthwhile." The baby didn't cry; her face was composed, quiet. "It's better, that way. It will never allow me to forget. I don't ever want to forget. If I do, it was all just a waste."

Maxie looked at Lulu for confirmation of this agreement, *never let me forget*, and Lulu held the small creature in her crisscrossed arms. The room in New York Presbyterian was cold and very white, like the walls at Serendipity. This was the hospital Lulu was born in and her sister and her father. This was the hospital Maxie and Alex were born in. This was where you went when you sliced your hand open cutting a bagel and your best friend got alcohol poisoning in the tenth grade. It was just one of those places you knew.

A leaf drifted down into her lap. Next year at this time the baby would be a toddler, and everything would be different again, just like it always was. She wouldn't know the person who'd sat on this bench and hated herself for being a coward. She wouldn't want to know her.

Lulu hailed a cab on Fifth Avenue and took it all the way up to Sarabeth's. She bought the cookie and ate it while she walked home, jam on her fingers and powdered sugar on her coat. When she got to her parents' house the lights were on, one window thrown open to catch the autumn air. It was late enough that the cold had started to drop down and blanket all of them, promising confidently that soon there would be winter once more.

CPSIA information can be obtained
at www.ICGtesting.com
Printed in the USA
BVHW040208060323
659764BV00005B/149

9 781800 165229